DEBT OF HONOUR

Gabe studied the pictures closely. One showed a plane in flight with its wing almost obscured by a great orange-and-yellow explosion. Two other pictures showed the same plane diving toward the ground, twisting and burning, trailing a funnel of black smoke. The fourth picture showed the instant of impact, trees and purple hills in the background, the airplane exploding like a fire bomb, pieces of debris raining down around the edges of the crash scene.

"All the planes he draws and paints now are exploding in midair, burning, and crashing," Kosta said. "And it's always the same plane. Always with Air Force markings."

Adam Kennedy is the talented author of a number of novels including *Somebody Else's Wife*, *Just Like Humphrey Bogart* and, most notably, *The Domino Principle*, which Harold Robbins described as 'Riveting suspense . . . I couldn't put it down'.

Debt of Honour

Adam Kennedy

Star

A STAR BOOK

published by

the Paperback Division of

W. H. ALLEN & Co. Ltd

A Star Book
Published in 1982
by the Paperback Division of
W. H. Allen & Co. Ltd
A Howard & Wyndham Company
44 Hill Street, London W1X 8LB

First published in Great Britain by
W. H. Allen & Co. Ltd, 1981

First published in the United States of America by
Delacorte Press

Reproduced, printed and bound in Great Britain by
Hazell Watson & Viney Ltd, Aylesbury, Bucks

ISBN 0 352 31175 4

For Susan,
I never write about her but she's in everything I write.

*How does it become a man to behave
toward this American government today?
I answer that he cannot without disgrace
be associated with it. I cannot for an
instant recognize that political
organization as my government. . . .*

HENRY DAVID THOREAU

Debt
of
Honour

Part One

On January 6, 1980, an H-14 jet aircraft, Simison Air International's flight 346, nonstop to Los Angeles, crashed, exploded, and burned while taking off from International Airport in Indianapolis. No survivors. Two hundred twenty-six dead.

Ten days later, on Wednesday, January sixteenth, passengers and crew boarded another H-14, Air Force Three, at Andrews Field in Washington, D.C. The plane, one of five operated for the convenience of the executive branch, members of Congress, and other government officials, took off at ten thirty-two in the morning. First stop Chicago. It was a clear and lovely winter day, crisp and cold.

Among the passengers on Air Force Three that morning were Chet Treptow, thirty-seven, a first-term United States senator from Illinois who had been elected in November 1978. Traveling with him were his wife, Evelyn, and their seven-year-old son, Sam.

Sam, pug-nosed, with prominent ears, freckles, and a helmet of brindle hair, had been a blue-ribbon talker for almost six of his seven years. He had begun to read when he was three and could read almost anything that interested him by age five. His memory was prodigious, his curiosity inexhaustible. He collected Latin-American stamps, built models of pre-1930 automobiles, and was a tireless archivist of all printed lore about the Chicago White Sox.

But, most surprising, he had learned the secret of silence. He knew how to listen. A few days after his seventh birthday, his mother said to Chet, "It sounds ridiculous, I know, but sometimes I feel as if Sam is my best friend in the world."

"Thanks a lot," Chet said.

"You know what I mean. He's a regular dingbat seven-year-old, thank God for that, but also I can sit down and talk with him and it's *fun.* He pays attention and he laughs at my jokes. And he's got a real nose for what's phony and what's not. He seems to know a thousand things that nobody ever taught him. I mean he has some way of fitting himself into all kinds of corners. When a situation changes, *he* changes. He's a dynamite kid."

That morning, as Air Force Three taxied to its takeoff lane, Sam, strapped in his seat between Chet and Evelyn, said, "Have you ever had two Christmases before? I mean in the same year?"

"Not me," Chet said.

"I don't think so," Evelyn said. "But it's not a bad idea, is it?"

"I guess not," Sam said. "I just can't get used to it. Because every Christmas I can remember, I was in Fort Beck. With Gabe and Helen and Grandpa."

"Well, this year we had to change things around a little," Chet said.

"That's why we spent Christmas in Philadelphia with *my* folks. You liked that, didn't you?"

"Oh, sure, Mom. It was terrific. But I just got used to seeing Grandpa Treptow on Christmas mornings. I always like to watch him unwrap his box of cigars and act like he's surprised at what I got him."

"It's just a matter of timing," Chet said. "Tomorrow we'll pretend it's Christmas Day. I talked to Gabe this morning and there's even some snow on the ground in Fort Beck. Gabe will bring Grandpa to his house and we'll all have our Christmas there. Just like every year."

"What about Aunt Helen?"

Evelyn glanced at Chet. Then, "What about her?"

"When we talked to Gabe the other day, he told me she wouldn't be there."

"Did he tell you why?" Evelyn said.

"He didn't have to. I figured it out myself. But he told me anyway."

"What did you say?"

"I told him I didn't like it."

"None of us like it," Chet said.

"Why do you suppose they did that?" Sam said.

"It just happens sometimes," Evelyn said. "There must be half a dozen kids in your class at school who—"

"I know that," Sam said. "But it's different when it's Gabe and Helen."

When they were airborne, when the pilot turned off the seat belt sign, Sam walked forward in the plane and got himself a drink of water. When he came back, he said, "Wait till you see Grandpa tomorrow morning. When he opens that present from me he's gonna bust. It's a big fancy cigar box. But inside it's not *cigars*. It's something else."

"Fish worms," Chet said.

"No. It's not a joke present. It's something great. Something Grandpa really *wants*. I can't wait to see his face. What time do we get to Chicago?"

"About noon, I guess. Chicago time."

"Then what time will we get to Fort Beck?"

"Gabe's meeting us in Chicago with the car," Chet said. "We should be home not later than three."

"And what time is it now?"

"It's not even eleven o'clock. We only took off a few minutes ago. You'd better simmer down or you'll be a nervous wreck before we hit Chicago."

Sam flopped down in his seat. "Grandpa's gonna go bananas, Dad. When he sees that present, he's gonna have the biggest surprise of his life."

At eleven fourteen the control tower at Andrews Air Base lost contact with Air Force Three. At eleven thirty-five the West Virginia highway police reported an explosion in the hills outside Elkins. At twelve forty-seven the burning wreckage was positively identified as Air Force Three. There were no survivors.

 Leo Hartwig graduated magna cum laude from Purdue University. Took his degree in aeronautical engineering. Six weeks later he went to work for Howard Hughes. He was a key member of the group who designed and built Hughes's plywood transport plane, a controversial aircraft whose flight time was logged in seconds and whose production costs added up to millions.

For thirty years Hartwig had only one employer. He became Hughes's advisor and confidant and was board chairman of Air Alternatives, Inc., an aeronautical research company functioning under the Summa Corporation umbrella.

In 1971, however, cut off from contact with Hughes and sensing the chaos ahead, he maneuvered free of Summa, allied himself with Tishune Industries in Okada and Peddicord Electronics, a British firm located in Liverpool, and created a new business entity: Hartwig Systems, offices in San Francisco and New York, production facilities ten miles east of Santa Clara, California.

Hartwig produced computer systems for military aircraft and space vehicles. But he expanded quickly to office units and home computers. And in June of 1973, his company announced the completion of a prototype passenger airliner, full production to begin in 1974, first deliveries due in 1976.

With forty first-class seats and two hundred sixty in coach, the new plane, called the H-14, would compete for sales with the Lockheed L-1011, the McDonnell Douglas DC-10, the Boeing 727, and the A-300 European Air Bus.

By January 1979 Hartwig had completed and tested forty-eight H-14's. But only eleven had been sold, four of them to the United States Air Force for use as executive jets. The other thirty-seven—gleaming, resplendent, and flawlessly engineered—sat in hangars alongside the Santa Clara testing grounds.

The explanation was simple. All the airline executives, after their pilots had tested the plane, admired it and praised it. But none of them wanted to go first. No one wanted to make the original investment till some other airline had flown the equipment in service for at least six months.

On Sunday, May 27, 1979, Hartwig was meeting with his British and Japanese associates in a board room in Brussels. Considering all alternatives, they concluded at last that they had only one choice: to shut down production on the H-14.

As they conferred and agonized and measured their losses, an American Airlines DC-10 crashed while taking off from O'Hare Field in Chicago. Two hundred and seventy-three people died. Passengers and crew. No survivors.

During the following weeks, as investigations of the DC-10 crash began and multiplied, Leo Hartwig sold all thirty-seven of the H-14's he had stored in his Santa Clara hangars. And he took orders for eighty-three more from sixteen different airlines.

"We're working three shifts a day," Hartwig told the press. "In four years we'll have two hundred planes in service."

But it didn't work out. The Hartwig sales phenomenon ended as it had begun. With disaster. The SAI plane crashed in Indianapolis. And ten days later Air Force Three went down near Elkins.

After completing their investigations, the National Transportation Safety Board and the Federal Aviation Administration, in a joint announcement, said that the H-14 crashes, like the DC-10 tragedy, were caused by structural flaws, that both design and manufacture were at fault.

Arthur Slayback, vice-chairman of NTSB, said, "In the DC-10, faulty engine mounts were the problem. In the H-14, it was total failure of the hydraulic system."

Two hours after he heard the government announcement, Leo Hartwig called a press conference. "Somebody made a serious mistake in judgment. There was *no* failure of our hydraulic systems. I defy the FAA and the NTSB to *prove* what they're saying. Those two H-14's crashed for only one reason—because somebody *wanted* them to crash."

Five days later, *Newsweek* announced that Leo Hartwig had taken an extended leave of absence for health reasons. "Roland Casper, chief executive officer of Peddicord Electronics, will function as president of Hartwig Systems until a successor to Hartwig can be appointed."

Ten weeks after Chet Treptow's death, his brother, Gabe, thirty-five, was chosen in a special **3** election to succeed him.

Christened George Albert, he was called Gabe from infancy. He and Chet grew up in Fort Beck, Illinois. After high school, Chet went to the University of Illinois on a basketball scholarship and Gabe enrolled at Foresby in Fort Beck.

Later Chet went on to law school at Northwestern and Gabe took his Ph.D. in American literature at Brown. Then he returned to Foresby to teach.

Chet was a political animal from the time he learned to talk. Gabe had no interest in politics. Except when he could be of help to Chet. Then he campaigned tirelessly. First when Chet ran for district attorney, later for the Illinois state legislature, and at last for the United States Senate.

During his own brief campaign after Chet's death, Gabe's

slogan was, "If you can't face the truth, don't vote for me. I'm too lazy to lie."

Ten days before the election, when Bert Culbertson came to interview him for a segment of *Forefront,* that statement was the first thing he challenged. The two men had a one-to-one lunch in the faculty room of the Foresby Union Building. Then they talked in front of the cameras in Gabe's office in the English department.

"What does that mean exactly," Culbertson asked, "that you're too lazy to lie?"

"Just what it says. The trouble with lying is, you spend all your energy trying to remember exactly what you said and who you said it to. If you tell the truth you don't have that problem."

"It's not an ethical matter then. It's more a question of enlightened pragmatism."

"I guess you could say that," Gabe said. "I mean *I* wouldn't put it that way, but you can if you want to."

"How would you put it?"

"I'm not trying to label myself in big letters as an *ethical* man. *If* I am, that's for somebody else to say. But I'm sure as hell not a pragmatist either."

"Let's not get away from this matter of *truth* in politics. In Washington they say politics is the art of the possible. How do you feel about that?"

"I think it stinks," Gabe said. "That definition is a big part of what's wrong in Washington. It sounds like the philosophy of a pickpocket."

"How would you define politics?"

"I think you'd better ask me that in a year or so. *If* I get myself elected. All I can tell you now is that the Latin word *politicus* means 'citizen' and the Greek word *politikos* means 'belonging to the citizens.'"

"'Of the people, by the people, for the people.' Is that it?"

"Doesn't sound bad to me," Gabe said. "Lincoln was no fool."

"Do you think of yourself as a party man or as a kind of populist?"

"Neither one."

"Does that mean you're not a loyal Democrat?"

"My brother was a Democrat and I always voted for him. And I am certainly running on the Democratic ticket. But I wouldn't support a second-rate man just because he was a Democrat."

"That's the kind of talk that makes some of your supporters very nervous. I've talked to a lot of shaky Democrats here in Illinois in the last day or two."

"That's what I hear," Gabe said.

"Some of them are very candid on the subject. They think they picked the wrong man."

"Maybe they did."

"You have to admit you weren't an obvious choice. Why do you think they chose you instead of Dumler or Hurst—some professional politician?"

"I *know* why they picked me. Because they want to win. And they decided they have their best shot with me."

"How does that figure?" Culbertson asked.

"Because the Republican candidate is Roy Spiker. Former governor and a two-term senator. He has a lousy voting record, but everybody knows his name. Chet barely beat him in 'seventy-eight. Spiker would murder Dumler or Hurst, and the Democrats all know it. So they're taking a chance with an unknown guy. With *me*. I may not be a winner, but I've got the same name as a winner. Chet never lost an election. So that's it. It's as simple as that. Half the people don't know who they're voting for anyway. They see a name they recognize and they pull the lever."

Culbertson smiled. "Well, you're a new kind of politician. No question about that."

"I'm not a politician at all. I'm just a professor of American literature who happens to be running for the United States Senate."

"But why? That's what doesn't figure. If none of this means anything to you, why bother to run?"

"It *does* mean something to me. Otherwise I wouldn't waste my time. I had a lot of faith in my brother. I believed in what he was trying to do. He felt that changes had to be made. He was dedicated to the idea of making certain things *happen*. So am I. By that I don't mean that I think I can *replace* Chet. I know I couldn't fill his shoes if I stayed in Washington for thirty years. But if I can do 10 percent of what he wanted to do, then it's worth a try."

"Do you really think you can get elected if you keep saying exactly what's on your mind?"

"I doubt it. Most people don't want to hear the truth. It scares hell out of them."

"And what if you *do* get elected? Do you think you can buck those high-powered people in the Senate? They won't just roll over and play dead, will they?"

Gabe shook his head. "I don't think so. I don't know what they'll do. But it'll be interesting to find out."

The Illinois voters saw the Culbertson interview on television three days before they went to the polls. The Republican Committee to Elect Roy Spiker made a transcript of the program, printed five million copies, and circulated them throughout the state.

There were handbills, too, headlined "The Gospel According to Treptow," with bold-type excerpts from the Culbertson interview. And Spiker taped a television message where he quoted a few of Treptow's outspoken opinions. During the last hours of the campaign, that message played in every major city in Illinois.

 Rafer Isbell, the senior senator from Illinois, was born in Lake Forest, Illinois, April 12, 1920. His grandfather Carl Isbell had gambled and bullied and swindled his way from Cicero to LaSalle Street. When he died, he left his son, Theron, three million dollars in government securities and four city blocks in Chicago's financial district.

By the time Rafer graduated from law school, his grandfather's original holdings had quadrupled in value. After long discussions with his father, Rafer decided to concentrate on tax law.

The company he formed, Isbell, Pellegrini, and Elam, did just that. His client list came to include some of the wealthiest men in Chicago. Most of them, like Rafer himself, paid no income tax whatsoever. And thanks to Rafer's wisdom it was all legitimate. Flagrantly legal.

When Rafer decided to run for the Senate in 1952, his clients were delighted to support him. The fact that he was running as a Democrat disturbed them, the memories of Franklin Roosevelt still raw and painful in their hearts; but they concluded that the *man,* a man who understood them and their needs, was in this case more important than the party. They muscled, maneuvered, and bought Rafer Isbell his first Senate seat. And they never regretted it.

They marveled, in fact, at his resourcefulness. While continuing to serve and further enrich these demanding gentlemen who had sponsored him, he managed to emerge as an articulate and indignant champion of the South Chicago blacks, the West Side Poles, and the tenant farmers and coal miners in the southern part of the state.

These supporters of Isbell later discovered and encouraged Chet Treptow. They saw him as an attractive right bower to Isbell's king. A downstate young and vigorous senator to team with their mature and experienced Chicago man. After Chet was elected, Isbell said, "Illinois will have *two* Democratic senators for many more years. I guarantee it."

After Chet was killed, the party leaders met in Springfield. They concluded after two days of argument and frustration that Roy Spiker could beat any candidate the Illinois Democrats might put forward.

It was Rafer Isbell who said, "Let's go for the long shot. Let's try with Chet's brother." And it was Isbell who finally persuaded Gabe.

After saying no the first half-dozen times Isbell asked him, one afternoon Gabe said, "What if I said yes, what do you think the odds are that I could make it?"

Isbell didn't hesitate. "A hundred to one against you."

Gabe laughed. "That did it. You sold me. I can't resist the odds."

Since no professional politician, Republican or Democrat, thought Gabe had any real chance, they let him campaign in his own way. For three weeks he drove back and forth, up and down, around the state. Talking to people, asking and answering questions, saying what he thought.

After the first week or so, when some of his statements cropped up in local papers, a busload of reporters and television people began to follow him wherever he went.

When an aide pointed out to Spiker how much press coverage his opponent was getting, Spiker lovingly adjusted his crotch and said, "Suits me fine. Every time that sucker opens his mouth, I get another vote."

The Democrats felt the same way. The day before the election, Isbell sat in a hotel suite in Springfield with Shirley Goodpastor, his executive assistant, Dwight Mather, his press secretary, and Armand Dooley, the state party chairman.

"It's not a case of winning," Dooley said. "Not anymore. It's just a question of how much we get humiliated. He's having the time of his life and we stand to lose a few hundred political appointments. Plus a Senate seat."

"Listen to this," Mather said. He picked up one of the flyers the Spiker people had scattered over the state, Gabe Treptow's picture at the top, and the headline "Is *this* the man you want to represent you in Washington?" Under the picture a dozen quotes from Gabe's speeches.

Mather began to read from the printed quotes. " 'Abortion is a private matter. I think government should stay out of people's sex lives. If a woman wants to have a baby, that's *her* business. If she *doesn't* want to, that's also her business. And if that woman happens to be on welfare, if she's entitled to government medical care, then she's also entitled to a free abortion. If that's not *medical* care, then somebody will have to explain to me what it is.' "

Shirley picked up one of the flyers and took a turn reading. " 'Instead of fighting birth control, the Catholic Church should encourage it. There's nothing Christian about babies sleeping cold on the bare ground, dying of exposure or malnutrition. The greatest social evil I know of is a starving kid.' "

Mather again. " 'I understand that one third of all the United States senators are millionaires. Does that make sense? Not to me it doesn't. Not unless one third of the country's population are millionaires. How can he understand—a man with a million dollars in the bank—what it's like to feed a family on minimum wage?' "

Mather looked up from the page. "Can you believe this?" He started to read again. " 'There is *no* nuclear energy question. The question has already been answered. It's too dangerous, so who cares if it's cheap? Only a lunatic would rather be dead than give up his electric toothbrush. There is no safe way to get rid of nuclear waste. It's as simple as that. And if you reprocess it you end up with plutonium. So however you look at it, it's a killer. Let's get rid of it before it gets rid of us.' "

"Jesus," Dooley said. "We'd better get rid of *him* before he gets rid of us."

"A little late for that," Isbell said. "The polls open in less than twenty-four hours."

"So far this candidate of ours has scared the shit out of every special-interest group in the state. The farmers, labor, the church, the bankers—he's taken a crack at everybody. If somebody had paid him to wreck his own chances, he couldn't have done a better job."

"There's no point crucifying ourselves," Shirley said. "It was always a calculated risk. We took a flyer and it didn't work."

Mather lit a cigarette, turned to Isbell, and said, "I suggest we find a nice congressional junket. Preferably one that leaves tomorrow. We'll inspect the radish fields in Bulgaria. Or maybe I can arrange a two-week audience with the Pope."

On the subject of Gabe Treptow, the columnists and the television commentators all agreed. He was a breath of clean air on the political scene. No question about it. He was honest and bright and fast on his feet. And Jessica Savitch thought he was sexy.

Several experts said it was a pity that the political structure, particularly the Senate, could not include an attractive maverick like Treptow. But they all concurred. It was, as things stood, impossible. It wouldn't happen.

Accommodation, everyone agreed, was the Senate watchword. Compromise and adjustment and finesse. No iconoclasts need apply. There was no niche or cranny in the Senate's private club for the original thinker. Logical conclusions and simple solutions were not the stuff of high-level politics. No bumpkins welcome. Certainly not intelligent ones who were capable of looking you in the eye and saying, "I've never heard such a line of crap in my life."

The Chicago Sun-Times said Treptow would be lucky to get 10 percent of the popular vote. The *Tribune* said he was likely to prevail only in his home precinct.

Roy Spiker smiled grandly when he showed up at his polling place and said, "I have great respect for Professor Treptow. If I wanted to study up on Bret Harte or Carl Sandburg, I'd go straight to one of his classes. But he's out of his league here. We're talking about government. And lawmaking. The people want experience. Established know-how. We expect to win by a substantial margin."

When all the polling booths were closed, everyone was startled to hear that there had been a record turnout. And they were absolutely stunned by the results.

Treptow had captured 63 percent of the precincts and 68 percent of the popular vote. His plurality had been nearly half a million votes.

In his victory speech from the front steps of his house outside Fort Beck, Treptow said, "I didn't make any promises when I was campaigning, and I don't make any promises now. Politics is a profession and I'm an amateur. When I finish my term in Washington, I have a hunch I'll still be an amateur. At least I hope I will be.

"We have a lot of national problems. Serious problems. I wish I could tell you that I have the solutions to those problems. But I don't. That's all right, though. Because I'm sure my fellow senators and their millionaire friends who got them elected know *all* the answers. They'd better, because I sure as hell have a lot of questions."

Two days before he was scheduled to leave Fort Beck and move to Washington, Gabe drove to Macomb to see his father. Following a week of early spring rain, it was warm now suddenly, the sky high and clear, fast-moving white cotton clouds, the cattle lazy and silent in the fields.

The nurse brought Howard Treptow to the sun room in a wheelchair. As soon as she left, he got up carefully and shuffled a few steps to a couch beside the window.

"Are you supposed to walk like that by yourself?" Gabe said.

"Not supposed to do anything in here except eat oatmeal and die. You got to get up a petition before they let you take a leak."

"Just try to take it easy. You don't want to break your hip again."

"That's right. I sure don't. But that doesn't mean I *won't*. I didn't want to break it the last time either, but that didn't keep the damned thing from breaking."

Gabe moved his chair over closer to his father. "Well . . . how you doing?"

"No good. Not worth a damn to tell you the truth. They tell you that getting old is a million laughs. And maybe they're right. But *being* old is a pain in the ass."

"Maybe it's just this place."

"No, it's not. I grunt and groan about it, but this place is just as good as any other place."

"You don't have to stay here, you know. You can come and live with me. You could have lived with Chet and Evelyn. And Helen and I must have asked you a hundred times. We meant it. I still mean it."

"I know you do, and I appreciate it. But that wouldn't be any good for you. And it wouldn't work for me, either. Misery loves company, you know. Whoever said that knew what he was talking about. I look around me here, I see people stumbling back and forth and slobbering on themselves, and I think I'm not so bad off. I mean I'm in brand-new shape compared to some of these derelicts."

"Well, I wish you'd think about coming to Washington with me. I'd like to have you around. I'm gonna need all the advice I can get."

"Not from *me*. Don't hand me that. Any brains you and Chet inherited you got from your mother. You got my size and you both resemble the Treptow side of the family, but your mother's people had the gray matter. They could handle figures and quote Shakespeare, and Thelma's uncle spoke three languages. He was an asshole but he sure could talk."

"I just don't like leaving you here by yourself."

"I'm not by myself. That's what I'm telling you. There's almost two hundred old farts living here. And thirty deadbeats, more or less, on the staff. Nothing but company whether you want it or not. Besides, your Aunt Nancy only lives twenty minutes away, and Homer's just over in Pekin. So don't start feeling sorry for me. I'm not desperate. I'm just old."

Gabe got up then, walked across to the corner of the lounge and got a cup of coffee. When he came back and sat down, he said, "I didn't get you any. I figure you're still on the wagon."

"That's right. No coffee. No tea. Nothing but skim milk and tap water. I used to dream about naked women. Now all I dream about are pork chops and doughnuts."

He gripped the chair arms with his knobby leather hands, raised himself up, and shifted his body farther back in the seat. "I must say, you don't seem very shot in the ass with yourself," he said then. "After everything I saw in the papers and heard on the radio, I expected you to come tooting in here with a big cigar and a gold hat."

"No you didn't."

"That's right. I didn't." He put his hand on Gabe's knee. "But I think you've got a right to feel puffed up a little. You sure made jackasses out of the experts. According to them you were due to get tarred and feathered. Shipped to Oklahoma or something."

"I think it was all Chet. I think the fact that I'm his brother had a lot to do with it. It was Chet and me together. A three-legged race."

"Maybe so. But not as much as you think. For every vote he got you, he might have lost you one. Remember—you beat Spiker a lot worse than Chet did. So I say you did it on your own. You said what you thought, and a lot of people liked what they heard."

A nurse walked up to them then, a solid, gray-haired woman with a pink face and gold-rimmed glasses.

"Congratulations, Mr. Senator." She shook Gabe's hand. "You had a lot of people rooting for you around here. Your dad probably won't admit it to your face, but I think he's real proud of you."

"I'm not too sure of that," Gabe said. "I think he's waiting to see how I get along in Washington."

"No he's not. He's proud as a rooster. You really picked him up. He's had a tough winter."

"Everybody had a tough winter," Mr. Treptow growled.

As soon as the nurse walked away, he said, "I can't stand that old heifer. She's all over me like a suit of underwear."

"She's just trying to be nice, I guess."

"That's the excuse everybody uses. But they ought to be smart enough to know that feeling lousy is a one-man job. You don't need anybody to help you. I know I said misery loves company, but it doesn't *always* work that way. Sometimes the worse you feel, the less you want to talk. Take you, for instance. I know how you feel about what happened to Chet and Evelyn and Sam. But I can't make it any better for you by yapping about it. Any more than you can make it better for me. All we can do is just stand here, like two old dogs caught in the rain, and get wet."

He looked out the window, then turned back to Gabe again. "Everybody keeps telling me I have to *forget.* But I don't *want* to forget. I want to *remember,* for Christ's sake. I·don't want to get over feeling bad. It's the only connection I've got left with your mother and your brother and Evelyn and Sam. I want it to last. I want it to last as long as I do. And I sure as hell don't want to *share* it. I want to keep it to myself."

Later in the afternoon, before he left to drive back to Fort Beck, Gabe pushed his father back to his room in the south wing, helped him into bed, and hung his robe on the back of the door.

"What's happened to Helen?" his father said then. "Have you heard anything from her?"

"Not since the funeral. I think she's out in California, but I'm not sure. I heard she was in Palm Springs."

"Damned shame," his father said. He adjusted the back rest on his bed and repositioned his pillows. "But . . . I guess you'll have women falling all over you once you get to Washington. I read in *Reader's Digest* there's something like six females there for every man."

"There you are. That's all the more reason you should move to Washington with me."

His father winked at him. "Maybe I should at that. I'll give it some serious thought."

 It was late in the afternoon, close to sunset, when Gabe drove down the southbound river road leading into Fort Beck. At the edge of town he turned in through a stone gate with a brass plate on one of the gateposts: ST. THOMAS CEMETERY.

Getting out of his car, he walked up a grassy slope to a cluster of sycamore trees at the top. Chet's headstone, and Evelyn's, were in a shady clearing side by side. Across the top of their burial plots, like a dolmen, was Sam's grave.

Walking past the graves, Gabe stopped at the wrought-iron

fence crowning the hill and looked through the heavy vertical bars at the city below. From there, Fort Beck seemed very much the same as it had when he was a kid in the early fifties, roaming the hills with Chet, swinging on vines, stealing hickory nuts and apples and pears, swimming in any pond or stream they stumbled on.

In Gabe's lifetime, Fort Beck's population had more than doubled, from thirty thousand to seventy-two thousand. But from where he stood, the visible growth changes were not in proportion to the population increase. The residential areas had spread out easily and almost gracefully up and down the Boone and back into the fields and hills at the edge of town, the city expanding by one house at a time, it seemed, rather than by great raw-edged and bulldozed developments.

In the older parts of the city, however, along the original river streets and around the courthouse, on the four-square-block grid that had been for many years the business and shopping core of the community, the changes of the past few years were stark and ugly. Empty stores or naked lots where business buildings had been razed. Pornographic book shops at addresses where the wealthy residents of Park Place or Holloway Street had once bought sterling dinnerware and ropes of pearls.

Dirty gutters, unswept sidewalks, and broken windows. No place to have a meal. No place to buy a book. Only long rows of red-brick nineteenth-century commercial buildings, 30 percent occupancy, many of them empty altogether, the remains of some years-ago window display still visible through the dirt-streaked plate glass; cars rolling down Ashby Street toward the Front Street Bridge, but only an occasional solitary pedestrian on the sidewalk.

Standing there, at the edge of the cemetery, Gabe could see his own house, far off to the left, across the town and across the Boone, three quarters of a mile upriver from North Beck. It sprawled across a knoll two hundred yards above the river, sycamore and elm, oak and black walnut trees studded around it like sentries.

He turned away from the fence, paused for a moment at the top of Chet's grave, and read, as he had a hundred times before,

Sam's headstone. Born March 13, 1972. Died January 16, 1980.

He moved on downhill then, to where he'd left his car, just inside the cemetery gate. He sat behind the wheel watching the sky grow dark. Then he started the engine and drove slowly home.

 A family counselor, upon examining the circumstances of Gabe's childhood, and Chet's, would have concluded, almost certainly, that the two boys would grow up twisted and confused. The pattern was classic. Motherless boys in a single-parent home.

Their mother died when Chet was six and Gabe was four. Sudden pains in the night, a burst appendix, and she was dead. Before the sun came up.

Their aunt Nancy Furman, Howard Treptow's sister, decided that the only sensible solution was for Howard and the two boys to come live with her and her husband. "Or if that don't sound good to you, we'll rent our place out and move over to Fort Beck. Wayne can do his carpenter work anyplace he wants to. One thing's sure, Howard. You can't handle those two little colts by yourself. They need to be cooked for and kept clean and looked after. Thelma would have done it for any kid of mine if it was me that was taken. So it's the least I can do for her."

The boys' Uncle Homer, their mother's older brother, and his wife, Enid, had pretty much the same idea. "Our kids are grown-up and gone, so we got room to burn. You just sell your place here, Howard, and move over to Pekin with us. There's plenty of construction going on in the good weather, and you won't have any trouble getting inside work when the winter turns nasty."

Howard Treptow sat listening, drinking coffee, and eating a piece of the pecan pie the neighbors had sent in. But when the funeral-home vigil and the funeral itself were over, and the burial, he sent everybody home. "Let me think about it a little. I've got a lot on my mind now. I'll get in touch with you in a week or so."

When they were inside the car, heading back toward Pekin, Homer said to his wife, "Forget it, Enid. Howard's bound and determined to raise those boys by himself."

For the first few months after Thelma's death, Gabe's father did all the cooking and the cleaning and the yard work. But the boys were always hanging on him, watching him work, asking questions.

Everything he did he carefully explained to them. He showed them how things worked—the vacuum cleaner, the gas oven, and the washing machine. He taught them how to oil the lawn mower and sharpen the blades, how to light the pilot light when it went out, how to put the chute in the basement window when the coal truck came, and how to take the ashes and clinkers out of the furnace.

By Chet's seventh birthday, he could cook breakfast. Ham and eggs and potato cakes. Or flapjacks and sausage patties. Less than a year after his mother died, he could make a meat loaf with mashed potatoes; he could shell peas and cook them, and make cowboy coffee. And he could iron a shirt so the only wrinkles were in places that didn't show.

Gabe did the janitor work. He stood on an apple box by the kitchen sink and washed the dishes. He dusted and mopped, washed windows, and ran the vacuum cleaner. And after his dad put a short handle on the lawn mower, he cut the grass. When he was seven, that late spring, he planted lettuce and carrots and green onions in a twenty-foot-square plot in the backyard. He hoed and weeded, and when the rabbits began to eat the carrot tops, he and Chet built a chicken-wire fence to protect the things he'd planted.

The boys did their homework after school. Or they did it after supper. Their father never asked if they had schoolwork to do and he never checked to see if they'd done it. "I'm not a police-

man. Besides, I don't know what you're assigned to do. You're
the only ones who know that. I mean you can horse-shit *me*
about it, but you can't horse-shit yourselves. The only *free* thing
you'll ever get in your life is what you learn in school. So anybody that don't take advantage of that is a dumbbell."

Until they were ten or twelve, he took them to Sherman Park
every summer Sunday to see the doubleheader. But then, gradually, he eased away from that. "You guys are growing up. I'm
not your playmate. I'm your dad. I don't want to hang around
so much you get sick of me. So get busy and branch out a little.
Meet some people. Learn a few things. Then come home and
tell me what you found out."

Their father was a tireless reader. There was a radio in the
kitchen, but except for the World Series and University of Illinois football games it was seldom turned on. Instead, Howard
spent his evenings and weekends with great stacks of books.
James Fenimore Cooper, Mark Twain, Jack London, Zane
Grey, Rafael Sabatini, Georges Simenon, Graham Greene, and,
surprisingly, Joseph Conrad. "I don't know what the hell he's
getting at half the time, but I feel like I'm in good hands. He's
a Polack, that bozo, but he writes English like he was born to
it."

Almost every night, just before bedtime, the three of them
played cards for half an hour or so. Hearts or euchre mostly. Or
casino. And once a week, usually on Thursday, they walked
downtown after supper and went to the movies. But Howard
eased away from that, too, little by little.

"The three of us don't want to grow together like Siamese
triplets—three bodies and one head. Nobody likes to be by
himself all the time, but you have to be *able* to be. I mean,
there's nothing or nobody in the world that can't be taken away
from you. All you can keep and protect is what's in your head.
What's in your skin. What you've taught your hands to do.
Everything else is up for grabs."

From the beginning, both Chet and Gabe were good students. They had an instinct for achievement, stimulated constantly by their awareness, each of them, of how well the other
one was doing.

Their father, professing ignorance of all things academic, but paying close attention nonetheless, praised them when they got high marks or earned some scholastic honor. But otherwise he stayed out of that part of their lives.

Athletics were something else. He insisted that they play the games. "I'm not trying to turn you into Luke Appling or Jay Berwanger. I don't care if you're all-state or all-city or all-nothing. But you have to take your licks and hand out a few. It's good to learn that. You have to hang in there and mix it up. Because you'll find out there are some places your brains can't take you. Sometimes you just have to back into a corner and slug it out. That's what you learn from playing football or baseball or lacing on the gloves."

When Gabe was eight and Chet was ten, he bought them each a set of twelve-ounce gloves. Then he took them out in the yard and taught them to box. Carefully. Properly. When they started to swing wildly at each other, he took their gloves off, put them back in the hall closet, and sat down with his book. "Any gorilla can throw a haymaker. If you don't want to jab and hook and counter, don't waste my time."

So they jabbed and hooked, learned to move to their left, to block and feint and slip punches. Both of them had broken noses before they were eleven. But neither of them ever got into a street fight, never brawled on the basketball court or on the football field. "You got the idea," their father said. "You _know_ what you can do. You don't have to prove it to every loud-ass you meet."

Howard Treptow didn't believe in sex education. Certainly not from father to son. He respected their privacy and expected them to respect his. When he strolled two blocks south on Hairston Street to while away an hour or so with Rachel Marlin, a forty-year-old widow who'd moved north from East St. Louis after her husband was cut in two in the railroad yards, Howard didn't expect Gabe or Chet to giggle or smirk or make any reference to it whatsoever. And they didn't.

One evening, however, when Chet was eighteen, when the three of them were sitting at the supper table, he said, "It wouldn't surprise me if you got married again, Dad. You'll have Gabe and me out of your hair pretty soon. I mean if the word got around that Howard Treptow was available, I'll bet there'd be a line of women outside here a block long. What do you think, Gabe?"

"There'd probably be a line halfway to the courthouse."

"What do you say, Dad?"

"I say you're both full of horse manure. I was lucky to talk your mother into marrying me. You two better stick to your own tomcattin' and leave me in the box stall. I'll save up my energy for being a grandfather."

 As the years passed, as Chet and Gabe grew up, they remembered less and less about their mother; Gabe particularly could not put clear pictures together from the first four years of his life. But they were curious about her, both the boys; they asked questions endlessly, and never tired of hearing the same stories over and over.

"Tell us about how you met Mom the first time," Gabe would say.

"You must know that one by heart by now."

"No we don't. Tell it."

"Well . . . I was working on a construction job over in Indiana. We were building a cement plant at the edge of Frankfort. Actually we were a mile or so out of town."

"And Mom rode by on a horse. Right?"

"That's right. Riding bareback on a little roan mare, with her skirt hiked up and her hair a-flying."

"What did you say to her?" Chet said.

"I didn't say anything. I just stopped work and watched her go by."

"Did she see you?"

"I don't think she did. Not that first time. But after that she used to ride by every day or so and we'd all look at her, and one afternoon, the foreman, a man named Chad Winger, let out a big laugh and said, 'Treptow, I think that little cutie has her eye on you.'"

"Did she?" Chet said.

"No," Howard said. "I've told you before, your mother came from good people. She didn't need to ride around the country looking for some hayseed cement finisher on a construction gang."

"Come on, Dad," Gabe said. "You're no hayseed."

"So how'd you meet her then?" Chet said.

"The only day we had off was Sunday. So I used to go into Frankfort and check out books at the city library so I'd have something to read at night. And one Sunday your mother was there so we started talking."

"And she said, 'Wow, who is this great-looking guy?'" Chet said.

"No, she didn't. I don't know what she thought when she first saw me. But I'll tell you one thing. I had to talk like a son of a gun before I could even get her to go out with me. I don't know to this day how I talked her into marrying me. She could have had her pick of a hundred guys. All smarter and better-looking than me. And drawing better wages."

"But she picked you. Right, Dad?"

"No. *I* picked *her*. And I wouldn't let her alone till she finally broke down and said she'd marry me. She wouldn't even tell her folks. She knew they'd find a way to stop it if they found out about us. So we just kept it to ourselves for a while, and then one Sunday I borrowed Winger's car and your mother and I drove down to Kentucky and got married."

"How'd you feel then, Dad? Pretty good, huh?"

"Felt lousy. I was scared to death. To start with I was a good fifteen years older than she was. And I was taking her away from her family and the town where she grew up, a big house with a woman who cooked and an old Filipino man who took care of the flowers and the shrubs.

"I felt like a pretty poor stick when we drove back up to Frankfort and she took me into the house and said to her folks,

'This is Howard Treptow. He and I just got married last night.' "

"Tell about what Grandpa said then."

"He took a good look at me and said, 'Well, if you take *my* advice, you'll get *unmarried* tomorrow.' "

"So what happened then?"

"Your mother and I got on a bus and came over here to Fort Beck. We rented a little flat down on Crockett Street near the square, and from that day till the time she died she never heard a word from her folks or any of her brothers and sisters."

"Except Uncle Homer," Chet said.

"That's right. Homer was another family outcast just like Thelma."

Howard Treptow never fully recovered from that one meeting with Fred Wilder, his wife Dorothea, and the multilingual uncle, Foster Wilder. Their assessment of him became, for many years, his secret assessment of himself.

Each time he and Thelma moved to a different flat or upstairs apartment, even when they settled at last into the little frame house on Linville Street where both the boys were born, as he plastered and painted, hung wallpaper and scraped floors, always at the back of his mind was the memory of that wide hallway and carpeted parlor in Fred Wilder's house in Frankfort.

He never stopped measuring Thelma's life with him against the life she had left in Indiana. The fact that she never mentioned her parents, never made an attempt to get in touch with them, convinced him that they were never out of her mind, that she missed them, that she missed that life, that somewhere inside her, there was a tiny gemstone of regret and resentment. The fact that she showed no evidence of discontent convinced him that she was not content, that she had taken a critical misturn, that she had married beneath her.

Through the eight years from their marriage till her death, he loved her totally and selflessly. She remained as fragile and fresh and appealing to him as she had been the first time they talked in the Frankfort library, as she had been the first time they lay in bed together in a tourist cabin just outside Chester, Kentucky. But the guilt that had clutched his guts as he stood all that long time ago in the parlor of her father's house had stayed with him too, had continued to burn and grow like a tumor. Even her death didn't end it. It simply changed the tense. Present guilt became past guilt and continued to rot his insides.

The guilt ended suddenly, however. Unpredictably. Almost six years after Thelma's death. Rachel Marlin stopped to chat one early July evening when he was trimming the hedge, and introduced herself. Then, before she strolled away, in her shantung summer dress and white pumps, she said, "I've always got a big jug of ice tea in my kitchen. Come over some evening if you want to and I'll pour you a glass."

Two weeks later, walking downtown with Chet one sultry Saturday, he saw her again, wearing a soft blue dress, walking with another young woman. She smiled as she passed and said, "That ice tea is still waiting. Whenever you want it."

"Who was *that?*" Chet said.

"I don't know. Some woman from East St. Louis. She's living a couple squares down from us."

"She's some hot-looking lady."

"What does *that* mean?"

"I just mean she's the best-looking woman I've seen in Fort Beck for a while."

"Twelve years old," Howard said, "and you're a lady's man."

"Not *me. You.* You're the one she's inviting over for ice tea."

Having assured himself that neither Rachel Marlin nor her ice tea appealed to him, he decided not to take an evening walk down to Hairston Street. But on the following day, a hot and sweltering Sunday, he watched Gabe and Chet bicycle off to a double-feature movie at five in the afternoon, and at five thirty he changed his shirt and strolled along to Rachel Marlin's house.

She was sitting on the porch, fanning herself and drinking lemonade. "Come on up and sit down," she said. "I'll get you a glass of something cool."

When she came back she said, "I decided maybe you didn't like ice tea, so I made up some fresh lemonade instead." She smiled and sat down on the glider beside him. "Just in case."

They sat there talking till the sun went down. She told him about her husband, how he'd been thrown between two switching freight cars and run over. "My little girl's staying with her grandma. If my job pans out here at Corn Refining, I'll bring her up in September so she can start to school in Fort Beck. Otherwise I'll hightail it back to East St. Loo and find some work there."

As the sky started to darken, she said, "We'd better get inside or the mosquitoes'll eat us up. I've got an electric fan up in my kitchen. That should keep us cool."

They sat in her kitchen talking for almost two hours. And when he got up to go, she said, "I'll tell you the truth. I'm not looking for a husband, and like I say, I may not be living in this town after September. But while I'm here I hope we can see something of each other. I haven't looked at another man since Marion got killed, but I don't mind admitting to you I get lonesome sometimes. Especially since I've been up here, away from my little girl and not knowing anybody. From what you told me, I'd guess you've been by yourself a lot too since your wife died. So it seems to me it wouldn't do anybody any harm if we spent some time together. Like we did tonight."

He went to see her often after that. At least two evenings a week. Sometimes three or four. After the first few visits they moved from the kitchen to the bedroom where they lay for long late-afternoon and early-evening hours on her soft white bed, shades drawn to keep out the August heat, the electric fan whirring softly in the doorway.

She was free and relaxed with him. She slipped out of her clothes as unselfconsciously as a three-year-old child, clung to him, kissed him, touched him tenderly, and made love to him fiercely with her tiny, muscular body.

After the first time, as they lay back on the crisp sheets, her head on his shoulder, she said, "I don't want you to think I'm some kind of a stray dog. All my folks are as poor as churchmice and Marion's were the same. But they're decent people and I'm a decent woman. Maybe you think I'm not good enough for you and you might be right. But I guarantee you I'll not give you any reason to be ashamed of me. Or ashamed of yourself."

After she went back to East St. Louis to take a job there in a department store and be with her daughter, Howard measured in his head the total time he had known her. Seven weeks and four days. He had taken her to the Greyhound station the day she left, and just before she got on the St. Louis bus, she said, "I wish I didn't have to go, but I do. It looks like I'll be in East St. Louis from now on, at least till Bonny grows up. And you've got yourself anchored here in Fort Beck. So we'd better not kid ourselves about anything. I'd rather say good-bye to you right now than to have it all peter out somewhere down the line. You know what I mean?"

"I guess so."

"I just want you to know that it's meant a lot to me. You made me feel better about myself. I needed to laugh and have some fun again and feel like I could be valuable to somebody."

They didn't write to each other. But fourteen months after she left Fort Beck he had a letter from her.

> *I'm not sure if it's a good idea or not for me to write like this. But I wanted to tell you I'm getting married next week. Maybe that's something that doesn't interest you. But it matters to me. I mean I didn't want you to just hear about it in some off-hand way. The man's name is Ralph Hemerling. He worked in the freight yards with Marion. He has a daughter ten and a boy twelve years old and he lost his wife two years ago so he's in the same boat with me.*

> *I never thought you and I would end up together. It just wasn't in the cards. But I won't ever forget that summer we had. I hope you won't either. You got me believing in myself again. You showed me that all my luck hadn't run out.*

Howard kept that letter in his shirt drawer for a long time. And every few months he'd get it out and read it. When he sold the house, when he was sorting through his things before he went into the nursing home, he read the letter one last time. Then he put a match to it, watched it burn, and dropped the black ash in the metal wastebasket by his desk.

Helen Leacock Treptow was born August 12, 1950, on a country estate twenty-five miles west of London. Her father, Gerald Leacock, was a career diplomat in the United States Foreign Service, an economics specialist assigned to the embassy in London.

Helen, an only child with an eccentric mother, was raised by an English nanny and schooled by tutors. Later she went along to Cambridge, where she studied archaeology and museum science and fell in love at the age of nineteen with a thirty-year-old alcoholic from Seattle who had spent his entire adult life in colleges from Berkeley to UCLA to Michigan to Heidelberg to the Sorbonne to Cambridge. His name was Jess Miley.

He had a remarkable flair for Slavic languages and he excelled at every university he attended. When he met Helen, he had doctorates from UCLA and Heidelberg, and he was working toward a third one at Cambridge. In addition to his unusual scholarship and his absolutely Wagnerian drunkenness, he was bisexual and a skilled artist on the cello.

Helen was mesmerized by the wonder of this man. Although his talents and achievements were electric, his faults were the hooks that captured her. He was flawed and wounded. And irresistible. Two weeks after they met, they drove north to Aberdeen and got married.

Helen—all of whose nineteen years had been solid, warm, and undangerous, who had been endlessly catered to, who had learned to expect that kind of concern and careful treatment but was nonetheless bored silly by it—found, with Jess Miley, a totally new rhythm. The mistress became the servant, the patient became the nurse.

Her instincts and her upbringing had taught her order. She had learned that chaos could be avoided or muted by a careful attention to detail. As a ten-year-old, when she was being punished by her nurse, or when she was angry with her father for some imagined slight, she quieted herself by taking all her stockings and underclothes, blouses, sweaters and nightwear, out of her drawers and stacking them on the bed. She would reline the drawers then with fresh paper, carefully refold each article of clothing, and put it back in its proper place.

Her schoolwork, too, had reflected her drive for order, her need for it. Her mind was not quick or profound. She didn't have strong curiosity or a genuine passion to learn. But she had a retentive memory, a talent for organization, and a need to excel, a very specific desire not to make a fool of herself. So her notebooks were exemplary, her papers neat and well researched. And she was always carefully prepared for written examinations.

Helen's school marks, invariably high, reflected her self-discipline rather than her intelligence. She was a perfect student. Hampered by no theories of her own, no preconceived notions, she could be taught anything. By the time she reached Cambridge, her mind was an extremely expensive intellectual file cabinet.

From this carefully contained slow dance of security, she was plunged suddenly into a maelstrom of days without meals and nights without sleep. Blasting Bartók and Shostakovich for hours on end. Then white silence. Long periods of study when Jess could not, *would* not, be disturbed or distracted by any sound more penetrating than the folding of a towel.

After their wedding trip, a headlong ten-day drive among the hills and lakes of West Scotland, Helen always driving, Jess more often than not either drunk or asleep in the backseat, his cello in front beside Helen, after that trip ended, when they returned to Cambridge, she realized at once that she would have to withdraw from her own classes.

There was no possibility of adjusting their schedules, hers to his or his to hers. If she was to see him at all, be with him ever, she saw that she would have to chart his moves, try to anticipate his ever-changing itinerary, and insinuate herself into that tumbling, back-and-forth swirl as much as she could.

Jess was careless and self-serving. But there was no cruelty in him. His sins were sins of omission. Helen simply did not know, ever, where to find him. Or when to expect him. Or if she could expect him at all. Cambridge is not a huge city. His circle of friends was not great. But he could not have been more difficult to locate, more impossible to track, if they had lived in Tokyo or Calcutta.

He never lost his temper. In their off-and-on more than three years together, she never saw him angry. He would agree to anything, promise anything, laugh if laughter seemed appropriate, or weep if that seemed the thing to do.

"I just want you to be happy," he said. He said that very often. Then he would smile like an urchin, make love to her, play for hours on the cello, and drink a bottle of Bombay gin. And if she woke up at two in the morning, he'd be gone.

The pattern of their physical life together was set during their wedding trip. For more than a week he drank constantly, in the car, in their hotel rooms, or in the highland pubs. They never *went* to bed together. She put him to bed. He went to sleep or passed out in chairs, on the floor, wherever he happened to be when the gin finally overpowered him. Each night she lifted and pulled, half-carried him to the bed, and rolled him, heavy and half-dressed, under the down comforter.

Two days before they were to start back to Cambridge, however, she woke up one morning in an inn called The Golden Gull on a hill road near Kinlochleven. Rain was pounding against the window, and Jess was standing naked beside the bed.

Clear-eyed and smiling, he said, "Don't you think you've put me off long enough? We didn't get married so we could live like a brother and sister. I demand my marital rights."

Making love to her slowly and lazily, he aroused her to craziness before he pulled her to him, thrust firmly inside her, and broke the membrane. Then, while it rained and blew and pounded outside, he whispered and laughed in her ear, stroked her softly, and stayed inside her for more than an hour, bringing her past the first pain and up to a tentative quivering climax.

Then he punished, pounded, and rocked her through an endless chain of orgasms, her breath rasping in her throat, her arms flung wide and limp, fingers twitching, her body soft and heavy and helpless except for an animal upward driving, spasmodic, pushing and bucking up from the bed, her inner muscles contracting and releasing, squeezing him, holding him, breaking loose inside herself then, groaning and whimpering, hurting, aching and breaking loose again till at last, still twitching like a dying animal, she lost consciousness and lay dead still, with some fragile web of nerve endings still alive, feeling him move heavily in and out of her, while the chambermaids clattered tea trays in the corridor and the rain slashed down endlessly, streaking across the leaded windows.

When they were back in Cambridge, in their third-floor rooms in a stone house overlooking the river, his arrhythmic, unpredictable sex patterns persisted: long periods, weeks sometimes, when he came and went, drunk or sober, laden with books, lugging his cello more often than not, when he charmed and chided and teased her, patted her, kissed her warmly on the cheek, but never turned to her in the bed, never responded to whatever tentative overtures she found the courage to make.

She accepted those long lapses because some primitive female wisdom told her she had no choice. And she accepted, eagerly, the explosive, violent turnarounds when he abandoned everything else—classes, friends, drinking, music—and engulfed her, stifled her, crushed her with unrelenting physical love. Rolling and twisting and turning her into every possible position, he teased and tantalized and punished her with his hands, his mouth, and his penis, on the floor, in the tub, on the table, in her car, in the fields, or standing up in dark doorways on their way home at night from the movies.

It was a frenzy, a sexual frenzy, as overpowering and physically shaking as an attack of epilepsy. But it was real and recurrent. And she was caught up in it at least as thoroughly as he was. It became her rhythm as well as his: long periods of cool abstinence, the details of the days and nights meshing together in some predictable manner, followed by a harsh and sudden, almost ugly period of naked combat, two white, glistening bodies at war, locked together, fused, fighting and loving and trying to die, struggling on the edge.

It was an imperfect way to live, a pattern conceived by a four-year-old. All indulgence on one side, self-indulgence on the other. A kind of emotional hide-and-seek. A child's game in grown-up clothes. Grown-up words spilling out of baby mouths. And a grown-up bed for a playpen.

Still, they served and fulfilled each other in many real and critical ways. The masochist had found her gentle sadist.

Helen believed, without question, that Jess was truly brilliant, a genius perhaps. So allowances had to be made. A man whose intellect could carry him, swallow-swift, to the far dark corners of whatever philosophical or philological maze anyone might contrive, and bring him back singing with the proper, sought-after sprig of laurel in his beak; a man who could slump in a chair, pale and exhausted, adjust his battered cello between his knees, and transport himself, and anyone else within earshot, to some peak level of soaring, multi-colored sensual ecstasy that could not be described later or reproduced ever, such a special person had to be catered to, dealt with gently, considered, and cared for. Even when pain was involved.

After two nervous and apprehensive meetings, each of which ended in a sodden shambles, there was no longer any question of bringing her father and Jess together. It was the same with her friends. Her best friend, Judy Carbondale, summed it up. "It's hopeless, Helen. The man's a maniac. It doesn't matter if he's brilliant. He should be confined. Francis and I love you. You know that. But we can't handle him. We don't even want to try."

It was the drinking that finally undid them. It had always been difficult for her. Because there were strong armatures of control in the way she conducted her own affairs, it was agonizing for her to see him so often and so totally out of control. The unexplained absences the gin brought on were almost more forgiveable in her eyes than the ugly chaos he dragged home with him.

She reached a point where she simply could no longer stand the stink. His clothing damp and yellow with urine and stiff with vomit. Sour sweat, foul breath, and the sweet sickening smell of the gin itself.

Each time she undressed him, wiped him like a child, bathed

him, and dragged him to the solitary cot he called "the drunk bed," it seemed like the ten-thousandth foul-smelling repetitive time. And each time as she washed herself in the bathroom, like a soldier after a filthy battle, when she heard the neighbors through the window referring to her and Jess as "those nasty bloody Americans," each time she said to herself, It's the last time.

But each time he charmed and seduced and shamed her away from the truth. He knew her well; he knew that, whatever revulsion or disgust she might feel, he could turn her full around by simply looking up from the floor where he lay in a pool of his own piss and saying, "Help me. I'm sorry. But *help* me."

He was right, of course. When he was helpless and hopeless, unable to walk or control his bladder, she couldn't turn her back on him. Trying not to breathe and forcing herself to function like a benevolent robot, she drove herself through the familiar routine, transforming what seemed to be a survivor of war on a dung heap into a cleaned-up, smelling-of-soap, dead-asleep, but apparently civilized man.

Finally, however, one October afternoon, catching him quiet, at home, in a chair by the window with a book, she said. "You're forcing me to leave you, Jess. Don't you see that? You're driving me away. If you don't stop drinking like a lunatic, I'll *have* to leave. No choice. I can't help it."

He sat there looking at her. Finally he said, "I can't stop drinking. I'll *never* stop drinking. I don't even *want* to. It's how I get through everything."

"What does that *mean?* What is there to get through?"

"Nothing, I guess, for you. That's why I drink and you don't."

She started crying then, and slumped down on the floor by his chair. He leaned over, put his arms around her, and held her close to him for a long time. She got up finally and went into the bathroom to splash water on her face. When she came back into the sitting room, he was gone.

She heard the car engine start downstairs. As she came to the window and pulled the curtain aside, he backed out along the carriage path and turned left onto the street. Through the rear window of the car she could see his cello.

Five weeks later she had a picture postcard from him, mailed in Milan, a limerick scrawled in red ink on the back:

> There once was a dandy named Dan
> Who humped a divan in Milan
> The results were quite scary
> The child was mohair-y
> Its ass made of braided rattan.

Ten days later she received another postcard. From Venice this time, the picture a reproduction of "The Doge" by Bellini. The carefully printed message said:

Dear wife:
I miss you a lot. I think concessions are in order. All of them by me. Although I never promised I'd be perfect, I know I can be a lot more perfect than I have been. I'd like to try. It's worth it to me if it's worth it to you. I love you more than a hundred.

Jess

That was the last she heard from him. A week or so after the second card arrived, her father drove up from London. Word had come through embassy channels that a Jess Miley from Seattle had been in an accident in Venice. He was dead.

Helen and her father flew to Venice that night. A man from the U.S. consulate there took them to the police station, where they were told the details. Jess had been found floating in the canal. Stripped naked. With his throat cut.

When they searched his hotel room in the Monaco y Grande Canale, they found that all his clothes had been hacked to pieces, his cello had been smashed, and someone had defecated in the center of his bed.

The day after Helen flew to Seattle with Jess's body, his family had him cremated. They left his ashes in a synthetic brass urn in a garish mausoleum in downtown Seattle.

There was no religious service. "We're not church people," his father explained to her. "We believe that life is simply a series of cycles. There may be some order to it all, but there's no clear evidence even of that. Food spoils, milk sours, and people die. And that's the size of it."

On the plane from Seattle to San Francisco she started to cry and couldn't stop. The memory of the Miley family wouldn't go away. The bone-thin parents with lipless mouths, milky gray eyes, and voices like corn husks rubbed together. And the two sisters, twins, white-skinned and obscenely fat, eyes like tiny pierced holes in a suet ball, their pink fish-mouths opening and closing constantly on morsels of sweet ugly food.

How Jess could have come from such a place, from such loins, from such frightening people, baffled Helen. And it saddened her. How had he transformed himself? Where did all that energy and fire and creativity come from? All his flaws and failures and perversions seemed like triumphs now when measured against the putrid, self-satisfied decay of his family.

"No wonder he stumbled and floundered," she thought. "No wonder he drank like a maniac. What a miracle that he was able to function at all."

In San Francisco Helen found a job in an art gallery. She rented an apartment in an old frame house on a hill looking north. And she stayed there for almost two years. She made no close friends. She avoided, in fact, any intimate associations. She was open and warm to all the people she met through her work. At least she pretended to be. But at the end of the day she went home alone to her apartment.

Just as she had as a child, she occupied herself totally with the details of her life. She cleaned her apartment, waxed the floors and washed the windows, did her own laundry, and looked forward to the evenings when she listened to classical music, wrote letters to her parents, and did the ironing.

She went to the theater and the ballet and to concerts. But not on a regular schedule. She liked to decide at the last minute, go to the theater late, and take a chance that there would be a single seat available. It was a new kind of recklessness for her, one of her few excitements. When there were no seats—it happened rarely—she took the cable car back to her neighborhood and went to a movie. Or she sat in the coffeehouse just down the block from her apartment building and read a mystery novel.

She did not think of herself as a damaged person. She did not define herself to herself in any way at all. She simply attended to her job and to her own needs and resisted any impulse to plan ahead.

All the same, she knew she had not set a permanent template to her life. Without wishing or planning for anything specific, she knew that at last some fresh avenue would open up. Some job, some place, some person. She would know it when it happened. Until then she was simply Helen Leacock Miley, young widow on her own. Learning to live by herself.

In November 1974 the Society for American Studies held its annual convention in San Francisco. The University of California gave a reception for the delegates at the Fairmont. Also invited were local writers, artists, museum and art gallery people. Helen went, along with two of her associates from the gallery. She met Gabe there.

Four of the five nights he was in San Francisco, they had dinner together. At Christmastime she went to Fort Beck and stayed for a week with Chet and Evelyn. In February Gabe flew to San Francisco during a semester break. And in April they got married in the chapel at Grace Cathedral. Chet and Evelyn were there for the ceremony.

Later, after they put Gabe and Helen on the plane for Honolulu, as they were driving back to their hotel, Evelyn said, "Well . . . what do you think?"

"I think they've got it taped," Chet said. "World by the ass. What do *you* think?"

"I think you're right. You've got a lucky brother."

"Wrong. You've got a lucky sister-in-law."

Everyone agreed, it seemed. Especially Gabe and Helen. "We *fit*," she said. And they did. No storms. No collisions. They laughed a lot, cared about each other, and lived a fine warm life in the house on the slope that led down to the Boone River. For almost five years.

Then, on December 27, 1979, Helen flew to El Paso, crossed the river to Ciudad Juarez, and got an instant divorce. No one knew why. Except Gabe and Helen. And even they were not totally sure.

 When Chet was in law school at Northwestern and Gabe was in his final semester at Foresby, they lay awake late one Saturday night, in Chet's Huron Street apartment, after a five-hour pub crawl up and down Rush and Wabash on the near north side. Boasting and lying about their sexual victories, dead tired but exhilarated still from countless mugs of Michelob and Meister Brau, they lay in the two beds on opposite sides of the room, laughing, listing their triumphs, and pondering their splendid futures.

"Only one problem," Chet said. "What if we marry two girls who hate each other?"

"Couldn't happen."

"Sure it could. Happens all the time. Family feuds result. Civil war. The Hatfields and the McCoys."

"Well . . . if that happened, I guess we'd just have to get rid of them and get two new ones."

"I thought of that," Chet said. "But I decided it would be simpler if I kept mine and you got rid of yours."

"Jesus, Chet. You've got to stop sacrificing yourself for me. When are you going to start thinking about what's good for *you?*"

"Never, I guess. That's just the way I am."

"You're a saint. That's what you are."

"You're right," Chet said. "But don't spread it around. They'd never let me take the bar exam."

As it turned out, they could not have selected two women more chemically and psychologically different than Evelyn and Helen. Both were intelligent and well educated, both were attractive. But beyond that, all points of comparison were stark and conflicting. Or so it seemed. Black and white. Severe as a woodcut. No soft middle tones.

Helen's childhood had been cool and formal. No brothers or sisters. Governesses and boarding schools and tutors. Careful attention to dress and manners and social decorum. Rules and standards always in evidence. Few opportunities for improvisation.

Intent on slipping into the mainstream of upper-class English life, her parents, with her mother in the lead, had become, like Henry James's pilgrims, more British than the British. Admiring the conservative clothes of their country neighbors, they began to wear garments that were even *more* subdued. Soft wools in tones of gray. Tweeds from Scotland, brown and smoky, shades of heather.

They developed a taste for boiled vegetables and overcooked beef or mutton, for Stilton and port. And whiskey without ice. Having installed a magnificent heating system in their country home, they made amends by keeping the temperature at fifty degrees.

Without admitting to anyone that she was making the effort, Helen's mother carefully acquired the rhythms and the vocabulary of Etonian speech, cultivated a kind of offhand indignation that seemed proper, changed the pitch of her laughter—laughed very little, in fact, after her first few weeks in England—and quickly learned the credo of upper-class English parents: Children must not be spoiled or confused by too much parental affection. And they should be sent off to a proper school as soon as they're old enough to signal for permission to visit the water closet.

Evelyn, on the other hand, Chet's wife, had been smothered from infancy with attention and affection. The youngest child and only daughter in an upper-middle-class family in Philadelphia, she had been fondled, spoiled, and catered to by her parents, her two older brothers, and a small tribe of childless aunts and uncles.

Pretty and plump, a cherished and contented child, Evelyn had skipped along from one peak of acceptance and popularity to the next, from kindergarten through her undergraduate years in the speech department at Northwestern.

She tap-danced, toe-danced, gave dramatic readings, excelled in the backstroke, sang, played the violin, and displayed herself in school theatricals from sixth grade up to and through college. She made the dean's list, won scholarships and awards, and from age fourteen on was a perennial and voluptuous beauty contest winner, prom queen, and a sought-after guest for house parties and ski weekends.

When she graduated from Mrs. Upshaw's School in Bryn Mawr, under her photograph in the yearbook it said, "Evelyn has it all and she's going for more." Four years later, her college yearbook noted, "Nothing can stop Evelyn. Except Evelyn."

This prediction mystified her and disturbed her. After a lifetime of approval, some nameless yearbook staff writer had questioned her suddenly, felled a tree across the road, hung up a cardboard cloud. Those six casual and silly words burned themselves into her consciousness and stayed there. She was suddenly unsure about tomorrow, next month, next year. Most important, for the first time in her life, someone had echoed her own secret evaluation of herself.

Six weeks later, however, early in August, she and Chet Treptow got married. And Evelyn's tomorrows became solid and sure again. In her diary the night before the wedding she wrote, "Nothing can stop Evelyn. Not even Evelyn." She wasn't sure what it meant, but it made her feel better, as though she'd found a voodoo doll, an exact replica of herself, and destroyed it before any pins could be stuck in its heart.

So . . . by a dice roll, by the random circumstance of their marrying two brothers, Helen and Evelyn came together, in a small city surrounded by hills and meadows and cornfields.

Sisters-in-law. They had a relationship and a label almost as soon as they met. A label that implied warmth and trust, that seemed to demand intimacy before there had been time or opportunity for even simple friendship. What were the odds against this apple and this orange tumbling into a bowl together, rolling to the center, and remaining there, easy and smooth, the rough peel of one against the high gloss of the other? Insurmountable odds. A thousand to one? Probably.

But they did come easily and agreeably together. And they stayed that way. They never named it or discussed it, but each of them sensed from the start that they complemented each other. In a simple but most unexpected way.

From a childhood spent very much alone, with no strong family life or sense of place, from a chaotic first marriage, Helen had emerged miraculously whole, tempered, it seemed, by both the shortcomings and the excesses of her life so far. She had seen herself sink to the bottom and come up again. Her fantasies had been destroyed, many of them, but she had survived. She sensed a foundation under herself. She inhabited her own skin.

Evelyn's situation was simpler in a way. But harder to understand. And harder to fix. She had managed to pirouette her way through twenty-plus years of health, beauty, love, admiration, achievement, every kind of fulfillment and acclaim she could have possibly envisioned, and had come out at the end adrift and unsure, out of touch with herself and her needs, feeling strangely guilty and unwanted.

A lifetime of approval had given her nothing except an appetite for more approval. It angered her that she needed it and it angered her when she didn't get it. And it frustrated her that she felt free to confide in no one. Not even Chet. Then Helen appeared, and everything changed. Evelyn talked and Helen listened, and in some inexplicable way each of them was nourished by the process.

A few weeks after Gabe and Helen came home from their honeymoon trip, Chet called Gabe at his office one afternoon and said, "Remember when we used to be worried that we'd marry a couple of bimbos who wouldn't like each other?"

"Yeah. I remember."

"Looks like we can forget about that," Chet said.

"Yeah. I guess we can."

 Both Evelyn and Helen detested the structured activities that the ladies of Fort Beck created to help themselves kill time and spend money. They avoided the bowling league, the bridge club, and the quilting society. Also the literary club, the dramatic club, and the ladies' auxiliary to the Junior Chamber of Commerce. They used the pool and the tennis courts at the country club, but they gracefully avoided the gaggle of ladies with blue hair who spent four afternoons a week in the bar overlooking the eighteenth hole, gossiping about television performers and sipping Polish vodka with orange juice.

Although Helen was by nature a listener and Evelyn was by necessity a talker, those psychological circumstances did not dominate their relationship. In fact, once Evelyn knew that there was at last one person she could talk freely with, once the lid had been loosened and the pressure released, she no longer felt that raw drive to unburden herself, to babble and cry and scream, to blurt it all out before the moment passed, before the listening person got away. She knew Helen was permanent and unchanging. At least in relation to her. Two sisterless women had discovered a sister. Or so it seemed to Evelyn. Where once she had needed to tell everything, to confide, to struggle for understanding and guidance, now she took pleasure in carefully parceling out her thoughts, her anxieties, the hoarded facts about herself and her family. Small portions, a little serving at a time. Making it last.

"I always felt as if my parents had divided up their responsibilities the day I was born. My mother would make me beautiful, teach me grace and manners, how to run a house and deal with servants. And my father would teach me to be somebody important. Somebody special. Somebody with a gift. I don't know what got into them. I know they always wanted to have a daughter. From the beginning. But when I finally came along they'd already been married for sixteen years. Two sons and three miscarriages. But no daughter. Not till me. By then I guess they'd waited so long that *just* a daughter wasn't enough. I had to be the *best* daughter that anybody ever had. Everyone had to notice."

Another time, when they were driving into Springfield, Evelyn said, "It's funny how kids get things screwed up in their heads. We all think if we love our children enough they'll never have any problems. But I'm not so sure. I was loved so much I was stifled by it. My folks, my brothers, my teachers, my friends. I can't remember any time in my life when people weren't falling all over me.

"And all the time I was studying, taking lessons, learning to *do* things so even *more* people would love me. And it worked. Except I got it all turned around. I didn't say to myself, 'Gee, I'm important to a lot of people, so I must be valuable.' I said to myself, 'My job is to *make* people love me. More all the time.' What I *didn't* say, but what I *felt*, was that if *one* person didn't think I was the greatest thing since ice cubes, then I was a complete failure. I mean I'd got myself into such an idiotic *approval* pattern that I was like an addict. I needed bigger doses. Stronger jolts. Thank God I got out of the acting thing. That would have really flipped me over, I think. If I hadn't met Chet when I did, God knows where I would have wound up."

Very often, Helen responded with something like, "You're

really crazy. Do you know that? Every woman who knows you envies you."

"You don't."

"That's because I know you're paranoid and psychotic and a fruitcake. But everybody else, including Chet, thinks you're Cinderella."

"Bull."

"I mean it," Helen said. "To start with, you've got a great bod."

"Big boobs. Who needs them? Ever since I was fourteen I've been wishing I could wear a B cup."

"Fantastic legs."

"A little thick in the ankles. Too much ice skating. When I was eight my dad had a fix on Sonja Henie."

"Beautiful hair. You can't deny that."

"I found three gray hairs yesterday," Evelyn said.

"And on top of all that you've got a world-class husband."

"That's true. No argument there. No complaints."

"Your only real problem, as I see it, is Sam. It's tough to have a second-rate kid. No personality. Not too bright. Somebody you have to hide upstairs in a closet."

"That's right," Evelyn said. "Poor old Sam." Then, "We should all have Sam's problems."

"You mean *no* problems?"

Evelyn nodded. "Eating the world with a spoon. I think an angel kissed that kid. I can't imagine him ever wanting something and not knowing how to get it."

"Take some credit. Good breeding stock."

"Not me. What Sam got from my side of the family you could put in a thimble. He's a Treptow. Ninety-nine percent pure."

It was *that,* Helen decided, that explained her reaction to him. Always, when he crawled up in her lap or when she saw him laughing and tangled together with Gabe in a deep chair or on the floor by the fireplace, she felt an aching throb down inside herself. Part of that feeling she understood. Another part of it she didn't comprehend at all.

13 There are five small and independent sheikdoms on the west shore of the Persian Gulf: Kuwait, Qatar, Bedaki, Oman, and Bahrain. In international political chambers and in angry boardroom discussions of the Gulf, Texaco, and Standard Oil companies, these five are referred to as the United Arab Emirates.

Each is oil-rich beyond comprehension, bare and desolate and culturally geared to another century. Each functions as a conservative monarchy, all power vested in the sheik, the emir, the Arab sultan or prince. A ruler who was once gifted annually with his weight in gold and precious stones now receives many times that amount from oil revenues. Not in one year as before, but in the time it takes him to sip a few cups of sweet, thick coffee.

Dependent on outside sources for almost everything, these countries also need to import foreign labor. This makes them vulnerable to their neighbors and to their enemies, to radical Arab groups of all persuasions, hot-eyed political and religious activists who feed on local minorities and grow strong as they spread dissent.

Consider Bedaki, a tiny lozenge of a country, less than one thousand square miles, not even a third the size of Kuwait, but second only to Kuwait among the emirates in the size of its oil reserves.

Largely desert, but with marshland areas along the coast, Bedaki is one of the world's leading oil producers. Sir Ronald Fraser, then president of British Petroleum, who made the first oil explorations there in 1937, said, "The entire country, from one border to the other, is like a bottomless sea of crude oil, crusted over with a bit of earth and a thick layer of sand."

Fraser's company, however, did not profit greatly from their find. In 1941, following a complex international trade-off between British Petroleum, Dutch Petroleum, and Aramco, all the drilling rights in Bedaki were assigned to Aramco. The sheik, Abu Khamufa, then a young man of twenty-three, would share equally in the Aramco profits.

In 1966 the Abu, now an enormously wealthy man with thirty-one wives and nearly two hundred children, declared himself a prince. His subjects, many of them still living nomadic, penniless lives, others glutted with automobiles, electronic playthings, and free health care, made no objections.

But a group of dissidents had begun to form. Foreign workers, students, Islam purists, and a handful of professional terrorists began to put together what would come to be a sustained program of dissent.

Soon rumors began to circulate about police brutality, about losses of freedom; leaflets were printed and distributed listing inequities and what had begun to be referred to as "crimes against the people." Portable radio transmitters blasted out a litany of abuse against Abu Khamufa, his brother Ibn, and all the male members of the sheik's family.

The dissenters by now had named and identified themselves as the NPC, the New People's Committee. Its leader, educated at Princeton, a longtime exile in Iraq, was Ishaq Rashid.

Some oil lines were bombed then, a tanker was partially disabled, and soon the letters *NPC* began to appear in the world press, linked sometimes with Italy's Red Brigade, sometimes with the PLO, and most often with the far-left forces in Iraq.

Castro mentioned the NPC in a speech to the nonaligned nations, called Rashid his brother, and condemned the United States for continuing to support Khamufa. A prominent French motion picture actress identified the NPC as "an inspiration to all the world's subjugated peoples."

Abu Khamufa was not concerned. He expanded his secret police force, the Kaskar, and occupied himself with other matters. His program of highways and social reforms. His campaign to assume greater personal influence in the United Emirates. His constant bargaining for increased arms shipments from the

United States, France, and the Soviet Union. And his program, begun in 1969, to fully nationalize Bedaki oil.

Following the example of his Saudi Arabian neighbors, he allowed Aramco to continue pumping from Bedaki fields, but only on a contract basis. He, the Abu, would now own all the oil. Aramco would receive an exclusive right to purchase at a figure just under the world market price. Having captured Aramco's 50 percent, Khamufa was willing to give them back perhaps 2 percent. More or less. Temporarily.

In September of 1979, when the NPC surfaced suddenly in surprising numbers, armed with Soviet grenades and automatic weapons, when the radio stations, the newspapers, the oil fields, and all government buildings were seized and occupied in one hour and twenty-seven minutes, when the Abu and his family, alerted two days before, were able to flee to Zurich, where he had carefully deposited, through the years, billions of Swiss francs, the prince told a complex story of who was to blame for his fall.

Iraq, he said at first. Then he implied that Turkey perhaps, and certainly Iran, had a hand in his overthrow. And Aramco, of course, was never to be trusted.

Only Cuba, which admitted publicly that it had sent advisors to help Rashid, and the Soviet Union, which had unquestionably furnished the NPC weapons—only those two nations escaped the Abu's censure.

In *The New York Times* Sidney Harbaugh suggested that the Abu was not perhaps as displeased by his forced exile as one might suspect. He had gone to school at the University of Chicago and later at M.I.T., at least two of his wives were American women, and he had never concealed his affection for American luxuries and American automobiles.

"Time will tell," Harbaugh wrote, "what effect this new government will have on the Bedaki people. Mideast observers will be slow to draw conclusions till they have more specific signals from Rashid. There will be a series of trials, no question about it, involving some of the Abu's top officials as well as members of the detested Kaskar. But government leaders around the world have made it clear to Rashid that they will look with extreme disfavor on the kind of bloodbath justice that followed the Shah's departure from Iran. Since Rashid has always been an outspoken critic of Khomeini, no one expects him to repeat the Ayatollah's mistakes.

"As for Abu Khamufa, we suspect he will buy the Hearst castle, the Waldorf, or some such suitable maison, install himself and his considerable family and proceed to lead the good life. After all, he'll be sixty-two years old next month. Perhaps, like many of us, he's decided that early retirement isn't a bad notion after all."

Rumors persisted that the Abu and his family either had left Switzerland and come to America or would do that soon. But security was tight in Switzerland, and hard facts were difficult to come by. At last, however, the Swiss government announced that the Abu's party had indeed taken off from Geneva, in two chartered 747's flown by Varig airline crews, destination not disclosed.

That same day, Ishaq Rashid announced that Abu Khamufa and all the adult males of his family were considered by the NPC to be enemies of the Bedaki people. Any country harboring them would be committing an unfriendly act toward Bedaki.

"This does not mean that my government will send gunmen halfway around the world to assassinate the Abu or members of his family. This is not Iran. I am not the Ayatollah. I would never give such a barbaric order. We will make every effort to bring Abu Khamufa here for trial. But if we fail, I will not send men to kill him.

"I do *not*, however, guarantee his safety. No one can make such a guarantee. The Abu Khamufa, his father before him, and his grandfather, made many enemies. Thousands of Bedaki people suffered and died as a result of their commands. Many families still bear those scars. If we are not able to bring the Abu to trial, if we cannot recapture the riches he stole from our country, will some angry patriot take the law into his own hands? I cannot answer that. There is an ancient Persian proverb: 'A man with bloody hands leaves a bright trail.'"

At the end of his speech Rashid said, "We are a small country. A peaceful people. We do not perform hostile acts or threaten our neighbors. But our principles are important to us. As new leaders of a people who have been oppressed for centuries, it is critical that we demonstrate to them how we propose to activate our programs, how we will make practical decisions that reflect our political ideals.

"In that spirit, I make the following announcement to the leaders of the world's nations. Bedaki produces four million barrels of oil each day. This oil is sold freely to those who need it. The United States, for example, buys 2.2 million barrels every day.

"We will continue this policy of free-market sale. With one exception: Any country that gives asylum to Abu Khamufa and his family will no longer be able to buy oil from the wells of Bedaki. Never again as long as I am the leader of this nation."

Eight days after Rashid's speech, the President of Costa Rica announced that the Abu and his family had arrived there the day before. They had asked for asylum and it had been officially granted.

Later, films were released showing the Abu's new residence, a huge walled estate in the wooded hills north of San Jose. Limousines were seen coming and going, and uniformed guards manned the gates and patrolled the grounds.

Between Constitution Avenue and C Street on Capitol Hill is the Richard Bernard Russell Senate office building; just behind it, fronting on First Street, the Everett McKinley Dirksen office building. One block north, on D Street, is the Monocle restaurant.

The Monocle never appears on the constantly revised lists of the capital's ten best restaurants. It is seldom mentioned in newspaper gossip columns as a place where one is likely to see

Goldwater or Proxmire or Jack Javits. The Palm, the Prime Rib, the Sans Souci, and the Lion d'Or are more often regarded as the watering places of the mighty.

The fact is that in the Monocle, particularly at lunch time, day in and day out throughout the year, one is likely to count coups on more senators, representatives, and other greater and lesser kudu than in any place outside the Capitol dining rooms themselves.

From just before noon till well after two in the afternoon, the downstairs bar and two-level dining area, as well as the upstairs dining room, are filled and busy, the air humming with advice, admonitions, warnings, directives, and considered counsel. Power speaks to power. An almost three-dimensional sense of urgency is present. The problem must be clarified before the entrée, the solution presented before the coffee arrives. And some understanding, some accommodation must be reached before the brandy glasses are drained and the cigars stumped out. Otherwise . . . God knows what.

On his first day back in Washington after Gabe Treptow's election, Rafer Isbell had lunch with his two closest friends on the Senate side: Richard Basenfelder, the senior man from Nevada, and Owen Bright, in his fourth term from Mississippi.

Isbell prided himself on the fact that he had many close friends in the minority party. He had engineered critical legislative compromises with Fletemyer of Kentucky and Harvey Kitchin of Montana. Those two, as well as half a dozen other Republican senators, were frequent guests in Isbell's Bethesda home. Early in his Senate career he had been quoted as saying, "Our similarities and our common goals must be stronger than our party differences. Otherwise, our constituents suffer for it, *we* suffer for it, and the country suffers for it."

In his private moments, however, secure and heavy in his chair, his belt one notch looser than normal, no important votes or committee decisions scheduled before mid-afternoon, he preferred the company of these two men, Basenfelder and Bright. In a world where caution is king, where one useless word or unqualified statement can wreak havoc, these three knew that with each other they could be as careless and unqualified as they pleased; they could abandon caution and speak whatever private heresies they wished. In an upstairs private corner at the Monocle, they could, with each other, come as close to the truth as their instincts and experience would allow.

"I would give a lot if I could have seen Spiker's face when those returns started to come in," Basenfelder said.

"I saw him on television," Bright said. "He was so green around the gills I got up to adjust the set. But the more I adjusted it the greener he got. I just wish I'd put a couple of thousand on that sideshow. Fletemyer offered me ten to one. I could have ended up with twenty big ones."

"Only if Fletemyer's wife countersigned the check," Isbell said. "She controls the money in that house. And everything else. She even tells Arthur how to vote. When she takes a leak, he flushes the toilet."

"Don't kid yourself about the money," Basenfelder said. "Arthur's a slick proposition. Did you ever see that duck-hunting jacket he keeps in the basement? He's got enough fifty-dollar bills wadded up in those game pockets to keep us all going for five years."

"He didn't go to divinity school for nothing. Every time he goes home to Kentucky to make a speech he winds it up with a prayer. Then he passes the collection plate."

"That's why he keeps giving those showboat television interviews saying we should divulge our assets. Because he's strictly cash-and-carry. He's like Lyndon used to be. Everything in his wife's name."

"According to him, he's always broke. Dimestore ties and J.C. Penney suits. But I guarantee you he's got half a million dollars folded up in his underwear drawer. And another million stuck in paint cans in his garage."

They ordered coffee then, and Isbell passed his cigar case around.

"What really happened out there in Illinois?" Basenfelder asked. "I talked to Sam Donaldson yesterday and he said it was the political miracle of the century."

"Told me the same thing," Bright said. "And he gives you the credit, Rafer."

"I'm happy to take the credit," Isbell said. "But I don't deserve it. I don't know *what* happened. I'm tickled to death to see us keep that seat, but don't ask me how we did it. I didn't think Treptow had a chance in a thousand. And neither did anybody on my staff."

"He must be a high-powered jaybird."

Isbell shook his head. "None of us thought so. But he certainly kicked the shit out of Spiker. And he didn't do it with mirrors. He just got the votes. The money people in Chicago didn't go for him, and he lost a lot of the Catholics, and the Polish vote up north, because of his stand on abortion and birth control. But every other section—white collar, blue collar, the farmers, the unions, the young voters, the old cockers—they all went for him."

"It had to be the name," Bright said. "His brother was a popular guy. It's Jack and Bobby all over again. Same old song."

"That's why we picked him," Isbell said. "We thought we could drum up some emotional votes. And we leaned hard on the fact that he's not a pro. Not a politician. An intelligent, responsible citizen. That old routine. But _that_ didn't do it. _He_ did it. He won the election with his mouth. He came down as hard on our party as he did on the Republicans. He took Carter apart like he was boning a fish. Said he was the only Democratic president ever elected by the Republicans. And one night in Chicago he did an hour and twenty minutes on the Trilateral Commission. He tied Carter and the Rockefellers and the oil companies and OPEC into a tight knot you couldn't blast apart with nitroglycerine. And he was just warming up. The next day he stood up in front of five thousand black truck drivers in the south side of Chicago and called Jesse Jackson a racist. And he made it stick. He carried the black vote in the state five to two."

"What's the poop?" Bright said. "Is he just reckless or is he smart?"

"Both," Isbell said. "But his big edge is he doesn't give a damn about being reelected. He says he's in office just to finish out Chet's term. He made it a campaign promise. He said, 'Hot or cold, when 1984 rolls around, I'm gone. Until then I'm gonna tell you the truth, whether you like it or not. But when 1984 comes, you'll get a chance to vote in another lopsided lawyer with mush in his skull and his hand in your pocket.' "

"Jesus," Basenfelder said, "if this guy sets a trend, we'll all have to go home and go back to work."

"I've known him for eight or nine years," Isbell said. "I met him when he campaigned for his brother for the Illinois legislature. No big fireworks when he comes in the room, but he does his homework. If he tells you how many cars General Motors recalled in 1979, you don't have to look it up."

"He looks like a rugged guy in his pictures."

Isbell nodded. "Six feet. One eighty-five, one ninety maybe. Easy going. Low-key. But when some red-neck came at him with a knife one night in Hoopeston, Gabe tossed him through a plate glass window."

"How's he gonna fit in on the Hill?"

"He's not. You can't negotiate with a man who doesn't *want* anything."

"Can you handle him?" Bright said.

Isbell shook his head. "Not a chance. I can *talk* to him, but I can't handle him."

"Will he vote with us?"

"He will when he feels like it, I guess."

"Maybe we'd have been better off with Spiker. He's in the wrong party, but at least you can scare him. You can scare the shit out of Spiker with a toy mouse."

Basenfelder chuckled. "You tell Spiker he's about to lose his parking space on the Hill—he'll put on a false beard and vote straight Democrat."

Bright called the waiter over then and ordered three Rémy Martins. Easing back in his chair, he twined his fingers together and said, "If I ran a department store in Hattiesburg and this Treptow was my son, I'd make him assistant manager of the fertilizer department and give him some time to educate himself. But we don't have time for that. We've seen these high-powered assholes before. They come and go. If Mr. Treptow wants to shoot craps with us, he has to roll *our* dice. If he's as smart as you say he is, he'll get the picture."

Basenfelder grinned. "We'll have the Steering Committee give him some assignments where he can really be useful. Things like Merchant Marine Standards. Or Post Office–Civil Service."

"You can't keep him off all the major committees."

"That's right," Bright said. "We'll put him on Judiciary, Richard, where you can keep an eye on him. You can give him something with a lot of paperwork. Like Immigration and Naturalization."

"I think you're underestimating him," Isbell said. "You can't bury this guy. He'll go public on you."

"Maybe he will and maybe he won't," Bright said. "I guarantee you he won't get much newspaper space or air time by talking about the problems of wetbacks or what we have to do to get the mail delivered faster."

"Right now, Treptow looks like a winner," Basenfelder said. "But if we stick him in a corner with a dunce cap on his head, he'll look different. He'll catch on. If he gets his act together, we'll give him a key to the men's room. Otherwise he can piss in the street till it's time for him to pack up and go back to Illinois."

 Late in the afternoon, the day before Treptow was scheduled to leave for Washington, Helen called him.

"Guess who's in Chicago."

He carried the phone to the chair by the bedroom window and sat down. "I thought you were in Palm Springs."

"I couldn't stand Palm Springs. Have you ever been to Palm Springs?"

"No."

"Don't go. You'd hate it. I stayed three days. Then I went to London to clear my head."

"How was London?"

"Good. I saw my folks. At least I saw Dad. Mom was off on what she called a cultural mission. Six weeks in Bucharest looking at icons or something. She left the day after I arrived and came back two days before I left. Par for the course."

She paused. When Gabe didn't say anything, she went on. "I've been in New York the last few weeks. Since the end of February actually. You remember my cousin Maribel who works for *The Wall Street Journal?* I stayed with her. I just flew into Chicago about an hour ago. Checked into the Airport Hyatt. I want to ship that stuff I left in storage there in Fort Beck."

"You didn't have to make a special trip for that. I could have handled it for you."

"It's all right. It was on my route. I'm going out to California again." Another hollow pause. Then, "If you're not all booked up, I thought maybe I'd drive down there tonight. I got a sexy red Thunderbird from Avis. Did you eat yet?"

"It's only five thirty."

"I'm still on New York time," she said. "I could pick up some Kentucky Fried Chicken. Or some hamburgers maybe. You have any beer?"

"Everything's pretty well cleaned out, I'm afraid. I'm leaving for Washington tomorrow afternoon."

"Then I'll bring a six-pack. What'll it be? Chicken or hamburgers?"

"I think I'd better pass. I mean, it's nice of you to offer, but I don't think it's such a great idea."

She answered quickly. "Okay. I can take a hint. Just thought I'd ask. . . . Listen—congratulations on the election. I think it's terrific that you won the way you did. I thought you'd win, but . . . look, I'm sorry I called. You're right. It wasn't such a brilliant idea. I just had an impulse. You know me. So, anyway . . . good luck in Washington."

The line went dead then. When he jiggled the phone, a dial tone buzzed through.

He hung up the receiver and crossed to the bed where his canvas suitcase lay open, another suitcase open on the floor;

stacks of folded shirts, jackets, and underwear were scattered about on chairs and on top of the low, brass-fitted military chests that stretched along one wall.

He began packing the shirts. Deliberately. One shirt at a time. Suddenly he stopped, walked back to the phone, and called the Hyatt in Chicago.

When the hotel operator answered, Gabe was stuck suddenly. He wasn't sure what name she'd be using. He said, "Give me the front desk, please." When a smooth, androgynous voice came on, Gabe said, "This is Gabe Treptow. I believe my wife is registered there."

When she answered the phone, Gabe said, "What's the matter?"

"What do you mean?"

"Your voice sounds funny."

"I've been—I was sneezing. You know me. When the seasons change, my sinuses get crazy."

"Did you hang up before or were we disconnected or what?"

"I didn't mean to hang up. I just felt like a jackass all of a sudden and I couldn't think of anything else to say."

"Look," he said then, "if you still want to drive down . . ."

"Thanks anyway. I think you were right."

"I didn't mean that. I just thought it wasn't such a good idea for you to—"

"I know what you meant. But I think maybe we'd better leave it lay, as some famous lady once said."

"I'm not doing you a favor."

"I know you're not. I just think . . . I decided to go on to California tonight. My flight leaves in forty minutes."

16 In Washington, Gabe checked into the Madison Hotel. He called no one. He had said to his father before leaving Fort Beck, "It's a big jump for me. I want to give myself some breathing room if I can. I think I'll sort of ease into town. Like a cattle rustler. I won't be sworn in till next Tuesday, so I'd like to settle in a little—talk to some cabdrivers and feed the pigeons."

Also he wanted to test himself. It would be the first time in the past four months that he had been completely alone. In that short period every foundation stone in his life had shifted. His marriage had exploded. His father's health had capsized. Chet and Evelyn and Sam were dead.

And now he was leaving his house, his town, and his job. The people, the places, the sounds, and the smells he had grown up with. His books, his students, the campus, and the classrooms. All that, he had chosen to abandon.

He didn't deceive himself, however, that this physical act, this nine-hundred-mile eastward move, would be in any way a panacea. On the contrary, he suspected that a new address would only sharpen focus on the devastation he had been trying to struggle through.

Those expectations turned out to be correct. Shutting himself away from the early-spring splendor of Washington, he lay in his hotel room with the shades closed and allowed himself to sink as far down as his instincts insisted he go. Making no effort to rationalize, with no impulse to heal himself, he lay on his back in the half-dark and stared up at the blank ceiling. For the first time since just before Christmas he loosened the bonds he had kept on his feelings and allowed himself to grieve.

The central icon of his loss slowly blurred through then, a clear but complex picture. It was the last time he had been together with his father and Helen, with Chet and Evelyn and Sam. The previous Thanksgiving Day. Piecing that day together like a mosaic, he forced himself to remember every image and moment, to recall each snippet of conversation, every family joke, each stumble or hiccough, each kitchen scent.

People slipped in and out of soft focus, a montage, their voices rising and falling, fading, then sharply claiming attention.

Sam said, "I like pumpkin pie the best. Anybody can tell that I like a piece of pumpkin pie with whipped cream as well as almost anything. But at Christmastime I like mince pie. If it's made with real mincemeat. Not just some kind of raisin goo with a bunch of other stuff stuck into it so it *looks* like mincemeat. Or smells like it. If it's fake, mince pie is no good. Dad says nothing's any good if it's fake."

Evelyn said, "We always had venison for Thanksgiving in Philadelphia. And squash pudding. And apple cider. And I hated it. We had dried ears of corn on the table and bouquets of autumn leaves and everything *authentic*. So much so that I didn't believe any of it. I never knew what Thanksgiving was like till I moved out here. You have to *see* all those cornstalks and pumpkins in the field before you have any idea of what Thanksgiving started out to be. If you're stuck in a city and you've never seen anything *grow*, how can you know what a *harvest* is, what it means to plant the food people eat, to watch the weather and be afraid of it, to pray for a good crop?"

When Howard rolled his wheelchair back from the table finally, he said, "Well, I've made a hog of myself, and I'm not sorry. The thing I'm thankful for today is that I've got two daughters-in-law as pretty as dancing girls, they're both crazy about me, and they *cook* even better than they *look*, if such a thing is possible."

Evelyn had come over early that morning to help Helen prepare the dinner. When Gabe woke up at eight thirty, he could hear them laughing and talking downstairs in the kitchen. When he called down on the intercom, Evelyn answered. "Go back to sleep. No men wanted in the kitchen. Your wife and I are getting bombed on cooking sherry."

When he got up later he found a note wrapped around his can of shaving soap. Held there with a rubber band.

Boy, did I hate to get up. My idea of a great Thanksgiving would be to spend it in our nice warm bed. Maybe we'll do that tomorrow. Or Saturday. Or both.

Love—Me

When Chet and Sam and Howard showed up at about noon, Sam and his grandfather went straight to the library to watch a college football game they'd made a dollar bet on. Chet and Gabe sat in the den in the basement, drank beer, and watched the professionals play in Detroit. At halftime, when they turned the sound down, Chet said, "Take a good look at me. Maybe you should take a Polaroid shot. Because a year from now I may have my ears laid back and all my hair pulled out."

"What does that mean?"

"It means that starting next January, your big brother is going to start putting the screws to some people in Washington."

"Why January?"

"I'm giving them a year. It'll be a year in January since I was sworn in. I've been laying back, playing the game, watching and listening and taking notes. But when 1980 comes, I intend to start throwing grenades. They think they've got me house-broken. Isbell figures if he whistles I'll bark and eat a dog biscuit, but he's due for a big surprise."

"What have you got against Isbell?"

"It's not just him. It's the whole fucking Senate. I could tell you some stories that would curl your hair. In this past year, in just *one* year, if I'd had my hand out I could have made three times my salary. Easy. My phone rings twenty times a day and somebody says, 'We want to help you. What do you need? What can we do?' And technically it's all perfectly legal. They don't hand you a bag full of money. They just offer you *opportunities*. You put up five thousand dollars and in two years it's worth a quarter of a million.

"I'll give you an example. We have a senator on the Finance Committee. He's a key mover in energy legislation. But at the same time he owns a lot of oil and natural gas properties, more than a million dollars worth. They give him an annual income more than double his salary. How does that grab you? And that's just the beginning. Believe me. The tip of the iceberg. Look at Isbell. If anybody ever tried to untangle *his* finances—with the campaign contributions, legal fees, real estate investments, and the income from thousand-dollar-a-plate dinners all mixed up together like a plate of spaghetti—there'd be an explosion that would shove Cook County twenty feet out into the lake."

"So what are you planning to do?" Gabe said.

"Blow the whistle. Name names. Make waves."

"What's that going to do to your political career?"

"I'm not sure. It may wreck it. If it does, I'll practice law again. Or I'll teach school. Or I'll tend bar. But one thing I'm sure of. I'm not interested in hanging around Washington pretending to do a job I can't do because Isbell and his asshole friends won't let me."

"You've been in politics for ten years," Gabe said. "Are you telling me you never saw people on the take before?"

"No, I'm *not* telling you that. But I really expected something different in Washington. Maybe I was naive. But I was proud as hell when I was elected to the Senate. I thought it was an important job. Important work to be done. I still think that—that's why I can't just sit on my hands and watch what's happening. I may not be able to accomplish anything. They may burn my ass. But I've got to try. I still believe that if people find out what's going on, they'll raise enough hell so things will get changed. But maybe I'm wrong. We'll find out."

It was that speech, those words, remembering them, that got Gabe back on his feet, out of his hotel room, and into the streets of Washington, walking, thinking, planning ahead.

He realized how much Chet's few impassioned words had influenced his own campaign, shored it up, driven it forward. Those words were the real reason he was in Washington. When he'd told Isbell that he would make a run for the office, when he finally made that flippant remark about irresistible odds, it was the echo of those words of Chet's that had pushed him to decide.

Feeling alien and unarmed in Washington, two days away

from his swearing-in and from all the uncharted territory ahead, he fantasized that his maiden speech on the Senate floor would be, as nearly as possible, a playback of Chet's Thanksgiving words to him. The thought gave him a kind of reckless strength. But whatever political wisdom he had accumulated said no. Off-tackle might work. Or an end run. But it wasn't time for a straight-ahead plunge. Not quite yet.

 "Do you, George Albert Treptow, solemnly swear that you will support and defend the Constitution of the United States of America against all enemies, foreign and domestic, that you will bear true faith and allegiance to the same; that you take this obligation freely, without any mental reservation or purpose of evasion; and that you will well and faithfully discharge the duties of the office on which you are about to enter, so help you God?"

The day was April 22, 1980. Two weeks after Gabe's election. It was eleven fifteen in the morning, a light day in the Senate Chamber, perhaps thirty senators present, listlessly debating financial aid to the Virgin Islands.

After Gabe was sworn in, there were two welcoming speeches, one from Rafer Isbell and another one from Harvey Kitchin of Montana, the minority leader. Then Gabe was taken to lunch in the Senate dining room by Isbell and his friends.

"Bright, Basenfelder, and Isbell," Basenfelder said. "B, B, and I—Bully, Bruise, and Intimidate." He laughed. "Don't you believe it, Gabe. The fact is we're pussycats. Three of the gentlest souls in the chamber."

After lunch, mid-afternoon, the Virgin Islands discussion still piddling along, Gabe stood up at his desk, far to the left, second row from the top on the Democratic side, and asked the chair for recognition.

"I would like to lend my support to the bill in question," he said. "The amount we're talking about is comparatively modest. Six point two million dollars. And the need is real. No question about it from the evidence that was presented here this morning. Also, certain stipulations as to how this money should be spent have been carefully included in Senator Bagby's bill. I would hope that we could have an early vote on this and move along to more urgent matters."

There was an instant of quite remarkable silence on the floor and Gabe, after a pause, went on. "Mr. President, if I may, I would like to add a few personal remarks. As all of you know, this is my first day here. And like a schoolboy who's late getting to class, I'm anxious to catch up.

"I've been told that it's unusual for a freshman senator to take an active role in debate during his first few months in office. I respect that tradition. But in my case, since I'm late starting and since I'll be here only until November of 1984, I think it would be a mistake for me to hang back and waste time."

Gabe cleared his throat, took a sip of water, and glanced around the chamber. It was three-quarters full now. "I am a political tenderfoot," he went on. "Many people are amazed that I'm here at all. But I *am* here. And as I take my first steps I trust my colleagues will be patient. When I played football in college, the scouting reports on me used to say, 'Not too quick. But very durable.' I suspect that's the way things may work out here. But all the same, I promise you I'll be as quick as I can."

The senators had warmed up noticeably by now, a combination of Gabe's disarming remarks and whatever they'd had to drink for lunch. They settled back, easy and relaxed.

"I understand that Robert Kennedy made a major address on this floor during his first week as a senator. I have no intention of doing that on my first day. I do want to define myself a little, however, and perhaps correct some misconceptions. When I met with my staff for the first time yesterday, they informed me that a certain reputation, I should say *reputations,* had preceded me here. Some of the labels they mentioned were 'half-baked liberal' and 'right-wing hawk.' "

General laughter at this point. And Gabe went on. "Seriously, whatever credentials I bring here, whatever public service I may be able to perform during my term in office, I want my beginning position to be clear. I am proud to be here as a senator, I am honored to be included, because I know I am in the company of honorable men."

Now there was a spontaneous burst of applause.

"Many people criticize the Congress. They find fault with the Senate. I disagree with those critics. I disagree with *The Congressional Quarterly* when it says, 'At least fifty-four senators have personal financial interests that could conflict with their committee responsibilities.'

"Charges such as these can't possibly be accurate. If they were, it would mean that the senators in this room are not true representatives of the people who elected them. It would mean that the lawmaking process itself is not working.

"If such charges were true, it would mean that our entire system of individual rights and constitutional guarantees is coming unglued. We all know that can't happen. The reason it can't happen is that this chamber is filled with men who would prevent it. One hundred honorable men. I am proud to be included in such a group, and I pledge that I will do my best to uphold its high standards."

Gabe's speech was quoted in part that evening on the Washington, D.C. television news. And the next day, in both the *Post* and the *Star.* That afternoon a telegram came to his office.

YOUR BROTHER'S DEATH NO ACCIDENT. BOMB ON PLANE.

The telegram was signed R. M. KOSTA.

When his secretary showed it to Gabe, she said, "This is your typical crackpot telegram. Every senator gets a few of these every week."

The first day Gabe went to his headquarters in the Everett Dirksen Building, when everyone squeezed into his private office for a meeting, he announced that he planned to keep the staff intact.

"That doesn't mean you can't quit if you want to. But I hope you won't. I'd like you all to stay on."

His chief assistant was Judson Rimmer. Jud had been Chet's friend since law school. They had roomed together in Chicago, dated sisters for two years, and later each of them had been best man at the other's wedding.

After school, they'd formed a law partnership in Fort Beck. And as soon as Chet got into politics, Jud became his campaign manager and chief advisor. They considered themselves a team, through almost ten years, through the local and state political offices Chet had held. When he won his Senate seat, Evelyn was on one side of him on the victory platform, Jud on the other.

Smiling and waving his hands, Chet had shouted to the crowd, "The three of us are going to turn Washington upside down." In Washington, however, Jud began to sense, for the first time, the amount of space, both width and depth, that separates a senator from his staff. Remaining fiercely loyal to Chet, he nonetheless began to plan ahead.

Nona Sugarman was a fifty-one-year-old widow. She had been Chet's first secretary when he began to practice law in Fort Beck, and she'd stayed with him. No one had ever questioned her devotion to Chet or to her job. In private Gabe called her

Desdemona. "Some day she'll stick a letter opener in you," he told Chet. "All that unrequited love—"

"What makes you think it's unrequited? She's a little out of proportion, but I'm sure she'd be willing. If you were any kind of a brother, you'd audition her and give me a full report."

"—all that unrequited love," Gabe went on, "will come bubbling out of her like detergent. She'll rip your picture down from her bedroom wall, drink a bottle of Southern Comfort for breakfast, and carve you up with a letter opener when you walk in the office."

"Not Nona. She's saving me for her old age."

"Starting next year."

"That's right," Chet grinned. "She *is* starting to sag a little."

So Nona was there in the Washington office. With Chet she had insisted on being both his personal secretary and his appointments secretary. But when Gabe arrived, Nona hired him a new personal secretary, Monica Cullen.

Monica was a tall, slender girl, originally from Red Wing, Minnesota, who could type faster, without errors, than most people could talk. She was reputed to be a young woman with a chancy personal life, but she was a quiet, almost solemn model of decorum in the office.

There were five legislative assistants, four men and one woman, all young, bright, and aggressive and all from eastern schools—except for Dave Matlock, who came from Granville, Ohio, and had gone to DePauw on a tennis scholarship. In his junior year he switched from economics to political science and transferred to the University of Michigan. From there to Yale Law School. From there to Clark Clifford's law firm in Washington, and from there to Treasury. At last, with a cool eye on his personal political future, he had joined Chet Treptow's staff.

Gabe's press secretary was Patty Ingledow—short yellow hair, granny glasses, and thirty pounds overweight. Born in Springfield, Missouri, she had studied journalism at the State University, then put in two years on the *Kansas City Star* and three years on the *Indianapolis News* before joining Chet.

The rest of the staff, twenty-odd people all together, were secretaries, typists, general office assistants, research people, and two speech writers. All of them were crammed into five rooms clustered around the senator's office. Three of those rooms were subdivided by plywood panels, providing the illusion, if not the fact, of privacy.

In another building three blocks away, seven more clerks sorted and answered routine mail. And when Gabe's committee assignments came through, he would have at least a dozen more assistants scattered here and there. In Illinois he would keep four regional offices which did case work for constituents. These offices employed ten more people.

Checking over the personnel list with Jud and Nona his second day in the office, Gabe said, "We're a light industry. I was expecting to deal with eight or ten people. A dozen at the most."

"We'll be adding more soon," Jud said. "We're understaffed. If you have half the energy Chet did, we'll all be up to our ears in work."

"Senator Treptow," Nona began. "I mean, your brother, Chet, had two senior advisors. One was Vincent Pointer. He'd been a longtime lobbyist for the coal industry. The other one was Glenn Patterman. He's a retired federal judge. At one time, during Johnson's administration, he was an under secretary of commerce."

"They're both gone now," Jud said. "We should be thinking about some new people to fill those jobs."

"I think I'll go slow on that," Gabe said. "I have a hunch that advice is something I'm going to get a lot of."

"The thing is," Jud said, "those jobs are in the budget. We're funded for them. If we don't spend up to our allowance, we'll be dead when we ask for an increase next time around."

"If we're not spending what we're allotted, why do we need an increase?"

Jud and Nona exchanged a look. No comment in it, just simple eye contact.

"That's just the way it works," Jud said. "The bigger your budget, the more people you have working for you, the more influence you have on the Hill. And the more chance you have to get your ideas and programs across. If you're not spending more money and pushing for more staff, everybody assumes there's no action in your office. Makes it tough when election time comes along."

Gabe sat quietly for a moment. Then he said, "Jud . . . I'll tell you the truth. I don't give a damn what anybody *assumes* about me *or* this office. I'm not trying to learn somebody else's rules. I'm not trying to win a friendship trophy. And more important —I am *not* trying to be reelected. I am *not* campaigning for 1984."

Nona smiled and said, "A lot of us think you may change your mind about *that.*"

In his office at the State Department, Mark Dalrymple sat behind his desk, the Lincoln Memorial framed in the window oehind him, James Lasker, his associate, sitting just in front of him.

"I can't believe it," Dalrymple said. "They promised me we wouldn't have a problem."

"I know."

"What kind of a dance are we doing here? Don't they know we're squatting in a bonfire?"

"They know, all right. Newquist has tried to reach me half a dozen times since I got back to the office. I wanted to report to you before I returned his calls."

"They're not leveling with us. Somebody made a secret deal. I mean that bastard's not going to look us in the eye and tell us to take a flying screw unless he has strong support. And there's only one place that kind of support could be coming from."

Lasker nodded. "That's right."

"But Newquist says no. Isn't that what he keeps telling you?"

"Not exactly. He won't let himself get boxed in. He denies

there was any agreement made in secret. Then he shoots the whole thing down by adding, 'according to my best information.' "

"Which means if the President made a deal, he didn't tell Newquist about it."

"That's the way I read it. What about the Secretary?"

"What about him?" Dalrymple said.

"What does he say?"

"Dead silence. He's not crazy. He knows I've been lying my ass off to Rashid. So he's covering himself. If this thing blows up, he wants to be able to say it's all news to him."

"Is there any way you can protect yourself?"

"Sure. I could call Dan Rather over at CBS or write a letter to Ben Bradlee. I could also cut my throat, but I'm not going to. If the President talked when he should have listened last winter the Secretary knows about it. You can bet on that. You can also bet he doesn't want me to *remind* him that he knows it."

Lasker took a cigarette out of a lacquer box on the desk and lit it. "So what do we do?"

"We're in a corner. Where there's nothing to be done, you do nothing."

"You never know. Maybe we'll get away with it."

"Maybe we'll sprout wings and turn into eagles."

"I mean it. I think time's on our side now. The FAA thing held together. Bedaki's off the front pages. And we seem to have Rashid quieted down."

"Bullshit. He's an Arab. He's just waiting. He caught us with our pants down before. He'll do it again. But next time he'll keep his promise. I guarantee it. If we humiliate him in front of his people, he'll cut us open like coconuts."

Dalrymple lit a cigarette. "Set up a meeting with Newquist. Let's dump this on him."

Joseph Newquist, Jr., sat at his desk in the Executive Office Building, the window behind him looking out on Lafayette Park. He was thirty-four years old, but he looked twenty-five, his cheeks pink and clean-shaven, blue eyes innocent and clear, and freshly barbered hair parted on the left and brushed fifty strokes each night since he was nine years old.

Facing him, across his desk, were Dalrymple and Lasker.

"Are you saying we have a problem?" Newquist said.

"Of course we have a problem. We all know that. And we'll continue to have one until—"

"I'm not talking about that," Newquist said. "We've dealt with that. At least we've done what we can for the moment. I mean is there something new? Are things coming unstuck?"

"We hope not. But we're getting little bubbles. Questions and rumors and crackpot guesses."

"We expected that."

"That's right," Dalrymple said. "And I'm sure we've got everything bottled up. But the fact remains—we're sitting on a powder keg. It's a volatile son of a bitch."

"Mark, you're saying exactly what I've been saying since January. But I can't call the tune here any more than you can over at State. The President and the Secretary are hanging tough. I think they're wrong and I've told them that. *You* think they're wrong. But unless they do a fast turnaround and decide to be forthcoming on this thing, you and I have no choice but to stay in a holding pattern."

"The *time* thing is the problem," Lasker said. "We've been lucky so far. But we can't keep a secret like this forever."

"You're right. But we can't *not* keep it either. Remember, you three men at State, the two men at Justice, one man at the bureau, and the President and I, are the only ones who know how all the pieces fit together."

"It's just that *one* piece I'm worried about," Dalrymple said.

"How do you think *I* feel? I hate to look at the headlines in the morning." Newquist picked up a photocopy sheet from his desk. "Did you see this in the *Post* this morning?"

Dalrymple took the page and read it, then passed it to Lasker. One section had been circled in red:

It is becoming increasingly evident that the OPEC nations present a future economic dilemma that is greater than the present energy crisis. Before 1973, for example, those nations held *six* billion dollars in cash reserves. Four years later those reserves had grown to one hundred forty-five billion. In 1985, according to a World Bank estimate, OPEC countries will hold combined reserves of 1.2 *trillion* dollars.

These oil nations *save* $115,000 per *second*. At that rate, after fifteen years and eight months, they could buy all the companies on *all* the world's stock exchanges. In just ten months they could buy all the companies listed on the London Exchange. To buy all the companies on the New York Stock Exchange would take about nine years and three months. The *total* Rockefeller family wealth is equivalent to just *six days'* oil production.

If the OPEC nations decided to float a mere forty billion of the almost two hundred billion they have deposited in hundreds of international banks, the world economy would collapse.

"That's the ballbreaker," Dalrymple said. "We're screwed no matter what we do."

"Not necessarily," Newquist said. "We're buying time. And the more time we buy the better chance we've got. If things broke loose now it's a cinch we'd have trouble trying to function. We'd have labor on our ass, NATO, and the oil companies. We'd be fighting Congress, the Pentagon, and the whole Soviet Bloc. Even people who *agreed* with what we've done would be forced to disagree in public. Suddenly it becomes a *moral* issue."

"I thought you were on *my* side," Dalrymple said.

"I am. I agree with you. Sooner or later we'll be stuck with the truth. Then we'll have to patch things back together and go on from there. But *we* can't make the first move. All we can do is *wait*, mind the store, and play the cards they dealt us."

Three weeks after he was sworn in, Gabe stood up in the chamber, eleven twenty in the morning, only fifteen other senators at their desks, and made his second Senate speech.

"I released some material to the press this morning. And now, if there is no objection, I would like to read that same material into the record. I believe it's vital for the mechanic in Louisville and the housewife in Missoula to know that some of the questions they're asking each other are also being asked on the floor of the United States Senate."

What Gabe read, what was printed later that day in the Washington papers and the following day in papers around the country, was a list of questions:

Number One:

Why have Senate office staffs doubled in size in the past ten years, increasing that part of the budget from $150 million to $550 million?

Number Two:

So far we have spent $385 million on the Chrysler XMI tank. First stage of a projected ten-billion-dollar program. But the turbine engine in this tank is vulnerable to sand and dirt. It breaks down after less than 150 miles. Why have we just appropriated $189 million more for this project?

Number Three:

When John Kennedy was assassinated in Dallas, three men were arrested at the scene. They were photographed, identified simply as "bums," and quickly released. Who were those men? What are their names? Why were they arrested and why were they released?

Number Four:

How can a federal judge have lunch at his club, where the only nonwhites are waiters and porters, then return to the bench that afternoon and make a fair judgment of racial questions?

Number Five:

In government statements concerning the necessity for nuclear power, why is it not made clear that at present it accounts for only 4 percent of our total energy production?

Number Six:

Polychlorinated biphenyl was banned in 1976. Why is it still in wide use in electrical transformers and industrial machinery? How can one million eggs be poisoned and four hundred thousand chickens killed by a substance that both theoretically and legally is not in use?

Number Seven:

The Central Intelligence Agency admits that it kept files on ten thousand Americans and gathered data on three hundred thousand others. What guarantees do we have that this illegal surveillance is not still going on?

Number Eight:

In our eagerness to burn more coal, why has it not been adequately explained that the resultant carbon dioxide buildup could create disastrous climatic changes all around the world?

Number Nine:

Do people realize that eighteen million tons of sulfur dioxide are released in the atmosphere each year? Do they know that air pollution causes 140,000 deaths annually?

Number Ten:

In the world's wealthiest country, why do we have between 18 and 64 million adult illiterates? In at least nine states, why have more than half the adults not completed high school?

When Gabe left the chamber, Rafer Isbell followed him to the cloakroom, put a hand on his shoulder, and said, "A lot of good stuff in that little speech."

"Thanks."

"You just have to be careful not to move too fast. Don't try to cover too much ground. We've got some conservative people here in the chamber. I'd hate to see anybody tag you as a grandstander."

Gabe smiled. "Thanks for the tip. But as long as I stick to documented facts I think I'll keep out of trouble. You know what I mean? The truth never killed anybody."

"Maybe not. But let's make sure it doesn't kill *you*. We don't want you to turn into a lame-duck senator before you even get started. Some of these old bulldogs around here can really chew you up if you're not careful."

22 A few minutes later, when Gabe started out of the cloakroom, the attendant handed him a note. Across the top of the page was printed, in small type, LOBBY FOR HUMAN SURVIVAL.

Dear Senator Treptow:

I have been trying to see you or talk to you for almost three weeks. But those camp followers in your office won't give me a tumble.

I also sent you a telegram about the H-14 crashes. Did you get it? Probably not. You've got a receptionist I'd like to hang up on a hook.

Anyway, I've been watching you on the Senate floor. And I saw you on television during your campaign. Big question: Do you believe those things you're saying or is somebody just writing them out for you?

If you do believe them, if you're ready to do something besides talk, then I'm giving you a chance to put your money where your mouth is. If you want to line up with the good guys, you'd better get around town a little. Because all those turkeys you're sitting with in the Senate Chamber are on the other side. I guarantee it. Cufflinks and cigars and five-hundred-dollar suits specially tailored to cover their fat rear ends.

Am I making contact? If I am, call me up. Or come on the phone when I call you. Like I said in that telegram those H-14 crashes didn't just happen. Hartwig said so and I say so. I'm really on to something. I'm sure of it. I'm going

*to dig it loose whether you help me or not. But with you
behind me it could happen faster.*

> *Yours truly,*
> *R. M. Kosta*

When Gabe saw the signature, he remembered the telegram
that had come earlier. He folded the note, put it into his pocket,
and made a mental note to ask Jud about R. M. Kosta. But it
slipped his mind until six that evening, when he and Jud were
sitting with Dave Matlock discussing a bill that was supposed to
come out of committee the following week, a bill that would
give substantial tax benefits to a farmer who retired and sold his
farm.

"It breezed through committee and there doesn't seem to be
any real opposition on the House side," Dave said. "Nobody
wants to dump on the small farmer."

"That's the problem," Jud said. "There's *no* problem. If the
bill's a shoo-in the way it seems to be, that means half a dozen
guys will try to tack amendments on it."

"Like what?" Gabe said.

"No way of knowing for sure till it hits the floor. But there's
some talk about a couple of things. One of them is the foreign
investor restriction that's been kicking back and forth for a
couple years. It seems to have some muscle behind it this
time."

"It prohibits any land sale of more than fifty acres," Jud said,
"to non-U.S. citizens. Ireland did it a few years ago to squeeze
the Germans out. It might make sense as a rider on the farm tax
bill. At least there's some connection."

"Then there's old man Veach," Dave said. "I heard at lunch
that he's planning to try with his favorite amendment. No porno
shops or X-rated theaters allowed in cities under a half-million
population."

"Every city in his state is smaller than half a million," Gabe
said.

"That's it. Veach thinks nobody noticed that but him."

After Dave had gone and Gabe and Jud were about ready to
leave, Gabe remembered the note in his pocket.

When Jud had read it, he tossed it on the desk and said, "That one is bad news."

"How so?"

"I've got a report on her if you want to read it."

"Her?"

"That's right. R. M. Kosta is a female. When we got that telegram from her a few weeks ago, I sent it over to Justice for a routine checkout. It turned out they have a file on her. They sent me a report the next morning. She's a ding-a-ling. Brilliant but a wacko. Late twenties, but looks like a kid. Comes from someplace in Virginia.

"She got a scholarship to Brandeis and raised all kinds of hell when she was up there. For four years she never missed a demonstration anyplace between here and Boston. She chained herself to a policeman during some kind of a fracas in Baltimore, led a sit-in inside the Statue of Liberty. Stuff like that.

"She was arrested a dozen times while she was in school. Disturbing the peace, resisting arrest, you name it. After she finished school she spent a year traveling around the country in an old bus with a dozen other lunatics. An antipollution crusade, they called it. They painted signs on a lot of walls and demonstrated in front of some little plants and factories in the South and the Midwest where the people had never *seen* a picket sign before. A lot more arrests on that trip. Thirty times at least she and her friends got thrown in the can. After that she spent a year in Denver on an underground paper, then two years in New York working for Jack Newfield. She's been in and out of Washington since 1977."

"Doing what?"

"She's an investigative reporter. Does articles for papers like the *Voice* in New York, *Rolling Stone, Mother Jones.* And she did a series in *Ramparts* on Carter. She also feeds column items to Arthur Garrigus from time to time. So she has press credentials. She can get into a lot of places and she does. But nobody takes her seriously."

"Why not?"

"Too crazy, I guess. She's an ERA freak. Women's lib. Calls herself Kosta—no first name. And she's conspiracy happy. According to her, Kennedy was killed by some CIA guy and a couple of Cubans, Bobby Kennedy was shot at least once by one of his bodyguards, J. Edgar Hoover had a hand in Martin Luther King's murder—stuff like that. She has a real hate-on for Hoover. She wrote a piece called 'Memoirs of a Bigot' and signed it J. Edgar Kosta."

Gabe picked up the handwritten note and looked at it. "What's this Lobby for Human Survival?"

"That's something recent. Henigar over at Justice says it's half joke, half serious. She wrote a piece last year about how lobbyists distort the lawmaking process. She called it 'Everybody Has a Lobby Except the People.' Some radical bird in the House read part of it into the *Congressional Record* and there was a lot of heat about it. So after that, Kosta and some of her friends formed this group, the Lobby for Human Survival. It's like an offshoot of Nader's Public Citizen thing. Kosta's very thick with the Nader people."

"What do you think she wants from me?"

"The same thing every other nut in Washington wants. A little edge. A little power. A chance to get on the inside. She's looking for credibility. Something to break her loose from the underground. Something to give her a bigger audience. Just talking to you for ten minutes, talking to *any* senator, one-to-one, could give her a leg up. Next thing you know you'd be quoted in some magazine with Che Guevara's picture on the cover. She wants to use you. She wants to get her hooks into you. It's as simple as that. That's why we keep sluffing her off."

Twenty minutes later, Lasker hung up the telephone in his office and called Mark Dalrymple on the intercom. "Remember the Kosta girl? The reporter who was trying to nail the FAA?"

"What about her?" Dalrymple said.

"She's back in action. Trying to stir up the H-14 thing again. Trying to get that new senator, Gabe Treptow, to come in with her."

"You'd better get hold of Newquist."

"I already put in a call. He'll get back to me."

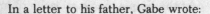

23 In a letter to his father, Gabe wrote:

It was great to hear from you. Four pages. Keep up the good work. You've got a wicked pen, though. If those nurses knew what you wrote about them they'd pour rubber cement in your socks.

I'm glad to hear you're walking around a little more. Pretty soon the weather should be nice enough so you can sit outside. When I get a few days to come back to Fort Beck we'll take some long rides in the car.

I'm getting settled in here now. Like I told you on the phone, I found a place to live. I rented the top floor of an ancient brick house in Georgetown. In case you don't know, that's not a separate town. It's just an old residential part of Washington. Very pretty. Very nice. And it beats hell out of living in the suburbs.

A lot of people who work here drive halfway across Virginia to get home every night. Makes no sense to me. I sure as hell don't want to spend a big hunk of my life in a car getting to some house in the country with nobody living in it but me.

So that's it. I'm right in town. On a nice side street with maple trees. It looks like the old part of Fort Beck. On Holloway. Or Chandler Street maybe.

My landlady is a lady named Clara Pettigrew. Transparent skin and bones like a bird. She's almost ninety years old. Has a nurse and a handyman living on the premises.

Her great-grandfather was a senator from Massachusetts

and he built the house. Miss Pettigrew (she's never been married) was born right here, in the back bedroom on the second floor, and she's never lived anyplace else.

Anyway, she lives on the ground floor now. I live on the third floor, and the second floor is closed off, only used for storage. So if I decide to roller-skate from the kitchen to the bedroom, I won't disturb anybody. Also, the entrance to my place is by an outside stairway, so it's completely private.

I bought myself a coffee pot, a case of Scotch, and some sheets and towels, and I leased a new Pontiac. So I'm all set.

If you're worried about me living like a monk, don't be. I have people coming out of my ears all day. Breakfast meetings, lunch meetings, dinner meetings. And I always have work to do when I get home. So I'm fully occupied, no question about that.

I've been thinking a lot about Chet. But not sad stuff. Just remembering some things about when we were kids. The sparring matches in the side yard and the ball games we went to on Sundays. All the stuff the three of us used to do together. It's a damned shame that Chet couldn't live to be a hundred and do everything he'd hatched in his head since he was six years old.

Remember those timetables he used to tack up on the wall? "Here's what I plan to do by the time I'm twenty-four" or "Here's how much money I'll have when I'm thirty years old." He didn't have as much time as he planned on but he sure as hell didn't waste the time he had.

I've been thinking about Sam a lot, too. Can't get him out of my head. Sam was . . .

Gabe sat there staring at the letter. He capped his pen and read through what he'd written. Then he carefully copied the last page on a fresh sheet of paper. When he came to the final two lines, the part about Sam, he left it out. He told himself that he didn't want to remind his father, didn't want to start him thinking about his grandson.

The fact was, he was afraid of the subject. Afraid to explore it. As close as he'd been to Chet, as locked together as their lives had been for all of Gabe's thirty-five years, it was Sam's death he couldn't handle, Sam's coffin he couldn't watch being lowered into the ground.

And he couldn't talk about it, couldn't tell anyone how he felt. Not even his father.

Part Two

24 Newquist stood at the wide window of his office, late afternoon, the sky gray, turning slowly dark. When he sat down behind his desk, he said, "I don't know. My first reaction is that we have to go easy. I'd hate to see us overreact. On the other hand, we can't sit back and let things snowball."

Across the room, Dalrymple sat on the couch against the wall, Lasker in a deep leather chair. "It could be nothing," Lasker said. "Or it could turn into a real pain in the ass."

"How do you read it?" Newquist said.

"The Kosta woman is one thing. I think we can contain her. It bothers me that she's picked up on Hartwig's line about the H-14's being sabotaged, but at least she hasn't started writing about it yet. So far there's just this letter to Treptow and that telegram a few weeks ago that we decided to ignore.

"She can't hurt us with *theories*, especially if they don't get published. She's bush-league. It isn't as if she had a big paper behind her. Or a network. She may be a nuisance, but I don't think she can come up with ten cents' worth of hard evidence. We've covered every base."

"What do you think, Mark?" Newquist turned to Dalrymple.

"I think Jim's right. I don't think she can get to anybody that Tunstall hasn't covered already. We sweated this one out last winter. We handled it then and we can handle it now."

"What about Treptow?"

"That's what throws me," Lasker said. "I don't know what she figures he can do for her. I mean, his brother was on Air Force Three, everybody knows that, but she can't take *that* to the bank."

"Remember, she hasn't talked to him yet," Dalrymple said.

"And she's not going to if Rimmer can manage it."

"We can't depend on that, though," Newquist said. "If she keeps pecking away, sooner or later she'll find a way to get to Treptow. What we don't know is what she'll say to him and how he'll react. Does she just want a fast story, or does she really *know* something?"

"The problem with Treptow," Lasker said, "if she manages to sell him a bill of goods, the problem then is, he gives her credibility. If she can link him up with whatever half-assed theory she's trying to push, we could get a lot of people saying there must be something to it."

"Have you talked to the Secretary about this?" Newquist said.

"No. He doesn't want to hear. If it's *not* a problem, he doesn't want to be bothered. If it *is* a problem, he expects us to handle it." Dalrymple lit a cigarette. "I think you said the key word, Joe. *Overreact.* That's what we have to steer clear of. If we jump the gun on this thing we could *make* more problems than we solve."

"So what are you saying?"

"I think we have to keep our eyes open and wait. Once we see what she's up to, then we'll know what we have to do to fight it."

"Counterpunch?"

"Something like that."

"There's only one problem with that," Newquist said. "If you get knocked out with one swing, you never get a chance to counter." He turned to Lasker. "Do you go along with Mark? You think we should hang back and see what happens?"

Lasker glanced at Dalrymple, then back at Newquist. "I don't think we have much choice."

"Sure we do," Newquist said. "We always have choices. We'd *better* have. What if we decide we don't want to hang back and wait, then what?"

"The other alternative," Lasker said, "is to assume the worst. That Kosta knows more than we think she does, that she gets Treptow all steamed up, and the two of them get the H-14 thing on the front pages again."

"All right," Newquist said, "let's assume that. That's the last thing we want to happen. How do we avoid it?"

"That's not my field," Lasker said. "That's Tunstall's baby."

"Forget about Tunstall for the moment. How would *you* handle it?"

Lasker looked at Dalrymple again, got no help there, and said, "Well . . . if there's going to be a firefight, we have to be sure we've got an edge. If Kosta and Treptow are going to be the enemy, we'd better get the jump on them. Stop them cold if we can. And if we can't stop them, *contain* them. Or discredit them. It's a thousand-to-one shot that they could uncover the *real* stuff, the things that could hurt us. But if there's even a remote chance of that happening, we'd have to have the muscle to stop them. We'd have to be on top of them all the time. And we'd have to start now."

"Is that what you're suggesting?" Newquist said.

"No, it's not," Lasker said. "You just asked me to give you an alternative and I gave you one. But I don't think it's right. Not at this point. It's overkill. And like I said, if we're going that route, you need a commando. You need Tunstall. Maybe we should talk to him about it."

"I *did* talk to him. I called him this morning."

"What did he say?"

"He said exactly what you just said. He said we have to plan a counterattack. Even if we're never forced to use it. If they're going to take us on, we need to know what we're up against, what the weak points are. We have to know where they're vulnerable."

"Maybe he's right," Dalrymple said. He looked at Lasker. "It can't hurt us to be ready."

"No, I guess not."

"There's only one hitch," Newquist said. "Tunstall can't take it on. He'll advise us, but he can't be the architect the way he was in Indianapolis. He wants to stay out of sight. He won't leave California."

"What does *that* mean?" Dalrymple said. "Since when is Tunstall calling the shots?"

"There must be half a dozen guys we can get to handle that California situation," Lasker said.

"That's right," Newquist said. "But that's not the problem. The problem is that the last time Tunstall was in Indianapolis, somebody recognized him. Knew his face and knew his name. McCann, the guy who ran the underground newspaper. Tunstall says McCann won't blow the whistle on him, but he doesn't want to risk somebody else tying him to the H-14 business. And I think he's right."

"So where does that leave us?" Lasker said.

"No big problem. We move ahead. And somebody else fills in for Tunstall."

"Jesus, we can't bring somebody in cold and brief him on everything that's happened on this thing in the last six months."

"That's right. Somebody will have to double up. Take over for Tunstall."

"Like who?"

"Like you, Jim."

Twenty minutes later, in Dalrymple's car heading back to the State Department, Lasker said, "I'd like to know what the hell is going on."

"What do you mean?"

"You know damn well what I mean. I have a rotten feeling that somebody's hanging me out to dry."

"Who?"

"How the hell do I know? Newquist. The Secretary. *You* maybe. But it's not going to happen. I promise you that. I'm up to my ass in this thing already. But so are a lot of other people. I mean, as of now we're all in the same boat. Except Tunstall. He's worse off. He really has dirty hands. So anybody who thinks I'm going to put on rubber gloves and slip into his routine has got another think coming."

"Why didn't you tell Newquist that?"

"Because I wanted to tell *you*. I work with *you*, not Newquist. As a matter of fact, I thought *you'd* say no *for* me."

"I can't pull rank on Newquist. You know that."

"Does that mean you knew what was coming? Did you know he was going to throw that at me?"

Dalrymple shook his head. "News to me. All kinds of things happening that they don't copy me on."

"Then what do you think? Am I right?"

"Jesus, I can't answer that one, Jim. You have to make up your own mind."

"I have made up my mind. That's what I'm telling you. But I don't want to get dumped on. Will you back me up, or am I gonna be naked in church?"

"What do you want me to do?"

"Whatever you can."

"All right," Dalrymple said. "Why don't I call Newquist as soon as I get back to the office? I'll tell him you don't want to take on the job. And I'll tell him I agree with you."

"I thought you said you couldn't buck Newquist."

"Maybe I can't. But I'll take a crack at it. You want me to back you up, that's what I'll do. You're not in prison, for Christ's sake. Nobody can force you to do something you don't want to do."

Ten minutes after he got back to his office, Dalrymple called Lasker on the intercom. "I talked to Newquist. I told him how you feel."

"What did he say?"

"What could he say? He was disappointed, but he said we'd have to work out something else."

"He wasn't pissed off?"

"Didn't seem to be. He likes you. Thinks you're a first-rate guy."

At six that evening, when Lasker was packing his briefcase getting ready to go home, his secretary called him from the outer office and said, "Miss Hollenbeck called from the Secretary's office. She said he'd like you to come up for a drink if you can make it."

"When?"

"Now, she said. But if you're tied up it's okay. She said it's nothing pressing. You can make it another time."

"No . . . it's all right," Lasker said. "Tell her I'll be upstairs in ten minutes."

He waited in the reception room for forty minutes. When he was ushered in finally, the Secretary, a slight, ruddy man with a shock of white hair as stiff as a brush, came around the desk to shake his hand. "I'm sorry, Jim. I had three back-to-back calls I couldn't dodge." He turned to his assistant, a tall, balding man in a dark suit, and said, "I think we could use a drink, Justin. Mr. Lasker will have . . . ?"

"Scotch," Jim said. "A little water."

"And I'll take a brandy and soda."

The Secretary went back to the chair behind his desk. Glancing at a card tucked in one corner of his desk blotter, he said, "How are Carol and the boys?"

"Just fine," Lasker said. "Couldn't be better."

Before anyone was ushered into the Secretary's office for an interview, a meeting, or a visit, one of the staff people went in first and left a file card listing personal information about the guest, his career, and his family.

Sitting in front of the Secretary's desk, watching his glance flick down to the card on his blotter, Lasker tried to guess what details of his own life were listed there.

NAME: James Guinnup Lasker

BORN: Stamford, Conn., June 12, 1950. Only child.

FATHER: Martin Lasker—attorney

MOTHER: Adrian Guinnup

WIFE: Carol Sue Whitson, b. 1952, Boston, Mass.

CHILDREN: Roger (b. 1974), Stacey (b. 1976)

EDUCATION: Williams College—1971, Harvard Law—1973

WASHINGTON EXPERIENCE: Clerk for Justice Byron White, 1973–4; Special Counsel, Labor Dept., 1975–6; State Department since 1977.

They were into their second drink before the Secretary came to the point. "I've been hearing some excellent reports on you. Dalrymple is impressed. The White House is impressed. And so am I. There's no shortage of brains in Washington. What we never have enough of is men who can take charge, men with enough guts and imagination to get the job done. We've all been aware of what you've been doing for us in this . . . this situation we've had to deal with in the past few months. Now Joe Newquist tells me you've volunteered to take on some additional work. He's tickled to death about it and so am I. That's why I asked you up here this evening. I wanted to thank you personally and tell you how much faith all of us have in you."

As soon as he was back downstairs in his office, Lasker called Dalrymple at home. "What the fuck is going on?"

"What do you mean?"

"Did you know the Secretary was going to talk to me this evening?"

"Yeah, I did. He told me just before I left the office."

"Why didn't you tell me?" Lasker said.

"He told me not to."

"Do you know what he wanted to talk to me about?"

"He didn't tell me, but I've got a pretty good idea."

"I thought you told me you called Newquist."

"I did."

"You said everything was settled."

"No, I didn't. I told you Newquist said we'd have to work out something else. That's what he did. He bypassed me and went to the Secretary."

"Well, it won't work, Mark. I told you I'm not going to do it and I'm *not.*"

"Did you tell the Secretary that?"

"No. I wanted to talk to you first," Lasker said.

"I told you I'd go to bat for you with Newquist and I did. Now you're on your own. I can't take on Newquist *and* the Secretary."

"This afternoon you said nobody could force me to do something I didn't want to do."

"That's right. Nobody can."

"So how do I handle it?"

"No problem. You can resign."

"What the hell does that mean?"

"Just what it sounds like. You can quit."

"Are you telling me that's my only alternative?"

"Not as far as I'm concerned. But Newquist doesn't like people to say *no* to him. Neither does the Secretary."

"Jesus, I can't believe it."

"I know how you feel. It's horse shit. But that's the way it is. People like you and me are hired for one reason. To solve problems, to clean up somebody else's mess. If we don't want to do it, there are people lined up outside who are dying to do it. This is a whore's town, baby. *Everybody's* doing the trick for somebody."

During the last week in May, after the third group of what had come to be known as "Treptow's Questions" was released to the press, Gabe appeared, Tuesday evening, on Bruce Hinshaw's *D.C. Overview.*

Hinshaw, after introducing his guest, opened up with a quote from that day's *Washington Star,* from Paul Alkire's column, "The Senate Side":

"'Gabe Treptow, the recently elected junior senator from Illinois, has set some kind of record on Capitol Hill. Although he has held office for just a few weeks, Senate observers say he already has a legion of enemies in the chamber.'"

Looking up from the clipping in his hand, Hinshaw said, "How about that, Senator? Do you agree with Alkire's assessment of your popularity?"

"I read his column every day. He seems to be right about most things."

"But what is your reaction?"

"First of all, I'd like to read *you* something. Something that

Edmund Burke said in 1774. He was talking about the English Parliament, but I think the parallel is clear. He said, 'A representative must not be ready to take up or lay down a great political system for the convenience of the hour. . . . He is in Parliament to support his opinion of the public good, and does not *form* his opinion in order to get into Parliament, *or to continue in it.*' "

"How is that relevant to your problems with your fellow senators?"

"I don't *have* problems with my fellow senators. But they seem to have a lot of problems with *me*. I say the job of a legislator is to legislate, that only the quality of his service should determine whether he remains in office or not. My colleagues don't like to hear that."

"You don't feel that's an ingenuous position to take, the realities of politics being what they are?"

"The *realities* of politics," Gabe said, "are what have to be changed. The Constitution doesn't provide for lobbyists. No mention is made of special interest groups. Or of political campaigns that go on for a year or two. I don't believe it's ingenuous to suggest that five or six million dollars is too much money to spend on one man's campaign for an elective office. How can we defend an expenditure like that at the same time we're cutting back on food stamps? The hungry people of the world are shocked by that kind of extravagance. And so am I."

"Will Rogers said, 'We have the best Congress money can buy.' Is that your position?"

"Will Rogers was a humorist. I take the situation more seriously. Laughing at a problem doesn't make it go away." Gabe looked down at the clipboard on the table in front of him. "Let me read you another quote. Something Karl Marx wrote more than a hundred years ago. 'There is a strict correlation between a society's economic substructure and its political superstructure.' "

"Does that mean we're getting the Congress we deserve?"

"I think that's too pat," Gabe said. "It creates an illusion that there's no need to think about the problem anymore. I'm not saying that Marx's ideas in 1918 have specific relevance for us today. I *am* saying that we have to think in terms of basic *values*.

"When our economic substructure feeds on greed and dominance, dishonesty and opportunism, we can't be surprised if our political superstructure and our elected representatives exhibit those same characteristics."

"Let me ask you this," Hinshaw said. "By taking this adversary position against your colleagues, how can you hope to function as a legislator?"

"I'm not sure I can. I'm already in Coventry in the Senate. I'm being assigned to unimportant committees. I'm excluded from party caucuses and bipartisan planning sessions. And I'm sure it will only get worse as I continue to speak out."

"That's my point exactly."

"It looks discouraging. I admit that. But this very situation we're talking about may have a positive side. If people like yourself and Alkire, for example, along with my constituents and some informed people around the country, if a *lot* of people notice what's going on and start asking questions, just the way *I've* been doing, if people begin to say, 'Why are they so mad at this guy? What are those other senators afraid of?'—if *that* starts to happen, then maybe things can begin to turn around.

"What I'm saying is this. We're off the rails. We're facing a crisis. And I can't solve it. No single person can. But what I hope I *can* do is make people think, get them to wake up and admit that there *is* a problem. A serious problem. Until that happens, there's no way for anyone to solve anything."

"Do you see any parallel between yourself and Jimmy Carter?"

"In what way?"

"He sees himself as a *teaching* President. A moralist. An idealist."

Gabe shook his head. "I see myself as a realist. I'm not talking about theories and concepts. I'm talking about making things *work.* Let me put it *this* way: Somebody in the Carter administration said, 'If it's not broke we don't fix it.' I say a hell of a lot of things are broke. And we'd better find a way to fix them."

The next morning Kosta called the studios of WETA and talked to her friend Nellie Arvidsen, an assistant program director. "This is Kosta, Arvidsen."

"I thought you'd run off to Bogotá. Where have you been?"

"Chasing around the country," Kosta said. "Sorry I missed your birthday party."

"It's your loss. We had one broken arm, three citations for disturbing the peace, and at least two guests got pregnant. For a while there I thought I might make it three."

"But you didn't?"

"Not this time," Nellie said.

"Congratulations."

"For *what?* I'm dying to get pregnant. The only trouble is I've got a new rule. I won't go to bed with any guy who wears cologne or a suit with a vest. So I'm sleeping by myself a lot."

"Listen," Kosta said then, "I need a favor. *D.C. Overview* last night. I missed it. I understand Senator Treptow was on."

"Right. He doesn't wear cologne and he doesn't wear a vest."

"Meaning what?"

"Meaning nothing. I tried to look available but he didn't notice."

"Can I whip over there and look at that tape?" Kosta said. "When?"

"Right now if I can. As soon as you can set it up."

"It'll be ready when you get here. Studio 3G. You have a lunch date?"

"No."

"Good. Some macho lawyer was going to do me a favor and

take me to Bagatelle but I guess he got a better offer. He just called up and said he has to fly back to Cleveland. His cocker spaniel lost a contact lens or something. You know what I mean? One of those really outstanding human beings. A guy you can count on."

Kosta sat in the studio an hour later and watched Hinshaw's interview with Gabe. Then she had it rewound and watched it again. During the discussion about the Trilateral Commission she took notes on a five-by-seven pad she took out of her bag.

"There's nothing secret about the Trilateral Commission," Hinshaw said. "I seem to recall a kind of social note that appeared in the *Post.* It said the President had entertained thirty members of the commission at a White House luncheon."

"That's just the point," Gabe said. "There *have* been references to it. But beyond that nobody seems to be curious. Nobody asks any questions. The newspapers and the television reporters don't seem interested either."

"Are you suggesting there's something sinister about this organization?"

"No, I'm not. I *can't* do that, because I'm almost as badly informed as everybody else. But what I *do* know stimulates my curiosity. When a President of the United States, his Vice-President, and more than a dozen key members of his administration are *all* members of a powerful international group that most people in this country have never even *heard* of, it seems to me that bears some examination. When *The Atlantic Monthly* suggests that Carter was the first Democratic president in history who was elected with Republican money and Republican political backing, you have to admit that's an odd interpretation of the two-party system."

"Haven't the left-wing organizations always maintained that people like the Rockefellers are the powers behind our national elections?"

"Yes, they have. But the election results, more often than not, have seemed to disprove the theory. Men like Roosevelt and Truman and Kennedy weren't chosen by the bankers and the oil men."

"But Carter *was.* Is that your point?"

"Let me put it this way. Bank revenues have never been

higher. Oil profits have never been greater. And for reasons that baffle most of us, oil prices have been decontrolled, so profits can go up even more. Since the founding members of the Trilateral Commission are international bankers, industrialists, and oil men, and since Carter and his key people are also members, a person doesn't have to be paranoid to suspect that there's some connection."

27

"What are you working on?" Nellie asked. She and Kosta were having lunch at Bagatelle. "Still the FAA?"

"In a way. I can't tell you the exact details because I'm not sure where I'm heading."

"That DC-10 crash in Chicago—wasn't that what got you in gear?"

"That and a few other things. The San Diego midair collision. All those complaints from the flight control guys. And most of all the doubletalk that the National Travel Safety Board and the Federal Aviation Administration were handing out. I decided there was a dirty story there someplace. But I couldn't get a handle on it. I kept pushing till I got to the point where I was getting the same scenario from everybody I talked to. When that happens you're dead. Either everybody's telling the truth or they've all been rehearsed. Whichever it is, the story's shot."

"Does that mean you're off on something else?"

"In a way it does," Kosta said.

"Why don't you just tell me to mind my own business?"

"Because that's not what I mean. I think I'm into something scary. It started in a way with the DC-10 crash in Chicago, but it's a different story now. If there *is* a story."

"Where does Treptow fit in?"

"I'm not sure he does. But I *hope* he does. Because I need help. I'm running into closed doors and dead telephones. I need some muscle."

"Don't we all?"

"You know what I mean," Kosta said.

"And you know what *I* mean. What did you think of him on the Hinshaw interview?"

"I'm not sure. I want to go over that transcript you gave me."

"I didn't ask what you thought about what he *said*. I asked what you thought of *him*. The particular person."

"I don't know. What do *you* think?"

"No vest," Nellie said.

"I know. You told me that before."

"I'd like to have him for breakfast. Skip the cream and sugar."

"Is he for real?" Kosta said.

"What does *that* mean? Who *cares*? Show me a sincere man and I'll run like a burglar."

"I mean, did you talk to him?"

"Just hello and like that," Nellie said. "He was in the studio once before. Two weeks ago."

"So . . . what's he like?"

"He looks *lazy*. I'm really queer for that look. Sort of flops down in the chair with his legs stretched out and makes you want to capitulate."

"That's a new word for it."

"New or old . . . blue or gray . . . at home or away . . . whoopee."

When she got back to her apartment that evening, Kosta took a shower, got into bed in her pajamas, and looked over the Hinshaw transcript. She flipped through to the part about the Trilateral Commission.

TREPTOW

It's common knowledge that Henry Kissinger was brought into public life by Nelson Rockefeller. They were close friends and political allies. And there's certainly nothing wrong with that. It's less well-known that Zbigniew Brzezinski is also a protégé of the Rockefellers. Nothing wrong with that either. But apart from his academic and government activities, he has other functions. He is the key philosopher and tactician for the Trilateral Commission. His theories are the foundation stones of the organization.

HINSHAW

What are those theories?

TREPTOW

As I said, the commission's membership is drawn from the highest levels of banking and industry in Japan, West Germany, and the United States. The thesis is that only these three countries, among the democratic nations, are powerful enough to alter world affairs by whatever unilateral action any one of them might take. Economic or military. The commission further theorizes that world *business,* the maintenance of international trade and economic stability, is too important to be put in the hands of elected governments. So we're talking about an international alliance that functions autonomously. *Outside* government supervision or restriction.

HINSHAW

In other words, presidents and other world leaders come and go but the Trilateral Commission goes on forever.

TREPTOW

That's the idea.

HINSHAW

Like a gigantic Chamber of Commerce. Or an international trade association.

TREPTOW

Not exactly. You see, the commission wants to have it both ways. Governments have no control over *them,* but they propose to have whatever control they can manage over governments. They admit openly that a key part of their long-range program is to influence national elections in those three countries I mentioned. West Germany, Japan, and the United States.

HINSHAW

Many organizations would like to do that. I could name a dozen.

TREPTOW

That's right. But most of them simply don't have the power and the money to make any real impact. They can influence voters, but not on a broad enough scale to affect the results of a national election.

HINSHAW

Then why do you think the Trilateral Commission could pull it off?

TREPTOW

I say they've already done it. In 1976.

HINSHAW

How so?

TREPTOW

There's a lot of evidence. And most of it is hinged to one fact. In 1974, the Trilateral Commission was a fairly young organization. Its membership was small. All the members were immensely wealthy and powerful men, representing the largest banks and industrial conglomerates in the world. It was truly an elite group of multimillionaires. Led by David Rockefeller. But strangely enough, sandwiched in among these financial giants were two comparatively undistinguished men, Jimmy Carter and Fritz Mondale. Two years before they became President and Vice-President, these two little-known politicians were members of the Trilateral Commission. Does that have some significance? It certainly does to me.

In any competition to select a nondescript, totally forgettable man, Oscar Tunstall would have been a winner or a close runner-up. He was square and solid, in his mid-fifties, it seemed, hair thin on top, his eyes flat and innocent behind steel-rim glasses. His torso was thick, his arms and legs short. Pink, soft hands with stubby fingers.

His clothes were inexpensive and ill fitting, clean but worn. A drab gray suit. A pale blue shirt with a brown tie, gray socks showing below his too-short pant legs, heavy brown oxfords with waterproof soles. And a lightweight, dark-colored raincoat, neither black nor blue, which he rarely took off, and a soft gray hat, snap brim, a relic from the forties.

When he got off his TWA flight in Kansas City, two in the afternoon, when he marched through the exit tunnel to the reception area, carrying a battered and peeling leatherette-covered briefcase, he seemed to be a traveling drummer from another time, a man selling roofing paper or bathroom fixtures. Looking failed and hopeless, he attracted no attention whatsoever.

At the first newsstand he bought a copy of the Kansas City *Star,* rolled it in a tight cylinder, and put it in the left-hand pocket of his raincoat. Holding his ticket envelope in his right hand, his briefcase under his right arm, he marched to the coffee shop, went inside, and took a booth by the window overlooking the landing area. Taking off his hat and putting it on the seat beside him, he signaled to the waitress and ordered coffee and a plain doughnut. As soon as she brought the order and left, Jim Lasker got up from the counter, dead center in the room, walked over, and sat down in the booth, across from Tunstall.

"How was your flight from Los Angeles?" he said, careful to say the memorized question exactly as planned.

"Fine," Tunstall said. "How about the flight from Chicago?" Also careful. Clear and distinct.

"No problems. But I came from Washington."

"I came from San Francisco."

Tunstall said no more till the waitress had brought Lasker a cup of coffee and left again. Then he took a folder of blueprints out of his briefcase and spread them out between himself and Lasker.

"How old are you?" Tunstall said.

"Old enough. Don't worry about it."

"I worry about everything. They tell me you didn't want this job."

"Who told you that?" Lasker said.

"It doesn't matter. Is it the truth?"

Lasker nodded. "That's right. I didn't want it. But I agreed to do it. That's all you have to know."

"I'm afraid not. What I have to know is whether I can work with you. Whether you can work with me. If this thing heats up suddenly, we'll have to move fast. I'll be in California and you'll be in Washington or wherever else you have to go. It's a coordination problem. There won't be any time for philosophical bullshit. You know what I mean?"

"I already had this discussion before I left Washington. Here's the way it was laid out for me. If things start to pop, if we get problems, you and I will be in constant communication. You'll recommend what you think should be done. I'll carry it out. When I need help, you'll get me the people I need. Or you'll contact them direct."

"Do you buy that?" Tunstall said.

"No choice. I already bought it."

"That's not good enough. Can you live with it?"

"If I can't," Lasker said, "you'll be the first to know."

Tunstall called the waitress over for a coffee refill. Then he said, "All right. Here's what I've done in the past couple of days. I've got some people doing profiles on Kosta and Treptow. By the end of the week we'll know more about them than they know about themselves. Everybody they know, everything

the receptionist asked for her number and said someone would get back to her. But no one called. There was no acknowledgment of her telegrams or her letters. Even her dossier came back to her, neatly enclosed in the same gray envelope she had mailed it in, her handwritten note still clipped to her photograph.

Finally, frustrated and angry, she tracked down Patty Ingledow at a cocktail party at the Overseas Press Club.

"Will you tell me what's happening in that cockamamie office where you work?"

"What do you mean?" Patty said, three pretzels in one hand, a banana daiquiri in the other.

"Come on, spook. This is *me*. Remember? It's bad enough I'm spinning my wheels trying to see some freshman senator nobody ever heard of, a hotshot whose biggest committee assignment is watchdogging the workers in the Senate cafeteria— *that's* bad enough. But when I can't get *you* on the phone, somebody I could nail to the cross by leaking just one percent of her sordid private life, *that* is really the lowest."

"It's not *me*, booby. *I'm* not the villain."

"Then who *is?* You're the press person. If you can't shuffle me in, who can? I mean, do you handle the press or don't you? What's the problem?"

"You're getting a little piercing, aren't you?"

"No," Kosta said. "Not yet. But I'm capable of it. You people are really starting to bore me. I hate to be bored. It makes me mad as hell. And when I get mad I do crazy things. How would you like me to call Liz Smith and drop a blind item on her about your hayseed senator?"

"Come on, Kosta. You're a class act."

"No I'm not. I'm only a class act when you treat me like one. When people like that pain-in-the-ass Jud Rimmer start to dump on me, I turn into a mean Greek. I can even get *you* in the papers if I concentrate on it. How's this? 'A certain towheaded press person around Washington just flunked her Wasserman.'"

Patty started to laugh. "Oh, for God's sake, Kosta . . ."

"Wait a minute. I'm not finished. There's more. 'The problem is, she's not sure who to get mad at—her boss, a freshman senator from the corn belt, or a certain Rumanian soccer player.' "

"You're really *weird* . . . you know that? A Rumanian *soccer* player?" She took Kosta by the arm. "Come over here in the corner for five minutes and I'll tell you how the world works."

They sat down on a couch in front of a window, looking out on Massachusetts Avenue. "Okay," Patty said. "I'll level with you. But if you quote me I'll murder you."

She lit a cigarette. "We have an unusual situation in the Treptow office. None of us are quite sure how to deal with it. We've got a boss who's scaring the bejesus out of a whole lot of people. I mean, we're there to help and support him. But he doesn't *want* help. And he loses support every time he opens his mouth. We can't control him and we can't shut him up. What we *can* do, what we're *trying* to do, is slow him down a little, cut down his exposure, cut down on the number of chances he gets to alienate people. Jud thinks he'll settle down after a while. He'll get tired of tilting at windmills and end up reasonable and civilized. Ready to do the job he was elected to do. But for now he's like a bull on roller skates. Heading downhill with his tail flying."

"What's all this have to do with me?"

"Nothing so far. But it could have. You're a street fighter. So is Treptow. And right now he doesn't need any new battles, thank you very much. He needs to shift down and get back into his own pattern. Do his homework and memorize the rules. So for now you're a bad influence. Potentially at least. Everybody knows what you're like when you get your teeth into something. That's what makes Rimmer jumpy. He doesn't want anybody inciting his senator to riot."

"Too bloody bad about him. I don't care what Rimmer wants."

"You asked me who the villain is. I'm telling you. Jud is the one who's keeping you away from Treptow. He told him you were trying to *use* him."

"That's right. I *do* want to use him. But not the way Rimmer's talking about. I need help. I need some friends who can help me. At least *one* friend."

"Give us a break. There are ninety-nine other guys in the Senate. Why pick Treptow?"

"I *didn't* pick him. He's already involved. He just doesn't know it yet. If this thing unravels the way I think it might, nobody will be more interested in the outcome than Treptow."

The next day Kosta changed her tactics. Except for lunchtime, she was in the press gallery of the Senate Chamber from nine in the morning till adjournment in the afternoon. Each morning, a dozen red carnations were delivered to Treptow's desk, always with the same message typed neatly on a florist's card:

> The world is so full of a number of fools, I think we should all be as happy as ghouls.
>
> Your friend—
> the Glamorous Greek.

Each afternoon or early evening when Gabe left his office and went to the subterranean garage for his car, he found Kosta's photograph stuck under the windshield wiper. And his left rear tire was always flat.

After the third or fourth day, one of the pages came to him and said, "There's a lady in the press gallery who's really staring at you. She's been there all week. Every day. *All* day."

When Gabe looked up and saw her, he recognized her from the photographs. When their eyes made contact she didn't look away. After that, each time he glanced up at the press gallery he saw her there, cool and composed, staring at him.

Early the following week, Tuesday afternoon, when he looked at her, she held up a small, neatly lettered poster that said HAD ENOUGH?

That evening, just before she left the office to go home, Nona Sugarman called to report Senator Treptow's automobile problems to the police.

Two detectives from the district's motor vehicle division came to Kosta's second-floor apartment one morning at eight o'clock. She was in her robe making coffee.

"Are you R. M. Kosta?" one of the men said. He was stocky and black. He wore tinted aviator glasses.

"Yes, I am. And you are unmistakably from the fuzz house."

"I'm Lieutenant Starks and this is Detective Sergeant Crider."

The man at his shoulder, tall and angular, short-cropped red hair and a neat brown mustache, nodded his head.

"Come in," Kosta said. "Free coffee today."

They sat in her dining alcove looking down on the rear garden. She brought three mugs of coffee to the table and sat down with her back to the window. "What's up?"

"Senator Treptow's office called us," Starks said. "There's a pattern of harassment that seems to be upsetting the senator's people."

"And . . . ?"

"Your name came up," Crider said. "They seemed to feel you might be involved somehow."

"I'm a big fan of the senator's," Kosta said. "I've never met him, but I certainly like the things he says."

Starks took a notebook out of his jacket pocket and glanced inside it. "His staff says you've been trying to see him for some time now, that you've called his office on many occasions, and that you've gone there trying to arrange a meeting."

"That's true. Did they tell you why?"

"No."

"I'm a reporter. I've been trying to interview Senator Treptow."

"What paper are you with?"

"No particular paper. I'm free-lance."

"I see," Crider said. Then, "Senator Treptow's secretary, Miss Sugarman—"

"She's crazy," Kosta said. "She eats Twinkies for lunch and washes them down with Dr Pepper. Don't pay any attention to her."

"She says," Crider went on, "that you've been in the Senate Chamber every day. Staring at the senator and trying to attract his attention."

"Like I said, I'm a newspaper person. I'm entitled to sit in the press gallery and stare at anybody I feel like staring at."

"Is it true you send him flowers every day?"

"Only on weekdays."

"Do you mind telling us why you do that?"

"Tricks of the trade, boys. There are all kinds of ways to skin a cat. You want some more coffee?" She went to the stove for the coffeepot and refilled their cups. "Some lady reporters have been known to send senators their apartment keys. I'd rather send flowers. Or a nice stainless-steel nutcracker maybe. They're reminder gifts, you know what I mean? Like a funeral parlor sending out calendars every year."

Crider and Starks looked at each other. Then Starks said, "I hope you don't think this is funny. We're not here for our health."

"I don't think it's funny at all. I think it's a pain in the neck. But I'm trying to be sweet. Giving you fresh-ground coffee and pretending I like to see policemen before I've had my shower in the morning. I mean, I'm being very nice. But if you start getting snotty I won't be nice anymore. It may surprise you guys, but I've got better things to do than to sit here in my pajamas shooting the breeze."

"What do you know about the damage that's been done to Senator Treptow's car?"

Kosta slid one hand inside the pocket of her robe, crossed her fingers, and said, "I wouldn't recognize his car if it ran over me. I don't even know what kind of a car he drives."

"A Pontiac," Crider said.

"Somebody's been letting the air out of his tires," Starks said. "Every day. For over a week now."

"Is that what you mean by *damage?*" Kosta said.

"Whatever you call it, it's damned inconvenient. Every time he leaves work he has to get the attendant to inflate his tires."

"Sounds like the garage attendant's the one who's being inconvenienced."

"We're talking about specific violations," Crider said. "Illegal trespass, harassment, and interference with the duties of a government official. Plus malicious impairment of a private vehicle."

"Are you accusing me of doing nasty things to the senator's car?"

"We're trying to get information." Starks took a photograph out of a manila envelope and put it on the table. "This is a picture of you, isn't it?"

Kosta picked up the picture and said, "Such a face. I mean, lots of smart little chickies can write political stories, but how many people have a drop-dead face like that one?"

"Somebody sticks one of these pictures on the senator's windshield every day," Starks said. "At least one of his tires is flat, and a picture like this is stuck under the windshield wiper."

"That's weird," Kosta said. "At least fifty of those pictures were swiped out of my car a month or so ago."

"Why do you need fifty pictures of yourself?"

"Publicity. Promotion. I order two hundred at a time. Lots of editors I work for like to run a picture of the author. You know what I mean? With a fancy caption. 'R. M. Kosta, dissident, journalist, and intimate friend of the famous. Equally at ease with indigents and rich folks.' Stuff like that."

"You're saying that somebody else has been leaving your picture on Senator Treptow's car and then letting the air out of his tires?"

"I'm not saying anything. *You're* the detectives. All I said was that a gang of those pictures was pinched out of the bonnet of my Volkswagen."

The two men got up to leave then. At the door Crider said,

"We talk to bright people all the time. They start out trying to outsmart us and they end up outsmarting themselves."

"There must be a lesson in that," Kosta said.

"I wouldn't be surprised," Starks said.

When Kosta was arrested a few days later, it wasn't Starks and Crider who took her in. It was Patrolman Mendez and Sergeant Hahn.

 Gabe was more amused than annoyed by Kosta's shenanigans. He even found a painless way to deal with his deflated tires. He left a standing order with the garage attendant to check his car every day at four thirty and put air in any tires that were low.

As for the flowers and notes and her constant presence in the Senate press gallery, those things were a kind of diversion, a change of pace from the pressure of his schedule, from the driving energy of his staff.

She seemed always to wear either a red sweater or a navy blue one. And usually, classic as a uniform, the collar of a white shirt edged above the bright red or the dark blue.

Her glasses were pushed up to the top of her head. Vanity, he thought. Later, however, she told him, "I don't even *need* glasses. I have eyes like an eagle. But I like the look. They give me clout. People *expect* a keen intellectual like me to wear glasses. Also, in case my eyes *do* go bad, when I'm eighty years old or something, then I'll be ready. I'll have the habit, if you know what I mean."

Gabe was convinced, however, that Jud's assessment of Kosta had been correct. Whatever the surface glitter, she was an arriviste. Upwardly mobile. A gung-ho contraption wired for sound. She would use him, he had no doubt, if she could.

If she could package him with Che Guevara as Jud had suggested, she would. If she could use him as a case history to prove that men in high office are tone-deaf, color-blind, or sexually aggressive she would probably do that.

The first time he saw her face to face, when he came out of the Jockey Club late one night and found her standing by his car, he was suddenly angry. When she started to speak, when she said, "Senator Treptow, I'm—" he interrupted. "I *know* who you are. And to tell you the truth, I'm not crazy about your tactics. If you have something to say to me—"

"*If* I have something to say to you? What do you think I've been trying to do? I could have had an audience with the Pope in the time I've been trying to reach you."

As he drove away, he could see her in the rearview mirror, standing by the curb, watching him go. She stood absolutely still, like a child, her arms down at her sides. He was tempted suddenly to turn and go back. But he kept going ahead.

Two days later he saw her again. When he came home she was sitting at the top of the outside stairway that led to his apartment.

It had rained early in the evening, and she was wearing a yellow fisherman's slicker. As he came up the stairs, she said, "Don't start yelling at me again."

"I'm not going to yell at you."

"You yelled the other night."

"I'm just going to ask you to respect my privacy. I'm not public property."

"You're *not?* You're a senator, for Pete's sake. What's more public than that?"

"I don't want to have a debate here on the stairs. And I'm sure as hell not going to argue with you."

"Ahhh . . . he swears a little," she said. "That's a good sign."

"Look—"

"Please . . . just give me a minute. I'm not what you think I am. Just because I'm not very old and not very big doesn't mean I'm not serious. I'm so serious I give people toothaches. Be a sport. Just ask me in for half an hour. Or fifteen minutes. I'll talk fast. Just let me say what I have to say, and if you're not interested I'll be gone like a herd of turtles. And I promise I won't bug you anymore. That's reasonable, isn't it?"

"It might be if you hadn't turned this into some kind of a contest. I don't have much patience with people who think they're going to wear me down."

"I don't want to wear you down," she said. "I just want—"

"I know what *you* want. Let me tell you what *I* want. I want to stay clear of any scheme you may have for capitalizing on my brother's death. I don't want anything to do with *that.*"

"You've got it all twisted," she said. "I'm on *your* side."

"No you're not. You're on your own side."

"Jesus—for somebody who never said ten words to me before tonight you sure have a high opinion of me."

"I don't have *any* opinion of you. It's not a question of that. I know what you're up to because you told me. In that first telegram you sent."

"Are you telling me you don't even care why your brother was killed?"

"I *know* why he was killed. He was riding in a plane and the plane went down. That's it."

"But that's *not* it," she said. "That's what I'm trying to tell you."

"And *I'm* telling *you*. I won't let you use my brother for a cheap headline in some underground paper."

She stood there looking at him for a long moment. Then she said, "I know how you feel. But you're all wrong about me." She turned and started down the steps. A few steps down she stopped suddenly and turned around. "I know things you don't know. And I won't be satisfied till I tell you what they are."

She ran down the rest of the stairs then to the side yard. Hurrying along the driveway to the street, she turned right toward Wisconsin Avenue.

Two days later, when Gabe was in Chicago speaking to the South Side Democratic Club, Kosta slipped into his office at lunchtime, chained and padlocked herself to the leg of his desk, and announced that she would stay there till Senator Treptow gave her the interview she wanted.

An hour later a police squad arrived, broke her chain with bolt cutters, and drove her to jail. The *Washington Star*, in its late edition, carried a picture of her looking through the bars of a cell.

By dinnertime, one of Nader's lawyers had arranged her release, but her picture and the wire story of what she'd done were picked up in papers all over the country. Gabe, having breakfast at the Drake the next morning, saw it in the *Chicago Tribune*. The headline said, SENATOR TREPTOW'S OFFICE OCCUPIED BY RADICAL WRITER.

In the photograph, Kosta did not look radical. She looked as if she'd been crying. The story said that one of the magazines she normally contributed articles to had canceled all work contracts with her. The editor was quoted: "We do not support illegal actions, no matter what the ultimate objectives may be. We will not tolerate such behavior from our contributors."

32 Arthur Garrigus was not amused by the treatment of his fellow journalist and sometime stringer.

When a newspaper reporter or a serious political writer goes to jail for some alleged crime or misdemeanor committed in the pursuit of his or her profession, that action should be carefully examined by all of us, the ones who write and the ones who read.

A responsible colleague, R. M. Kosta, recently spent several hours in a Washington, D.C. jail. The crime? After weeks of frustration trying to arrange an interview with a member of the United States Senate, the reporter in question chained herself to the senator's desk. Did she hope that she would at last get her story, or was it merely a protest be-

cause she had been blocked off, for some reason, from a valid news source?

Whatever her motive, attention must be paid. The facts behind this story should be examined. A young woman who is simply trying to do the job she is paid to do, even if her actions are extreme or eccentric, does not deserve to be dealt with as a criminal, to be fingerprinted, locked in a cell, and photographed there. Nor are her private political convictions or previous political activities at issue.

The question, as we see it, is this: Does a public servant, an elected legislative official, have the right to deny access to his opinions and judgments to a qualified member of the press?

We are constantly reminded of the obligations of the media. In fairness it should be noted that people who have chosen to become public figures have an undeniable obligation to the media. The electorate has a right to be informed. Journalists have a right to gather information, to publish the facts, and to draw conclusions about those facts. They have, in short, a right to practice their profession.

In the case of Kosta, it is particularly ironic that the senator who refused to see her or talk with her is Gabe Treptow, the new man from Illinois.

Treptow, in his short time in Washington, has established himself as the most vocal iconoclast in the Senate. He has systematically attacked and debunked every sacred precept on Capitol Hill. He has been called an inept grandstander by some, a dedicated public servant by others. He has demonstrated both the desire and the ability to communicate, an instinct for avoiding the cliché congressional channels and going directly to the public with his views.

The irony is this: A reporter was arrested for criminal trespass and disturbing the peace because she protested her

*inability to make contact with a senator who needs, per-
haps more than any other man in the Congress, the support
and cooperation of the press corps. In such a circumstance,
everyone loses. And the public, I suspect, loses the most of
all.*

"What do you think?" Lasker said.

Dalrymple closed the folder stuffed with press cuttings and looked up. He grinned. "So far so good."

"Better than that. That picture of her broke all over the country. It even ran in a paper in London. And in *France-Soir* in Paris."

"Who set up the arrest?"

"As soon as we heard from Rimmer we told him to call the police, and they came and got her. Then we tipped off an AP photographer. He saw her being taken in and he maneuvered his way inside to get the shot. Then we set up the quote from the magazine editor saying he wouldn't hire her. Pie in the sky."

"For a man who didn't want this job you seem to be getting a hell of a kick out of it," Dalrymple said.

"I know when I'm outmaneuvered. When that happens I try to make the best of it."

Dalrymple grinned. "Don't hand me that. I know you. You like to win."

"Who doesn't? And that's what we're doing. It's forty to nothing in our favor and the game's barely started. She's made herself look so bad we may not even have to put on our cleats."

"I see. That's why you're so high all of a sudden. Everything's going to fall in your lap and you won't have to play dirty."

"Dead wrong, Mark. I didn't want the fucking job, but I took it. You know me. Once I sign on, I'll stick with it."

"I know that. I was just kidding you."

"What do you think about the Garrigus piece?"

"Looks like another piece of cake to me. He bails Kosta out a little, but he certainly doesn't pin any roses on Treptow. Maybe we didn't bat a thousand on this one, but I'd give us about eight fifty."

"Do you think she'll still try to get to Treptow?"

"Hard to say. What do you think?"

"I'd guess no. I'd bet she's really pissed off at him."

"We'll have to wait and see," Dalrymple said. "But so far we're looking good."

The Saturday following Gabe's trip to Chicago, he went to see Kosta at her apartment. She came to the door barefoot, wearing a short terry-cloth robe, her hair in curlers.

"I tried to call you," he said, "but your phone's not working."

"It's working. I just turn it off on Saturdays." She stood in the doorway with her hands in her robe pockets, looking up at him.

"I thought you were taller," he said.

"Five three. I'm tall enough."

"Look . . . I'm sorry to bother you. . . ."

"No problem. I just washed my hair. Now I'm going to sit under the dryer."

"I can come back later if that's better for you."

"I won't be home later."

"I was out of town for a few days," he said then, "but I've been reading about you in the paper. I wanted you to know I'm sorry about what happened."

"No big deal. I've been in jail before."

"I mean, if I was responsible in some way—"

"Forget it. I knew what I was doing."

"I feel as if maybe I could have prevented it."

"You could have," she said. "But you didn't. It was a contest. Just like you told me that night outside your house. Me against you. And you won."

"I've been thinking over some of the things you said that night."

"Too late. I changed my mind. I'm gonna junk the whole story."

"Just like that?"

"Just like that. It's too much for me. I can't handle it by myself."

"You said you wanted me to help you. Let's at least talk about it."

"I don't want to talk about it. Like I said . . . I changed my mind." She eased back a step and put her hand on the door knob. "I have to dry my hair now."

When the door closed, he walked down the stairs to the garden, through the gate, and along N Street to the Potomac. He was just opposite St. John's Church when he stopped walking suddenly, staring straight ahead. He turned then and walked quickly back to her building.

When she opened the door, he said, "I didn't finish what I had to say. I just want you to know that you're a hardheaded pain in the ass."

"You're a hardheaded pain in the ass."

"You're spiting yourself just to get even with me. That's stupid. If you're on to something, stick with it. If I can help you I will."

"I told you. I don't want your bloody help."

"I'll be at the Georgetown Inn at"—he looked at his watch — "at twelve thirty. I'll buy you some lunch and we can—"

"I already have a lunch date."

"Then *break* it. Or *don't* break it. It's all the same to me." He turned and walked away, down the steps to the garden, and out into the street. He didn't hear her door slam behind him. It closed easily. He decided that was a good sign.

 It was ten minutes past one when Kosta walked into the Four Georges restaurant at the Georgetown Inn. The headwaiter led her to the table by the window where Treptow was waiting, halfway through his second Cutty Sark and soda.

"I decided you weren't coming."

"I wasn't," she said.

"What made you change your mind?"

"You were right. You said I was spiting myself just to get back at you. And I was."

The waiter came then with menus and they ordered lunch.

"You want some wine?" Gabe said.

"Sure."

"Red or white?"

"I don't care."

"How about Muscadet?"

"That's fine."

"What do people call you?" he said then.

"The people I like call me Kosta. Other people call me all kinds of different things."

"What do the initials stand for?"

"I was christened Rosemary but I always hated it. So did my dad. He started calling me R. M. But when I was in school it got to be Arm and then turned into Army. When I started to write and get a credit line I went back to R. M."

"They named me George Albert after a couple of uncles. But nobody ever called me anything but Gabe."

The wine arrived then, Gabe tested it, and the waiter half-filled their glasses.

"You a big drinker?" she said.

"Depends on the occasion. I've lost a few weekends here and there. But if I decided to go on the wagon tomorrow it wouldn't be any problem for me."

"That's what they *all* say."

"What do *you* say?"

"I say I hate drunks. But I don't trust people who never take a drink. Show me a teetotaler and I'll show you a weirdo."

"You hungry?" he said when the waiter brought the food.

"Starving. I'm always starving. I've got a screwed-up metabolism. If my size reflected the amount I eat I'd look like Mount Whitney. I really burn it up. Five meals a day and I'm still hungry. And I wear the same size dress I wore in high school."

After they finished eating, when the table was cleared, he said, "I'm ready to listen if you're ready to talk."

"I'm still not sure what turned you around."

"Very simple. I decided I'd made a mistake."

"Don't be too sure. I know you thought I was trying to use you."

"Who told you that?"

"I have spies in every corner," she said. Then, "The fact is I *am* trying to use you. I need your name. I need the power of your office and I need money to go where I have to go and find out what I have to find out. If this turns out the way I expect, it will be a tough nut to crack. It's gonna take time and patience and chutzpah. You know about chutzpah?"

"Yeah. I do."

"Good. That's what it's gonna take. Am I scaring you off?"

"Not yet."

"One thing I don't need," she said, "is to have my head patted. After I tell you what I know and what I suspect, if you think I'm crazy, I expect you to tell me so. If you're not *with* me, you're no good to me. You know what I'm saying?"

"I'll tell you what I think. You don't have to worry about that."

"Good. Let's get out of here. I never tell secrets in restaurants."

 They walked up Wisconsin Avenue to P Street, then over to the Georgetown University campus. It had rained the night before. The morning had been misty and gray. But now the sky was bright. They found a bench in a grove of trees and sat down, sun streaks slanting down around them through the foliage.

"I don't have all the facts," she began. "I don't have many facts at all. I don't even have a respectable theory. What I *do* have are a lot of questions and a very funny feeling in my gut that *somebody* is *managing* events. You know what I mean? A scenario has been written and everybody involved has memorized it. It's over five months now since those two H-14's crashed. There's been plenty of time to stuff everything into a big container and screw the lid down tight."

"So how do you lick that?"

"That's the trick. We've got two things going for us—*one*, the information that came out before they started to rearrange things, and *two*, the fact that those months *have* passed. My hunch is that *if* there was a cover-up, whoever put it together thinks it's old news by now. I mean, I'm sure they consider it a *closed* operation."

"Who's 'they'?"

"Ahhh . . . that's a good question. When we know the answer to *that* we'll know it all. Or *I'll* know it all. Just because I say 'we' doesn't mean I'm assuming anything. After I tell you what I think, *then* you can decide if you want to go along with me."

"You already said that."

"I know I did. Now I'm saying it again. I mean, it's moment to moment as far as I'm concerned. You'll be involved only as long as it makes sense to you. When it doesn't—zip."

"That's fair enough."

"Here's what I think," she said then. "Two H-14 jets crashed last January. The SAI commercial flight on the sixth and Air Force Three, the executive plane, on the sixteenth, the one your brother was on. I think both those planes were sabotaged. I believe there's a connection between the two. If there was a bomb on the first plane, and I think there was, then there was probably a bomb on the second one."

"How do you connect the two crashes? Outside of the fact that they were both H-14's?"

"I think there was a pattern to the way the FAA and the NTSB handled the two accidents. When the SAI flight went down, the first *official* announcement said it looked like pilot error. They even speculated that the pilot could have suffered a heart attack. SAI officials denied this. They said the pilot was *not* at fault, that even if he had been sick, the copilot would have taken over and flown the plane safely. Then, a few days later, the airline people suddenly changed their story. They said the pilot *had* been at fault, that something had gone wrong in the cockpit during takeoff. They decided that since the plane *was* taking off, since it had only climbed a thousand feet or so, a few seconds of confusion or indecision could have been enough to throw the plane out of its climbing pattern and cause it to crash."

"Didn't the president of the Airline Pilots Association deny that could happen?"

"At first he did. But he had a sudden change of heart. He decided the FAA conclusions were correct. Human error. Okay, so much for that. Then the second plane crashed, the Air Force jet. It had taken off from Andrews Air Base half an hour before. It was in full flight. This time there was no mention of pilot error."

"Didn't they link it with that TWA flight that suddenly dropped thirty thousand feet a year or so ago?"

"That's right," Kosta said. "That was their first theory. But then they decided it was a mechanical problem, a failure of the plane's hydraulic system. The manufacturer screamed bloody murder, said the plane's hydraulic system *couldn't* fail like that. Leo Hartwig said it. He was the president of Hartwig Systems. He'd helped design the H-14 and his company had built it. Then all of a sudden Hartwig Systems released a statement saying the FAA was right. The hydraulic complex *had* failed. Just about then the FAA changed its mind about the first crash. It hadn't been pilot error after all. A failed hydraulic system had caused that accident too. Everybody nodded their heads and agreed and the two investigations were formally closed. Hartwig Systems was the official goat, Leo Hartwig was replaced as president of the company, and everyone seemed satisfied.

"It was a familiar pattern. People were accustomed to it. The electric refrigerator stops making ice cubes. The new toaster burns the toast. A giant airliner falls out of the sky. I mean, they just don't build things the way they used to. That's the song. *C'est la vie.*

"Well . . . for me it doesn't wash. Too much choreography. It's too neat. When people started knocking the design of the DC-10 after the Chicago crash, McDonnell Douglas fought back. They're still fighting. So why would Hartwig Systems roll over and play dead? Even the insurance companies paid all the claims with a smile. It was like the order came down. Don't make waves. Let's put this thing to sleep."

"What makes you think sabotage is the answer?"

"Logic. If it's not pilot error and if you think the hydraulic system excuse is a little too convenient, what's left? It also explains why there'd be a big scramble to cover up the truth. Remember what Leo Hartwig said? 'Those two planes crashed because somebody *wanted* them to crash.' "

"Later he denied saying that, didn't he?"

"No. A spokesman for Hartwig Systems denied he said it. But I've heard the tapes. He said it, all right. And since then he hasn't said *anything.* No interviews. No statements. He's holed up outside of Watsonville, California, in a beach house. As far as I know, nobody has even talked to him for four or five months."

"What makes you think he's there?"

"A guy from the *San Francisco Chronicle* took some tele-photo shots. Hartwig walking by the ocean. A couple of men walking with him. Bodyguards they look like. But you can't tell if they're keeping people away from Hartwig or Hartwig away from people. If he thinks he needs protection, that's one thing. If somebody wants him out of circulation that's something else again."

She turned to look at him. "I know what you're thinking. It's all guesswork. You're right. I *am* guessing. A *lot.* But there are some other things. When the SAI plane crashed outside Indianapolis I was in Lexington, Kentucky, in a rented car, heading for the Cincinnati airport. I had the car radio blasting and I heard the first news report from Indianapolis. They quoted witnesses, two or three of them, who lived near where the plane crashed. They said the plane had started to climb after taking off, there had been an explosion, and one wing fell off. Then the plane dived straight into the ground, exploded, and burned."

"They said there was an explosion when the plane was still in flight?"

Kosta nodded. "But you didn't read that in the papers. Because it wasn't there. After the first radio reports nobody said anything about a wing falling off. But a friend of mine, Dick McCann, has an underground newspaper in Indianapolis. He tracked down one of the eyewitnesses, a farmer named Avery Buck, and he told Dick the same story he'd told before, that he'd seen an explosion when the plane was in midair."

"Have you talked with this guy Buck?"

"Not yet. But he's at the top of my list."

"How about the other witnesses you mentioned?"

"A few days after the crash everybody ended up telling the same story. The plane had gone down, hit the ground, and *then* exploded. When McCann asked the authorities about those earlier reports, they said the witnesses had decided they'd been mistaken."

"That kind of thing happens all the time, doesn't it?"

"It happens *some* of the time," Kosta said. "People get befuddled and they're not quite sure *what* they saw. And it's possible that's what happened this time. I won't know for sure till I talk to some of those people. But whatever they saw or thought they saw, that won't solve the riddle of the missing passenger."

"What's that all about?"

"When SAI made the first announcement after the crash in Indianapolis, they said the total number of victims was two hundred and twenty-six. Passengers and crew. Two days later the FAA revised that down to two hundred twenty-five. That's how many names were on the published list. But by then the emergency teams had recovered two hundred and twenty-*six* bodies.

"At first the FAA said that extra person was someone on the ground who'd been hit when the plane crashed. But then somebody leaked the SAI flight manifest, and sure enough there were two hundred and twenty-six names on it.

"The FAA hemmed and hawed for a couple of days, and finally they said the passenger they'd overlooked was a man named Ralph Benedict from New York City. But when it was time to release the bodies, Ralph Benedict's body was the only one that wasn't claimed by a relative or finally identified by anybody other than the government investigators.

"Next time I was in New York I checked out all the Ralph Benedicts in the telephone directory. None of them took off from Indianapolis that day. All of them are still alive."

"Does that really prove anything?" Gabe said. "Maybe he wasn't from New York. Maybe he just *said* he came from New York."

"Maybe he did. Because there's no record of a Ralph Benedict on any passenger flight out of New York for a month before that crash in Indianapolis. I've got a cousin in traffic control at Pan Am. She runs a computer that can tell you how many freckles Kissinger has on his left thumb. She also told me that no Ralph Benedict flew *into* Indianapolis during that same period."

"So?"

"So is there a real Ralph Benedict or isn't there? Was he on that flight or wasn't he? Did the FAA make a mistake or are they doing some kind of a number?"

As they walked back toward her apartment, Gabe said, "What's your next move?"

"I'm flying out to Indiana Monday morning. I'll spend a few days there. Then I'll stop in West Virginia on my way back."

"I'm still not sure what you want from me."

"That's easy. I want you to jump up and down and tell me how smart I am. But I know you're not going to do that. Not from what I've told you so far. I know I need more facts."

"I'll tell you the truth. From what you've told me I can't see any real link between those two crashes."

"Maybe there isn't one," Kosta said. "Maybe I'm crazy. But I've got this creepy feeling about it. Like when I used to see pictures of Nixon and his cronies having a good laugh together. I mean, I smell something rotten. Whether I can dig it out is another matter. But I'm sure gonna give it a rumble. If I'm on to something big it won't take long to find it out. As soon as somebody starts to scare me off or buy me off I'll know I'm getting warm."

The next morning Lasker called Dalrymple at home. "I guessed wrong. Kosta and Treptow spent the day together yesterday. And last night she made a plane reservation for Indianapolis."

"Have you talked to Tunstall?"

"Three times. And he's been on the phone to Indianapolis. He says everything's buttoned up."

 On Monday, at the airport in Indianapolis, Kosta went to the office of Don Gulliver, SAI's customer relations officer. She had talked with him before on an earlier trip.

Gulliver was affable, tall and slender, thinning brown hair, and dark eyebrows that looked as though they'd been reshaped with tweezers.

"How you getting along?" he said.

"Not too great. I may give up writing and open a massage parlor."

"Why not? I'll be your first customer."

"Television's wrecking everything," she said. "It's rough to find an idea for an article that can hack it against the tube. I sure wouldn't be poking through the ashes of that airline crash if I could find something better to write about. I mean, I think I'm bats to be doing a piece on Ralph Benedict this late in the game. But I'll bet you a cigar I can sell it. Blood and guts. The mystery victim."

"He's not much of a mystery anymore, is he?"

"I guess not," Kosta said. "But all the same it gives people chills to read about somebody dying a long way from home and nobody ever shows up to claim the body. Or maybe somebody *did* show up since I talked to you last."

Gulliver shook his head. "Nobody showed up."

"It's odd. What do you do with the body in a case like that?"

"Cremation."

"How long do you wait?"

"That's not an SAI decision," he said. "I assume the county coroner decides."

"I guess so. How long did you say they waited?"

"Five days. They took him to the crematory on the fifth day."

"Five days after the crash or five days after he was identified?"

He hesitated. "All those files have gone to our Chicago office, but as I remember, it was five days after the crash."

"But it was three or four days after the crash before they identified him."

"Something like that."

"That means he was cremated almost as soon as he was identified."

"Like I said, those decisions were made by the local medical people."

As soon as Kosta left his office, Gulliver called his superior in Chicago. "You asked me to keep you posted on Kosta, that girl from Washington. She was just here. Just left my office. She's still asking questions about Ralph Benedict."

On her way downtown from the airport, driving a rented Mercury, Kosta stopped at the Marion County coroner's office. She identified herself as a writer working on an article about public attitudes toward cremation. She was ushered, after a short wait, into a private office, where a husky, auburn-haired woman wearing a brown pants suit and shell-rim glasses shook her hand and invited her to sit in the chair beside her desk.

"I can only give you an educated opinion," the woman said. "Our duties here are quite—what shall I say?—*clinical*, I suppose, is the best word. The crematories and the morticians try to present death as something better than it is. We deal with it as a simple fact. My feeling, however, is that the *idea* of cremation has begun to take hold here in the Middle West. It took a while. Many of these people come from rural backgrounds. They are quite traditional in their beliefs. Viewing the remains, great baskets of flowers—all that. But more and more we're seeing simpler ceremonies. Less pageantry. Less expense. Many people still shudder, I think, at the idea of burning their dead relatives. But as they discover that cremation costs one-half or one-third as much as a traditional burial, I'm sure many people will find a way to accept it."

"When you have unidentified remains, unclaimed bodies," Kosta said, "what is your policy?"

"Our office does not make policy. The county medical board—"

"Yes, of course. I just wondered if those people who must be dealt with at county expense—"

"All county-funded services are cremations."

"Is there a time schedule? How long after death . . . ?"

"When the victim has identification, the body is normally kept in the county morgue for at least two weeks after notice of death is published in the newspapers. In special circumstances, bodies have been kept for as long as a month."

"Recently I wrote an article about the airline accident that took place here last January," Kosta said carefully. "I was surprised to find out that one of the victims was cremated the day after he was identified."

"I'm sure our department had nothing—"

"Yes, I believe it did. The airline people told me the county coroner's office ordered the cremation. The name of the deceased was Ralph Benedict."

The woman adjusted herself in her chair and said, "I am not familiar with that case."

"Perhaps I should talk with Dr. Springer then. I believe that's the coroner's name. I would prefer not to use this Benedict incident in my article without double-checking it with the person in charge."

The woman was gone for almost ten minutes. When she came back she said, "Dr. Springer sends his apologies. He's anxious to talk with you, but this is a bad morning. Will you be in Indianapolis for a few days?"

"I'm at the Holiday Inn downtown," Kosta said. She wrote her name on a card and gave it to the woman.

"Good. I'm sure Dr. Springer will call you tomorrow."

 After she'd checked in at the hotel, Kosta drove out Meridian to Dick McCann's office. He worked in an abandoned grocery store on Forbush Street, two blocks off Meridian, a mile and a half out from the Circle. Across the front of his building hung a twenty-foot-long sign, his paper's name, *The Belated Truth,* printed on it.

When Kosta parked at the curb and got out of her car, she saw the sign had come loose at one end. It angled sharply down toward the ground. Through the front windows, streaked and dirty, she could see that the store was empty.

The war surplus desks and file cabinets, the odd chairs and bits of furniture from the Salvation Army, the phones and battered typewriters, were all gone. Papers and posters and hand-lettered signs were scattered around the floor, a sign reading Kunstler For President was propped in a corner, and huge photo blowups of Paul Robeson, Bertolucci, and Trotsky were still stapled to the walls. On the back wall, floor-to-ceiling, in five-foot letters, someone had painted with a broad brush THE SUPREME COURT SUCKS.

Stuck with drafting tape to the inside of the front-door glass was a neatly typed five-by-seven-inch file card:

> *The Belated Truth* is now deflated and deceased. Having survived poverty, brutality, harassment, indignity, prosecution, and humiliation, we have now capsized on the shoals of public apathy.
>
> It's true. The cruel fact is that no one any longer seems to give a shit. The barefoot idealists are now fully occupied, wearing seventy-dollar shoes and kissing corporate asses. The college girls who fought the police with their fists are content to shop long afternoons at Blocks and Ayres and write an occasional snotty letter to the *Indianapolis Star*.
>
> So . . . we pack it in. *We*, meaning Dick McCann, founder, editor, typesetter, janitor, and publisher, through the bad days and worse days, of *T.B.T.*
>
> My creditors, who are legion, can kiss my bankrupt ass. My friends, those who are left, out of jail and out of pocket, will know where to locate me. I will be easily recognized in my double-knit suit, button-down shirt, and turd-bird necktie. There will also be a small American flag pinned to my lapel.

Turning back toward her car, Kosta saw two young black men leaning against the side of a magnificently mangled 1964 Plymouth parked at the curb two doors down the street.

"Dickie who?" one of them said when she asked if they knew McCann. He was wearing a Scotch-plaid beret with a red pom-pom on top. His friend wore a pale-blue cowboy hat. They looked at each other and giggled.

"Forget it," she said. "I don't want to play games with you

two comedians. I owe Dick fifty bucks and I want to pay him. But if I can't find him I'll just be fifty bucks richer."

When she turned and started toward her car, the two young men were quickly beside her. She stopped abruptly and said, "Don't get overstimulated. I don't have the fifty on me." She slipped her hand into her shoulder bag. "What I *do* have is a five-dollar bill and a thirty-two caliber automatic. If you try to *take* the five, I'll kill you. If you tell me where I can locate Dick McCann, I'll *give* it to you."

They walked with her to a phone booth on the corner while she checked out the number they'd given her. As soon as McCann came on the line, she handed the folded bill to the man in the cowboy hat, and he and his friend hurried away.

She met McCann for lunch at a restaurant called The Chop House just off the Circle behind the state capitol building. When he strolled in and sat down across from her, she said, "I don't believe my eyes."

"Metamorphosis," he said. "The reptile sheds his skin."

"How long have I known you?"

"Ten years, plus or minus. You were in your first year at Brandeis."

"Second," she said.

"Whatever. And I was one year out of U. Mass."

"Do you know I've never seen you without a beard? Never seen you with a civilian haircut. If I'd met you on the street I wouldn't have recognized you."

"That's the idea. A new life. A new leaf. A new face."

"What about Hazel?" Kosta said.

"What about her?"

"What's she say about all this?"

"I guess she liked the old face better. She packed up her portable loom and went back to Pasadena."

"You're kidding."

He shook his head. "Straight stuff. Back to Daddy and clean sheets every week. Fresh-squeezed orange juice in the morning and a four-car garage with all the stalls occupied."

"I just saw you guys two months ago."

"Three months," he said. "A little over."

"So when did all this happen?"

"Eight weeks ago yesterday I took an honest job. Eight weeks ago tomorrow Hazel took off for the father house."

"Why, for God's sake?"

"You'll have to ask her."

"You two were together eleven years."

"Twelve," he said.

"Were you slipping around?"

He shook his head. "Nothing like that. You know me. Old dog Trey. Bring in the paper. Sleep by the fire. Fetch the lady's slippers. No, it was nothing *personal* like that. At least not by my definition. But it sure as hell seemed *personal* to her. She said I was selling out. 'You're fucking selling out'—she said that about a thousand times. She didn't want me to fold the paper and she didn't want me to take this job I took. You know Hazel. She can scream it up pretty good when the spirit moves her. And the spirit sure as hell moved her. Finally she said it was the job or her. If I was going to ditch everything I believed in she was bloody well going to ditch me. And she did."

"Was the job that important to you? *Is* it that important?"

He lifted his glass and took a slow drink. Watching him, she had the odd sensation of seeing his eyes cloud over. As though a lizard's transparent eyelid had slid down slowly, veiling the iris and the pupil, giving Dick a screen to hide behind.

"You said you stopped by the old office. You must have read the card in the window. That's the story. That's what I tried to explain to Hazel. I just figured I'd come to a dead end."

"It always *was* a dead end, Dick. And you knew it. We were always butting our heads against the bricks. I'm still doing it. Not because it makes any sense. Only because the alternatives are so scary. If everybody reads nothing but the government handouts; if all of us accept Walter Cronkite as the ultimate good and the final truth, then we really are up shit creek. Somebody has to keep asking the tough questions."

"You sound like Hazel."

"No I don't. I sound like *you*. She learned it from you. And so did I."

"Well . . . listen, Kosta . . . don't wreck my lunch." He looked at his watch. "Let's just say that all that stuff used to make sense to me. But it doesn't anymore."

Kosta smiled. "It can't be money, can it? Are they paying you a ton of money?"

"They sure as hell are."

"How much?"

"A lot," he said.

"What are you doing exactly?"

"It's a government job. The regional office of Health, Education, and Welfare. Public relations section. Mostly I'm writing. Just like I always did. Remember, I always said the only real integration was integrated neighborhoods, that busing wasn't the answer. Well, that's what I'm working on now. A series of pamphlets with that idea as the foundation."

"You mean to tell me HEW is taking a position *against* busing?"

"Not exactly. Not yet. This is sort of a pilot program. They feel they have an obligation to explore all aspects of the problem."

"Like how much more oil we have to import if we're going to run a school-bus program?"

"Don't try to dump on me, Kosta. I paid my dues. They say an ethical man can either sleep well or eat well but not both. I don't buy that. I've been sleeping well all my life. Now I want to eat well too. And that's what I'm doing."

After they finished lunch, when they were having their coffee, she said, "How'd you fall into this job? Did you answer an ad or what?"

"A guy came to see me at the newspaper office. He said he was from HEW in Washington."

"I know quite a few people over there," Kosta said. "What was his name?"

"It's not important."

"What do you mean? It might be important to me."

"Too bad. I'm not going to tell you. I don't want you screwing up my act."

"You're a bastard. You know that?"

"I *always* knew it," he said. "You're just finding it out. Anyway, this guy said he'd read a lot of my articles through the years. Said he didn't usually agree with what I said but he liked the way I said it. He told me there was always a place for a guy like me at HEW, that I could reach a lot more people through their publications and mailing pieces than I could with *T.B.T.* And I wouldn't even have to relocate, he said. I could stay on in Indianapolis. A couple days later we talked about it some more and a week later he offered me a job."

"And you jumped at it?"

"Not exactly. I thought about it for a while. And Hazel and I hashed it over. But in the end they sold me on it. I mean I sold myself. And I'm still sold."

When they left the restaurant, she walked back to his office building with him. "I'm still trying to get an angle on that H-14 crash," she said.

"Forget it. I went over that mother with a fine-tooth comb."

"No luck?"

"It wasn't a question of luck," he said. "I just decided the FAA was shooting straight. Once the manufacturer admitted there was a failure in the hydraulic system . . . "

"What about those witnesses? The ones who reported an explosion before the plane went down?"

"Nothing to it. Some dingbat farmer and a couple of Looney Tunes ladies who wouldn't recognize an explosion if it happened in their kitchens. As soon as the government investigators started asking hard questions they changed their stories in a hurry. I interviewed two of them myself. They were so screwed up they didn't know *what* they'd seen."

"Were they sure they *hadn't* seen a midair explosion?"

"Absolutely. When I talked with them last they both said the same thing. What they'd thought was a midair explosion was probably the sunglare reflecting off the wing when it angled around suddenly."

"They *both* said that about the sun glare?"

"That's right," Dick said. "If you're still trying to beat a story out of that thing, you're wasting your time."

"It looks that way. I just thought maybe you had some new stuff on it."

He shook his head. "It's a dead duck. They've closed the book. There was a plane crash in Lisbon last week. One in Hong Kong the week before that. What happened in Indianapolis last January is about as exciting as a 1936 weather forecast. If I were you

I'd write an update on Spiro Agnew. Or dig up a new angle on Rebozo."

She stood in the mid-afternoon sun and watched the young man walk briskly away from her toward the entrance to his building. He was trim and lean in his well-cut suit, his collar gleaming white; his shoes, rich brown and burnished like a Spanish saddle, clicked importantly on the sidewalk. She tried to connect him with the scraggly, unwashed, ink-stained pilgrim she had known and followed and listened to for ten critically important years of her life, tried to find the anger and outrage and excitement of that man behind the neatly pressed and reasonable facade of this one. But she couldn't do it. She felt sad suddenly. Used and misled. And frightened.

 Avery Buck, Arloa Anderson, and Ellen Perigo. Those three people lived just west of the Indianapolis airport. They had reported, each of them, that they had seen a midair explosion, a burst of flame along the left wing, just before the H-14 lost power and crashed in a pasture barely outside the airport boundaries.

All three, Kosta found, had changed addresses in the past five months. None of them were listed in the Indianapolis telephone directory. During the next days, however, she was able to locate two of them.

Beulah Anderson Wick told Kosta that her sister, Arloa, had a history of nervous disorders. "Ever since she was a toddler we knew she wasn't just right. Not a crazy person, mind you. Nothing like that. Arloa is as sweet-tempered a woman as you could ever meet. And a pretty little thing. Always was. My mother used to dress her up like a doll. We lived on a good-sized farm down by Wingate then. Mom had kitchen help. So it left her all the time she wanted to sew and embroider and the like. She had a workroom on the north side of the house, looking out over the orchard, and she'd be in there five or six hours a day, pumping the treadle on her old Singer. And more often than not she'd be making something for Arloa. Pretty little jumpers and aprons and bonnets. All trimmed with lace and ribbon and ricrac. Bows and rosettes sewed on and tiny white buttons shining like pearls.

"Me . . . I was kind of a horsey kid. Never in the house. Tagging after my brothers mostly. Doing men's work when they'd let me. Wearing bib overalls and gum boots. So Arloa was the only little girl my mom had to fuss over. And that's what she did.

"Arloa never got married. Never was courted or went out with a man at all. Just stayed on in the house with Mom and Dad till he died. Then it was just her and Mom together in a little house in Crawfordsville till Mom was taken. And after that she moved in here with Lon and me. By then our kids had up and gone and we were tickled to have her around for company.

"Lon always liked Arloa. Said she was the prettiest thing he'd ever seen. She was always smiling, it seemed like. Quiet and sweet. And she kept herself clean as a pin. Washed up good every morning and was able to iron and look after her clothes as good as anybody. And she could sew like a whip. Just like Mom.

"A person that didn't know—somebody that just saw Arloa walking around in the garden, or sitting out in front of the house of a summer—wouldn't have noticed anything different about her at all. But we knew.

"The poor soul just couldn't manage. Couldn't make any kind of a decision for herself. When she felt boxed-in for some reason she couldn't deal with it at all. She'd just sit with her hands in her lap and cry. Not making any noise. Just staring straight ahead with big tears rolling down her cheeks. Lon couldn't stand to watch her when she felt bad like that. Made him feel awful.

"He used to say there wasn't as much wrong with Arloa as

there was with the rest of us. He said we were the crazy ones. All she knew was to smile and be nice and make pretty things with her hands and never yell or be nasty to anybody.

"But . . . like they say, the majority rules. When it's one person up against a lot of others, when they all say that somebody needs to be watched over and put away where doctors and trained people can look after their needs, then that's what has to be done, I guess. My cousin Hulda up in Rapid City says we should have fought it in court, but Lon and I didn't know anything about such-like. And our kids are scattered every which way, from San Bernardino to Orlando to Albany, New York. So they couldn't be any help.

"Finally we decided it was best just to leave it up to Dr. Causey. He's looked after all of us for years ever since we moved here to Indianapolis. He sat me down one day and said, 'Beulah, we've got to put Arloa over in Longcliff now. She'll be better off that way.'

"In case you never heard about Longcliff, it's the state mental home over by Logansport. And it's not nearly as bad as I was afraid it might be. It's close enough so we can drive over every week or so to see her and bring her things. Fudge and fresh fruit. We miss having her with us in the house. But Dr. Causey says that more than likely Longcliff's where she'll be from now on."

"Have you noticed much change in her since they put her in the hospital?" Kosta asked.

"No change exactly. Mostly she's just gone back to the way she used to be. Before that plane crash you were asking me about. That's what made her so jumpy, I think. Nervous and bug eyed and crying all the time. Like I told you, she seen the whole thing as clear as anybody. Sitting by that big east window in her bedroom upstairs, she saw it plain, right in front of her, like some scary picture show.

"Lon and I were downstairs in the kitchen. We didn't see a thing. But we heard the crash and the explosion. The whole sky went yellow and white and the heat from the fire took paint right off the east wall of our barn."

"That must have been an awful shock for your sister."

Beulah nodded. "The odd part was she didn't seem too

affected by it till later. When people started to show up, asking her all kinds of questions. You see, Lon made the mistake of telling the neighbors that Arloa had seen the whole business. And the next thing we knew, people were coming in droves. Mostly police and government people from the East.

"I think all the commotion just wore Arloa out. She started yelling and talking back to people in a way we'd never seen her do before. She used to say to me, '*I'm* the one that seen it. Not them. *I* know what I saw. But they say different.'

"Two different times we had to drive her all the way in to the center of Indianapolis so she could tell what she saw to a roomful of men. They kept asking her the same things over and over and I guess it was just too much for her. At least that's what Dr. Causey said. He told us all the excitement had got her mixed up and mad at everybody and the only way she could get better was to have a long rest in a quiet place. It made sense the way Dr. Causey put it to us, so we signed the papers. And a couple days later they came and took her away.

"I cried my eyes out for weeks after that. I mean it all happened so quick. One day she was upstairs, humming to herself and walking around with light little steps, and the next thing I knew she was gone. But at least she missed those last hearings they held about the airplane crash business. Thank God for that. I'd have hated to see her go through all that questioning again, people contradicting her and going at her and getting her mixed up in that sweet little head of hers. I really would have hated to see that happen."

As soon as Kosta left, Beulah Wick telephoned Dr. Causey. "You asked me to let you know if anybody came here asking about Arloa." Then she told him about her talk with Kosta.

"God knows it's high time things started going my way," Ellen Perigo said. "I've been pickin' shit with the chickens so long it's a wonder I ain't grown a beak."

She sat tilted back in a reclining chair, her feet up, her frizzy hair bleached champagne blond, pink satin mules on her feet, a red-tipped cigarette in one hand, her other hand holding a brightly painted beer stein, the kind that's sold in airport souvenir shops.

Her stomach and hips and her mammoth thighs bulged dangerously under orange nylon slacks. Her breasts and upper arms struggled against the fabric of a hip-length Japanese kimono made in Newark, turquoise rayon with a red-and-gold dragon appliquéd on the back.

"After what happened to Newt I wasn't worth a damn. I mean, I wasn't fit for nothing for three years after that. I'd never been a drinking woman in my life. My folks was strict Baptists. I never saw a drop of liquor in our house when I was growing up. So I never got started on it. Cigarettes were something else. I smoked like a chimney from the time I was eleven or twelve. But when it came to drinking I never developed a taste for anything stronger than some sweet wine. A little Tokay or Muscatel.

"Even when Newt and I were going out and later on when we got married, I most always settled for a Gatorade or an RC. Newt was proud of it that I didn't drink. God knows he put away enough for the two of us. But he bragged to anybody that would listen that his little wife Ellen didn't booze it up. 'She'll do anything else you want to think up,' he used to say, 'but when it comes to the joy juice, just deal her out.'

"It was the truth. That's how I was. All the time we was married. Never back-doored on Newt and hardly ever took any kind of a drink. But then . . . when he died the way he did, choking to death and coughing up black, hacking and spitting his life up in a pan by the bed—when that happened, I just fell apart like a two-dollar shoe. I came straight home from the cemetery, found a bottle of Newt's Ten High whiskey in the kitchen cabinet, and finished it off. From then on I didn't draw a sober breath for almost three years.

"Finally, though, Newt's life insurance money petered out and I had to leave our little house there in Cagle and come up to Indianapolis where I knew I could get work. Newt's sister, Clara, was a cook in one of the dormitories at Butler College and she got me on there. After a couple of years I was ready to go back to Tennessee. I was so homesick for Cagle I couldn't see straight. But by then I didn't have anyplace to go back to."

"What happened to your house?"

"Flooded out. Just lifted up off the cinder blocks and floated down the gulch. Strip mining. That's what caused it. Some Pennsylvania company came in with bulldozers and peeled the top right off of all the hills around Cagle. Cleaned off the trees and grass and topsoil slick as a gut. The arrangement was that they would replant everything after they'd finished their mining. But they didn't do it like they promised. So when the snow melted and the spring rains came, half the houses in Cagle got washed away. And the ones that were left were three feet deep in mud.

"There was a big stink about it. Just what you'd expect. Threats and lawsuits and lots of letters to the newspapers. The government said the mining company was liable, no doubt about it, but then the company turned around and went bankrupt.

"So . . . all of us have been sweatin' it out since 1967, waiting for the courts to act, hoping for some kind of a settlement. Matter of fact, most of the people had high hopes. There were stories in the papers saying all of us were entitled to heavy damages. And the politicians dropped by every few months to shed a few crocodile tears and tell people what they wanted to hear. Every time I got a letter from somebody down in Cagle, most of them living in campers or bunking with relatives, they told me that justice was just around the corner. Big money was on the way.

"Well . . . I wasn't buying any of it. I'd already been through that same line of horse shit with the black lung people. I was entitled to a heavy pension, they said, because of what happened to Newt. But quite a few years had gone by since he'd coughed himself to death, so I'd given up on the idea of any of that money.

"After I left my job at the college I went to work at the Indianapolis airport. Working night shift. Short-order cook in the employees' coffee shop. I lived in a furnished room with a hot plate less than a mile from my work and I'd decided that was where I was going to stay, like it or not.

"But *now*," she said, waving one hand to indicate the splendor of her double mobile home—two bedrooms, two baths, washer-dryer, twin-door refrigerator, shag carpet, and a twenty-foot living room with a picture window— "just look at me. I fell in the outhouse and came up with a rose."

"What happened?"

"A miracle. That's the way I look at it. By that I don't mean I got anything I wasn't entitled to. But the miracle is how fast it all came. All at once. Like a bathtub running over. Within the space of ten days, two weeks at the most, Newt's black lung pension came through. Five hundred a month I get. For life. Besides that they gave me a check for all the back payments I was entitled to and never got. That came to a hundred and two thousand dollars. In one lump. I no more than got *that* money in the bank till a government man came to the door and handed me a check for another hundred and eighty-six thousand. Compensation for losing our house and ground in Cagle.

"Last Christmas I was so strapped it was all I could do just to mail a few dime-store cards to people at home. Now I've got so much money I don't hardly know what to do with it. I bought me this mobile deluxe home for forty-one thousand, bought myself a closetful of clothes and twenty pairs of shoes, picked out that white Chrysler sedan you see parked outside, laid in enough frozen steaks and Southern Comfort to last me a year, and I've *still* got close to two hundred thousand on interest in the Plainfield bank down the road.

"I mean, I could take out over a thousand a month just in interest if I wanted to. But I don't need it. I just sit here with my feet up watching my RCA, switching programs whenever I want to without even getting up, and all the time I'm earning a few dollars an hour from that money I've got sitting in the bank. You think I'm not lucky?"

"You're lucky all right."

"Like I said. And the funny thing is, I wonder if any of it would have happened if that big airliner you was asking about hadn't gone down here last January. Don't get me wrong. I don't mean there was any *real* connection. I'm a churchgoing woman, and it would just about kill me if I thought the good things that happened to me were linked up in any way with all them people getting killed like they did. But all the same I can't help thinking that those newspapers writing up my story had something to do with everything that happened later.

"I must have half a dozen clippings around here telling about how Newt died of the black lung and about our house getting flooded away because of that strip-mining company. I wouldn't be surprised if some of those Washington white-collar men read about me and decided I'd got a pretty raw deal."

"Maybe they did," Kosta said. "You were an eyewitness to that crash, weren't you?"

Ellen nodded. "I was hanging up some wash in the backyard. It was one of those clear days we don't get very often in January. Bright sun and not too cold. So I figured it was a good chance to let the sheets blow out a little. I was looking over the clothesline and I saw that plane from the time it took off. It angled right up the way they always do. Then it just keeled over and dived straight down to the ground. It was the worst thing I ever looked at in my life."

"Didn't somebody testify that the plane exploded in the air? Before it crashed?"

"*I* did. That's what I told them at first. I thought I'd seen a red flash like an explosion before the plane started to fall. But I was wrong. Later on I figured out that what I'd seen was the bright sunshine reflecting off that shiny aluminum wing."

"You're sure about that?"

"As sure as I can be. There wasn't ever any explosion till the plane hit the ground. That's what the investigators decided and that's the way it was."

As soon as she got back to her hotel, Kosta placed a call to Hazel Metzger in Pasadena. A cool voice said she was not at home. She had gone to Big Sur for a month.

"I'm a good friend of Hazel's. It's very important that I get in touch with her. Do you have a number where she's staying?"

When the Big Sur number answered, a man's voice, laughing, said, "Hazel went out in the woods looking for pinecones. Or maybe she's looking for *hazel* nuts."

"Will you take my number and have her call me? It's very important."

"There's no pencil here to write the number down with. I'd just call later if I were you. She should wander back in a half-hour or so."

Kosta called three more times. On the third try Hazel came on the phone, laughing, more laughter behind her in the room. "My *God,* Kosta, where are you?"

"I'm in a motel room in Indianapolis. Where are *you?*"

"We're having a nonstop party out in the woods. It's a blast. Like the old days. Vino and grasso and who-gives-a-damn-o."

"I need to talk to you. And I can't hear a word you're saying."

"Hold on. There's a phone upstairs. I'll go up there."

"That's better," Kosta said when Hazel came on again. "I called your house and they told me where I could reach you."

"What are you doing? Why don't you come out here? We're all screwing ourselves silly. Somebody brought a sixteen-year-old Mexican kid and he thinks he died and went to heaven."

"I had a long talk with Dick. That's why I'm calling. I thought you might be down in the dumps."

"I was," Hazel said. "That's why I took off from Pasadena. Too much time to think."

"I couldn't believe it about you two."

"Neither could I. The best years of my life and all that crap. But there was nothing else to do."

"He said he didn't want you to go," Kosta said.

"That's right. He didn't. Cried like a Barbie doll. But Jesus . . . he's trained me too well. I couldn't just do a backflip and turn into a junior executive's wife—or roommate—or whatever I was. And if that wasn't bad enough, he had to take a *government* job. And such a job: *I* couldn't believe it. I said, Jesus, if you're going to sell out you might as well go the whole hog and go to work for my father. In two years you'll be the yogurt king of Orange County. We'll have a box at the opera and you can wear a necktie to bed every night."

"Did it really happen as fast as he said it did?"

"Him taking that crummy job or us breaking up?"

"Both."

"Well, it sure seemed fast to me. When he told me about it first we just joked about it. Bounced around on the water bed and had a good laugh. But the next thing I knew he was getting serious. And the next thing I knew after that he said he'd taken the job. That's when I said it was HEW or me and that's when he cried a lot. But he wouldn't let go of that fucking job. So I left."

"I still don't get it. Dick never gave a damn about money."

"That's what *I* thought. But he turned out to be like a lot of other people. Money's not important till somebody offers you some. That was the first offer Dick ever got. And he jumped at it."

"But *you've* got money to burn. So what's the problem?"

"That's different. Dick always said he liked to screw me so much he didn't want to ruin it by taking money for it."

"Did you ever meet this guy from HEW, the one who gave him the job?"

"Never laid eyes on him. He never came to call. Dick always met him somewhere. Away from the house."

"Did you know his name?"

"Not from anything Dick said. He was silent as a stone. But I saw the name Fenton scribbled on his desk pad. John Fenton. I think he was the weasel in the chicken house."

Before she started looking for Avery Buck, Kosta called Nellie Arvidsen in Washington.

"I need a favor," she said. "Is this a cool phone?"

"No. I'll call you back. What's your number?"

The phone in Kosta's hotel room began to ring almost as soon as she hung up. "That was fast. Are we off the switchboard?"

"Clean as a whistle. Nobody listens on this line except the IRS. What's up?"

"I'm in Indianapolis."

"I know that. I just called you back. You're the only person I know who goes to Indianapolis on purpose. What's the favor?"

"Between you and me. No leaks."

"Right."

"Have somebody in your research department run a check on John Fenton."

"F-E-N-T-O-N?"

"Right. The word is he's with HEW. If you don't find him there, do a general sweep. Let's see what we find out."

"Should I call you or will you call me?"

"I'll call you."

There was no listing for Avery Buck in the current Indianapolis telephone directory. But in the 1979 book Kosta found his name. When she dialed, however, a recorded voice announced that the number was no longer in service. She called both information and new listings. No number registered for Avery Buck.

There were fifty-four people named Buck in the telephone book. Sitting on the bed in her hotel room, Kosta called twelve of them before she found someone who knew Avery. It sounded like an old man's voice that answered. "I never met him but I've heard of him. Far as I know we ain't related. There's quite a few Bucks in Marion County. This man, Avery, if I'm not mistaken, is a farmer. Seems to me he had a place out west of town."

She dialed seventeen more numbers before she located another Buck who knew something about Avery. This time it was a woman's voice, sounding foggy. As if she'd been asleep in the middle of the afternoon. "He's my husband's uncle. My father-in-law is Herman Buck, Avery's brother. Is he in some kind of trouble?"

"No. I just need to talk to him if I can. It's a personal matter."

"Well . . . he's moved to Arizona. And I can't tell you exactly where."

"I see," Kosta said. "Is there any way I could talk to your husband?"

"He manages the Kessler shoe store down on the Circle. He has to work late tonight. But he takes a supper break at five thirty. Maybe he could talk to you then."

"What's his name?"

"Melvin Gary Buck. But he just calls himself Gary."

At five thirty Kosta was sitting in a cafeteria with Gary Buck. Just down the block from the shoe store. She was drinking a cup of coffee while he ate a Salisbury steak with mashed potatoes and peas.

He was a husky young man in his thirties, thick brown sideburns and heavy hair that looked as if it had been teased and sprayed. He wore a gold-tone sportcoat with gray-green slacks, a pale-yellow shirt, and a raspberry-and-gold striped tie.

"This is not a place I'd eat in usually," he said. "I prefer something a little more . . . you know . . . with some service . . . and an à la carte menu. And I like to have a Manhattan or two before my supper, but tonight I'm short of help in the store. I may have to wait on some customers myself. And I don't think it's good business to have alcohol breath."

When she told him she was writing a follow-up story on the H-14, when she asked about his uncle, Gary said, "Like I told you walking over here from the store, we're all proud of my Uncle Avery. My dad came from a big family, eight children, and Avery was the most successful of any of them. He was a big influence on me. He directed me into my career in retail sales. He used to say, 'We're all selling something, Gary. And the better we sell it, the better we do. It's a long winter without a good supply of acorns.' I guess I heard him say that about acorns a thousand times. My mother used to say that Avery knew how to get it and how to keep it."

"Your wife told me he's moved away from Indianapolis."

"Yes, he has. Sold his farm early this year and moved to the Sun Belt. Bought a fine home there, I understand. Uncle Avery never got married, never had children, so he's got nobody to look out for but himself. I guess he'll have a fine life, spending his autumn years down there in New Mexico."

"Your wife said he was in Arizona."

"No, I don't believe so. I think Bev is mistaken about that. I'm quite sure he's in New Mexico."

"I guess you don't have his address then?"

"No, I don't. I'm sure he gave it to me, but I must have misplaced it." He smiled and sipped carefully from his coffee cup. "Our family's never been much to write letters. We're more likely to just pick up the phone every week or so and talk long distance for an hour." He smiled again. "But I don't have his telephone number either, if that's what you're wondering."

As they walked back toward the store, Kosta said, "How large was your uncle's farm?"

"Not that big. A little over a hundred acres. But I understand he got a very good price for it."

"You don't happen to know who bought it?"

"No, I don't."

When they stopped in front of the shoe store, he said, "Will you be writing up any of the things I told you?"

"I don't think so. Don't misunderstand me. You've been very

helpful and I appreciate it. But I really wanted to talk to your uncle."

There was a greenish-yellow light coming through the display window, shining on the young man's face. As he stood there, the easy salesman's presence, his color and his energy, seemed to bleed out of him. A nerve twitched at the corner of his eye and his arms hung stiff at his sides.

"Well," he said, "if you manage to locate him, maybe you'll give him a message for me."

"I'd be happy to if—"

"Tell him his brother is still getting his disability checks. So there's no need to worry about him. And tell him his nephew, Gary, is doing first-rate. Paying the mortgage and feeding four kids and just doing great. Those five-dollar raises come through once a year just like clockwork. Tell him we're all thinking about him and hoping he's having a good time. Be sure to tell him that if you see him. Tell him we think about him all the time."

The next morning after breakfast, Kosta wrote a note to Gabe and mailed it to his home address in Georgetown.

Dear Senator:

"Everything's up to date in Indiana . . . I've gone about as far as I can go . . ."

Don't you believe it. I am making magnificent progress. I will save the details till I see you in Washington.

Remember after Jack Kennedy's death in Dallas when anywhere from seventeen to thirty critical witnesses (de-

pending on who's counting) died sudden, accidental, mysterious deaths?

Later on, someone put this question to Lloyd's of London: What are the odds that such a large number of people, all linked together by the Kennedy assassination and nothing else . . . what are the odds that so many of them would die suddenly and strangely within just a few months?

The odds, Lloyds said, were a trillion to one. I've been thinking about that. I've been thinking about it a lot. There are some strange odds here in Indianapolis too. See you soon.

Your Greek friend—
Kosta

At nine that morning Kosta drove to the Marion County Courthouse, located the office of deeds and titles, and spent an hour there.

Later, back at her hotel, she called the coroner's office and spoke to the woman she'd talked with before.

"I thought maybe Dr. Springer had been trying to call me."

"I'm sure he tried," the woman said.

"I guess he didn't leave a message then."

"I couldn't say . . . " the woman began.

"It's all right. I'm sure we just missed connections. I've been very busy. Out a lot. If he's there now maybe you'd be good enough to transfer me."

"I'm afraid he's not in today. He had to drive over to Anderson."

"I see. Is there a number in Anderson where I can reach him?"

"I'm afraid not."

"Are you sure?" Kosta said.

"Quite sure."

"When do you expect him back?"

"Later today, I hope."

"But you're not sure?"

"No, I'm not."

"All right," Kosta said, "in case I'm not able to reach Dr.

Springer before I leave town maybe you'll give him a message for me."

"Of course."

"Tell him I found the information I was after. Tell him I managed to get photocopies of all the documents I needed. I expect the story will appear in the Washington and New York papers early next week. If he misses it I'll send him a copy."

After she hung up, Kosta clicked the receiver till the hotel operator came on. "This is Miss Kosta in 311. I've been getting some annoying calls. If anyone calls within the next hour don't put them through until you've told who it is."

In less than five minutes the telephone rang. The operator said, "There's a Dr. Springer calling you."

"Is it a long-distance call?"

"No, it isn't."

Smiling like a small and extremely pretty tiger, Kosta said, "Please tell Dr. Springer that I've already checked out of the hotel." Then she hung up.

She was booked on a two o'clock flight to Pittsburgh, connecting with a commuter flight to Clarksburg, West Virginia, and picking up a car there for the drive to Elkins, where she'd reserved a room in the Tygart Hotel.

At twelve forty-five, as she was packing, her door buzzer sounded. When she opened the door a slender, light-haired man in a denim sport jacket was standing in the corridor, a pretty girl in her late twenties beside him. "I'm Sergeant Felstad," he said, flipping open his wallet to show his badge. "Indianapolis police."

"Terrific," Kosta said. "Who's your friend?"

The girl showed her badge. "Detective Junior Grade Freedman. Are you R. M. Kosta?"

"That's right. What's the problem?"

"I'll have to ask you to come to the station with us."

"You mean you're arresting me?"

"No," Felstad said. "We'd just like to ask you some questions."

"About what?"

"There's been a complaint," Freedman said. "Soliciting for prostitution."

"I don't believe it," Kosta said. "Don't you people ever learn any new tricks? Read me my rights and let's go. And never mind the dime for a phone call. I have my own dime."

As soon as they arrived at the police station she called the Citizen's Action office in Washington. "Who's this? . . . Hi, Debbie, this is Kosta. I need an ACLU lawyer. . . . No, I'm in Indianapolis. . . . That's right. The sooner the better. I already missed one plane. I don't want to miss the next one."

Kosta sat on a bench in the waiting room with Detective Freedman. In twenty-five minutes her lawyer walked in, a tall black girl, cool and sleek. "I'm Lena Goslin," she said. "Washington told me all about you. Just sit tight. You'll be out of here in thirty minutes."

When Sergeant Felstad walked up, the lawyer said, "I hope for your sake you didn't book her yet."

"Sure, we booked her. What do you think?"

"Oh, Jocko, am I gonna burn your tail! You tell Lieutenant Magnuson to struggle out here or my entire organization is going to unload on this department like a truckful of dirty mud."

As soon as Lieutenant Magnuson, a tall, gray-haired man looking ill at ease, walked into the interrogation room, Lena Goslin said, "Lieutenant, may I say something?"

Magnuson turned to Felstad. "What's the complaint?"

"Soliciting."

"Repeater?"

"Not in our records."

"Lieutenant," Goslin broke in, "believe me, I can save you a lot of grief. This young lady lives in Washington, D.C. She is a professional journalist. She writes articles that appear in national magazines and newspapers. It looks to me as if somebody's trying to make a fool of you people. This girl is *not* a hooker. And if she were I guarantee she wouldn't be working out of the Holiday Inn in downtown Indianapolis."

"Not funny," Magnuson said.

"I agree," Goslin said.

"Who made the charge?" Magnuson said then.

Felstad checked his notes. "John T. Skeen."

"Local?"

"Chicago."

"What's he doing in town?"

"Tourist."

"Bring him in," Magnuson said.

"He prefers not to confront the accused."

Goslin broke in. "The accused prefers not to *be* accused. The accused would prefer to be on an airplane right now."

"I'm stretching procedures now to give you a break," Magnuson said to her. "Don't push me or we'll go back to doing it by the numbers." He turned to Felstad.

"Bring Skeen in here."

In a few minutes Felstad was back, looking pale and tentative. "He's not here. He left."

"He what?"

"The man at the desk said Skeen walked out when the four of us came in here. Said he had to get back to Chicago."

"Are you telling me," Magnuson said slowly, "that a man came in here to register a vice complaint, we picked up the subject on his say-so, and before we can even talk to her, the man disappears? Is that the situation?"

"Yes, sir. That's the way it looks."

Magnuson turned back to Goslin. "It happens sometimes. I'm sorry." Then to Kosta. "I think we owe you an apology, Miss Kosta."

"Forget it," she said. "I've been hassled before."

"What does that mean?"

"It means that if you do a follow-up on Mr. Skeen you'll find there's nobody by that name at the Chicago address he gave you. He doesn't even *know* me. He's a zombie."

"Then what's the point? Why would he—"

"Ms. Kosta is a troublemaker," Goslin said. "She's like me, Lieutenant. She keeps asking questions that nobody wants to answer. Instead of answers, you get hassled. Your phone gets tapped, your lights and gas get turned off, and sometimes you get picked up by the vice squad."

"You're not saying we had anything to do with this, are you?"

"No, I'm not, Lieutenant. That's what hassling's all about. Nobody ever knows how it starts or who's behind it."

An hour later, before Kosta checked out of her hotel to drive to the airport, she sent a telegram to Gabe's apartment in Washington.

NOW WE'RE GETTING SOMEWHERE. THE FOX IS STARTING TO CHASE THE DOGS.

Part Three

44 From the time their mother died, both Chet and Gabe began to develop what would become at last an easy self-confidence. They were able to *do* things, to learn new skills, to *function*.

It started with their father. Watching him work, seeing him measure and saw and hammer, seeing him glue broken furniture, replace windowpanes, straighten bent nails, they aped his movements. He convinced them that anything broken could be fixed, anything worn out was only partially worn out. One new bolt or washer, one rebuilt part, could bring back to life what had seemed to be a piece of worthless machinery. Countless times they saw him pick up a broken toy or an injured pet and say, "Now . . . what can we do about this?"

The habits they'd learned at home they took with them to school. They simply did their work, did it so systematically that they became known as students who could get first-class marks without studying at all.

In athletics it was the same. They built their own gym in the basement, competed with each other in push-ups and pull-ups. In football, they learned to block and tackle and run hard. And they learned how to fall. In basketball they drilled each other for hours. Carrying a ball with them everywhere, handling it till it was like an extension of their arms, they could pass it, catch it, or shoot it without hesitation. By hard work they developed what appeared to be pure instinct.

Once they had an objective, they set about reaching it, bottom rung first. They did not theorize at the beginning or congratulate themselves at the end. They believed what their father had told them:

"I work with my hands. My dad and all our people did the same thing. You guys are workers too. It's bred in you. That doesn't mean you have to grub and sweat and push a wheelbarrow. It's just a matter of how you look at yourself. If you just say, 'I'm a worker, I get my work done,' you'll make out all right. And you'll feel good about yourself. That's the important thing. If you can't find a way to feel good about who you are and what you're doing, you won't be worth a damn to anybody."

Contrary to the negative theories about single-parent families, and contrary to the clearly expressed nay votes of both their aunts, Nancy and Enid, Gabe and Chet came away from their bachelor childhoods, from their bunkhouse life with their father, strongly reassured, feeling valuable and needed.

"If your mother hadn't been poorly," their father told them, "if she hadn't died so young, I guarantee you we'd have had a houseful of kids. She loved to have things crawling around over her. Cats and dogs and guinea pigs. And most of all, *kids*. I used to tell her we needed at least five boys and she'd say that was all right with her, just as long as she had three or four daughters to fuss over. So that makes eight or nine, right there, that we were planning on.

"I guess if a man can compose a great piece of music or paint a museum picture, or write books like Joseph Conrad—I suppose maybe a guy like that feels different about having a family. But for suckers like me, our kids are all we have to contribute, the only thing we can leave behind so somebody knows we were here."

So there was no question that someplace up the line there would be families for both Chet and Gabe. They joked about it from fourth grade on. "When my kids take on your scrongy kids, I guarantee you it will be a slaughter," Chet said. "Fifty-four to nothing, probably. That's if we're playing baseball. If it's basketball or football, my boys will really run up the score on you."

"What makes you think you'll even *have* any boys?" Gabe said. "*I'll* have all the boys. I'd bet on it. I see you with a houseful of girls, all skinny and bowlegged. I figure you'll be lucky to scrape together a croquet team out of that squealin' tribe of girls."

When Chet got married, Gabe was the toastmaster at his bachelor dinner. Toasting Chet, he said, "My brother's been trying to get the best of me for twenty-three years. As most of you know he's never made it. I beat his ass in marbles, I beat his ass in tennis, and I taught him everything he knows about women. He did pretty well in basketball over at Illinois, but that's only because *I* wasn't there. So here's a toast to my brother. He finally got the jump on me. He's getting married first. That is, unless Evelyn gets smart and changes her mind. I'm sure Chet also thinks he'll be a father before I am. *That* remains to be seen. If he's no better at *that* than he was at shooting marbles, I may beat his ass at that too."

A year later, when Gabe got his doctor's degree at Brown and came back to Fort Beck to teach, Chet and Jud were practicing law there. Jud's wife, Hope, had just given birth to a baby girl. Chet and Evelyn were still childless. Jud and Gabe joked with Chet about it whenever they met for lunch or played tennis at the country club.

"I'm just waiting for the duffers to get off the course," Chet said. "Jud here had something to prove. I mean, he's got hair on his chest and everything, but let's face it, the man's a bookworm. Wears glasses all the time. Even when he drinks. He's not exactly a guy who gets his picture pinned up in the girls' locker room. He'd be the first to admit it. Right, Jud? So what happens when a man like that gets married? We all assume he's scoring with his wife, but just in case somebody *doubts* it, what does he do? He says, 'Cock-a-doodle-doo, look at me—my wife's gonna hatch a chicken.'

"Don't get me wrong, Jud. I'm not knocking it. We *all* understand what you're up to. But some of us want to have a little fun first. You know—postpone the Pampers and the babysitters for a year or so. But I guarantee you, when you and Hope are stumbling in the homestretch, Evelyn and I will pass you like you're standing still. And as for you, Gabe, don't knock your betters. The way I hear it you haven't found a girl who'll kiss you on the mouth yet."

A year later the three of them were still joking about it. But the jokes had become repetitive and a bit strained. By August 1970, when Hope Rimmer gave birth to twin boys, Chet settled for "They run in the family, for Christ's sake. Hope has twin uncles and twin brothers. She'd have had twins if she lived in a convent in Tibet." From then on the childbearing jokes gradually petered out.

Later that year, one afternoon during Christmas week, when Chet and Gabe were having lunch at the country club, crystal icicles hanging from the roof edge outside the window and a great coverlet of drifted snow spread white across the golf course, Chet said, "You want to hear something ridiculous? I went to a doctor when I was up in Chicago last week and he told me I can't have kids."

"You can't or Evelyn can't?"

"She can but *I* can't."

He explained everything the doctor had told him. A chemical imbalance. Possibly inherited from the mother's family. No danger otherwise. No effect on a happy sex life. But total infertility. Permanent.

"If I were you," Gabe said, "I would get about twenty-five second opinions. Who *is* this guy?"

"He's the best man in Chicago. And he's the fifth doctor I've talked to."

"Jesus. I can't believe it."

"To tell you the truth, I wasn't all that surprised. We had Evelyn checked out over a year ago and there's nothing wrong with her. For a while everybody pretended it was psychological. But finally I had to admit the problem might be me. It was and it is."

"What about artificial insemination?"

"What about it?"

"They have sperm banks, don't they? Just like blood banks?"

Chet shook his head. "Evelyn doesn't want to have a test-tube baby. Fathered by some turkey neither one of us ever laid eyes on."

"I didn't mean that exactly. They can use the husband's sperm, can't they?"

"You're not paying attention," Chet said. "In this case the husband's sperm is the problem. Three quarts of my sperm wouldn't make a gopher pregnant. I'm not impotent, lunkhead. I'm sterile."

"You say it's hereditary?" Gabe said. "Does that mean I'm . . . ?"

"I said it *could* be hereditary. That's what Dr. Elleman told me. He's the guy in Chicago. But you'd have to take all the tests to find out for sure."

"I don't know. What do you think?"

"It's up to you," Chet said. "But if I were you, I'd want to find out. If it's bad news we can always turn it into a plus. We'll start a whispering campaign saying you can't get anybody pregnant and you'll have women hanging on you like cobwebs."

Three weeks later Gabe drove to Chicago for a day of tests and an examination in Dr. Elleman's clinic. As soon as they told him the results he called Chet in Fort Beck. "It may be hereditary but I didn't inherit it."

Chet didn't answer for a moment. Then he laughed and said, "We're a great parlay. I'm sexy and you're fertile."

The following spring, when Chet was starting his campaign for district attorney, when he and Gabe and Jud were driving around five counties speaking to any women's club or civic group that would listen, one night, two in the morning, when Jud had gone to sleep in the room next door and Gabe and Chet were getting ready for bed, Chet said, "I want to ask you a question."

"Shoot."

"Two things you have to promise. One, you won't punch me in the mouth, and two, you won't give me a smart-assed answer before you've had a chance to think about it."

"I promise I won't punch you. I'm too tired. The smart-assed answer I can't guarantee."

Chet sat on the edge of one of the twin beds. Pointing to the other one, he said, "Sit down a minute."

"Nothing doing. If you're gonna get serious in the middle of the night, I think I'd better take it standing up."

"Give me a break, Gabe. This is tough going for me."

When Gabe sat down on the bed facing him, Chet said, "It's complicated. So don't start yapping at me till I finish what I have to say. Okay?"

"Okay."

"All right . . . here's the situation. I'm a healthy man with a healthy wife. We want to have a family but we can't. We could adopt children and we will if we have to, but it's not our first choice. We could also go to the sperm bank. That way at least one of us would be the real parent. It wouldn't be *my* kid, not biologically, but it would be Evelyn's. Like I told you before, she's not wild about that idea, but she's willing to do it if there's no other choice."

"What other choice is there?"

Chet took out a cigarette and lit it. Then he said, "This isn't some wild idea. It's not off the top of my head. Matter of fact, Evelyn and I have talked about it. We've talked about it a lot. We want you to help us have a kid."

"What does that mean?"

"Just what it sounds like. I can't be a father. *You* can. I want you to be the father to *my* kid. Or I guess I mean that I want to be the father to *your* kid."

"Are you saying what I think you're saying?"

"Why not? We've talked about adopting a baby whose parents we'll never lay eyes on. Or using sperm from some college kid who's trying to make a few bucks from the sperm bank. If you say *those* are far-out solutions, I agree with you. But *this*—

what's so strange about it? If I lost both my eyes in an accident, would you give me one of yours?"

"It's not the same."

"The hell it's not. This is not even a sacrifice we're talking about. It's a *gift.* It's a kindness. I mean we're *brothers,* for God's sake. We look a lot alike. We *are* a lot alike. We've got the same blood. The same ancestors. I could look at a kid of yours and feel as if it were mine. It *would* be mine. I know it sounds crazy, but it's not crazy at all when you really think about it."

"I *am* thinking about it," Gabe said, "and it's crazy. It wouldn't work, Chet. That's why people adopt kids they don't know anything about. That's why the sperm bank idea works. There are no other names or faces involved. You can look at your kid and say, 'I may not be his *real* father, but I'm the only father he's got.' And *that's* the important thing. I mean, how the hell could you look at a kid and say to yourself, 'Gabe's kid looks like he's catching cold' or 'Gabe's kid needs a haircut'? It just wouldn't track, Chet. It would screw up your life and mine too. And God knows how it would affect Evelyn."

Chet didn't answer for a moment. Then, "I told you. We've talked about it. We've been hashing it over for a couple of months. And believe me, there's no drawback you can bring up that we haven't considered. You know Evelyn. She's a planner. She hates surprises. She doesn't do anything without working out the plus and minus columns. And in this case, almost everything's in the plus column."

"Almost—that's the key word."

"You're the only minus factor," Chet said. "We had no idea whether you'd agree or not. And even if you *do* agree, Evelyn's worried about how you'd live with it. Later, I mean. She thinks you're the one who could have a bad emotional hangover. Seeing a kid you knew was yours and not being able to live with it or claim it. She thinks *that's* the main problem. And I think she's right. But that's someplace down the road. And Evelyn and I are being selfish. We're thinking about *now."*

The next morning, when they were getting dressed, Chet said, "Did you think about what we talked about last night?"

"Half the night, you bastard."

"What do you think?"

"The same thing I thought last night."

When the room service waiter brought their breakfast, when they were sitting across from each other at the table, Gabe said, "Even if I was wacky enough to go along with you, I don't see how it could be handled. As far as I know there are no artificial insemination clinics in Fort Beck. And even if there were, a lot of people know who we are. They certainly know who *you* are. So we'd have to go to Chicago or St. Louis. And we'd have to use fake names. You say it all seems logical to you and Evelyn. But most people wouldn't see the logic at all."

"You're right. In fairness to everyone, it would have to be a secret. But I don't see that as a problem. You won't tell anyone. And Evelyn and I certainly wouldn't."

"It's not that simple."

"Yes it is," Chet said. "Nobody would know except the three of us. Because Evelyn doesn't want to have artificial insemination. And I don't want her to. If this works out it will probably be the only child Evelyn will ever have. That's important to her. And to me. We don't want the child to be conceived in a laboratory."

"You may not *want* it, but—"

"Wait a minute. Let me finish. Evelyn is not in love with you. She's in love with me. But she loves you. And she'll love her child when it's born. So she wants it to come from an act of love."

"Jesus, Chet . . . "

"And so do I," Chet said.

"We can't . . . I mean how could I . . . ?"

"If you come to a point where you understand that you would be doing us, *both* of us, the greatest possible kindness, if you decide it's something you can find a way to feel good about, the way Evelyn and I do—"

"Look . . . wait a minute—*hold* it! I know how important this is to you. If I didn't know that, we wouldn't be having this conversation. But that's all it is. It's just *words*. I mean . . . I really don't think it's crazy. I said I did but I don't. As I told you, I thought about it half the night. And I understand everything you've been saying to me. But it's still . . . it's just an *idea*. I mean, I can't just sit here with a plate of ham and eggs in front of me and make some kind of a *deal* with you to—"

"I know you can't," Chet said. "I don't *want* that. You don't have to agree or promise or even nod your head. You never have to say a word. I'd rather you didn't. But if you don't say no, if you don't call me by the end of this week and say no, I will know that you mean yes. Regardless, whatever you decide, you and I will never discuss it again. Is that fair?"

"I don't know. You're going too fast for me."

In the next few weeks Gabe saw Chet several times every week and he saw Evelyn at least once a week. No mention was made of his earlier conversations with Chet. No reference to those talks. No acknowledgment whatsoever.

Late in June Chet and Evelyn went to New York City for a week. Then Chet went on to Washington for a three-day conference on juvenile crime and Evelyn came back to Fort Beck. That afternoon at four o'clock she called Gabe to tell him she was home. "Chet told me to be sure to call you. He thinks you worry about us."

"He's right."

That night Gabe went to a Haydn concert at the university, and later he had supper with two friends from the English faculty. By the time he got home it was almost one in the morning. He'd started to undress when the telephone rang. It was Evelyn.

"Hi. I tried to get you earlier but I got no answer."

"I just got home a few minutes ago."

"Can you come over?" she said then.

"Are you all right?"

"Yes. I'm fine. I've been taking my temperature every day and today I'm fine. Today I'm perfect."

Half an hour later, Gabe parked his car in Chet's driveway, went in through the kitchen door, and switched on the lights. On the cabinet just inside the door a note was stuck up with Scotch tape.

I'm upstairs. Come up. Ev.

Jiggs, the Airedale, came out of the family room and nuzzled him. Then he turned in a circle and flopped down on the kitchen floor. Gabe walked through the dining room, crossed the sunken living room, dark except for the dim light that filtered in around the window shades, and climbed the front stairs.

In the upstairs hallway, a small lamp was on. Gabe walked along the carpeted corridor to the master bedroom at the back of the house. The door was open a few inches. He knocked softly, but there was no answer.

Pushing the door open, he saw Evelyn, half-lying, half-sitting in the wide bed, two pillows behind her. The sheet was pulled up to her waist. Her upper body was silvery pale and naked in the bluish night light.

He stood in the doorway. She lay absolutely still in the bed, looking at him. Very softly then she said, "Close the door so Jiggs can't come in." Except for the instant, a few minutes later, when she moaned and whispered Chet's name, those were the only words she said.

When Gabe started to undress, she folded the top sheet back away from her and lay motionless, watching him, the pillows behind her shoulders still, her eyes shining in the soft darkness.

She reached out for his hand then, pulled him down on the bed, on top of her, slipped a pillow under her hips, and guided him inside her, her legs over his, her arms around her neck, her body quivering.

He came almost instantly, burning and unending and too soon. Then again, just moments later. And she, feeling him gush inside her, squealed softly like a winter animal, and came too, her face buried in his neck, her voice half-sobbing, whispering Chet's name in the soft dark.

Eight and a half months later, March 13, 1972, Evelyn gave birth to a baby boy. They named him Sam.

 Before their wedding, when Gabe and Helen were planning their honeymoon trip, with Chet and Evelyn giving reckless advice, Helen, responding to Evelyn's insistence that they must avoid Honolulu and hole up in a secluded condominium on Maui, said, "Nothing doing. You guys have been there before. This is *my* first time. I want to do all the corny stuff. Waikiki Beach, the Royal Hawaiian hotel, a lei around my neck . . ."

"You hear that, Gabe?" Chet said. "You think you can manage that?"

"Don't talk dirty," Evelyn said.

". . . hula dancers and Don Ho," Helen went on, "Mai Tais for breakfast, lunch, and dinner, and a midnight swim every night at midnight."

Their suite at the Royal Hawaiian, part of the wedding gift from Helen's father, looked out on the beach. And their ten days there followed Helen's clearly stated program. They were indolent and barefoot, he in white pants and Hawaiian shirts, she in a series of brightly patterned muumuus with savage blossoms stuck in her hair, shell necklaces around her neck, and a coral ring on every finger.

"We must overeat, oversleep, and never be totally sober," she said. "We will lie in the sun till we're brown as bears, swim till we're waterlogged, and all the rest of the time we will thrash around naked in our Royal Hawaiian bed and have a Royal Hawaiian time of it. It is absolutely vital that we not say or do anything civilized or sensible. Not if we can help it."

One afternoon, as they sat on the beach in front of the hotel, she said, "It's not fair, you know."

"What's that?"

"I haven't shut up for a minute since we left San Francisco. I have told you everything I've ever thought or done or been. You know every tiny detail about my mother and father, my first husband, my adventures in field hockey, and my appendectomy scar. No cabinet has been closed to you, no page unread, no record unplayed. You are now the custodian of my entire biography. Fingerprints, astrology chart, and cranial measurements. Am I right? Is there any possible single thing you could possibly want to know about me that I haven't told you?"

"I guess not."

"You see. I've blabbed and chattered away a woman's most precious commodity—mystery. Seven days we've been married and my infinite variety has been totally dissipated. I'm like a broiled fish on a platter."

"You're bonkers," he said. "Three in the P.M. and you're drunk as a daisy."

"Not so. I am only relaxed and easy. Able to see the light. Able to see the truth. And the truth is that in just one week of marriage, starting on even terms, we have become gloriously unequal. In addition to the wear and tear on my poor old body, you have stolen my soul, chewed up my entire life history and swallowed it. You have wolfed me down while I have been given only a taste of you."

"I am available to be wolfed down anytime you say."

"Don't talk tacky. I am speaking symbolically. And you know I'm right. You know everything about me and I still know almost nothing about you."

"Wrong. You know about my relatives, my job, my friends, my enemies, and my blood type. I've told you who I like and *what* I like, where I've been and where I want to go. You are privy, you should pardon the expression, to all my thoughts and all my speckled past."

"Aha," she said, "now we're getting somewhere. That's what I'm talking about. You have no past, speckled or otherwise. You are that rarest of all creatures, a virginal and untouched man of twenty-nine."

"Bull's-eye," he said. "You say you know nothing about me and then you come out with my biggest secret."

"Horseradish, Treptow. That ain't the way I heard it."

"Chet?"

"No. Not Chet. Evelyn."

"All she knows is what Chet tells her and all he knows is what I tell him."

"And all I know is what you tell me. And that's zero."

Gabe called the waiter over and ordered two more Mai Tais.

"Oh my God," Helen said, "what's to become of me?"

"What do you mean?"

"I mean I'm flying low already. One more drink and I'll be a basket case."

"I guess I'll have to take you upstairs and put you to bed."

"Sounds reasonable to me," she said.

When the waiter brought their drinks, Gabe took a long drink out of his glass, then leaned over and kissed her. "I think you're right," he said then. "You do deserve to know something about me. I always thought that wives preferred *not* to know. But maybe I was wrong about that. I suppose it's better for you to know the facts, from *me*, than to pick up little stories from other people in supermarkets and on street corners."

"Or written on walls," she said. "That happens sometimes."

"That's right. The only thing that worries me is . . . well, I don't want it to change anything between us. I don't want you to think of me as used merchandise."

"Heaven forbid."

"On the other hand, there are some people, even doctors, who say it's a good thing if the husband has had some sexual experience before marriage."

"Hear, hear."

"I assume that's the way *you* feel," he said.

"Let's assume that."

"Good. That makes me feel better about things. I was afraid you might not understand. Especially about Mrs. Agase. You remember her. You met her at Christmastime when you came to Fort Beck. Sort of a plump, gray-haired woman."

"Plump? You mean gross. She must weigh three hundred pounds."

"A little more than that, I think. With her clothes off, she's something to behold."

"You mean she . . . ?"

Gabe nodded. "When I was twelve years old. Chet and I used to do chores for her on Saturdays. First she did it to Chet, when he was twelve. Then two years later it was my turn. She had a daybed down in her basement and she took me down there. Chet didn't like her much, he said. Too much blubber. But it didn't bother me. For a long time I didn't like skinny girls at all. I liked Mrs. Agase best and her daughter second best."

"Her daughter?"

"Kate," Gabe said. "Shorter than her mother. Five three maybe. And not as fat. But still, by the time she was seventeen, I guess she weighed close to a hundred and ninety. Very firm, though. Not like her mother. Chet liked Kate a lot. But she liked me. Wouldn't have anything to do with him."

"So you were having a little do with Kate *and* her mother?"

"That's right. The funny thing was that Kate was jealous of her mother, didn't want me to go near her, but Mrs. Agase wasn't possessive at all. She was tickled to death about me and Kate. Gave us the run of the house. But anytime she and I got together we had to manage it when Kate wasn't home."

"How long did all that go on?"

"Till I was fifteen. Kate was eighteen by then, and she got engaged to some guy who worked at Sears Roebuck. He was jealous as hell, so she decided she'd better not keep up with me. But that was all right. It took the pressure off me and Mrs. Agase."

"You kept on with her then?"

"Oh, sure."

"How long?"

"Not since I met you if that's what you mean. As soon as Mrs. Agase heard about you, that was the end of it. She's a romantic woman. She said she didn't want to mess up my life."

"That's nice of her."

Late that night, when they were lying in bed not quite asleep, Gabe said, "You want to hear some more true confessions?"

"I don't think so. Not for a while. I think I'd better give you a chance to work up some more material."

"You mean you don't believe anything I told you this afternoon?"

"Sure I do. I believe everything you say."

She rolled closer to him and kissed him. "Good night, Sport."

He put his arm around her shoulders. "Tomorrow I'll tell you the good stuff."

"That's nice."

"No holds barred."

"I've got a better idea. Why don't you wait till we're a couple of old souls sitting on a terrace somewhere? Watching the grass grow and popping nitroglycerin pills? Why don't you save the really sexy stuff till then? It'll give us something to talk about."

"That's not a bad idea," he said. "Maybe I'll do that."

 There is bestiality in the world. Incest and sadism. With each new generation there are legions of people who accept viewpoints and behavior patterns that were abhorred, found totally obscene, by their parents or grandparents.

Nonetheless, in a world that has become in some eyes altogether godless, the Christians remain—millions of them, structured and decent—who believe, along with the Moslems, the Jews and the Buddhists, that evil never triumphs, that every sin, at last, is punished. Followers of Islam are neither surprised nor offended by the sight of a thief whose hands have been severed by the state.

Such persons would not have been dismayed by the fate of Gabe Treptow. In some perverse, fundamentalist way they might have felt fulfilled. What *is* the proper punishment for a man who has carnal knowledge of his brother's wife and fathers her only child? In Iran, death certainly. In uncharted corners of Borneo, perhaps, his offending member would have been sliced off, pickled in brine, and hung on a cord around his neck.

In Fort Beck, however, the natives are civilized. Christianity is tame and docile. No eyes are sacrificed for eyes. No teeth for teeth. Still, many Presbyterian ladies there, or Baptists, or Catholics, or Methodists, if they had known the true facts of Sam Treptow's parenthood, would have trembled surely, and recited whatever catechism had the most profound meaning for them.

Had these ladies been asked to recommend a punishment for Gabe's share of the sin, many of them unquestionably would have said, "No child of his own. Not ever. That's what he deserves. Punishment that fits the crime. That's the ticket."

Gabe would have scoffed at such foolishness. He was a Christian, both by upbringing and by instinct. But when he was asked to explain the phenomenon of Christ during a fourth-grade Bible class, he offended the teacher and caused his fellow students to giggle by saying, *"Conscience.* That's what Christ means. People who don't have a conscience aren't Christians. *God* means *good.* And conscience makes a person do good more often than bad. That's all there is to it."

He got a low mark in that class. Still, those early convictions stayed with him. Gabe did not believe in divine justice, heavenly vengeance, or bolts from on high. He was not a mystic, not a utopian, not a seeker after truth in astrology or tea leaves. He was also not a classic or academic existentialist. But those tenets reminded him very specifically of his own beliefs.

Coolheaded as he was, however, or imagined himself to be, during the four and a half years of his marriage to Helen—childless years—he could not help thinking at times that he was sniffing the fumes of Old Testament vengeance. "A man who casts his seed, et cetera."

Reason told him there was no possible connection, physical, psychological, or spiritual, between what had happened with him and Evelyn, and what was happening now, or failing to happen, between him and Helen. But still he smelled the smoke.

The very real problems that had prevented Chet and Evelyn from having a child were not there for Gabe and Helen. Early tests confirmed that each of them was sound and normal and fertile. But once each month the telephone in his office rang like a tolling bell.

Helen was as eager for children as he was. They had discussed it before they were married. And they discussed it afterward. Frequently. During the first year of their marriage the doctor felt that Helen, perhaps, was too anxious, trying too hard. He recommended a mild tranquilizer, but she said, "No thanks, I'd rather not." To Gabe she said, "I don't want to go to *sleep,* for Pete's sake. I want to get—what is that darling expression—I want to get *knocked up.*"

When he remembered it later, when the words and the anxieties of the past months waltzed back and forth through his mind, after Helen had gone off to Mexico for the divorce, the most agonizing thing of all was how completely and devastatingly he had been deceived, how perfect the details had been, how thoroughly she had immersed herself in the role she had chosen to play.

The fun, the passion, the laughing sexual lunacy, all seemed in retrospect to be vital parts of the senseless charade. "How about a romp in the bubble bath? We may not make a baby but we'll end up very clean." Or "We've got to change positions. It's as simple as that. If I can't get pregnant with you on top of me, then I'll get on top of *you* and *you'll* get pregnant."

Gabe and Helen never said *"if* we have a baby." They said, always, *"when* we have a baby." They believed that. At least Gabe believed it. And he was convinced, beyond any question, that Helen believed it too.

So the shock, when it came, was total. The previous December, around the fifteenth, Helen had driven to Chicago for some last-minute Christmas shopping. Several times a year she went there, either alone, with Evelyn, or with some other woman friend. She spent the night at the Drake, went to the theater, shopped, and drove home the following afternoon. Their ritual was that he called her exactly at five, at the hotel, and she called him, after the theater or dinner with her friends, before she went to bed.

On this occasion, however, when he telephoned, he couldn't reach her. She was not registered at the Drake. A reservation had been made, the desk clerk said, but it had been canceled at noon.

When Gabe called Evelyn, she said, "Don't worry about her. She probably decided on another hotel at the last minute. Every time we go to Chicago we say we're going to try the Ritz or the Whitehall or someplace different. But we always seem to end up at the Drake. It's only five twenty. You'll hear from her in a minute. She's probably trying to call you right now."

Gabe stayed downstairs in the den and read the evening paper. At seven o'clock he called the Drake again. She wasn't there. This time he called Chet. "If anything happened to her, you'd have heard something. She just changed her plans for some reason and she hasn't had a chance to call you yet."

"You're probably right," Gabe said, "but do me a favor and check with your friend Rucker at the state police barracks. Ask him to look over the accident sheet between here and Chicago today."

Gabe went upstairs then. As he started to change clothes, he noticed his portable cassette recorder resting on a pillow in the center of their bed. On the bedspread just beside the pillow was a note.

> *I hope you find this as soon as you come home. When you listen to the tape you'll know why I'm not staying at the Drake. But I'm all right. At least I'm as all right as I'm going to be. I love you.*
>
> *H.*

He sat down on the edge of the bed, staring at the tape recorder. He felt cold suddenly, afraid to hear whatever was there to be heard, afraid to know whatever it was that Helen couldn't tell him face to face. But he was more afraid *not* to know.

He picked up the recorder and carried it to the table by the window. He put on a heavy sweater, sat down on the chaise longue with his feet up, and pressed the forward button. Her voice sounded unfamiliar. Dry and husky:

> I hate these damned things. Buttons and needles and lights flicking on and off. I feel like an idiot sitting here by myself in the kitchen, doing such a crappy thing in such a cowardly way. I don't like myself much right now but that's nothing new.
>
> If I knew any other way to handle this, something that would be less cruel and ugly, I would have chosen that way. I can't stomach the idea of corny letters pinned to pillows or tied to steering wheels. I wouldn't *do* that. *Couldn't* do it. But I also can't do the obvious and proper thing . . . sit down across the table from you, cry my eyes out, and explain everything to your face.
>
> I know I'd never get past three sentences without collapsing into a blubbering mess. So here we are, me by myself talking, and you by yourself, sometime later, listening. Very modern and sophisticated and electronic. And *hateful.* But as I say, it's the best solution I can find to an impossible problem.

There was an empty space then, almost a minute's silence. Gabe could feel the room's presence on the tape, hear breathing and the kitchen clock ticking, and the clink of a cup in a saucer. Finally Helen spoke again.

> As you can probably tell, I'm crying like an idiot, getting tears on my nightgown, and blowing my nose. And I'm trying to find some words that will make what I have to say seem . . . I don't know . . . to make it seem . . . but there's no way to do it. I'll just have to blurt it out and be thankful that I don't have to look at you as I say it.

There was another pause, shorter this time, then:

> During the first year and a half we were married, when we were having a marvelous time in bed every night, laughing

and screwing our heads off and trying to pick out names for our first eleven children, during that crazy, ecstatic time in my life, I had three abortions.

That's right. Three of my trips to Chicago were not to shop or look at paintings or go to the theater, but to get myself unpregnant. Since that time, since October of 1976, I haven't been pregnant. Because I've been on the pill. Fanatically. Religiously. Never missing a day. Through all the talking and planning and sensational screwing, I have made damned sure that the baby you were hoping for, and that I *pretended* to be hoping for, was never going to be conceived. Or if it was conceived, it wasn't going to be born.

Gabe reached out and switched off the recorder. He sat very still, staring across the bedroom, dark now except for the soft spill of light from the lamp by his chair. He got up finally, walked to the bathroom, turned on the faucet, filled a glass with water, and slowly drank it. He studied his reflection in the mirror. It was the same face he'd seen when he shaved that morning, when he combed his hair and brushed his teeth. No scars or welts or oozing wounds. Just those familiar, irregular features, living lives of their own apparently, unmarked by events, unchanged, it seemed, by shock or pain or turmoil.

Walking to the liquor cabinet on the wall at the foot of the bed, he poured some Scotch in a tall glass and filled it with water. He switched on all the lights in the room then, and walked back to the chair by the window. Sitting down again, he turned on the tape recorder.

Wouldn't it be simple if I were just saying I don't love you anymore, that I want to be a liberated female, on her own? A silk shirt, leather britches, and no underwear.

Or if I said I was crazy about Tag Easter, the pro at the country club? Things like that really *happen* to people. We all know they happen. So when it's our turn most of us can clear the wreckage away and end up not hating the other person. Not hating ourselves.

But what I'm telling you is not like that. It's *not* simple.

There's no way to talk it away or *understand* it or *make* it simple. I've tried to imagine how I'd react if I heard of someone else doing what *I've* done. I can't be objective, but I've tried to be. The quick reaction is to say, "God, that woman is *sick*. She's really deranged."

But that's too easy, isn't it? It covers too much and doesn't really cover anything. What I would say, I think, if I were somebody else judging me, is that it seems to be a kind of vengeance. Some act of hatred. Against you. Or against myself.

But that doesn't work either. Because I don't hate myself. And God knows I don't hate you. My stomach still does a flip-flop when I hear your car turn into the driveway. When someone underestimates you or doesn't appreciate you I have an urge to kill. And going to bed with you is just as mysterious and lovely and delicious as it was the very first time.

So why have I lied to you and betrayed you in the most horrible way possible? I can't explain it. Not really. All I know is this: I am psychologically unable to be pregnant, to *stay* pregnant, to bear a child, to be a mother. I have known it for a long time, since I was married to Jess, but I thought it would change, that *I* would change. When I met you, when I fell in love with you, you transformed everything else for me. I thought *that* would change, too.

But it didn't. After the first abortion, even after the second one, I told myself that the pattern I'd fallen into would finally redesign itself. But when I drove home from Chicago after the third time, feeling ashamed and drained and humiliated. I realized I was permanently flawed, that nothing would ever change the way I felt, the way I was, the way I *am*.

I decided then that the only civilized solution was never to *get* pregnant. Then the problem would be solved. Not for *you*, of course. I never kidded myself about that. I knew it was disaster for you, no matter what I might do to mesmerize myself. But I ignored that. At least I *tried* to. I told myself that we were happy together and that was enough. But it wasn't. It never is when one person has a secret and everything depends on that secret never coming out.

Anyway . . . there it is. All of it. Now you know. You know everything except *why*. And I don't know that either. I hope you're as disgusted with me as I am with myself. At least that will make the mechanics easier. I know you won't want to stay with me now. And even if you did want to, I couldn't hack it. I know you too well. I know what you're like. I've never doubted that you love me. I don't doubt it now. But I couldn't bear to see it turn into something else.

The tape spun on to the end of the reel in silence. The player clicked itself off. Just then the telephone rang. It was Chet.

"Rucker just got back to me. No highway problems between here and Chicago today. Certainly nothing that sounds like Helen's car."

"It's all right," Gabe lied. "I just heard from her. She got hung up in a store on Michigan Avenue and couldn't find a phone that worked."

"Is she at the Drake?"

"No. She told me where she's staying but we had a bad connection so I didn't get it. She's gonna call me again before she goes to bed."

"Good. I figured she had everything under control."

"Yeah," Gabe said. "She's fine."

At ten o'clock Helen did call. "I guess you've listened to the tape by now."

"Yeah. I did."

"I'm sorry. . . . Look, I don't want to have a big conversation on the phone. I'll see you tomorrow afternoon."

"Where are you staying? I tried—"

"I'm all right, Gabe. Don't worry. I'll see you tomorrow."

49 In Venice the city morgue is located sixty meters south of Teatro la Fenice and a bit west of Scuola di Santa Maria della Carmine, in a damp and crumbling sixteenth-century building, its aspect gloomy and dark, perfectly fitted to the building's function. No hint of past splendor attaches to its façade or its interior. And no hope for the future when one examines the rotting blocks of stone at its foundation.

Lying in her hotel room in Chicago, just after talking on the phone with Gabe, that crumbling building, that whole heart-breaking time in Venice with her father, kept pushing forward in Helen's memory.

After identifying Jess's body she and her father had stepped out of the grim dampness into a fiercely bright October afternoon. The morning had been gray, raining when they walked from their hotel to the police station, still raining when they were motored along the Grand Canal to the dock beside the morgue. But suddenly the day turned clear and golden.

The police inspector and the young man from the U.S. consulate stayed behind to oversee the paperwork necessary for shipping Jess's body to the United States. So Helen and her father were by themselves, stumbling silently through the narrow streets in the general direction of their hotel. At last her father said, "How would you like to sit in the sun and have a drink?"

She nodded. "Any place except Piazza San Marco."

They crossed two narrow canals and found a small outdoor café in the Campo San Angelo. When the waiter came toward them, her father said to her, "Coffee, Cinzano, or something serious?"

"Something serious."

"Gin," he said to the waiter. "Two."

They sat in the bright yellow sunshine, sipped their drinks, and watched the people moving back and forth across the paved piazza. Finally her father said, "I'm proud of you, Puss."

"I didn't do anything. I just managed not to fall apart. That's nothing to be proud of."

"Yes it is."

"It's not my strong character, Dad. Nothing like that. I'm just all cried out. When we were flying here from London I thought I'd never stop bawling. But I did. It all drained out of me. Now I feel as if I'll never cry again."

That evening they had dinner at their hotel. They sat at a table by a tall window looking out on the Grand Canal. Her father drank more than she'd ever seen him drink, he ate more than she had ever seen him eat, and he never stopped talking.

As she sat watching him and listening to him, she felt suddenly old and quiet, as though he were the child and she the parent. She knew he was trying to distract her and reassure her, but it was an unfamiliar role for him. *She* was unfamiliar to him.

Sitting there across from her, one of the few times they had been alone together as adults, he realized, as she did, that there was no way to catch up. But he seemed determined to try, to pull her to him somehow, to rewrite history if necessary, to fill in the empty spaces.

"What a delicate little thing you were when you were born. You didn't really perk up till you were four or five."

"Mother says I cried a lot."

"I know she says that. But I never noticed that you cried any more than other babies. When we were in Denver one time for Christmas your grandfather said, 'You don't pick her up and hold her enough. That's why she cries.' Mary didn't like that too much. She had a theory that you spoiled children if you picked them up all the time."

"My nanny used to hold me on her lap. I remember that."

Her father nodded and smiled. "Miss Greenway had her own notions about child raising. And I didn't take sides either way. But I noticed you very seldom cried when your nanny was around."

"Here we are, talking about crying again. And I'm always the one who seems to bring it up. I think I'll change the subject."

"I'm sorry," her father said.

"It's not your fault. I've just thought about Jess and thought about myself and talked about everything so much, what might have been and what will never be, I just . . . you know what I mean. I keep hearing myself say the same things over and over, and nothing makes things any better. Or changes anything."

He poured some more wine in her glass. And in his own. Then he signaled the waiter for another bottle. "Medicine," he said to Helen.

"Not for me. I can only get high when I'm happy. Tonight I could drink the cellar dry and not even feel it."

"Good. At least one of us will stay sober. You can make sure I get upstairs in that Leonardo da Vinci *ascenseur.*"

"You're funny tonight," she said.

"Not me. Not a chance. I mix the drinks and your mother tells the jokes."

When they finished dinner, her father said, "Stroll me along the canal a little way. I ate too much and I drank too much and I'm not ready to tuck myself in yet."

Outside the hotel, the night was as clear and crisp as the afternoon had been. They turned left and walked slowly toward the Ponte dell'Accademia.

"You're a great talker," she said. "I'm impressed. I never knew you were such an outstanding talker."

"Never underestimate the old man."

"Old man? I've never called you that in my life. I hate that."

"I don't hate it yet," he said. "When I'm over fifty I'll probably hate it."

She took his arm and pulled him over to the rail at the edge of the canal parapet. She turned him to face her and put her hands on his shoulders. "I'm not a good talker at all, but I know what you've been doing tonight, what you were trying to do, and I want you to know it means a lot to me."

They walked on then, past the bridge, on past the Palazzo Ducale, and all the way to Santa Maria delle Pietà, before they turned around and came back to their hotel. As they went upstairs in the elevator, he said, "We walked too much. It sobered me up."

"That's good. You'll sleep like a baby."

As they got off the elevator and turned toward her room, he said, "The only trouble is I never got to the main subject. I stopped drinking before I could say what I really wanted to tell you."

She stopped at her door and said, "All right. We'll order you up a beautiful bottle of Corvo and you can start over."

"I don't think so. I've used up all my vocabulary and all my courage for one night." He unlocked her door, kissed her on the cheek, and said, "Will you be all right?"

"I'll be fine. I haven't slept for three nights, as you know. But tonight I think I'll sleep like a stone."

"Good. Whistle if you need company. If I really concentrated I could probably tell you a couple of your old bedtime stories."

"I'll remember that," she said.

Two days later, early in the morning, misty and gray, as they sat in the stern of a motor launch heading for the airport—he to return to London, she to fly to New York, then on to Seattle—he said, "I want to finish what I started to say the other night. But only if you promise not to interrupt me. If I don't say it all at once I'll never get it out."

They sat side by side facing the stern, the canal water foaming white behind the launch and the golden towers of Venice receding slowly in the morning grayness.

"I was trying to tell you something about your mother and me, the way we are together. The way we've always been. I mean I thought it might make things easier for you, help you to understand . . . " He paused. A long pause. Finally he went on. "When we were first married, I wanted to please her as much as I could. I suppose I felt that whatever made her happy would make me happy.

"I was an idealistic young clown. Very romantic. I thought that was what love meant. To care enough about someone to put their needs and wishes ahead of your own. I still think that's what it's all about. But now I know it only works if both the people involved have the same notion about it. It doesn't pan out at all if one person says, 'I want to *give*,' and the other person says, 'That suits me fine, because I want to *take.*'

"I'm making it sound all black and white, and it's never that way, of course. Relationships develop a little bit at a time. And if you care about someone, you don't notice. The days go by, and the weeks, and gradually you discover that something that was freely given has been redefined. The gift has become an obligation. Do you understand what I'm saying?"

"Yes, I do."

"In a marriage," he went on, "what seems at the time to be an unimportant concession or compromise can become, if it's repeated often enough, a rule of the house. A person who begins by teasing to have things their own way can become, very quickly, someone who *must* have their own way. One person decides. The other person agrees. Once that pattern is established, it's hard to change it. Very difficult to change the rules. To do that, I think you have to be willing to risk everything. You have to be able to say, 'I'd rather have nothing than what I've got.' I was never able to say that. Once Mary and I were married, once you were born, I felt as if I'd taken on a permanent obligation. I still feel that. But I also know I gave up a lot just to get what my father used to call 'a little silence around the house.' And a lot of the things I gave up, a lot of the battles I walked away from, affected you as much as they did me. More, maybe.

"When we found out Mary was pregnant, I wanted to go back to America so you'd be born there and grow up there. But she wanted to stay in England. So we stayed. And we gradually turned ourselves into synthetic Britishers. Mary's idea, not mine. Not my idea to have you brought up by governesses or tutors, either. Or to send you off to boarding school. I wanted you at home where I could see you and talk with you and watch you grow up. But I listened to your mother and pretended to agree with her when I didn't agree with her at all. I lost something I can never get back, and so did you.

"We shortchanged you, Puss. We didn't give you the things you should have had. I gave up something that was very important to me so your mother could be free to take badminton lessons and learn to play three Cole Porter songs on the piano. I know you're feeling rotten right now, and the last thing I want to do is make you feel worse. But I've needed to say this to you for a long time. I'm not trying to put the blame on your mother. Mary can't help the way she is. She's one of those people who never have second thoughts about what they're doing. She never feels guilty. Never has a bad conscience. She's like a beautiful cat. All impulse and no judgment. Follow your instincts and let the world get out of the way."

"Was she always like that?"

"Hard to say. Probably. But I underwrote it. I made it worse. The sad part of it is—well, that doesn't matter."

"Yes it does. What were you going to say?"

"The sad part is that the more I was willing to give up, the more she needed. Till now, there's nothing more she can take from me. So she's turned on herself like a snake swallowing its own tail. She's miserable now and she blames it on me. And in a way she's right. When a child has a crazy crying fit, what they really want is to be spanked. They want somebody to care enough about them to straighten them out. I never spanked your mother. I wasn't wise enough to see that her drive to dominate, to have her own way, was really something quite different from what it seemed to be. What she thought she wanted was not what she *needed*. Not at all."

"You're using the past tense a lot," Helen said. "Does that mean what I think it means?"

He shook his head. "It doesn't mean we're going to separate or divorce, if that's what you're asking. At least I don't think we will. I also want you to know that I'm not telling you all this so you'll feel sorry for me. I don't want that. I don't feel sorry for myself. Or for your mother. What I'm talking about is you. I know you missed a lot and I'm sorry."

She reached over and put her hand on his. Then she rested her head on his shoulder. "Don't be sorry. I'm not. I didn't miss anything important. I really didn't."

In her cool bed in Chicago, that Venice time with her father seemed a century away. But the words and the pictures were painfully clear. They flashed and flickered all night in her head. When morning finally came, she bathed and dressed and tried to prepare herself for the day ahead. For Fort Beck. For Gabe.

50 "Now that we're sitting here," Helen said, "I don't know what to say."

It was late afternoon. Gabe had just come home from his last lecture of the day. They were sitting in the living room, in front of the fireplace, in wing chairs, facing each other, eight feet apart. Helen had slipped her shoes off. They sat beside her chair on the carpet.

"Then don't say anything." He got up and walked to the bar. "You want a drink?"

"No thanks." Then, "I know you're angry. I expected that."

"I'm not angry. *Angry* isn't the word."

"What would you call it?"

"Once I lost six hundred bucks in a crap game. I used to love shooting dice. I knew somebody always had to lose. And sometimes it had to be me. So when I lost the six hundred it was no big tragedy. Then I found out the dice had been loaded. The game was fixed. I didn't mind losing, but I hated it that I never had a chance to win." He walked back to his chair and sat down.

"Don't try to make me bleed," she said.

"You asked me how I felt. I told you."

"My bags are still in the car. I can leave right now if that's what you want."

"Bullshit, Helen. It doesn't make any difference *what* I want and you know it. You told me on that tape that you couldn't hack it anymore. You're still dressed for the road and your bags are in the car. So it's not a question of *what.* It's just a matter of *when.*"

"You *are* mad. You're mad as hell."

"Suit yourself."

"I've never seen you like this."

"Neither has anybody else. This is a new experience for me."

"I wish you'd yell at me or knock me down or something. Don't just sit there being sarcastic. You're better than that."

"I'm not at my best right now. I don't expect to be at my best for quite some time."

"Jesus, Gabe . . . please . . ." Her chin began to quiver, her hands came up to cover her face, and she started to cry. He sat stiff in his chair, watching her but not moving. Finally he looked down at his glass. When he lifted it up to take a drink, he still didn't look at her.

Suddenly she got up, moved across to his chair, and sank down to the floor by his feet, her arms around his legs. "I can't stand it. That's why I couldn't tell you to your face. I couldn't look at you. I still can't. It kills me because I can't fix it. I'd do anything if I could just fix things. But I can't."

She started crying again. "Oh, God, how I wish I'd been born in this town. I wish I'd met you when I was ten years old. Before things got all tangled up and crazy."

He put his hand on the back of her neck and kept it there for a long time. Till she stopped crying. She was very quiet then. And dead still. As though she'd gone to sleep. Then, suddenly, her face still hidden against his thigh, her hand came up toward his face, and her voice, muffled and husky, said, "Handkerchief, please."

She blew her nose and dabbed at her eyes with his handkerchief. Then she stood up and walked to the powder room just inside the front door. While she was gone, he fixed himself another drink. And a vodka and soda for her.

When she came back, she'd washed her face and gathered her hair into a loose knot. Sitting down, she picked up her drink, sipped from it, and said, "Perfect timing." Then she pulled her feet up under her in the chair, cradled the glass in her lap with both hands, and said, "I told you I don't know what made me the way I am. And I don't. But there are some things . . . I'm not trying to make excuses . . . but if there's anything that might help you to understand . . . "

She took another sip from her glass. "I told you about Jess. The good and the bad. What that life was like. I was young and dumb and crazy, trying to be an instant grown-up. I had this thing about my mother too. Classic mother-daughter screw-up.

"Whether I was right about her or not is beside the point now. But it had an effect then. I decided she was an emotional cripple, that she didn't understand anything or anyone. Not me, not my father, not even herself. I decided I would top her in everything; I would make myself more attractive than she was, be a better woman, a better wife, and a better mother.

"It was all idiotic and vengeful, but just then it was very real for me. I was nineteen years old, smart as hell, I felt, and away from family restrictions for the first time.

"So when I met Jess, I was preconditioned, ready to fall, eager to show the world, particularly my mother, how grown-up I was, how capable and resourceful a girl of nineteen could be."

She paused and looked into the fire. Then, "I'm not saying I would have married any man who came along. I was wary of that. But Jess . . . I already told you how I felt about him. I was hypnotized. No question about it. I thought he was the most talented, most articulate, most unusual man on earth. Nothing but superlatives.

"What really attracted me, however, were his flaws. I know that now and I suppose I sensed it then. But it all dovetailed beautifully with my distorted image of myself. Let Helen fix it. Mother Teresa. All things to all men. *Ego*—that was it. Monumental nineteen-year-old ego. Out to prove what a truly superior woman could accomplish. Tenderness and intelligence would conquer all. Stones would sing. No sparrow would ever fall again.

"I'm exaggerating, but the core of what I'm saying is true. Truer than I like to admit. Anyway . . . all that magnificent self-deception didn't last long. Two months after Jess and I were married—in two *weeks* actually, that was all it took—the master plan was wrecked and discarded. From then on all I could do was hang on by my fingernails and try to survive. I needed all my energy and ingenuity just to get through the day.

"But I did grow up. I grew up very quickly. I found out about heartbreak and frustration, compromise and disappointment. And disillusion. All in a lump. But it never occurred to me to give up and walk away. Not till the very last. Through all of the grisliest, most degrading times with Jess, when I felt more like a zoo keeper than a wife, some shredded leftovers of my ego stayed intact. I kept telling myself I could do it, that somehow I would make things work.

"When I found out I was pregnant that first time, I was delighted. I thought it would be Jess's salvation, that as soon as we had a child he would become a different man. What an idiot I was. Thank God I had a miscarriage. I say that now, but I felt different then. I cried my eyes out for days. And so did Jess. He sat there dead drunk, a bottle of gin in his hand, and tears running down his cheeks."

She got up then, walked to the fireplace, and poked at the logs till a shower of orange sparks sputtered up the chimney and new flames began to lick and crackle under the dry wood.

She turned and stood with her back to the fire. "A few months later I was pregnant again. By then I knew some things I hadn't known before. But I played the game. I didn't tell myself that I was in an impossible situation, that it would be disastrous for me to bring a child into the chaotic life that Jess and I shared. I simply decided that the time was not right, that *later* would be better. When Jess had completed his work at Cambridge. When he had taken a teaching job somewhere and we could lead a calm and ordered life.

"So I had an abortion. The idea scared me to death but I did it anyway. A girl I knew in Cambridge drove me over to Bedford one morning and a midwife there did it. It was the grisliest thing that had ever happened to me. If I live to be a hundred I'll never forget it. I'll never be able to block out that dismal room with stained wallpaper, the operating table covered with paper toweling, the midwife skinny and surly with dyed red hair and the sour smell of sherry on her breath.

"I was twenty years old by then, frightened and sick and hemorrhaging. I went a little crazy, I think, between the time we left Cambridge and that night, almost midnight, when we got back. By then I was unconscious and half-dead from loss of blood.

"After a lot of transfusions, when I finally came to in a Cambridge hospital, I felt as if I'd died and had somehow come back to life. But there was some part of me that felt permanently dead. When I came home from the hospital, back to the apartment where Jess and I lived, I'd convinced myself that I'd never be able to get pregnant again. Three months later, however, I missed my period. I sat for hours in a hot tub, drank half a bottle of gin, and got violently ill. I also got my period.

"From then on, all the rest of the time I was with Jess, I wore a diaphragm. I mean *all* the time. An hour never passed that I didn't worry about getting pregnant. At night it kept me awake and anxious, like a presence in the room, as though some kind of sharp-toothed animal was living under my bed, skittering back and forth in the darkness.

"The mere thought of having a baby paralyzed me, made me chilled and nauseous. It penetrated into every corner of my life. Dominated it. Like a shrill, screeching sound you can't get away from. Or a putrid smell.

"It wasn't just the memory of that ugly day in Bedford. That was part of it, certainly. But not the main part. The thing I really couldn't deal with was the truth about my life with Jess. I realize now that no relationship between a man and a woman could ever have lived up to the fairy-tale standards I had hung on it. But I also know that even if I'd been older and smarter, even if I'd gone into that marriage with my wits about me, the ending would have been the same. There was no way to survive with Jess. There was no way for him to survive with himself. But neither of us could admit those things. To ourselves or to each other. So we struggled along, like people with wet gunnysacks trying to beat back a forest fire.

"All the time we were together, it seemed as though I lived with a mop and pail in my hand, scalding water and disinfectant, battling the stink of vomit and gin and urine. When I walked outdoors in the street I imagined I could still smell it, that people could smell it on *me*. I envied those homes that smelled of flowers and furniture polish, coffee and fresh bread. I baked great loaves of bread that we never ate, brewed coffee, filled our rooms with fresh-cut flowers, but nothing could overcome the smell of Jess's life. Nothing could mask or redefine the kind of lunatic existence the two of us were living together.

"So *that,* all that, got inside me, like some kind of growth on the brain. When problems couldn't be solved or even understood, when all kinds of ugly circumstances couldn't be changed, then substitutions had to be made. Black had to become white, contempt and bewilderment had to be processed somehow into affection. All the negatives had to be turned into positives. Survival demanded it. And in spite of confusion and indecision, one thing I was sure of—I wanted to survive.

"So the revulsion I felt for the life I was leading had to be rechanneled in some way. And it was. Pregnancy, the idea of it, became the scapegoat. All the other frustrations were picked up and transferred to that one emotional carton. Avoiding the areas I couldn't handle, I concentrated my attention on something I *could* handle.

"I told myself that if I could just avoid having a baby, then all the debris of my life with Jess could eventually be swept together, sorted through, and dealt with. *That,* and only that, was the solution. Avoid pregnancy. Avoid motherhood. I cultivated a revulsion for any nursery, for wet nappies and spilled food, for sour-smelling spit-up milk, for the general stink.

"It worked for me. I made it work. Cleaning up after Jess, I told myself how much worse it would be if I had a baby. When women showed off their children a voice inside me said, 'Better you than me,' and I believed it. I came to believe it totally. I transferred all my disgust with myself and my life to some unborn nonexistent child."

She turned and poked at the fire again, then walked back to her chair and sat down. "I was ill, of course. Crazy as a coot. I know that now. I think I sensed it then, but I wouldn't admit it. By the time Jess left me I was close to a real breakdown.

"Only after he was dead, when I'd taken his body back to Seattle, when I'd met the strange in-turned family he came from, it was only then that I began to understand some of his craziness. The drinking, the need to degrade himself and punish himself, to waste his talents and his education and wreck his health.

"When I left Seattle, I decided the best thing for me to do was to try to remember him at his best. All charm and persuasion and music coming out of his pores. His mind racing ahead, too fast for his speech to keep up. So I concentrated on that and it worked. In a few months I'd managed to forget most of the bad stuff.

"You remember . . . when I first told you about Jess, that first week when I met you in San Francisco, it wasn't a horror story, was it? As I remember, I told you he was very smart, very talented, and he drank too much. And he deserved a better life than he got. Didn't I say that?"

"Something like that," Gabe said.

"I meant it," she said. "By then I had no guilts about how I'd been with Jess. I'd dealt with it. I felt that I'd done all I could for him, for myself, for the marriage. I'd decided that long before we met, Jess was on a tragic headlong trip that nobody could have pulled him away from.

"What I'm saying is that when I met you I had no hangover from that other time. No emotional cobwebs to struggle through. After that first week I couldn't wait to start a life with you. I felt whole and solid and valuable. I knew I wouldn't disappoint you. I was eager to come here with you, to a place I'd never seen, and fit myself into your life."

She lifted her glass and swallowed what was left of her drink. "And it almost worked. I don't have to tell you how happy I was, how happy you made me. From the first day you brought me here, all I wanted was to stay put in this house, watch the river moving along at the bottom of the slope, and have a good life with you. And I was dying for us to have children. I couldn't wait to get pregnant. Then . . . I don't want to talk about it anymore."

They sat there in silence, their glasses empty, the fire burning weakly now on the grate. Finally Gabe said, "What if I told you that none of this really matters to me?"

"I wouldn't believe you."

"What if I said that our staying together is more important than anything else? Would you believe that?"

"Yes. I feel the same way. But it wouldn't work, Gabe. Not now. I couldn't face you every day. And I couldn't face myself. I've got a struggle ahead of me. I don't know if I can handle it or not. But one thing I'm *absolutely* sure of. It's not *your* struggle. I won't let it be."

Kosta was born in Brooklyn, New York. After age three, however, she grew up in the Shenandoah Valley of Virginia, first in Winchester, then, for eleven years, in Harrisonburg. Conceived before her parents left Greece for America, had she been born six months earlier, she would have been delivered by Anna Dukakis, the midwife of Almiros.

As it was, born in a Brooklyn roominghouse just north of Empire Boulevard, she was by age sixteen very much a Greek girl in her black-haired, dark-eyed appearance, but with a dash of saucy self-confidence that seemed to be pure Brooklyn. In all her years in Appalachia she had taken on few characteristics of the hill people.

She knew those people well, however, loved them, felt strongly at home and at one with them, admired and respected their clannish loyalty and sense of honor. As she approached the last leg of her trip from Indianapolis to West Virginia, her instinct told her that she must arrive in Elkins not as a journalist or as some pushy person from outside, but as the girl whose father owns and operates the Kosta lunch room and hot dog parlor in Harrisonburg.

Checking into the Tygart Hotel on Elkins's main street, she gave her home address as Harrisonburg and spoke deliberately in the soft hill rhythm she had heard most of her life.

"Did you drive over just today?" the desk clerk said.

"No. I came down from Clarksburg. Had some business to do up there for my daddy."

As soon as she'd gone upstairs and changed into her plainest clothes, she called down to the desk and said, "I sure would like to get a wash and set. Is there a beauty parlor around that could take me right quick?"

"We got The Beauty Fair just across the street by the motion picture house. But if I was you I'd try Mrs. Elizabeth Laidlaw. She's back down Ousler Street a square and a half. And she's more likely to take you without your calling ahead. Charge you less too, according to Bea and Mid that work downstairs here in the Java Shop."

Mrs. Elizabeth Laidlaw had her beauty parlor set up in the front room of her house on a side street not far from the hotel. When Kosta walked in, there was one other customer, a raw-boned, gray-haired woman sitting under the permanent-wave machine.

"Any chance I could get a wash and a set?" Kosta said.

Mrs. Laidlaw glanced at her wall clock. "I reckon I could work you in if you don't want anything too special. I'm pretty taken up with my regulars."

"Nothing fancy," Kosta said. "Just wash it good and put a couple of rollers in the front. If you've got a hand dryer I can blow it dry myself."

"Well, I may let you do that. If Myrna Gill gets in here when she's due, I'll have my hands full."

While she washed Kosta's hair, combed it out, and put the rollers in, Mrs. Laidlaw continued her conversation with the gray-haired woman. From what Kosta could pick up there had been an accident on a back road the night before. A man had driven into the ditch with a woman he wasn't supposed to be with. The gray-haired woman was indignant, but Mrs. Laidlaw seemed philosophical about it.

"Anybody who's surprised by Harley Boswell's shenanigans just ain't been paying attention, Clara. I mean, you got to give up your regular work if you aim to keep tabs on that jaybird. I went to high school with him, you know. So did Wad, my late husband. Even then he was busier than a closetful of squirrels. Wad always said Harley was carrying on with Ruby Constable, the woman from up at Buckhorn that used to teach us geography. Harley was no more than sixteen then, and Miss Constable was forty if she was a day. But Wad swore till the time he died that the two of them was riding up in the hills in that Oldsmobile of hers three or four nights a week.

"Since then it's been one woman after another for old Harley. Which ain't to say he's neglected his wife any. Audrey must have had a kid a year for the last fifteen, not even counting the times she miscombobulated. And all the while, Harley's combing the county like a bird dog, having himself a high old time with any skirt that'll have him. Tell you the truth, I don't know what *anybody* sees in him. Scrawny little runt. And Waddy said he's got hair all over himself like a circus orangutang."

"He's a peewee," the gray-haired woman said. "He'd have to tiptoe it to come up to my shoulder. I reckon that's what's eating him. I never seen a sawed-off man yet that didn't try to take on anything in skirts that gave him a second look."

After the gray-haired woman left, when Kosta had finished blowing her hair dry, Mrs. Laidlaw said, "Looks like Myrna got herself waylaid somewhere. Usually she rings in if she's not coming, but some days I don't hear a word. She's got a girl that's not quite bright. Almost twenty years old and pretty as a silk pillow but she don't know from straight up. Myrna has to watch her like a hawk or she'd be out in the grass with anybody that asked her. And there's plenty of people asking, I can guarantee you *that.*"

After she'd paid for her shampoo, when she was ready to leave, Kosta said, "I see you've got some coffee simmering over there. Could I have a cup?"

"You're welcome to it. More than welcome. I'll have some with you."

"I didn't get much lunch and I'm a little woozy."

After they sat down with their coffee cups, Mrs. Laidlaw said, "You're not from Elkins. I can tell that. Not unless you just moved in."

Kosta shook her head. "No, I'm from over in Virginia. Harrisonburg. And this is kind of a sad trip for me. A friend of mine had a sister who was on that plane that crashed here last January. Her family was awful broken up about it. You can imagine. They never felt satisfied about those newspaper stories that told how it happened. They still think there must have been somebody who saw the plane come down, somebody I could talk to and get kind of a firsthand version of what went on. Her family knows that nothing is gonna bring Shirley back, but it sure would ease their minds a lot if I could get them some kind of straight information from here."

"Well, it's nice of you to try to help," Mrs. Laidlaw said. "But I don't envy you the job. That was an awful thing to have happen. We've had our mine explosions and floods and such-like around here as far back as I can remember. But we never had anything to match that plane crash. All those government people and kids exploded into little pieces. And what's left of them burned up so bad you couldn't tell Joe from Charley."

"I guess you don't have a newspaper here in Elkins, do you?"

"Not so you could notice. Just a township paper once a week. And it's not worth anything for news. Just grocery store ads, mostly, is what they carry."

"I don't know where to start then," Kosta said. "I sure hate to go back to those people with nothing at all to tell them."

"Well . . . nine times out of ten I'd be able to help you out. I spend all day listening to one old hen after another telling me what's happening around Elkins. But all I can tell you about that crash is *where* it happened. About twelve miles straight west of here. A fella named Isley Pritchett runs a truck farm out there. Sixty acres, give or take a couple. And right there's where that plane went down, just at the north edge of Pritchett's place. All the oil and the fire and so forth ruined ten or twelve acres that he more often than not puts into sweet corn."

The next morning Kosta drove out to Isley Pritchett's farm. Elizabeth Laidlaw had called him the afternoon before to make sure it was all right for her to come.

The Pritchetts lived in a one-story cinder-block house a hundred yards back from the road. Isley was tall and thin, very erect. His wife, Sadie, also tall, looked enough like him to be his sister. But she stooped sharply from the waist, and her hands were twisted with arthritis. Both of them seemed to be in their late seventies.

There was also an eight-year-old boy playing in the yard. "That's our great-grandson, Arvid. He lives with us. His folks are up in Cleveland. His dad draws good wages at the asphalt plant there. But they think it's better for Arvid to be here with us. He was born deaf and dumb."

"Bright as paint, though," Isley said. "You can look in his eyes and see that. But he can't learn books 'cause he's deaf as a post, and not a sound has ever come out of his mouth. When he was a little tyke in his cradle they had to look at him close to see if he was bawlin', because there wasn't a tick of any kind of a noise coming out of his face."

"But the Lord Jesus Christ is watching," Sadie said. "He touched that boy and gave him a gift. What he's got is an eye like a chicken hawk. He don't miss nothing. He can take a box of Crayolas or some water paint and make you a picture that you couldn't find a better one in a Wheeling department store."

Isley drove Kosta out to the north boundary of his farm, showed her the great black field, burned off and oil soaked, with nothing growing on it. "The government agronomy man that came down here says they ain't nothing gonna sprout in that dirt for a long time to come. It's like it's been poisoned. He figures I got a claim against Washington, no two ways about it, since it was their air ship that done the damage. But so far I ain't seen a single dollar nor a promise of any."

Aside from that, Kosta learned nothing from Isley. He'd been in Elkins and hadn't seen the crash. Sadie had been busy in the house. "And if any of the neighbors seen anything they ain't said a word about it. There was government men and newspaper folks prowling around down here for days after. But they didn't flush out a single soul who said he'd seen anything. Not as far as *I* know anyway."

Back in the house, Sadie offered Kosta some coffee and a wedge of homemade pound cake. And just before she left, they took her into the boy's room to show her his pictures. They were stuck up with pins on the wallpaper, all four walls, from floor to ceiling.

It stunned her, this blaze of color inside a drab house sitting isolated in a potato field, this onslaught of brilliant, violent images that had exploded out of that beautiful, silent boy. The room was like a Gauguin hut, newfound, on some remote island in the Marquesas.

Kosta spent nearly an hour looking at the pictures. When she left at last and drove back toward Elkins, she could feel the warm blood in her cheeks. She knew now what she had needed to know.

 While Kosta was in Elkins, Gabe was in Illinois for a meeting with the governor, an address to the state legislature, and the unveiling of a plaque in Springfield, a memorial to his brother.

Saturday afternoon, on his way to Fort Beck, he stopped in Macomb. His father told him Helen was in town.

"At least I think she's still around. She drove out here yesterday morning to see me."

"How is she?"

"Seems all right to me. Likes her job, she says. Likes California."

"What's she doing here?"

"She didn't say. Just said she was staying at the Settler's for three or four days."

"Did you tell her I was due in town?" Gabe said.

"No, I didn't. She didn't ask and I didn't volunteer anything. I didn't know if you'd want to see her or not."

"Why wouldn't I? Just because we got a divorce doesn't mean we're enemies."

"Uh-huh. I've heard that tune before."

When Gabe got back to Fort Beck, as soon as he was inside his house he called the Settler's Hotel. When Helen answered her phone, he said, "The last time I talked to you, you asked me out to dinner. Now I'm asking you."

"What are you doing here?"

"I *live* here. What's your excuse?" he said.

"Remember last time we talked? I said I wanted to ship that stuff I left here in storage. Well, this time I did it. Sent it all off yesterday."

"That means you'll have to turn in your passport. You can't claim citizenship in Fort Beck anymore."

"I guess not," she said.

"So what about dinner?"

"To tell you the truth I was going to put on my pajamas, order up a sandwich, and watch some old movie on television."

"Come on. I'll buy you a bottle of champagne and we'll drink to the good life in California."

"I don't feel like champagne."

"Then I'll buy you a keg of beer."

There was a long silence at her end. Then, "You talked me into it. But one condition. Let's go to some tacky place where we won't see anybody we know."

After he picked her up at the hotel, they drove along the North River Road to a place called Slattery's. Catfish and beer and oilcloth table covers left over from another time. They sat in a booth in the back corner and drank draft beer out of heavy glass mugs. While the jukebox poured out an unending country lament. Death and heartbreak and betrayal.

"How's Washington?" she said.

"I'm not sure yet."

"Plus or minus?"

"I'm not sure."

"I followed your campaign, you know."

"No. I didn't know."

"I missed the beginning of it. I was still in England. But when I got back to New York, I found a newsstand there that stocked the *Chicago Tribune*. I bought it every day so I could read all the dirt."

"The *Tribune* didn't support me exactly."

"No, I could tell that." She sipped her beer and lit a cigarette.

"I thought you stopped smoking."

"I did, but I started again." Then, "Did you say all the things the papers said you did?"

"Like what?"

"Like you'd welcome a move to Washington because you'd just had a sad divorce. Did you say that?"

"Something like that."

"Why?"

"Because it's the truth."

"A *sad* divorce?"

"There's no other kind, is there?"

"I don't know. I guess not. It was just that one word. *Sad.* It threw me. It's not a word I associate with you."

"Why not? I'm not the tin woodman."

"I didn't mean that," she said. "I don't know what I mean. I was just there in New York, sitting in a room by myself, and I read that in the paper and . . . I don't know . . . it all got connected in my head with Chet and Evelyn and Sam and I wanted to call you up. But I couldn't. I just sat there watching it get dark outside and tried to figure out how so much bad stuff could happen so quick."

"Yeah . . . well . . . you have to find a way to steer clear of all that. Otherwise you'll drive yourself nuts."

"I'll never get over that funeral. I'll never get over what happened to them. I can't get it out of my head."

"Nobody ever gets anything out of his head. Drink your beer and tell me a couple of English jokes."

Sitting across the table looking at her, not having seen her since the funeral more than three months before, he kept hearing, over and over, like a tiny cassette playing in his ear, the last words she'd said to him before she left to fly to El Paso for the divorce. "Even if it *didn't* matter to you, Gabe, even if you managed to convince me of that, it would still matter to *me.* I can't explain what I did and the way I feel about it. I don't understand it myself. It's some kind of craziness. I realize that. But it's real. It haunts me. It paralyzes me. But I can't change it. Whatever it is, wherever it comes from, I'm stuck with it. But you're not. I won't let you be. If we tried to stay together now, now that I've told you the truth, it would wreck us both."

He sat looking at her, her eyes clear and gray-green, her

red-bronze hair pulled back in a loose knot, her skin tan and freckled, her cheeks as pink as an Irish urchin's. That clean, open beauty had startled him the first time he met her. It still startled him.

There was a newness about her. Something fresh-grown in a misty climate. When Chet and Evelyn met her for the first time, Evelyn said, "I don't believe it. *Nobody* looks like that."

Jack Slattery strolled over then with a platter of deep-fried catfish, home-fried potatoes, and a bowl of salad. "I'll bet you don't eat like this in Washington," he said.

"I guess not."

"I can't get used to calling you Senator."

"You don't have to," Helen said. "He's a man of the people. Just plain old Gabe. Poor but honest."

"That's right," Gabe said.

They ate the fish and potatoes, drank a lot of beer, and talked about things that didn't matter. He answered questions about the campaign, and she told him about California.

"I thought you hated it out there."

"I hate Palm Springs. But I'm living in Santa Barbara. That's a whole different story."

She'd been hired by the Santa Barbara Museum. Assistant curator for prints and drawings. "I went there for a few days between Palm Springs and London. Have you ever been there?"

"No."

"It's lovely. Like a postcard. Even if they do have oil derricks a mile off the beach. They say it's the only town in the world where they widened the sidewalks and narrowed the main street to cut down on automobile traffic. It's a neat museum, too. Perfect for that town. And the director seems like a civilized guy. So it should be an interesting job."

As she talked, tears glistened suddenly in her eyes and began to slide down her cheeks. "I found an apartment, too. A little bit like the one I used to have in San Francisco. Just big enough for me and a cat . . . "

"What's the matter?"

"Don't ask me," she said. "I don't know."

"Why are you crying?"

"How the hell do I know? It just happens sometimes. Maybe it's the beer."

"Remember when you called me from Chicago? When I called you back at the hotel, you'd been crying then, hadn't you?"

"Probably. I cry a lot these days," she said. "The clock strikes the hour and I start to boo-hoo."

"You want to leave?"

"No. I'm used to people staring. They stop after a while. I've decided that somebody crying is a boring thing to watch. One bucket of tears looks pretty much like the next one."

It was almost midnight when they walked in a curving line across the graveled parking area to Gabe's car.

"Are you holding me up," she said, "or am I holding you up?"

"I'm holding you up."

"Who's holding *you* up? We drank nine hundred dollars' worth of beer."

"It's all right. I'm a senator now. Slattery didn't give me a check."

"Terrific. That's what they mean by perquisites. Right?"

"I guess so."

"I just missed all that. I just missed being a senator's wife, didn't I?"

"Just barely."

"It's all right. I wouldn't be good at it anyway. I'm a very bad person with a teapot. I am famous for pouring tea on people's shoes."

When he took out his keys to unlock the car door, she said, "Don't drop me or I'll spill."

He helped her into the front seat, then walked around the car and slid in behind the wheel. When he put the key in the ignition, she said, "Don't start the car yet." She slid over in the seat, put her arms around his neck, and kissed him. Then she dropped her head on his shoulder, her cheek against his neck, and said, "If you give me a cookie I'll let you do anything you want to."

"I was right. You're drunk."

"That's all right. I'm fun when I'm drunk. Besides, I sober up as soon as I get my clothes off." She kissed him again. "Come

on, sport. Don't be a stick-in-the-mud. You'll have fun. I promise you. We'll pretend we're not quite divorced yet. Or maybe
we'll pretend we never got married."

As soon as they were inside his house, just inside the front
door, they took their clothes off and dropped them in a pile at
the foot of the stairs. Then they walked upstairs in the dark with
their arms around each other's waists. Inside the bedroom she
switched on all the lights and said, *"Voilà!* I don't want to hide
anything. Do you?"

She stood in front of him then with her hands down at her
sides and said, "See . . . I told you . . . I'm not drunk at all."
Putting her hands on his shoulders, she held herself back and
away from him, her tiny breasts arching up, her pelvis thrust
forward, almost touching him.

She let her hands trail down across his chest, then across his
stomach, until they came together between his legs.

He pulled her toward him, still standing by the side of the
bed. He lifted her up, she swung her legs around his waist, her
arms around his neck, and he slid, thick and slow, inside her.
Her legs tightened around his waist then; she moved quickly
against him and began to whisper in his ear. "You see . . . I'm
completely . . . sober . . . I may be . . . ohhh, Jesus . . . I may be
a little . . . tight . . . but I'm not . . . oh, God, honey . . . I'm not
. . . I'm not . . . oh, Gabe . . . oh, God . . ."

 When he woke up it was four in the morning,
almost four thirty, and she was gone. When he got
up and went into the bathroom, the light was on.
There was a piece of writing paper stuck with a
Band-Aid to the mirror over the sink. Pale-blue paper with her

name printed across the top, very small letters in Chinese red:
HELEN LEACOCK TREPTOW.

Three A.M.

Gabe sweetheart:

Don't be mad at me. I pinched your car to drive myself back to the hotel. I'll leave instructions for them to bring it back out here as soon as the world wakes up and has its coffee.

I've been lying in bed watching you sleep like I have a thousand times before. And all I could think was how marvelous it was to see you like that, cold outside but warm in the bed, everything dark and still and peaceful and parts of me still tingling from the crazy love battle.

I'd give anything if I could have met you before a lot of bad stuff happened to me, before I had to make adjustments that couldn't be changed back later. But . . . what the hell . . . nobody ever gets the whole banana, do they?

I know I didn't fool you with the story of why I came here. I take the Fort Beck paper so I knew you'd be home this weekend. That's why I showed up. I couldn't stand the thought of our seeing each other for the last time across three open graves on a raw and ugly January day.

I expect to be on my way to Chicago by the time you read this. I miss you a lot already. And I expect to go on missing you. But I'll try very hard to keep it to myself.

Thanks for all that marvelous beer. And the catfish dinner. You sure know how to treat a lady.

Love and kisses—

Helen

When Helen visited Gabe's father at the nursing home the day before she saw Gabe, it was the first time she had seen him since the morning Chet and Evelyn and Sam were buried. But they made no reference to that. For most of the time—she talked with him for almost an hour—they stayed clear of family matters, no reference to Gabe or the divorce or anything else that could be awkward or painful.

It was as though they had made a pact to stay out of all areas that could hurt either of them. Their conversation, once it got past Mr. Treptow's physical condition, restricted itself to safe channels, primarily an examination of where Helen had been since January and what she'd seen.

"For a man that's never been more than two hundred miles from Fort Beck I guess I've gone through more tour booklets and travel brochures than anybody alive," Howard said. "Always enjoyed reading about foreign places, seeing pictures of how other folks live. But I'm not sure I would have gone to any of those places, even if I could have afforded it. I mean I liked the *idea* of it, but I doubt if I would ever have packed up and gone off to Italy or Africa or New Zealand or anyplace I liked to read about even if somebody had handed me a ticket. Only place that really tempted me was England. Maybe because I knew I'd be able to talk to people there and be understood."

"It's my best place," Helen said. "It's like going home. I have to keep reminding myself that my parents are American and *I'm* American. When I'm buying a lipstick or looking for a new dress, I catch myself using some set of standards I learned when I was ten years old, some odd mixture that's half conservative and half crazy-eccentric. But that's what England is."

"I've done a lot of reading about London," Howard said, "and I guess I'd like to see it just for the history if nothing else. But when I used to think about going to England, it was always the *country* part that sounded best to me. The little towns and the farming sections and the like. I don't expect I'd feel any more at home in London than I do in Chicago. And New York is a place I couldn't live in if you paid me. Never been there and don't want to go."

"I don't like New York much either," Helen said, "but I've always thought it's because I've never lived there. There are some places that are no good at all to visit. They're too complicated. Too overpowering. You have to spend some time, get to know your way around, start to feel comfortable, before you can decide if it's a good place for you or not."

She told him then about California, plus and minus. And she described Santa Barbara in detail, the neighborhood she lived in, the stores where she shopped, the museum where she worked. At last she stopped abruptly. Then she said, "I feel like such a jackass. I keep jabbering on like a newscast and you're nice enough to listen. But I know you don't give a damn about anything I'm saying. I don't give a damn about it either. I just came here with the idea that—I don't know—I wanted to see you but I didn't want to bring up a lot of stuff that would make you unhappy. I thought I could . . . "

"What?"

"I thought I could pretend that all the bad stuff never happened. I told myself that you and I could talk and make nice on each other and neither one of us would think about the way things were just a few months ago, how perfect everything was. . . . "

"I think about that all the time," he said. "There's no way to steer away from it."

"That's what I mean. I think I'm going crazy sometimes. I can't get it out of my head. The harder I try to forget, the clearer everything flashes in my memory. I feel as if every minute that all of us ever spent together is recorded on film, and it keeps playing, nonstop, like home movies dancing on the wall, no matter what room I'm in, no matter what time of the day or night it is. Am I going to spend the rest of my life staring at the ceiling every night?"

Howard shook his head. "It'll go away. I don't mean you won't remember. But the pictures won't be so sharp after a while. Things start to fuzz over. Because that's the way we're made. So we can forget a little and keep on going. It's still too close. Not enough time has gone by yet. But it will. And you won't hurt so much. When the boys' mother died all of a sudden, here one minute and gone the next, I thought I was finished. I mean, I wasn't thinking about dying myself, I had Chet and Gabe to look after, but I knew for certain that all the heart had gone out of me. I knew that all I'd be able to do was just go through the motions, do the things I had to do. I didn't expect to laugh or have any fun again. Not the way I·had before. But like I say, it didn't work out that way. I came back to life, a little bit at a time. It didn't mean I cared any less about Thelma, it just meant we've got some kind of a healing system inside ourselves and it works. We're not intended to die from grief, or be crippled by it. We're meant to get well. Just like we do when we're sick."

Gabe's name wasn't mentioned till the very end, just before Helen got up to go. Finally she said, "I thought I wasn't going to say anything about Gabe. I was afraid to. But now that we've talked a little . . . I mean, I'll bet you're proud of him, aren't you?"

Howard nodded his head. "But not the way you might think. I'm proud because I know everything he's done these past few months is dead against his nature. Chet used to love the noise and the arguments and the attention. Gabe hates all that stuff. Chet liked to be in the middle of things. Gabe likes to be by himself. So that's the battle he's had to fight. A lot tougher than getting votes. He's had to battle with himself. He's still doing it. And he'll have to keep on doing it as long as he stays in Washington."

"Do you think he means it when he says he'll just be there for one term?"

"I know he means it. And if he keeps raising Cain the way he's been doing he may get to come home quicker than he planned."

She stood up then, picked up her purse and her scarf, and said, "I have to go."

"No rush."

"Don't want to wear out my welcome. If I don't stay too long, then you'll let me come back."

"Anytime," he said.

She bent down across the bed and kissed him. When she straightened up, there were tears in her eyes. "You take care of yourself now. Eat your oatmeal and mind the doctors."

"No choice. They got me surrounded."

Just before she left she said, "I don't know how to say this, but . . . it kills me being away from Gabe. If you thought it was one of those casual, friendly divorces . . . "

"I never thought that."

"There just wasn't any way . . . I mean, if there was any way in the world that we could have stayed together, we would have. I don't expect you to understand that. But I want you to believe it."

"I do believe it. I don't have to understand it."

In Harrisonburg for thirty-six weekend hours with her parents before returning to Washington, Kosta shed, as she always did when she came home, the vestiges of her life away from there. Like a chameleon, she took on the colors of the surroundings.

She dressed in her Harrisonburg wardrobe. Jeans and skirts and sweaters that she kept in her upstairs bedroom. Sneakers and loafers and the trench coat she'd worn in high school and all through her years at Brandeis. She had learned long ago that the people she'd grown up with, her parents' friends and neighbors, even the people her own age who had stayed on in Harrisonburg, were not interested in hearing about New York or Boston or Washington, not interested at all in knowing about her life or her work.

They sensed, a few of them, that there was something unique about her: they knew she had "caused a lot of trouble" when she was in school. And a few were aware that she was some kind of a writer. But almost none of them had ever read her articles or seen the publications in which they appeared. Suspecting that there was something foreign, even immoral, about what she did and what she wrote, they were not curious enough to go beyond those suspicions. Or perhaps because they did like her as a person, and did respect her parents, they felt it was best to leave well enough alone, best not to judge her or even to *know* her beyond what their eyes and ears told them, best to bracket her with the five or six other girls her age who had gone to Roanoke or Richmond to work or teach or be married and who came home occasionally to visit.

She knew that the highest praise she could receive in Harrisonburg was "That little Kosta girl never changes, does she? Nothing fancy or snooty about her at all. You see her walking down the street or working behind the counter in her father's place and you'd swear she'd never been away from Harrisonburg. They say she's got a lot of ginger, but she still acts like a hometown girl. I like her, no matter what anybody says."

Kosta also knew that this strange and diluted, half-complimentary acceptance of her was pleasing to her mother and father. In a community of eccentric people living eccentric lives, there was no higher praise than to be thought of and referred to as modest and plain.

Always, when she was at home, she put in some time behind the counter of her father's restaurant on the town square. Standing at the grill in her yellow-and-white checked uniform with a white ruffle-edged apron, she fried bacon and slabs of ham and thick sausage patties, cooked potatoes and eggs and made stacks of buckwheat cakes.

When her father took over the grill, she patrolled the counter. Joked and laughed and served coffee. And put together endless orders of the house specialty: a fat pink frankfurter in a steamed bun, a liquid, spicy mustard ladled on it, then a thick brown sauce made of ground beef, and fine-chopped raw onions sprinkled on top. Only tourists or fools added relish or catsup.

If any other taste was allowed to interfere, the only acceptable ones were the dark baked beans, soaked in molasses, with hunks of bacon in each individual pot and crisp bacon slices, smoky and hot, on the top.

Cole slaw was acceptable too, as a side dish for the frankfurters, but the true believers ate only the frankfurters on the soft buns. Washed down with coffee. Or a cold bottle of beer. Or a thick milk shake.

With her father, after they'd closed the restaurant and gone home, after her mother had gone upstairs to read for half an hour before she went to sleep—only with him, of all the people in Harrisonburg, could Kosta acknowledge that there was another world somewhere, a whole connected chain of other worlds, where she lived and struggled and earned her living.

Her father's curiosity was infinite. He was concerned and courageous and angrily political. He read three newspapers every day and subscribed to half a dozen journals that dealt with serious issues. But everything he read and mulled over was abstract and tentative in his mind till he'd had a chance to dissect and confirm it with his daughter.

Her firsthand details solidified his conclusions. When she rejected a theorem and told him why, he also rejected it. In their late-night, half-the-night explorations of politics, economics, and government evils, he devoured her, drained her, reveled in the intoxication of the moment, the child instructing the man. *His* child. His fearless and recklessly headlong daughter. Snake charmer and dragon slayer. When someone said to him, "How about that girl of yours? When's she going to bring you home a couple of grandchildren?" he flashed back, "Who cares? When she's ready, I guess. Now she has more important things to do. Now she's hunting tigers with a slingshot."

Also, when she was at home, when she could get up the courage, she borrowed her father's car and drove fifteen miles south to the national park in the foothills of Big Flat Mountain. Sometimes she couldn't make herself get out of the car once she got there. She sat behind the wheel, chilled and shivering, her eyes closed, her hands clenched in tight fists. Other times she forced herself, got out of the car, and climbed the trail to the hideous clearing she couldn't forget.

When she was in Washington, or in Harrisonburg, or anywhere other than that spot, she told herself it had to be faced and stared down, the place itself. It had to be seen fresh, not as a nightmare, not as a haunting ugly memory to make her flesh chill and her stomach turn over. It had to be looked at, in full light, reassessed and evaluated, properly defined. She could not let it continue to do what it had done to her, that place, that long-ago experience, for so many years. She had to conquer it.

But each time she stood in that clearing, sunshine patterns on the grass and the mountain wind ruffling her hair, when she was able to force herself to stay for a few seconds before she turned and ran back down the path, all she could feel was black nausea, a sharp, twisting pain between her legs, and a cold animal fear that made her tremble.

Frightened as she was, however, she persisted. Almost every time she came to Harrisonburg, she forced herself to drive those fifteen miles, climb that forest trail, and stand, for as long as she could, on that spot where she'd stood all those years ago. It was a mindless, primitive act; she despised herself for continuing to do it, for tormenting herself, for bringing back the pain. But she was determined to heal the wound, and she knew no other way.

This time, however, she did not go to the park and climb the trail. She made a specific decision *not* to go. She believed that this decision had nothing whatsoever to do with Gabe Treptow. As her father drove her to the Harrisonburg airport to catch her Washington plane, she told herself, Of course it doesn't. I mean, *that* doesn't make any sense at all. But she wasn't convinced.

As they turned into the airport parking lot, a weathered light-blue camper pulled in behind them, a young, red-haired woman at the wheel.

"Did you see that camper?" Kosta said. "The blue one with North Carolina plates?"

"Didn't notice. What about it?" her father said.

"I'd swear I saw it here at the airport when I came in."

"You probably did. There's a lot of traffic here. People come and go. Must be close to a hundred people that work here full-time."

"You didn't see that same camper on the road behind us when we drove home from the airport?"

"Not that I remember. You're just getting jumpy because you're heading back to Washington. The adrenaline's flowing."

She leaned over and kissed his cheek. "You know something? I think you're right."

 On her flight from Chicago to Los Angeles, Helen sat tilted back in her seat, eyes closed, for more than an hour, feigning sleep, putting up a silent barrier between herself and the stewardesses, between herself and anyone who might want to talk, to pull aside the wrappings, to puncture the protective film she needed just now.

Finally she opened her eyes, rang for the attendant, and asked for a cup of coffee and a pad of writing paper. After she finished the coffee, she uncapped her pen and began to write.

Dear Gabe:

God, what imperfect, stumbling boobs we are. Me more than thee, my darling. Me more than most people, I suspect. Here I sit, beginning a letter to you I know I will never mail. But driven to do it. Absolutely convinced that I must try to tell you now all the things I didn't manage to say over the past five years. Even though I know it's pointless, useless, self-serving, and too late.

Thank God you're an intelligent man who knows how to

see and smell and taste. Somebody who likes to touch and be touched. I can't imagine what it would be like to live with someone who was dense, someone who missed the point. Can you imagine sitting across the table year after year, talking to some clod and knowing from the expression in its eyes that it wasn't quite sure what you were saying? Trying all the time. Listening and smiling and nodding its head, but never for one moment really getting it.

Why am I off on this tangent? Only because I know as I write, no matter what I write, that if you were going to read it, if I were going to send it, if you were to be allowed to read it, you would understand what I'm saying as sparkling clear as if you had written it yourself. That's the best gift of all, isn't it, if you have that with someone. I met a Roumanian woman when I was in London a few months ago, in her forties, I suppose, handsome and elegant and no nonsense, a sculptor, and she said to a group of people at dinner, one of whom had proposed introducing her to a wealthy banker, "What would I do with him? What would we say? Do you think I would ever take off my clothes for a banker? Or sleep in his bed? I am an artist. I have always been an artist. Art is all I know about. All I care about. I have lived with five men in my life. All of them were artists. They work with tools and brushes. They make objects. They have hands and eyes. They can see. No woman who has lived in such a world will settle for something else. Not if she can help it. If I can't live with an artist I'd rather live by myself."

What does that have to do with you and me? Nothing, I guess. Or everything. In a different way I am trying to say what she was saying.

When I was too young to know anything at all about men and women and love and heartbreak but old enough to be curious I read in some odd little book, seventeenth century probably, that no two people are ever equally in love. One person always loves more than the other. I was depressed for days. I realized I loved my mother a great deal more than she loved me. And I knew that my father loved me blindly and totally in a way I could never match.

But I imagined that romantic love was another thing alto-gether, that the passion on each side was scientifically bal-anced. Otherwise it wasn't love at all.

I learned quickly. I saw the evidence all around me. And I accepted it. But I didn't understand it at all. When I was married to Jess, crying and suffering and feeling put upon and sinned against, I felt it was obvious to the world, at least to the city of Cambridge, that they were witnessing the case of a woman who loved with all her being someone who didn't care much at all for her. Now I see that I was in love with the notion of myself in love, painful and unrequited love. I was being noble. And I was very much enjoying the spectacle of my being noble. But when the spectacle ceased to fascinate me, I felt free to pack up my heart and leave. As it happened, Jess beat me to it, but not for the reasons I thought. He loved me enough to make him wrench his whole life apart and try to put it together again. He couldn't do it but he tried.

And what about us? God knows. I can't flap my wings and cackle that no woman could ever love you more than I did, more than I do. Right now I'm unable to boast about anything. You know without my telling you what kind of opinion I have of myself these days. But this much I'm sure of. However much I gave you, or little maybe, perhaps in your eyes, now that all the skeletons have danced out of the closet, it wasn't much at all; but whatever it was, it was my entire supply. I feel hollow and empty and burned-out now. I'm not being poetic. I'm trying sincerely to describe a real condition, a physical hangover, a state of mind, that is totally new to me. Foreign soil. Strange territory. It's not a question of pain. I'm not looking for sympathy from you or from myself. It's just like I say. The furniture has all been moved out, the power's turned off, and the lights don't work.

I'm sure I'll stumble around somewhere till I'm ninety years old, the women in my family live forever, and I'm not going to be miserable, not if I can help it, but I know, as sure as tomorrow, that the good stuff's over. I left too much of myself in Fort Beck, too many people I loved, too many years. Too many crazy nights with you, my love. Too much laughing. And too much crying when it all fizzled out.

I warned you this would be a self-indulgent letter. And it is of course. It's all about me, what I think, how I feel. But that's all I know right now. It's all I'm sure of. One other thing. The real reason I came to Fort Beck, the reason I had to see you, was because I couldn't make it be over. The divorce and being away from you didn't help. Maybe it sounds crazy, but it had to be good again, just once, before I could let go. I had to see you without the hurt and the confusion, I had to be naked with you with everything else forgotten or shut out. I had to hear you laugh and see you sleeping.

Now I can give you up. It kills me but I can do it. Now I can disappear and leave you alone and give you a chance to stitch everything together again. That's a promise. You don't know it but I know it. That's the important thing. And I mean it. Sleep warm.

On his flight to Washington later that same afternoon, Gabe had three drinks and read half a mystery novel. He wrote no letters to Helen or to himself. But he knew, as clearly as she did, that it was over. Because it had to be. Because there was no other answer.

"It didn't really surprise me," Kosta said. "I knew I was getting some hot material. Not one big head-line. But a lot of little things starting to stick to-gether. So when they arrested me and took me in I was tickled to death. It showed me somebody was watching.

I knew they were trying to send me a message—'Drop it. Buzz off. Get out of town.'

"If you're a man they try to discredit you by saying you're a homosexual or a womanizer or you hang out with Communists a lot. If you're a woman they get you booked someplace on a vice charge. Or they do the Jean Seberg thing. They circulate stories that you're screwing a Navajo Indian. Or an evangelist. Or a Socialist.

"It's all done to discredit you. So if you come up with something later on they can say, 'Who listens to a hooker?' It's amateur night but sometimes it works. They *do* scare people off. They really influence a certain percentage of dimwits. I've actually heard people say they stopped paying attention to Martin Luther King when they heard rumors he had a girl friend or two on the side."

They were sitting in a small restaurant, La Belle Jeunesse, on a street in Georgetown just off Wisconsin Avenue, Kosta and Gabe. Each of them had returned to Washington the night before, she from Harrisonburg and he from Fort Beck.

"What do you think?" she said then.

"I'm not sure. You've thrown a lot of stuff at me in the last hour. Let's try to stick it all together."

"Good," she said. "Number one. Three witnesses said they saw the SAI plane explode in midair before it crashed outside Indianapolis. Before the final investigation was finished, two of them had changed their stories and the other one had gone off to the funny farm. Also . . . the two who turned around suddenly became very rich. Ellen Perigo got a government pension that had been held up for years, plus all back payments, *and* a whopping settlement from a strip-mining company in Pennsylvania that had wrecked her house. Just a coincidence? Maybe."

"What about the farmer? Buck—is that his name?"

"That's right. Avery Buck. He got lucky too. Sold his pig farm for a bundle and ran off to live the good life either in Arizona or New Mexico, depending on who you listen to."

"How does that fit in?"

"It didn't. Not at first. It seemed odd to me that he suddenly sold his place just after he'd changed his tune about the plane crash. But that could happen. The thing that snagged me was this—he sold it for four times what it was worth. He had a hundred and ten acres, most of it hilly and *all* of it rocky. He'd made some money through the years, but only by raising hogs. The land itself wasn't worth zilch. And the heavier the airport traffic got the less it was worth. This is what two real estate men in that area told me. They said nobody would want that property if they couldn't rezone and subdivide. And even then it would be a risk, because not many people want to buy a home on the edge of an airport."

"So who bought it?"

"A company called Agronomy Research from Lafayette, Indiana. They specialize in hybrid grain development. Especially corn. So they bought this rock farm where it's impossible to grow grain crops, a place that neither of the real estate people I talked to thought they could sell for more than two hundred thousand dollars. And do you know what they paid for it? Nine hundred thousand."

"Doesn't add up."

"That's what *I* thought. *But* . . . it turns out that Agronomy Research, Inc., is not an independent company after all. It's totally owned by the United States Department of Agriculture. Operated locally but funded from Washington. Interesting? Damned interesting, I think.

"Now we come back to the mystery guest, Ralph Benedict. Who *was* this turkey? Why did they try to pretend he wasn't on the flight? Why does nobody know anything at all about him? What he looked like, what he did for a living, where he came from? And why was he cremated almost immediately after his name appeared on the passenger list? All good questions. But no answers.

"The cremation wasn't standard procedure. That's for sure. Somebody told the coroner what to do and when to do it. I'm sure that's why he wasn't anxious to sit down and discuss it with me. Not even hello and good-bye. He made himself very scarce till he thought I'd found out the truth and was about to publish it. Then all of a sudden he was anxious to find out what I knew."

"Did you talk to him finally?"

She shook her head. "No point. I knew he wouldn't tell me

anything. And I *couldn't* tell him anything. I ran a bluff to see if he'd respond and he did. I just wanted to find out if he's nervous about Benedict. He *is*. But anything he could tell us I think we'll pick up someplace else. I have a strong hunch already who gave the cremation order.

"You remember what I told you about my friend Dick McCann, how he got a cushy job with HEW just when he was starting to get curious about the SAI crash? Well, the man who contacted him said his name was John Fenton, an HEW official here in Washington. I checked him out. No such animal at HEW. But a funny thing happened. Everytime John Fenton's name went into the computer, the name Oscar Tunstall came out."

"Wasn't there a guy named Tunstall . . . ?"

"Right! Watergate," Kosta said. "That's what my friend reminded me of. Justice Department. He's been there a long time. He was a friend of Hoover, it turns out. Helped J. Edgar out a lot. Since he wasn't exactly in the Bureau, he wasn't hung up by any of the rules. When the Martin Luther King assassination committee was taking testimony about the FBI surveillance and harassment of King, Tunstall's name kept bobbing up. But he was never called to testify. During the Senate investigations of Watergate, at least half a dozen people, both witnesses and defendants, made some reference to Tunstall. But again he wasn't called. I talked to Naomi Guterman last night. She covers Washington for *The Village Voice*. And she gave me a real earful about Tunstall."

The waiter came then and poured what was left of the wine into their glasses.

"More vino?" Gabe said.

"Not me. Espresso."

"Two espresso," he said to the waiter.

"Tunstall is what they call in this town a 'manager.' Presidents come and go, administrations change, people lose their jobs or get reassigned, but these cats are always around. Sometimes they stay in one department for thirty years. Sometimes they're moved around. Their names never get into the papers. They don't make a great deal of money. Not officially, at least.

But the guys in the hot jobs, the key senators, the cabinet secretaries, the presidential advisors, all know who they are and how to locate them."

The coffee came then. When the waiter left, Gabe said, "So where exactly does Tunstall fit in?"

"It's hard to say. We're not far enough along. The big news is that he's involved at all. Because he doesn't do janitor work. They save him for the big games. Naomi says they only have three photographs of him. One picture with Sam Giancano, the Chicago mob guy who was shot to death before he could testify about some CIA attempts to assassinate Castro. Another picture on a boat in Florida with Howard Hughes, and a third one with Nixon when he made his last trip to China."

"Fast company."

"That's what I mean. That's why they call him a manager. When things have to be arranged, or rearranged, when a special kind of mechanic is needed, Tunstall seems to turn up. If he's really involved in this H-14 thing, then you can bet there's a big hunk of the iceberg that's still below the surface. There's something sticky that somebody doesn't want to see on the seven o'clock news. I'd bet money on it."

 When they walked back to her apartment from the restaurant and climbed the outside staircase to the walkway leading to her entrance, they found the door standing half-open.

"Act two, scene two," she said. She reached in, switched on the living room light, and they walked in.

"Jesus," Gabe said. "Somebody demolished this place."

"That's right. Right on schedule. First the hooker routine.

Now the break-in. Next shot the VD people will show up and tell me that three different derelicts have identified me as the lady who gave them syphilis."

"Where's your phone? I'll call the police."

She shook her head. "It's a wasted dime. Two cops will stroll in and make a list of what I lost. And that will be the end of it. Then a couple of months from now they'll find my briefcase and bring it back. Banged up and empty."

"You mean this has happened before?"

"This makes eleven times in the last five years," she said. "I predict an even dozen before the summer's over." She walked to the hall closet and opened the door. Everything had been pulled off the shelves, stripped off the hangers, and dumped in a heap on the closet floor. "Up there on the second shelf, behind the extra bath towels, is where I hide my briefcase. I always put it in the same place to make sure they find it. Once it was in my blanket chest in the bedroom and they missed it. It was a drag because they came back and wrecked the place again two days later.

"Since then I always make sure it's here in the closet. I keep some clippings from the Chicago Seven trial in it, a map of the Ho Chi Minh trail, and some copies of *The Daily Worker* and *Screw* magazine. Just so the goons will have something interesting to look at. Anything I really want to hide or hang on to, I keep in my car. Wait here a second. I'll be right back. Make me a drink."

In a few minutes she came back to the apartment, carrying a thick manila envelope. "The bastards are getting smart," she said. "They broke into my car too." She held the envelope up over her head. "But they missed the crown jewels."

"Where'd you have that?"

"I've got a Volkswagen bug. The trunk's in the front. They pried that open. Then they got into the car and broke open the glove compartment. But I had this stashed in a special place. In back with the engine. Where's my drink?"

"In the kitchen."

"Good. Let's sit back there. That's the only place that doesn't look violated."

"I know what you're thinking," she said, when they were

sitting across from each other at the kitchen table. "You're saying to yourself, 'Okay, the crash in Indianapolis is starting to look fishy as hell. But what about the Air Force jet that went down in West Virginia?' Am I right?"

"Right."

"It's a rough one. I admit it. Like I told you, I'm only riding a hunch. That plane dived thirty thousand feet, like a missile, right into the ground. And *nobody* saw it happen. That's the ball breaker. No conflicting reports like they had in Indianapolis. No reports at all. At least that's what everybody thought. That's what *I* thought."

She opened the fasteners on the big envelope and took out a dozen eleven-by-fourteen pages. Five or six of them she spread on the table in front of Gabe. "These pictures were made by an eight-year-old kid who lives on a farm outside of Elkins. His name is Arvid Pritchett. He's a mute. Stone deaf since birth. Not able to make any sounds at all. It's as if he had no vocal cords. No voice box. He laughs and cries like anyone else but you'd never know it if you weren't *watching* him.

"He can point and wave his arms, primitive things like that. Otherwise his only way of communicating is through his artwork. As you can see, each one of these pictures he did tells a story. Here's his great-grandmother in the chicken house collecting eggs from the hens' nests, his great-grandfather loading baskets of vegetables into a truck. Here's a pig being butchered. And cows in their stalls waiting to be milked.

"And here are a couple pictures of airplanes. They say he's crazy about airplanes. Always has been. Copies them from photographs or from commercials he sees on television. Or he makes up new airplane designs in his head and paints pictures of those.

"They told me he spends hours out in the fields or the woods, staring up at the sky, watching for planes. Apparently there are some Pittsburgh flights that fly over Elkins. And a few D.C. or Baltimore flights from Cleveland or Chicago. So he watches for those. He must have had fifty or sixty pictures like these two. Different colors and markings, different designs. But each one a low-angle picture of a big jet in flight."

She picked the pictures up from the table and put them to

one side, leaving just the two airplane pictures. From the envelope she took out four more bright-colored crayon pictures and spread them on the table.

"Then all of a sudden the pictures changed," she said. "For the past six months, all the airplane pictures that kid has made, dozens of them, look like these."

Gabe studied the pictures closely. One showed a plane in flight with its wing almost obscured by a great orange-and-yellow explosion. Two other pictures showed the same plane diving toward the ground, twisting and burning, trailing a funnel of black smoke. The fourth picture showed the instant of impact, trees and purple hills in the background, the airplane exploding like a fire bomb, pieces of debris raining down around the edges of the crash scene.

"All the planes he draws and paints now are exploding in midair, burning, and crashing," Kosta said. "And it's always the same plane. Always with Air Force markings."

She reached out and turned one of the pictures over, pointed to a date neatly written on the back. "Mrs. Pritchett writes the dates on his pictures. She has since he started making them when he was five years old. He brings them to her as soon as he's finished and she marks·the date on the back. I looked at all the pictures he's done of exploding airplanes, checked all the dates. The very first one I could find, and the first one his great-grandmother remembers him making, was dated January 17, 1980. Do you remember when your brother's plane went down?"

"January 16."

"That's right. It crashed on the Pritchett's farm. And *I* say there was a witness. I think that little boy saw it all."

59 Two days later Gabe held a press conference. Kosta sat beside his desk while he talked to the reporters.

"As all of you know, I'm sitting in this chair because my brother was killed last January in an airplane crash. I'm sure you followed the FAA and NTSB investigations of that accident as closely as I did. Their conclusions were that the crash that day was caused by a failure of the plane's hydraulic system.

"The SAI crash in Indianapolis ten days before was also caused, they said, by hydraulic failure. The planes in question were H-14's. Their manufacturer, Hartwig Systems, accepted responsibility for both crashes, and as far as I know, no one since has questioned the FAA conclusions.

"I *do* question them. That is the purpose of this press conference. This morning I sent letters to Ernest Mossler of the Federal Aviation Administration and Arthur Slayback, chairman of the National Transportation Safety Board, urging them to reopen their investigation of both these crashes.

"I have also contacted Senator Underhill, chairman of the Commerce Subcommittee for Aviation, suggesting that his group involve themselves in these matters. And later today, I will meet with officials of the Justice Department in an attempt to persuade them to cooperate fully with me and my people."

Sally Pfrommer of *The Chicago Sun-Times* asked, "Can you tell us what prompted you to reopen these investigations? Can you be specific?"

"Yes, I can. I have reason to believe there is a connection between the two accidents. I do not believe that all the pertinent information and evidence was released to the public. I do not, in fact, think they *were* accidents. I believe explosives were planted on both these planes, that they exploded in flight and crashed."

There was a moment of silence in the room. Then Norman Endicott of the *Cleveland Plain Dealer* said, "Are you saying that the FAA concealed evidence?"

"I may say that later, but I'm not saying it now. At this moment I'm simply saying there should have been further investigation before the final conclusions were reached."

Sally Pfrommer again. "Are you saying the FAA did not know there were midair explosions in both cases? Or are you saying they knew and chose not to divulge it?"

"I'm saying that one of those two statements is true. Which one I don't know. I prefer to believe that the FAA acted in good faith. Unless new evidence proves otherwise."

"What if they reject your midair explosion theory? What if they refuse to reopen the investigations?"

"As I said, I have also called on both the Commerce and Justice departments for support."

"What if they turn you down?"

Gabe grinned. "Then I'll yell a lot. I may accuse them of conspiring to deprive me of my civil rights. Then I will exercise my prerogatives as a member of the Senate and a citizen of the United States and move ahead with the investigation myself. Miss Kosta here, whom many of you know, has just joined me. She will continue these H-14 investigations with the assistance of my staff. That includes me. If we get no cooperation from other agencies in government, then I will be as active as I can in supporting Miss Kosta's efforts."

Irving Wiggs of the Associated Press said, "Forgive me, Senator, but aren't you afraid you'll be accused of fostering a kind of vigilante justice? Do you feel this kind of investigation is the proper function for a senator and his staff?"

"*Yes,* I think I'll be accused of all kinds of things," Gabe said. "And *yes,* I think this investigation is a proper function for *somebody.* I will take it on only if nobody else is willing to."

The press conference took place on a Wednesday. By Friday, spokesmen for both the FAA and the NTSB had replied to

Senator Treptow's invitation to reopen their investigations.

"All the evidence has been reviewed and we are convinced that our previous conclusions were correct," Ernest Mossler said. "All the concerned parties agree. The Air Force, Simison Air International, the commercial carrier involved, the investigative branches of both FAA and NTSB, and Hartwig Systems, the people who manufacture the H-14. With all due respect to Senator Treptow, we feel no purpose would be served by reopening these investigations."

Senator Underhill, of the Commerce Subcommittee on Aviation, said, "We have no reason to question the FAA conclusions."

A spokesman for the Justice Department said, "We have no public comment to make. We believe all decisions in these matters rest with the FAA and the NTSB."

Friday afternoon, Gabe's office sent out the following press release:

As a first step in our citizen's investigation of the H-14 airline lost January 6 in Indianapolis and of the subsequent crash of Air Force Three in West Virginia, we propose to interview the following concerned persons.

1. *Avery Buck.* Formerly of Marion County, Indiana. Present address unknown. Mr. Buck was an eyewitness to the Indianapolis crash.

2. *Ellen Perigo.* Formerly of Marion County, now a resident of Gosport, in Morgan County. Mrs. Perigo was also an eyewitness to the SAI crash.

3. *Dr. Evan Causey,* Indianapolis resident and personal physician to Arloa Anderson. Miss Anderson, too, was a witness to the above crash.

4. *Dr. Hugh Springer,* coroner, Marion County.

5. *Lt. Bailey Magnuson,* Indianapolis Police Department.

6. *Richard McCann,* former editor and publisher, *The Belated Truth.* Currently employed by HEW, Indianapolis regional office.

7. *Leo Hartwig,* former chairman of the board, Hartwig Systems. Present address: Watsonville, California.

8. *Roland Casper,* vice-president Peddicord Industries, acting president, Hartwig Systems.

9. *Preston Mavity,* vice-president public affairs, Simison Air International.

10. *Major General Craig Stecko,* United States Air Force. Commander, special flight operations.

. 11. *Ernest Mossler,* chief administrator, FAA.

12. *Wesley Duggan,* special investigator, FAA.

13. *Arthur Slayback,* chairman, National Travel Safety Board.

14. *Oscar Tunstall,* employee, Justice Department.

This witness list did not appear in the *Washington Post.* And in the *Star* it was buried in the third section, just next to an article listing ways to divert preschool children on rainy weekends.

The following Monday, however, Arthur Garrigus printed the press release, word for word, in his column. As soon as she read it, Kosta called Gabe at home.

"He printed the whole bloody thing. Either we're smart or we're lucky."

"Smart," Gabe said.

"I'm not so sure. We'll never get near any of those people now."

"Yes we will. Or maybe we won't have to. I have a hunch my phones are going to start to ring. I think people are going to start coming to us."

"Is that good or bad?"

"Don't worry. You're a senator's assistant. That's why I included you in that press conference. They'll think twice about hassling you now."

"They may think twice," she said. "But that doesn't mean they won't do it."

That afternoon the telephone in her apartment went dead. When she called the office they told her the bill hadn't been paid. She went in and showed them the canceled checks. They apologized and said there'd been a mistake. Service would start again immediately.

But it didn't. Not till Nona Sugarman called the executive offices of the telephone company and lodged a formal complaint on behalf of Senator Treptow.

That evening, Kosta's phone was working again. But every time she put the receiver to her ear, she heard a faint, muffled click.

 "Jesus Christ," Dalrymple said. "What is this guy up to? We thought we had him surrounded and suddenly he's on the front page."

"No he's not. The Garrigus column is a long way from the front page. Treptow's guessing. He's bluffing," Lasker said.

Dalrymple picked up a clipping from his desk. "Damned good guessing if you ask me. I look at this list of names and it scares hell out of me."

"I don't like it any better than you do. But we have to be careful not to overreact and make it bigger than it is. I think we have to stay loose, put some pressure on the media to stay away from Treptow, and then wait for him to run out of gas. He can huff and puff all he wants to but he won't find out anything."

"He won't, huh? What about this list? He may not know *what* but he's got a pretty good handle on *who*." He held up the clipping. "You think some of these people couldn't give him an earful?"

"They won't talk to him. And even if they do, even if *all* of them do, none of them knows the bottom line."

"They *don't?* What about Tunstall?"

"Treptow can't get to him," Lasker said. "And what if he did? Tunstall *invented* stonewalling. He wouldn't spill anything if you set his ass on fire."

"I wish I had your confidence. I wish the Secretary and Joe Newquist were as calm and fucking collected as you are. They're pissing blue. The Secretary has called *me* six times today. Joe Newquist has called me every twenty minutes. And always the same question—'How do we defuse this asshole?' "

"I was on the phone with Tunstall for two hours last night. He's got twenty ideas. We're not sitting on our hands."

"You already found out that Kosta doesn't scare easily. I don't think Treptow will either."

"Maybe he won't. If he doesn't we'll have to talk to him!"

"Talk to him? He's not stupid, for Christ's sake. What are you planning to say?"

"Give him the warm oil. Tell him we're taking him in on some top-level stuff."

"Then what?"

"We tell him the only reason we didn't level about the H-14 crashes was because we couldn't," Lasker said. "We give him an international scenario. For his ears only. Something to do with Latin America. The nonaligned nations. Venezuela maybe. Big threats of a takeover there. Somebody is about to fuck up the oil fields. Castro maybe. The scarier the better."

"How do we tie that into the H-14 business?"

"Ahh . . . that's the wienie. That's the part we can't come forth on. National security. Maybe we imply that there were hijackers on board. If he wants to think that hijackers blew up the planes, *let* him. He's not wacky enough to release *that* to the papers, is he? Not if we come on strong enough with the national security number. Threat of war with Mexico. Big oil cutoffs. We just have to give it all the muscle we can. Bring the Secretary into the meeting."

"Are you kidding?"

"We could clinch it if he sat in."

"Not a chance."

"What about Newquist?"

Dalrymple shook his head. "Not him either. Don't let that baby face fool you. Newquist knew more about survival when he was eight years old than we'll know when we're sixty. You're not about to make an accomplice out of him. That guy has made a profession out of *disappearing*. He only shows up after the race is over and the results are posted. If you win he was with you all the way. If you lose he doesn't know you. His secret is he only gives the President good news. If there's any catastrophe to be announced, somebody else ends up with the trumpet. That's why he invented those migraine headaches. When he thinks the shit is about to hit the fan, he gets a terminal headache and disappears in the wilds of Alexandria."

"All right. So we go it alone. We'll talk to Treptow ourselves."

"Then what? What if he tells you to crap in your hat?"

"He won't. Not if we present it right."

"What if he *does*?" Dalrymple said.

"If worse comes to worst, we tell him the truth."

"The *real* truth?"

"Why not? If he manages to dig it out by himself it's a cinch he'll blow it to the world. But if we confide in him, if we *tell* him, that would be something else. The man's not stupid. This really *is* a question of national security. He'll *see* that. I mean, he's not going to put the country in a bind just to prove a point, is he?"

"You wouldn't think so. But we can't forget one important thing."

"What's that?"

"His brother was on one of those planes."

"There's only one reason I can think of to blow up a passenger plane. To kill the people. Either all of them or *one* of them. Could be personal. Could be political. Or it could be money. If they'd both been SAI planes," Gabe said, "you could say that somebody was mad at the airline. Another airline maybe. Or an ex-employee who got fired and wants to get even. Two SAI planes go down in ten days and a lot of people get nervous. They change their reservations to TWA or United. So SAI loses prestige, customers, and a lot of money.

"Same kind of thing with Air Force Three. Somebody wants to get back at the government. Or strike a blow for Puerto Rican independence. Or some wack wants to get even with an Air Force captain who raped his sister in 1953. All kinds of reasons to go after the Air Force. Could be plain old terrorism. No motive at all except to disrupt things, wreck something, scare the shit out of people. Are you with me?"

"Keep going," Kosta said.

"The only trouble is, none of this works for us. Our theory is that there's a *connection* between the two planes, that the bomb on one had something to do with the bomb on the other one. If that's true, then the airline wasn't the target. And neither was the Air Force. So we're back where we started—*somebody*, some *person*, was the target."

"Or a group."

"All right. If we assume that one person or one group planted both bombs, then we can assume that an opposition group or an individual was the target. Maybe they were after the same person both times. They missed him on the SAI plane so they tried for him on Air Force Three. And they either got him or they didn't. Depending on a lot of things we don't know yet."

"I like the group idea," Kosta said. "I think the target on the SAI flight was Ralph Benedict."

"And somebody connected with him was the target on Air Force Three?"

"Makes sense."

Gabe shook his head. "It *might* make sense if we knew more about Ralph Benedict. Or if we knew *less* about the passengers and crew on Air Force Three. We've got those people cold. Chet and Evelyn and Sam. A couple of Air Force officers and their families. And a few high-level government people going home for vacations. Fourteen passengers. With all the facts laid out plain. From blood type to dental charts to date of baptism. Same with the crew. Not a kink or a secret in the whole plane-load. We've examined the fact sheets with a magnifying glass."

"Have you ever thought that your brother could have been the target?"

"I think about it all the time. I've gone over everything that was on Chet's desk when he was killed. His calendar and past agenda, appointment books, notes on all the legislation he was involved with. And all I can say is, I can't find any question marks there. Neither can Jud or Matlock. No new names or phone numbers. No mysterious notations. Just straight business stuff. Everything out in the open. Not even any stubborn legislative stands indicated, something that could have offended a special interest group. Or some nut. Nothing like that as far as I can see."

"What was the last notation on his calendar?"

"He didn't come into the office that last day. But sometime before, he'd written on that calendar page: 'Air Force Three to Chicago. With Evelyn and Sam. Andrews Air Force Base. One P.M.' "

"Was that it?"

"Just about. Underneath he'd written, 'Dog meat and sheep's eyes. Ha-ha. Full creative and culinary credit to Evelyn.' "

"What did that mean?" Kosta asked.

"I asked Jud and Nona. They didn't know."

"Nothing else?"

"Nothing."

"So we're back to Ralph Benedict," Kosta said. "Only how do you track somebody who used a fake name? And maybe used it only once? The only link is his airline ticket. If he walked up to the counter and paid cash for it, we're dead. If he paid with a credit card or bought it through a travel agent, maybe we can dig up something."

"What if you find out he missed the SAI flight in Indianapolis and took a later plane? What if you find out the real Ralph Benedict is running a flower shop in Colorado Springs?"

"Then I'll sell my Volkswagen and what's left of my grandmother's furniture and go for a long vacation in Greece."

 That night at nine thirty, Gabe's secretary called him at home. "It's Monica. I'm sorry to bother you, but I . . . well, I thought I should talk to you and I didn't want to do it at the office."

"What's the problem?"

"I'm not sure. But there are some things going on and I thought you should know about them."

She lived all the way east across the city, five miles from Georgetown. They met at a central point, an all-night bar called Jimbo's not far from the railroad station. She was already there when he came in, wearing black jeans and a cotton bush jacket over a plaid cowboy shirt. "Sorry about my outfit," she said. "I just came as I was. These are my Minnesota clothes. When I go home I don't wear a dress for weeks at a time."

She was drinking white wine. He ordered a second glass for her and a bottle of beer for himself. "I felt like a jackass," she said, "calling you at home. But I've been trying to figure out what to do for over a week."

She sipped some wine, set her glass down and said, "I hope you won't think I'm some kind of a troublemaker. I mean, I've worked in quite a few offices and I've seen some strange goings-on, but I've never had the urge to run to the boss before."

"Nobody's going to know we're having this talk, if that's what you're concerned about."

"I'm *not* concerned about that. I just don't want you to think I'm a nervous dumbo jumping at shadows. I can't show you copies of memos or prove to you that thirty dollars are missing from the petty cash box. All I know, what I'm trying to say, is there's a feeling in that office I don't like. It makes me uncomfortable. I get the heebie-jeebies every day now when I come in and sit down at my desk."

"What kind of a feeling are you talking about?"

"It's not my imagination. I've worked for two senators before and Charles Hammer when he was in the House. I know all about staff work. I know how a staff is supposed to function. And the thing I know best is that they're supposed to *support* the man they're working for. Back him up. When they *don't* do that, a lot of scary situations develop. First thing you know it's like a basketball game where two or three guys on one team are deliberately missing free throws. Am I making any sense?"

"Yes. But I'm not surprised."

"You're not?"

He shook his head. "Most of the staff worked for my brother. They all worked well together. I knew they'd be measuring me against him. That's the risk I ran when I decided to keep his people."

"That's not it," she said. "This is something different, the thing I'm talking about. It's an atmosphere of . . . I guess the word sounds silly in this context . . . but it's almost like *sabotage*. I've felt it for several weeks now. Something weird and negative. As if the staff, *some* of them, are not working *for* you. They're working *against* you. It's something—I can't explain it beyond that. It's like they're getting paid by you, but taking orders from somebody else."

The next day Gabe had a meeting with Jud and Dave Matlock.

"Ever since I walked in here with Kosta and told you guys and the staff about the H-14 thing, there's been a change of climate in this office."

"Better or worse?" Jud said.

"Worse. Lousy. What's going on?"

It was late afternoon. Very late. Most of the staff had gone home. Only Nona Sugarman and Monica Cullen were still working in the outside office.

"I wouldn't call it a change of climate. It's frustration, I think. And quite a bit of confusion," Jud said.

"Who's confused? Are *you* confused, Dave?"

"Don't get me wrong, Gabe. I'm here to help you in any way I can. But . . . "

"But what?"

"We've got a good staff, Gabe," Jud said. "They're all hard workers and they know their jobs. They were loyal to Chet and they're loyal to you. But . . . "

"But *what?*"

"You asked what's wrong so I'm telling you the truth. They can't *function*. Their whole work procedure has broken down. Their network of contacts, the people they've cultivated to help them get things done, *all* that has come apart."

"Basenfelder's people, Bright's people, Isbell's people, and most of the other staff advisors have cut us off," Matlock said. "We have to read the papers now to find out what's going on in our own building. You understand what I'm saying?"

Gabe nodded his head. "Keep talking."

Matlock went on. "I'm saying the professionals around here don't trust us anymore. The people who make the wheels move are looking the other way. They don't copy us on their programs and proposals and they don't return our phone calls."

"Dave is floating around out there like a zombie. He's a *whip*, Gabe. He's damned good at what he does. But all of a sudden he can't produce. It's like somebody tacked a quarantine sign on our office door."

"What do you suggest we do, Dave?"

"It's not up to me," Matlock said.

"Sure it is," Gabe said. "You and Jud must have discussed the situation. What do you think?"

Matlock looked uneasy. "Nobody expected you to be a carbon copy of Chet. Anybody who did would have changed his mind as soon as he heard you talk. We all knew you weren't going to come to Washington with your tail between your legs and kiss every available ass in the Senate cloakroom."

"You never deceived anybody about what you were after," Jud said. "You wanted to try something new. To cut through the double-talk and say what you meant, not what somebody *wanted* you to mean. Nobody questioned your honesty or your intentions, Gabe, and nobody questions them now. At least *I* don't. But the problem is—"

"The problem is it won't work," Gabe said. "The problem is that the odds are ninety-nine to one against me. Ninety-nine senators on one side of the hall and me on the other."

"That's right. The odds are rough. But that doesn't mean it *can't* work. I'm not saying that. I'm saying it won't work if we make a frontal assault. The only way we can hope to win this war is if we're willing to lose a few battles. Maybe a lot of battles."

"Compromise," Gabe said.

"I know," Matlock said. "You hate that word. But hating it won't make it go away. It's like the old story of the water glass. Is it half-full or half-empty? The practical definition of compromise is that both sides give up something but both sides also gain something."

"I know that definition. I give up the egg whites if you agree to give up the yolks. So we end up with an omelet without any eggs in it."

"That happens sometimes."

"Not to me. Not if I can avoid it."

"None of us have any quarrel with your principles, Gabe. I think you know that. But if you can't *function* as a senator, as a viable lawmaker, if *we* can't function as a staff, then where's the *profit?*"

"There *is* no fucking profit, Jud. That's the point. I know the rules. And I'm not stupid enough to think I can change them. But I *am* stupid enough to think there are some alternatives. Things that make sense to the people who are as impractical as I am. The pragmatists are always the majority. There's nothing new about that. But that doesn't mean that everybody else has to dry up and blow away. Nobody can convert a professional fool. There are too many even to count. But there are also a lot of people who have their heads screwed on right, people who know they're being dumped on and lied to from the cradle to the grave. Somebody has to tell those people they're not crazy. Somebody has to tell them that things really *are* as bad as they think they are."

The next morning Dave Matlock, three of the other legislative assistants, and Patty Ingledow all turned in their resignations, effective immediately.

 Two days later, Kosta called from New York. "My friend here has been working her computer overtime. But we're not making much progress on Benedict. It's what I was afraid of. No travel agent. No credit card. No traveler's checks. It looks as if he walked into some airline office and paid cash."

"Now what?" Gabe said.

"Not so fast. I didn't tell you the good stuff yet. It seems that Mr. Benedict insured his life before he got on that plane from Indianapolis. Two hundred thousand dollars. And the insurance company paid the claim. We just got the information an hour ago."

"Who collected the money?"

"That we haven't tracked down yet. But I should have the answer by the time I get back from California. Anything happening there?"

"Yeah. Half of my staff quit."

"You're kidding."

"No, I'm not."

"What happened?"

"I'm trying to find out. My guess is that somebody helped them decide."

"That's not a *guess*. That's the *answer*. I guarantee it. The gremlins are busy."

"Other than that I've been putting pressure on Justice, trying to flush out Tunstall. But no luck. So I called the bureau. Talked to a man named Roush. He's supposed to come see me later this week."

"Good. I should have something on Hartwig by then."

"You know anything about a guy named Haikal?" Gabe said then. "Harun Haikal?"

"Iranian?"

"I don't know."

"There was a guy named Haikal who was involved in the embassy takeover in Teheran. First they said he was one of the student leaders. But later he asked for asylum in the United States. So maybe we had him planted there. Why do you ask?"

"He's been trying to see me. Won't say what it's about. I think he's coming in tomorrow."

"Maybe he wants to sell you a rug."

"Maybe. I'll let you know."

"You know me," Gabe said. "I'm not an evangelist in a tent. I'm a practical son of a bitch. And the most practical thing I know is that you have to admit you're at the bottom before you can pull yourself up and try to climb again. The danger is not from guys like me who say everything is turning to shit. It's the utopian assholes we have to look out for, the ones who say everything is just dandy. America the beautiful. Pheasant for breakfast and four cars in every garage."

Jud Rimmer sat stiff in his chair and looked uneasy. "I know how you feel, Gabe. But we still have an operation to run here. We need a staff. When five key people bail out all at once we've got a problem."

"Are you saying they can't be replaced?"

"No, I'm not. We started interviewing yesterday and by sometime next week those jobs should be filled. But there's no way that we'll get people as good as the ones we lost."

"Maybe it doesn't matter," Gabe said. "The way you and Matlock were describing it the other day our operation has ground to a halt anyway."

"That's not true. Dave was giving you the basic picture, but he was exaggerating a bit just to make a point."

"What point was he trying to make? I had the feeling he was leading up to something but he never quite got there."

"I don't know about that. As far as I was concerned—"

"He never discussed the situation with you?" Gabe said.

"When do you mean?"

"Anytime. Before we had our little meeting or afterward."

"He didn't have to," Jud said. "I was aware of what was going on. What his problems were."

"Did he tell you he was going to resign?"

"No."

"Did any of the other people tell you?"

"No," Jud said.

"So you were as surprised as I was when those five resignation letters turned up on my desk."

"I wasn't surprised exactly."

"Why not?" Gabe said. "Either you knew they were going to quit or you didn't know."

"I didn't know."

"You didn't know but you weren't surprised?"

"I don't know what you're getting at, Gabe. Are you accusing me of something?"

"No. I'm trying to get information. You came in here this morning saying we have a problem to solve. I'm trying to solve it. I say it's unusual for five people to quit at one time without notice. To clean out their desks and take off without any discussion or—"

"Matlock explained his situation to you."

"That's right. You both did. And *you* didn't resign. Besides, the tone I picked up from Dave was that of a man trying to solve a problem. It didn't sound like an ultimatum to me. But the next morning he was long gone along with four other people. Is that the way things are done here in Washington?"

"Not as far as I know."

"Do you think those people were getting pressure from someplace outside our office?"

"What kind of pressure?"

"Pressure to do what they did. To quit."

"Why would anybody want them to do that?"

"Lots of reasons. To screw up our operation. To make me look bad. To kick off some kind of whispering campaign that I don't know what the hell I'm doing."

"I don't know about anything like that."

Gabe sat silent for a long moment, looking across his desk at Jud. "All right," he said then, "let me ask you this. When I was in Illinois last week, I heard a rumor that some recall petitions are being passed around out there, that there's a movement starting to get me out of office. Have you heard anything about that?"

"I haven't heard it and I don't believe it."

"No feedback from any of our offices in Illinois?"

"Not a word," Jud said. "Jesus, I wouldn't keep something like that to myself."

"No. I know you wouldn't. Look, I'm sorry if it sounded as if I was questioning your loyalty. I'm not. I know it's put a lot of pressure on you having these people leave. I just want to make sure it doesn't happen again. You can help me there. Just because I'm bullheaded doesn't mean I'm blind. If I've been coming on too strong, I want you to tell me. I know I can't accomplish anything without help. Maybe if I'd pulled back a little in that meeting with Matlock he'd still be working here. What do you think?"

"It's hard to say."

"There's something you're not saying. What is it?"

"It's pointless, Gabe. You don't want to hear it."

"Try me."

"Well . . . you said it yourself. In that last meeting with Matlock. You said that things had started to break down around here from the time you got involved in the H-14 investigation."

"And you're saying I was right about that?"

Jud nodded. "I'm not sure *why* it's true, but it is. Don't misunderstand me. You certainly have a *right* to do it. It's not that. But a lot of people seem to feel you'd be better off spending your time on legislative matters. I think the staff feels that. They think you have your hands full here. They like you, Gabe. They want to help. They don't want to see you make a fool of yourself."

"How do you feel about it?"

"I'm here to back you up no matter what you do."

"That's not what I'm asking you. If I told you I was giving up the H-14 investigation, what would your reaction be?"

"I'd say you'd made a wise decision."

"In other words you would advise me to give it up."

"Yes, I would. No question about it."

After Jud left his office, Gabe sat at his desk, slowly tapping his pencil on the desk top, staring at the opposite wall. Now we know where we stand, he thought. Now a lot of things are starting to make sense.

 Kosta took the night flight from New York to San Francisco. When she arrived it was three in the morning. She rented a car and drove south toward Watsonville, light traffic on the highway, the sun just beginning to edge up above the mountains to the east.

At a highway junction south of Gilroy, she stopped for breakfast at a diner called Goldie's. At six o'clock she went to the pay phone and called Gabe's home number in Georgetown. There was no answer.

After she finished eating she went outside to her car, checked the California road map and a smaller hand-drawn map she took from her purse. Then she drove west toward Watsonville.

It was twenty minutes past seven when she came to the gate in front of Hartwig's house. Forty yards away, up a tree-bordered driveway, she could see the house, all angles, stone and timber and glass, perched on a cliff edge looking out toward the ocean. But across the driveway there was a heavy chain blocking the entrance. And on the gate a sign said the house was for sale. But no real estate office was indicated. And there was no telephone number to call.

Leaving her car outside the gate, Kosta stepped over the chain and walked up the drive toward the house. It looked deserted. All doors and windows were closed, the garage doors down and padlocked, the flowers and shrubs brown and neglected, the parking area beside the house unswept. Scraps of newspaper blew back and forth and a soft-drink can rolled unevenly across the brick paving. From down below on the ocean side she could hear the surf rolling in. And the occasional squawk of a gull. But otherwise no sound. Nothing electronic or mechanical. No sounds of people.

Walking deliberately to the door facing the drive, she rang the bell. But she heard no sound from inside. No buzzing or ringing. No chimes. She knocked then. Firmly. Several times. But there was no answer. She had started to turn away from the door when she heard something. A dog growled. Just once. Then a muffled gruff command. Then silence again.

Back at the front door, Kosta took out her car keys and began to tap, metal against glass, on the panel at the top of the door No one answered. And there was no further sound from inside.

Finally she turned away again and started to walk around the corner of the house. A young man appeared suddenly on the side deck. He was tall and slender. He wore a neat gray suit, a light-blue shirt, and a maroon tie.

"I can't believe it," Kosta said. "I thought maybe this was the home for the deaf."

"If you want to look at the house—"

"I *don't* want to look at the house. I'm a friend of the Hartwigs. I want to see *them.*"

"I'm afraid they're not here."

"What do you mean? This is their house."

"It *was* their house. You saw the sign in front. It's for sale. The Hartwigs decided to sell it."

"But where are they now?" Kosta said.

"I don't know. They may be in San Diego. Or Mexico maybe. They mentioned Guadalajara."

"But you don't have their address?"

"No, I don't."

"Are you the real estate person?" she said.

"No, I'm not."

"Are you a burglar?"

No change of expression on his face. No smile or voice change. "No, I'm not," he said. "I'm just doing the Hartwigs a favor."

"Does that mean you're a house sitter?"

"I guess you could say that."

She turned and looked at the front of the house again, studied it carefully. Then she turned back to the young man. "All right," she said, "here's the way it is. I think you're lying in your teeth. If you can't tell me exactly where I can locate Leo Hartwig I am going to drive to Santa Cruz and tell the police you're holding Mr. and Mrs. Hartwig captive in their own house. How does that grab you? Would you like to relax in jail for a few days?"

"I told you—"

"I know what you told me. And you know what I just told you." She saw a flicker of indecision in his eyes. She turned and started toward her car, but his voice stopped her.

"If you'll wait a minute, I'll go inside and make a call. Maybe the real estate office has an address or a phone number for the Hartwigs." He turned and disappeared around the side of the house. Up in front she heard a sliding door open and close. And a lock snapped.

A few minutes later, the door to the driveway opened suddenly and Oscar Tunstall came out. "I'm sorry," he said to Kosta. "We didn't understand that you're a friend of the Hartwigs. The fact is, my organization has been hired to protect these premises while the Hartwigs are away on a trip. They own some valuable paintings and statuary and . . . you understand . . . an isolated house like this, it's an invitation to a break-in." He held out his hand. "I'm Bob Sheperd. I'm with the Guthridge Security System."

"I'm . . . uh, Melba Miller," Kosta said. Then, ʻYour office must know how I can contact the Hartwigs."

"Of course they do. If you'll tell me where I can reach you, I'll check with San Francisco, the office there will get in touch with the Hartwigs, and I'm sure you'll hear from them within a few hours."

"I'll be staying at the . . . what's that motel just this side of Watsonville?"

"The Santa Rosa."

"That's it. Tell the Hartwigs they can reach me there."

She walked down the drive toward her car then, till she heard the house door close behind her. Then she turned left and walked a hundred yards along the road. Angling toward the ocean, she crossed an overgrown, sandy field, found a steep footpath leading to the beach, and followed it all the way down to the edge of the water, carrying her shoes in her hand. Turning south then, she followed the beach till she came to a spot just below the Hartwig house.

Looking up, she studied the decks and windows for some sign of life. There wasn't any. But barely visible behind the railing on the house's highest deck, a pair of panty hose were stretched out to dry. And a woman's blouse flapped gently in the warm air blowing off the ocean.

As soon as she arrived in Watsonville, Kosta parked her car and found the local office for the Northern California Telephone Company. A gray-haired woman with a young face came to the counter. "May I help you?"

"I'm Leo Hartwig's new secretary," Kosta said. "I'd like to pay his last telephone bill."

"Do you have the bill with you?"

"No. That's the problem. It's been misplaced, I'm afraid. The name is Hartwig. H-A-R-T-W-I-G. It may be a new number. And I'm sure it's unlisted. I think he said they'd changed the number recently."

"Just a moment." The woman walked across the room to a bright orange file cabinet, opened the drawer, and flipped through the folders. Coming back to Kosta then, a piece of paper in her hand, she said, "This bill's been paid. It *is* a new number since January. And it's unlisted. But there's nothing due."

Kosta took the bill and studied it carefully. "You're right," she said. "No wonder we couldn't find it. Could I take this and show it to Mr. Hartwig?"

"I'm afraid we just have the one file copy."

"It doesn't matter. Just let me copy down the date of payment." She took a small pad out of her bag and jotted down the date. And as soon as she turned away from the desk she also wrote down the telephone number.

She drove back to San Francisco then, checked her rental car back in, and picked up a boarding pass for her flight back to New York. While she waited for the boarding call she placed a call to Naomi Guterman in Washington.

As soon as Kosta left the beach, as she climbed the steep dunes and walked to where she'd left her car, Tunstall, who had been watching her through the window, went to the storeroom behind the kitchen. Picking up a six-foot length of two-by-four, a claw hammer, and a small box of spike nails, he went upstairs to the third floor, knocked once, unlocked the door to the Hartwigs' bedroom, and went in.

Louise Hartwig, in a sweater and jeans and sneakers, was sitting by the window, writing on a clipboard. Hartwig, in another chair across the room, was reading a book. They barely reacted to Tunstall's presence. Their eyes flicked up as though a pet had wandered into the room, then went back to what they were doing. They seemed to pay no attention as Tunstall crossed the room, opened the sliding glass doors, and went outside to the deck.

He picked up the blouse on a hanger and the panty hose Kosta had seen from the beach, brought them inside, and laid them on the bed. There was a sense of ritual about his movements, something brittle and dehumanized.

Tunstall closed the glass doors then and locked them. Picking up the length of two-by-four, he wedged it tight, one end against the doorjamb, the other against the frame of the sliding door. Spilling the strong four-inch nails out on the carpet, he deliberately hammered all of them into the bar of wood and on through into the floor, nailing the glass doors permanently shut.

If he had expected some reaction from the Hartwigs, he got

none, either from the pounding or from his closing the draperies, shutting off the light from outside.

Picking up his hammer, he crossed the room to the hall door and unlocked it. He turned then and said, "We had an understanding. You were not to go out on that deck under any circumstances. Now I've fixed it so you won't be tempted. I am also asking you to keep those drapes closed at all times. If you don't do it, we'll nail plywood sheets across the window openings. Now at least you have some light. But if you try anything cute we'll turn this place into a cave." He stepped out into the hall, closed the door behind him, and double-locked it.

The room the Hartwigs were confined to was their bedroom. Twenty by twenty. With a dressing room and a large bathroom off the side opposite the ocean. Louise had designed and furnished the room with care and skill, artfully concealing the closets and cabinets so the room would have an open, uncluttered look.

Now, however, although she had tried to put it in some order, the room was a shambles. It looked like a storehouse for clothing and luggage and books. All these things had been carried upstairs and dumped in piles along the base of the walls. As many articles of clothing as possible had later been put into closets or drawers. And the books had been stacked in neat piles against the wall at the foot of the bed. But still the room resembled a church annex just before the annual charity sale.

The dressing room, once Louise Hartwig's favorite nook, had been converted into a kitchen of sorts. A folding table sat against one wall with a two-burner hot plate, an electric skillet, and a coffee pot plugged in, a few dishes, some plastic tableware, and two or three stew pans. In a corner, a small office-size refrigerator had been squeezed in, and on the floor beside it were boxes of detergent, bleach, breakfast cereal, crackers, and a supply of canned fruits and vegetables. Mrs. Hartwig, accustomed to a staff of five, had, for weeks now, done her laundry by hand in the bathtub and washed each day's dirty dishes and cooking utensils in the bathroom sink.

For a long moment after Tunstall left the room, she and Leo simply sat in their chairs on opposite sides of the room and stared at each other. Finally she said, "I'm scared, Leo. Before I was just mad. Now I'm starting to get scared."

"It's all right. We just have to hang on "

"I know we do. That's what we keep saying to each other. We've been saying it for weeks. But how much longer can we do it?"

"I don't know. As long as we have to, I guess. They're not mistreating us. We have enough to eat. And a comfortable place to stay."

"Oh, stop it, Leo, for God's sake. I'm not ten years old. We're *prisoners* here. We can't talk to anyone. We can't see anyone. No one can see *us.* What happened to our friends? Why doesn't somebody go to the police?"

"Maybe they have," he said. "But if these two guys are working for the government, if they represent some agency in Washington . . . "

"You don't believe that, do you? Wasn't that just something they told us so they could get inside the house?"

"I don't know, Louise. We've been over this a thousand times. I don't know what to think."

"Why would the government be interested in us? Why would they want to keep you away from everybody? Those plane crashes must be ancient history by now. And even if they're not, what stake could the government have in that? What harm could you do them? Just because you said those planes were sabotaged—how could that hurt the government? You said yourself you couldn't prove it. Isn't that what you told me?"

"I certainly couldn't prove anything now. Not six months later."

"Then why are we here? Locked up like this. I don't think it's the government at all. They must want money."

Hartwig got up then, walked across to the drapery-covered glass doors, and squatted down.

"What is it?" Louise said.

"I thought I saw a glint of something." He ran his hand along the thick-pile carpet just under the edge of the heavy drapes. "Yeah. Here we are." He stood up and turned to face his wife. When he held out his hand, she saw one of the four-inch spike nails Tunstall had used to seal the doors shut.

"Is that supposed to solve our problems?" she said.

"I doubt it. But it might get me as far as the phone."

Eighteen hours later, at three o'clock in the morning, Hartwig got out of bed. He shook Louise gently. When she woke up, he whispered, "I thought you weren't going to sleep a wink."

"I wasn't. But I did."

She got up in the dark and put on her robe. He went to the door, put his ear against it, and listened. "Dead to the world," he said. "If they're not asleep now, they never will be."

She flipped on a tiny, palm-sized flashlight and trained it on the door. Hartwig took the nail out of his pajama pocket. He'd wrapped it in adhesive tape from the first-aid kit in their bathroom. In his other hand he held one of his shoes, a heavy sock pulled over it. Carefully placing the point of the tape-covered nail under the head of the hinge pin at the top of the door, he tapped it twice with the muffled heel of his shoe. He stopped to listen.

"They'll hear you," she said.

"I don't think so. They're two floors down. It sounds loud to us but they won't hear it."

Working slowly and patiently, making as little sound as possible, retaping the point of the nail four times, he slowly tapped and pried, loosened and pulled the pins out of each of the three hinges. Pulling the center one last, he stood with his ear against the door, listening for sounds downstairs. Dead silence. Using the nail to pry with, getting leverage against the molding, he eased the door's back edge out of the frame and pulled it slowly toward him till there was room for him to slip outside into the hall.

On the carpeted stairs in his bare feet, he stayed away from the center of the steps. He descended slowly, pausing after each step, breathing silently, listening, then going down one more step.

At the second-floor landing it was dead black, all the window shades and drapes pulled shut. He stood motionless, listening, then started down the curving staircase to the main floor, feeling his way, counting the steps, hoping for some spill of light but finding none. When he stood with his hand on the brass octagon that decorated the bottom end of the stair rail, no familiar furniture shapes appeared in the living room. No shapes or forms at all. Just heavy darkness.

Gliding softly forward, trying to use his fingers and toes as antennae, Hartwig inched across the room to the spot where the phone jack was, in the corner opposite the fireplace. The furniture, he sensed, had been rearranged. But since most of it had been moved away from the room's center, it made his progress easier.

But the phone wasn't where it had been before. It wasn't on the table. It was nowhere in that corner at all. Dropping to his hands and knees, he crawled slowly along the baseboards, feeling for a cord, for the small metal box that meant the telephone would be close by. But his fingers told him nothing. Suddenly from the back corner of the house he heard the dog whimper. Just a shred of sound. Then silence.

He knew he couldn't prowl the edges of the entire living room groping for the telephone cord. There might not be enough time. He couldn't take the chance. He stood up, moved as quickly as he could toward the front foyer. Just inside it there was a wall switch. When he reached it, when his fingers barely touched it, he stood very still, bringing his concentration to sharp focus, opening his eyes, physically, as wide as he could, trying to will himself incredible speed and depth of vision. Then he flicked the switch for the ceiling light, on and off so fast that the light flash was little more than subliminal. But in that fragile sliver of an instant, he saw the familiar shape of the phone, on a table just at the bottom of the stairs.

Forcing himself to stay motionless, one shoulder lightly touching the wall where the switch was, listening now as acutely as he had tried to *see* a moment before, concentrating all his sensory strength in his ears, he tried to monitor any sound or motion from the rear of the house, where the guest bedrooms were. But he heard nothing.

He crossed quickly to the foot of the stairs, guided himself to the brass knob at the base of the railing, and when he touched it, reached down with his other hand and felt the familiar surface and shape of the telephone receiver. Listening again for a long moment, he bent over to raise the receiver to his ear. His arm made the proper movement; the correct impulse went down to his nerves and muscles. But the receiver refused to leave its cradle. When he applied greater power, the whole instrument lifted up heavily from the table and made a slight jingle when he quickly set it down.

At that instant a strong flashlight beam hit his face. A second later the dog began to bark back behind the kitchen, and all the lights on the main floor of the house flooded on.

In the kitchen doorway, holding the flashlight, was Oscar Tunstall, in sock feet, wearing just a shirt and trousers but looking crisp and unrumpled.

When his eyes adjusted to the bright light, Hartwig looked down at the telephone. A circlet of spring steel, fastened by a padlock, held the receiver firmly in its cradle.

"You went to a lot of trouble for nothing," Tunstall said.

Tunstall didn't go back to bed that night. After he'd rehung the Hartwigs' bedroom door, he attached hooks and screws to the outside so the door couldn't be taken off even when the hinges were removed.

At five in the morning he went into the kitchen and made a pot of coffee. Then he unlocked the telephone and called Jim Lasker at his home. They talked for almost forty minutes. After Tunstall outlined his plan that involved Rafer Isbell, Lasker spelled out the information he'd collected about Treptow's relatives and his ex-wife, where she worked in Santa Barbara and where she lived.

"Let's lay off the ex-wife," Tunstall said then. "I went over the material you sent me before. I think it's a dead-end. They're divorced. No kids. We've got nothing to work on. No reason to think that she'll try to protect him or he'll try to protect her. No pressure points. The Kosta situation is something else. Let's bear down on that."

As soon as he finished talking with Lasker, Tunstall direct-dialed a number in Harrisonburg, Virginia, and spoke with the red-haired woman Kosta had seen driving the blue camper.

Gabe got out of the cab on K Street, a warm summer rain pelting down, ran across the sidewalk, and pushed in through the glass doors of The Prime Rib.

It was early still for dinner, but the horseshoe bar was crowded. Well-groomed men and bright-faced young ladies clustered and gossiped and exchanged power tips with each other while a piano tinkled softly in the corner behind them.

Waiting for the reservations man to return to the door, Gabe glanced around the dimly lit room, a narrow one just in front on the street side, separated from the central room by a low partition topped with potted ferns, all the walls soft black, trimmed with gold, the chairs black leather with high backs, fresh flowers in giant vases, a richly patterned carpet, and Leda and the Swan coupling discreetly on a back wall.

"I'm meeting Senator Isbell."

"Yes, Senator Treptow. He's just upstairs on the second level."

Rafer Isbell was waiting in a corner booth of a private dining room. After Gabe sat down and they'd ordered drinks, Isbell said, "I have a bad conscience about you. I've really been remiss. I remember promising when you were elected that you and I would see a lot of each other here in Washington. You remember my saying that?"

"Yes, I do," Gabe said. He smiled. "But I didn't think of it as a contract."

"Of course not. But I feel guilty all the same."

Their drinks came then, and Isbell said to the waiter, "Check back with us from time to time. We don't want to feel deserted up here in the corner."

"Yes, sir."

"I'm sorry we can't have dinner," Isbell said after the waiter moved away. "Virginia's got a houseful of people she rounded up from somewhere." He sampled his drink. "Matter of fact, I guess you could drive home with me and eat some supper with us at the house. But I wouldn't recommend it. Not tonight."

"Thanks anyway. I'm meeting somebody for dinner."

"Some other time then."

"Fine," Gabe said.

"I understand you've settled in Georgetown."

Gabe nodded. "Nothing fancy. I just took an apartment."

"Nothing wrong with that. Besides . . . a good-looking bachelor in Washington . . . I doubt if you're ever home."

Gabe didn't answer. He took a slow drink from his glass, then set it down carefully, a peaceful expression on his face, his eyes straight ahead across the table. No message. No demands.

Uneasy with the silence, Isbell took out his cigar case, offered one to Gabe, then carefully clipped one for himself, lit it, and savored the taste. "You shouldn't pass up a good cigar. Especially a first-rate contraband beauty from Cuba."

Again Gabe was silent. Finally, watching Isbell smoke, he said, "What's on your mind, Rafer? It's all you can do to squeeze out hello when I see you on the Senate floor. Now all of a sudden you decide to stroke me a little. What happened? What's the message?"

Isbell resettled himself in the booth, studied his cigar for a moment, and said, "You're right. I admit I've steered clear of you. That's what I was talking about before. But I had to, Gabe. You didn't give me any choice. I know you don't give a damn how many enemies you make. You've made that clear. The first time you stood up and talked in the chamber you made it plain that you intended to take us all on.

"I'm not saying you're a hundred percent wrong. But you're not *right* either. I wouldn't sit here and try to tell you that we don't have any second-rate people in the Senate. Take a hundred men in *any* field—lawyers, teachers, whatever you want to pick—and you're bound to find a few bad apples. We're no different. Nobody who knows would tell you we've got a *perfect* Senate. But perfect or not, it's the only one we have. So that's what we have to work with. At least *I* do. That's politics the way I learned it. Try to make the best of what you've got and go on from there."

"No good, Rafer. That's the oldest song in public life and you know it—'We're all honest, hard-working men trying to do our best with an imperfect system.' That's bullshit. If the Senate doesn't track right, it's because there's something wrong with the *senators*. The *idea* that every state should have free elections to send two capable men to Washington to represent them is a *good* idea. If the men they elect turn out to be self-serving frauds with their hands held out to any interest group that wants to buy their votes, that doesn't mean the *idea*'s wrong. It means the wrong men are in office."

Senator Isbell smiled and nodded his head. "I'm not trying to convert you, Gabe. But you can't convert me either. Most of those men you're talking about I've known for quite a few years. I've worked with them and spent many hours in their homes. By and large they're honest men."

"By and large, they're looking out for number one. And that's *all* they're doing. You know it and so do I. It's a private club with private rules and nobody is allowed to rock the boat. Well, I *am* rocking the boat, and I intend to keep on doing it. You can pass that on to whoever sent you here this evening. Or if you want to give me the name I'll tell him myself."

The waiter appeared in the archway then, and Isbell signaled for another round of drinks. "If you think you can get me angry, Gabe," he said then, "it won't work. I have a job to do here in Washington and I think I do it well. I try to represent the people of Illinois in a way that will make them proud of their state. That's my responsibility as a senator."

"I don't want to hear it, Rafer. I'm not in the third grade."

"Just let me finish." He paused and took a long pull at his cigar as the waiter came back with fresh drinks and took away their empty glasses. "If you want to alienate your fellow senators, grandstand for the press, and put yourself in a position where you're unable to do the job you were sent here to do, no one can stop you. And I haven't tried. But when you suddenly announce a unilateral investigation, one that questions the competence and integrity of at least two responsible government agencies, then I feel bound to tell you that you're going too far."

"I say I haven't gone far enough. I say those responsible government agencies didn't go far enough."

"Those two accidents were investigated thoroughly."

"No they weren't," Gabe said. "They closed the book on the Indianapolis crash in three weeks. And the Air Force Three thing wasn't investigated at all. Not in any public way. Two days after the crash they announced what had happened. A little later Hartwig Systems took full responsibility, and that was that."

"Whatever the time scheme was, I guarantee you—"

"How can you *guarantee* anything?" Gabe said. "Do you have some information that wasn't released to the public?"

"No. I didn't say that. But I know both Ernest Mossler and Arthur Slayback. Know them well. They are diligent, ethical men. I have total faith in them and their organizations." He took a drink and set his glass down carefully. "I know their methods of operation. Thorough investigation and full disclosure. When we're dealing with public safety, nothing else is good enough."

"I agree with you."

"Only in situations where national security is involved . . . "

Gabe set his glass down. "Why do you say that?"

"No reason," Isbell said. "I was just giving you an example of a situation where full public disclosure might not be possible."

"Did somebody tell you there was a national security problem connected to those H-14 crashes?"

"You seem to think I'm acting as an errand boy for someone. Do you think somebody gave me instructions to talk to you?"

"Let me put it this way," Gabe said. "If you told me that was the case I wouldn't be surprised."

"Well, it isn't the case. The fact is I'm trying to do you a favor—"

"Thank you. I appreciate that."

"—trying to keep you from making a national ass of yourself."

"Thanks again."

Senator Isbell, well-known for his self-control, widely admired for that characteristic, was slowly getting angry. Starting at the edge of his white collar, a deep rose tint spread upward across his face. "You've made it plain to your constituents and to everyone in Washington that you intend to use your high office as some kind of springboard for your own notoriety. We're accustomed to publicity seekers here. But I must say I didn't expect it from you. First you attacked your fellow senators. Now you've launched an inquiry into two incidents that have been properly and officially dealt with."

" 'Dealt with,' " Gabe said. "That's *exactly* what happened. Those two crashes weren't investigated. They were *dealt with*. You call them incidents. I say two hundred and forty-five people died in those two *incidents*. One of them was my brother. So I am particularly interested in why those planes went down. And the more people like you try to discourage me, the more interested I *get*. If it turns out that what I suspect is *true*, then I am perfectly willing to make an ass of myself. You can report that to whoever sent you here."

"Don't you dare talk to me like that." Isbell drained his glass abruptly and leaned forward against the edge of the table. "Don't you dare underestimate me. I brought you to this town and if I have to I know how to send you back. You think you can take on the United States Senate but you can't. You think you can manipulate the press, you and that little second-rate—"

"Wait a minute . . . "

"It's the truth. There's a file on that Kosta girl that would choke a horse. Everybody sees through her except you. She's a user. She'll use you and the Senate and any other weapon she can get hold of to put the government in a bad light, to make the country look bad. If you want to *screw* her, that's your business, but don't *help* her with her nasty propaganda tricks. The girl's a tramp. Everybody knows—"

"Rafer, I'm warning you. You'd better get off this."

"I know what I'm saying. Ask her. Ask her if she wasn't arrested in Indianapolis less than—"

"How did *you* know that?"

"Picked up for soliciting in a downtown motel."

"Who told you that?" Gabe said.

"What's the difference? Word gets around. She's public property. Ask her about that gypsy trip she made around the country a few years ago. She and her pinko friends, male and female, all sleeping in a bus together like a bunch of hogs. Ask her about *that*. How many times she was arrested. How many nights she spent in jail. Ask her *that*. You'll get an earful, I promise you."

Isbell stood up from his chair suddenly, dropped a twenty-dollar bill on the table, and walked through the archway toward the stairs. Behind him his cigar lay smoking on the polished tabletop. Gabe picked it up and put it in the ashtray. His hand was sure and steady. But his veins stood out like blue cords. And when he turned his hand over, he could see a strong pulse throbbing in his wrist.

Isbell, on his way home, stopped at a telephone booth beside Arlington Avenue and called Joe Newquist. "I talked to him," he said, "but it didn't do any good. He's a bullheaded son of a bitch."

 Senator Isbell had been imperfectly briefed on Kosta. She had been a flagrant dissident since she was seventeen years old, she strongly supported socialist principles, but she was not a Soviet sympathizer. Her father, who was proud of her energy and her ideas and her fearless questioning of authority, often said to her, "*Theory* is one thing. *Practice* is something else. If you lived in Russia, you'd be in prison." Kosta agreed with him.

As she had told Gabe, she'd been arrested for prostitution. Several times. In the sixties and early seventies it was a classic police tactic. How does a small-city police force in Nebraska or Kansas or Minnesota cope with a vanload of long-haired young people, barefoot and wearing jeans, posters in their hands, bullhorns blasting accusations against local manufacturing plants?

A formula quickly developed. The young men were vagrants. The young women were prostitutes. The first arrest, a warning to pack up the posters and bullhorns and keep moving; the second, a guaranteed jail sentence.

The cross-country caravan Isbell described had indeed taken place. Rallies and speeches, handbills and posters. Picketing, graffiti painting, and frequent arrests.

And they had traveled together. The group, calling itself Pilgrims Against Pollution, had traveled in a converted and brightly painted school bus. For nearly a year they had lived, slept, cooked, eaten, and moved slowly westward, then back eastward, in that bus.

Nine young women between the ages of twenty and twenty-seven. Eight males between the ages of nineteen and thirty-four. The nineteen-year-old boy was married to the twenty-seven-year-old woman.

One other couple, the thirty-four-year-old man and a twenty-two-year-old girl from Youngstown, were also married.

Four other couples were living, sleeping, loving, and fighting with each other on a more or less permanent basis. Two of the boys were homosexuals, as proper and circumspect as George and Martha Washington, and two of the girls, as though Noah had selected a full range of preferences, were lesbians, private, shy, and outwardly straitlaced. The odd, leftover person, number seventeen in a total population of seventeen, was Kosta.

During that year on the bus there were unequal and unpredictable portions of sex, drinking, laughter, music, and fighting. Deep affection and profound dislikes. Love and sympathy and understanding, and in one case, something very close to hatred. But the orgies that were envisioned by the police in Davenport and Wichita and Yankton did not in fact take place. The wife swapping, girl sharing, husband trading, simply did not happen.

Only the two married couples provided any drama as the bus traveled west to San Francisco, south to El Centro, and back again to Boston via Phoenix, Dallas, New Orleans, and Atlanta. And they waited, these married couples, till the trip was almost over. Just north of Philadelphia, on the New Jersey turnpike, they announced that the thirty-four-year-old husband was separating from his twenty-two-year-old wife and would marry as soon as possible the twenty-seven-year-old woman who up till then had been married to the nineteen-year-old boy. The twenty-two-year-old abandoned wife then stood up in the bus and announced that she too planned to marry again. She had chosen the nineteen-year-old abandoned husband as her new mate.

It was not chance that had made Kosta the only free and unmated person on that ideological safari to the west edge of the continent and back again. She had planned it that way, as she always did, as she always had, since her early years in Harrisonburg.

At age eleven or so, Kosta had chosen her role. Starting then she became a tireless and adroit social engineer, managing events and relationships, giving advice, steering people together. She concentrated on being everybody's friend, offering help and guidance to boys and girls alike, accepting confidences, keeping secrets, helping to stick broken romances back together, becoming, in short, such a complete and invaluable friend to everyone in her school class, such a knowing confidante and convenient receptacle for the debris of ecstasy and heartbreak, that soon she was accepted and defined not as a flushed participant in the romantic athletics of her peers, but as a strangely wise, dependable spectator, an archivist, a kind of safe repository for the excesses, self-deceptions, joys, and frustrations of her friends.

By the time she left Harrisonburg and went north to college, she was clear and well rehearsed in her role. She picked it up without losing a step as soon as she began to make friends at Brandeis. As she became more politically aware and active, she used that, too, to keep herself stridently at the center of things, but personally apart. "He who lives to himself will be left to himself." This was her favorite literary theme. The first time she heard it, in an English lecture, she thought, "Yes—that's *me.*"

Ironically, the longer she abstained from the sexual circus, the more energy she invested in her academic life, in her speeches and articles, her marches and rallies and screaming demonstrations, the more she scorned any thought of a sensual life, the more attractive she became.

She crackled with electricity, with vitality, with shining, bright-eyed health. Boys her age, and older men, made very specific moves in her direction. Clear proposals and propositions were presented. Direct questions were asked.

Kosta responded, almost always, with something humorous, turning her lapel back to show a button, "Take a Rapist to Lunch," or saying, "I think you're the most attractive man I've seen in several hours and I'd love to go out with you. But I warn you I'm very serious. A year from now I want to be married and have a child." Or "I won't go out with you. I'm too busy for dates. But I wouldn't mind going to bed with you, I guess. How about today? I'm free between noon and twelve thirty. Then I have to meet my foot doctor for lunch." Or "If you want a girl who grinds her teeth at night, talks in her sleep, and sleeps in her socks, I'm for you. But to paraphrase Groucho Marx, I could never be attracted to anybody who would settle for *me.*"

She didn't fool her girl friends, of course. Not the ones who knew her best. They all said pretty much the same things about her. "Kosta is scared to death of men. That's where all that nervous energy comes from. It's sublimated sex. When she's seventy-five she'll still have her cherry."

She was *not,* in fact, frightened of men—not precisely. She liked the way they looked and she liked the way they thought. In any given semester, her favorite teacher was usually a man. Her political and academic role models were men more often than not. And her confederates in dissent were male, by a five-to-one ratio.

Her feminist instincts, her efforts toward equal rights, did not exclude or downgrade men. She did not feel that the road to equality had to be littered with the bloody remains of fallen males.

In short, Kosta *liked* men. In her way. She liked them a lot. She felt that she understood them, most of them. And most of them, she felt, understood her. And the thing they understood most clearly was that however willing and cooperative she was as a worker, a marcher, a conspirator; however tireless she might be, putting in punishing hours, doing donkey work if necessary; however amenable and selfless she was, showing up early, leaving late, working harder than anyone else; however totally available she willingly made herself—her physical self was not, nor would it ever be, part of the bargain.

She could be hugged like a comrade or kissed in moments of triumph. She would joke and swear, shove and jostle, and never be prissily offended by language or gestures or makeshift toilet facilities. When the wine was uncorked, or the tequila, or when a joint was passed around, she was a full and enthusiastic partner.

But when the ritual of sexual selection began, when people paired off in the dark, Kosta did not participate. She stood apart, stayed apart, slept apart.

All this was understood and accepted by the people who knew her. They called her Reverend Mother Cool and Susie Celibate and they drew up elaborate timetables and graphs designed to predict when she would fall. But no one was surprised that she didn't.

All through high school, and later, during the years at Brandeis, Kosta was a tireless reader of psychology texts, works on psychiatry, classic and experimental, and, especially, studies of abnormal behavior. This reading was prompted by her intellectual curiosity, by a hunger for general knowledge, but most specifically because she was anxious to shore up a particular theory. Kosta believed it was impossible for one single experience, one shocking moment, to traumatize a total life, to fix behavior patterns, to chart an emotional one-way route that could never be diverted.

Everything she read, the theories that supported hers, even the ones that seemed to refute it, strengthened her conviction that intelligence and free will could triumph over any trauma. With care and time one could erase any experience, push it back into the dark corners of consciousness where it would no longer have the power to distort or poison present life and new choices. She believed that. She came to believe it totally. No reservations whatsoever.

But when she applied the theorem to her own life, it did not work. It fizzled and spluttered, produced nausea and bewilderment, and didn't pan out at all. It stunned her and sickened her. She felt permanently caught on the jagged edges of one agonizing moment in her childhood that no amount of research or intellectual conviction could smooth over or cause to disappear.

When she was eleven years old, in the spring semester of her fifth-grade year at General Louis McClain School in Harrisonburg, her teacher took the class for a botany field trip and cookout in the National Park near Big Flat Mountain, fifteen miles southeast of Harrisonburg.

At four in the afternoon, when each student had a paper bag filled with leaves and grasses, nuts and acorns and odd pieces of bark, when the hamburgers and hot dogs had been eaten long since and the trash carefully cleared away and stuffed in plastic bags, when noses were being counted preparatory to climbing back inside the yellow school bus and returning to Harrisonburg, it was discovered that only twenty-three of the twenty-four fifth-grade students were present. Melissa Clegg was not there. Her nickname was Siksok. When she'd been brought to school for the first time, age five, she had wet her pants in a fit of frustration and anger, and her wet shoes when she walked up the kindergarten aisle had made that humiliating sound: *siksok . . . sik-sok.*

It turned out that Kosta had been with Melissa an hour or so earlier, in a thick ash grove half a mile up the trail toward Big Flat. So she and the teacher and two boys from the class went back up that way to find Melissa. When they came near the spot where she'd last seen her, Kosta ran ahead.

Melissa was still there in the clearing. When Kosta saw her, all the air in her lungs emptied out. She was dizzy suddenly. The ground seemed to tilt. With her eyes fixed on Melissa she stumbled against a tree trunk, held on to it to keep from falling, and struggled to breathe again. Then she began to scream.

Melissa lay on her back on the ground, white and naked, her eyes bulging, one of her stockings in her mouth, the other one knotted tight around her neck. One of her little-girl arms was twisted and broken, and her legs were streaked and smeared with blood. Her upper body, as slender and muscled as a boy's, was torn and bitten as if she'd been attacked by a dog. And her child's vagina had been ripped and slashed open. Bright blood still seeped out of her, and the handle of a hunting knife protruded from the angry red wound between her legs.

Part Four

70 Harun Haikal, a tiny, dark-skinned man twenty-four years old, sat on the edge of a narrow bed in a third-story front room of a rundown hotel near the corner of Potomac Avenue and Seventeenth Streets. Beside him on the bed were two automatic pistols, one thirty-two caliber, the other twenty-two.

At the window, Dami Hadi, a slender girl with black eyes, her dark hair bound up in a flowered scarf, stood looking down at the street. As she watched, a gray-green limousine slowly passed the hotel, moved on down the street for half a block, and parked at the curb. Jamal Hamad, a tall man in a dark suit, got out of the car and started walking toward the hotel, his driver just a step behind him. "Here he is," Dami said. "I will go downstairs to meet him." Harun Haikal sat motionless on the bed as she unlocked the door and went out.

When she crossed the dark lobby downstairs, she saw that Hamad had stopped and lighted a cigarette. He stood waiting on the sidewalk just outside the hotel entrance. As she came outside, Hamad gave a head signal to his driver, and the man moved a few steps away.

"Is he stupid?" Hamad said to Dami.

"No. Haikal is not stupid. It is not a simple issue after all. He is confused."

"Couldn't you explain it to him?"

"I did explain. But he was not easy with it. If he hears the same words from you I think he will be satisfied."

"If this man is not loyal I don't want him around. We don't need philosophers. We need loyal people who are able to follow orders."

"He is *too* loyal," Dami said. "You will see. If you order him to do this or anything else he will do it. But he will be more valuable to us if he understands."

The driver trailed a few steps behind them as they climbed the narrow, foul-smelling stairway to the third floor. Hamad, seeming to hold his breath, careful not to brush his sleeves against the walls, said, "This is the worst place I've ever seen. Why are you staying here?"

"I was ordered to stay here. We own this hotel.".

Inside the room, Haikal stood up quickly, greeted Hamad, and bowed stiffly from the waist. "I am told that you need to talk with me," Hamad said.

"I am sorry," Haikal said, "but I have questions."

"Do you want me to wait outside?" Dami said.

"No," Hamad said. Then he turned back to Haikal. "You understand what you've been ordered to do."

Haikal nodded. "I understand. But I am unquiet in my mind because I believe that what I do could be a benefit for the Abu."

"Do you think we would plan something that would be a good service for the Abu?"

Haikal looked uneasy. He seemed to struggle for words. But he persisted. "No, I don't think that. You see, if you ordered me to pick up one of those guns and put a bullet in my own brain, I would do it. But if I thought that it would somehow benefit Abu Khamufa, then I could *not* do it." His face grew pale suddenly. "May I sit down? I am very nervous."

Hamad nodded, and Haikal sat down on a straight chair. He said, "Is it not true that this man, this Senator Treptow, is trying to make public a secret that will do some harm to the Abu?"

"Yes, that is true."

"We also are working against the Abu, we are sworn to humiliate him, to reveal his cruelty, to reclaim the wealth he stole from Bedaki, to kill him and all his family if we can."

"Yes."

"If this man Treptow can damage the Abu, then he will help us. If we kill him, we kill a friend."

Hamad glanced over at Dami, positioned himself in front of Haikal, and spoke in an almost paternal tone. "We are aware of everything you say. But there are other factors to consider. The Abu is our enemy. But Ishaq Rashid is also our enemy. If this man, Senator Treptow, manages to uncover the things that we know, that the American President knows, and that Rashid knows, Rashid will quickly blame the Americans. He will make a thousand angry speeches and threats. And he will be a hero in Bedaki. He will use the incident as a weapon against our party. Our group will suffer most of all. At another time Treptow would be very valuable to us. Now he is a danger. It's all a question of timing. It is critical for us that *when* this scandal is uncovered to the people of Bedaki, *we* should be the ones to do it. We *must* do it that way. As we've planned it—the killing of Abu Khamufa, the announcement of this conspiracy between Rashid and the White House, and the armed uprising of our people in Bedaki. Each detail is critical. You have been selected for an important piece of work. Do you understand that now?"

Haikal nodded. "Yes. I understand."

"It is my hope that when we are finally face to face with the Abu you will be there too."

"That is *my* hope," Haikal said.

The following morning, at precisely ten thirty, Haikal, driving by himself, parked his car in the visitors' parking lot just behind the Everett Dirksen office building. As soon as he turned off the ignition key, a stocky young man in a dark suit appeared at the side of his car. When he identified himself with a secret hand signal, Haikal rolled down his window.

"I am Hamid Ar-Razi. Jamal Hamad sent me to meet you here."

The young man walked around the front of the car, opened the door opposite Haikal, and slid into the front seat. "It will be like this," he said. "Exactly eight minutes after you go inside the building, I will explode this car to make a diversion. By then I will also be inside the building to cover your escape. You will go out through the front entrance and turn right. At the bottom of that small park near Union Station, a car will pick you up."

As he spoke, Hamid Ar-Razi slowly lowered his right arm, the arm opposite Haikal. As he leaned forward then and feigned a fit of coughing, a knife slid down from inside his sleeve, into his right hand.

That afternoon, a Capitol security officer, Laurence Digby, and a Washington, D.C. homicide detective, Mel Stagg, came to Gabe's office. Jud ushered them in and stayed there while they talked to Gabe.

"About thirty minutes ago a dead man was discovered downstairs, in the visitors' parking lot," Digby said. "He was sitting in a rented car and his throat was cut."

"Who was he?" Jud said.

Stagg referred to his notes. "Harun Haikal. An Iranian with an up-to-date visa. He had a piece of paper in his pocket with Senator Treptow's name written on it."

"That's right," Gabe said. "He was supposed to be in my office at eleven this morning."

"Did you know him?"

"No. Just the name. He called several times asking if he could see me. So we made an appointment with him for this morning."

"Did you know anything about him?"

"Not much. Somebody said he was in Iran when they took over our embassy. I guess he was one of the student leaders. But I also heard that he might have been working for us."

"Who told you that?"

"I don't remember," Gabe said. He watched Stagg writing on his note pad. "I wouldn't store that information in the Smithsonian if I were you."

"Don't worry. We triple-check everything."

"When he called for an appointment," Digby said, "did he say what he wanted to see you about?"

"He told one of my assistants he had some confidential information that would interest me."

"That's all?"

"I'm in the middle of a tricky investigation."

"The H-14 thing," Stagg said.

"That's right. We thought maybe the information Haikal was talking about had something to do with that."

"But he didn't give any hints about it?"

"All they told me is what I've just told you."

"Do you think perhaps he was giving that impression as a means of getting into your office?"

"It's possible," Gabe said, "but what's the point?"

"The man was carrying two handguns. One in a hip holster and one strapped to his calf. Short-range, soft-nosed ammo. He could have been on his way to kill somebody."

"Senator Treptow?" Jud said.

"It's possible." Stagg turned to Gabe. "Have you taken any strong positions on the Mideast?"

"Nothing new. I'm pro-Israel. But I think the Palestinians have a right to locate someplace and stay there. And I've said we have to find a way to do without Arab oil, because sooner or later we'll have to give it up anyway. I guarantee you the American oil companies are more pissed off at me than the Arabs are."

When he saw Kosta that evening, Gabe told her, first thing, about Haikal. "Oh, my God," she said. "I'm starting to get scared."

Gabe shook his head. "He wasn't planning to potshot me. It doesn't make sense. If he *was*, he sure as hell wouldn't make an appointment, give his real name, and then start blasting away in a Senate office building. There are too many better ways. I'd be the easiest guy in the world to shoot. I live by myself, drive my own car, eat in tacky restaurants. I mean, here we sit, right now, in plain view. If somebody wanted to shoot me, all he'd have to do is stroll in here and do it."

"I know that," she said. "What worries me is—why did somebody kill *him?*"

"That's what I've been thinking about. If he really did have something important to tell me . . . "

She sat quiet for a long moment, looking past Gabe at the half-empty restaurant. Then, "I get crazy every time I hear about people carrying guns. I grew up with guns. All that crazy frontier horseshit about he-men bearing arms. Nobody gets to trespass on my property or dishonor my name. Cars and guns. Fake penises. Can you believe that people still think they can solve some problem by shooting a little hunk of lead into somebody's skin? Making a hole so all the blood will run out? Can you believe that?"

"I have to believe it. It's true."

"That's what gets me crazy."

He told her then about his meeting with Isbell. "In case you're worrying about your reputation, I guess I'd better tell you. The gossip is that you and I are having a hot romance."

"That's old news," she said. "I heard that right after your H-14 press conference. When you announced that I was working for you. My friend Nellie Arvidsen called me up two hours later."

"Maybe we should call another press conference and issue a denial."

"That's up to you," she said. "I've got nothing to lose. They've already run out of labels for me. Pinko pervert traitor hooker. And besides, I'm a Greek. If they said I was shacked up with a gorilla or a billy goat, that would be par for the course. Putting me in a senator's bed is a step up in class."

72 In an abandoned store on Jersey Avenue just north of the Washington navy yard, Dami Ḥaḍi sat in a dark back corner, three men and a young woman huddled close to her. She spoke in a whisper.

"Hamad believes that members of the Kaskar killed Haikal. It was the Kaskar pattern. But we must also think that this could have been a deliberate deception, that it was made to look like a Kaskar killing by some of Rashid's people. Either way we are in danger. All of us. Someone has penetrated our organization. We are a small group. All of us have been together since we were students. I will never believe that one of us in this room is a traitor. Hamad also believes that we five people are loyal patriots. He thinks there has been a betrayal in Bedaki. But until we know for certain, we must disappear. If there is a plan to liquidate all of us, beginning with Haikal, we must go underground until we know how we can make reprisals, until we know who our enemies are, and *where* they are. Hamad has found a farmhouse, an isolated place, more than a hundred miles from Washington. Mulla Khaldun will take us there tonight."

She held out her hand, and the other four reached out to clasp it. "There are very few of us," she said. "We must be strong and clever. And we must not despair. Justice and Allah are with us and we will have our way at last."

Twenty minutes later, Hamad's limousine pulled silently into the alley behind the store and stopped, Mulla Khaldun, Hamad's driver, behind the wheel, the headlights turned off.

From the back door of the store, Dami and the other four

filed silently to the car and got in, Dami in the front seat beside the driver. No one spoke until the car turned right on M Street and headed west. Then Khaldun switched on his headlights and said, "We should be there by six in the morning. Hamad will be waiting for you."

As he drove northwest up Maine Avenue, past the access road leading to George Mason Memorial Bridge, Dami said, "Aren't you taking the beltway?"

"No. Hamad said to go north on Fourteenth Street till I hit the Silver Springs highway."

Dami slouched down in the seat, tired and disturbed, her head resting against the seat back. Trying to cushion her anxieties and rest her mind, she focused on the buildings and monuments and parks as the car glided smoothly northward, past the Washington Monument, the Ellipse, the White House, and Lafayette Square, past Franklin Park and the traffic circle at the Massachusetts Avenue intersection.

Ten minutes farther north, at the corner of U Street, Khaldun slowed down suddenly and turned right.

"What's the matter?" Dami said.

"I don't like the way the motor's acting. I want to check it before we get out on the expressway."

He drove a block and a half east on U Street. Finally he pulled up and stopped just beside a late-model black sedan parked at the curb. He released the hood, opened the car door, and got out. "I'll just be a minute," he said. But as soon as he closed the car door behind him, he started to run, straight up the street, away from the car.

Instantly alert, Dami shouted "Get out!" to the people in the backseat. She pushed open the car door. But it jammed against the parked car by the curb. Not enough room for her to get out. As she started to slide across the seat to the opposite door, the darkness around her went suddenly yellow-white and the car beside the limousine exploded, hurling burning shards of steel hundreds of feet in all directions, totally decimating itself and all other vehicles within a forty-foot radius. Hamad's limousine folded in on itself, blazing white-hot, and the five people inside burned quickly in the blistering, melting heat.

Two days later, Mulla Khaldun's naked corpse was found in the basement of a construction site just west of Silver Spring, Maryland. He had been shot once in the head, his hands were missing, and his testicles had been cut off and sewed inside his mouth.

At seven in the morning Kosta called Gabe at home.

"I have to see you. Sorry if I woke you up."

"You didn't."

"There's a bagel joint at the corner of Thomas Jefferson and M Street. Can you meet me there in half an hour?"

"Why don't you come over here? I've got some coffee on."

She hesitated. Then, "I'll tell you the truth. There's something about me that drives men crazy early in the morning. Lots of problems with that in the past. Some real downers. You understand what I'm saying?"

"I know what you *think* you're saying. I'll meet you at the bagel place at seven thirty."

"Two hot developments," she said as soon as they were sitting across from each other in a second-floor booth looking down on M Street. "One . . . my computer-freak friend in New York City found something on Benedict. The company that insured him is Air Travel Assurance. Main office in Newark.

"Betsy, that's my friend's name, tracked down a girl who works there. She sniffed around a little and bingo, we know who the beneficiary was on Benedict's policy. Am I brilliant or am I brilliant?"

"You're brilliant. You're also lucky. You have a lot of nosy friends. Who are all these girls who pop up with information whenever you need it?"

"The new underground," Kosta said. "I mean it. It's like the Mafia going legit. All those girls who used to march and scream and lie down in front of police cars have square jobs now. They're typing and filing and running Xerox machines for the companies they used to picket. But their hearts are still with the SDS. Where there used to be a few dozen of us, now there are thousands. The ERA fight did it. Brought everybody into the fold. The kids who hated Vietnam and Nixon and Mayor Daley are grown up now. They're going after pollution, food additives, nuclear waste, and Dioxin. They don't want to have kids without fingers. I mean it. We don't have club pins or passwords and we don't pay dues. But I guarantee you I can bug my friends Nellie or Naomi or Betsy about almost anything and they can find me somebody on the inside.

"It's the new conspiracy. A conspiracy of women. And it works. If I come up with a specific question and if I can figure out what file cabinet or computer bank the answer is liable to be in, then nine times out of ten, if the answer's there, *somebody* will get it for me. Standard Oil, the Pentagon, Morgan Guaranty—it doesn't matter where. No office runs without women. And in every office there's always *one* woman who's more loyal to other women than she is to the windbag who signs her check."

"I'd better call my office and fire everybody."

"Don't worry. You're safe. You're with the good guys."

"What about that insurance policy?"

"The beneficiary is a company—Global Financial Horizons. Home office in Zurich. But there's an office here too. On Massachusetts Avenue." She reached inside her shoulder bag and took out a slip of paper. "On the corner of M and Massachusetts. The entrance is at 1900 M Street. I'm going there this morning to see if I can get a line on Benedict. That's number one."

She took an 8½-by-11-inch envelope out of her bag and put it on the chair beside her. "The second thing is Hartwig again. Remember what I told you about those two heroes who were guarding the Hartwig house? They smelled like Washington to me. Like *government*. Guys who never loosen their ties or take off their jackets. White eyes and button-down collars. The older one especially. High-school principal type. The good hands people. All that shit. A guy you wouldn't trust around the corner."

"Tunstall, you said."

"Tunstall, I _guessed_. I asked Naomi to copy those _Village Voice_ file pictures and send them along. They were waiting for me when I got home last night." She opened the envelope and slid the pictures out. "She only sent two. But two is enough." She put the pictures on the table in front of Gabe, one on either side of his cup. "There he is with Sam Giancano. And there he is in China with Mr. Dick."

"Is this the guy you talked to at Hartwig's place?"

"Bull's-eye," she said. "Not even a shadow of a question of a doubt. So that means that he and his friend are there to protect the Hartwigs because the Hartwigs asked for protection. _Or—_ the Hartwigs are being protected and isolated against their will. Kept away from their friends and the press. A kind of house arrest."

"Which _is_ it? You were there."

"If I had ten votes I'd vote ten times for the second choice. Nothing else makes sense. Somebody doesn't want Hartwig talking in public. The question is, how do we prove it and what do we _do_ about it?"

"Let me try a couple things," Gabe said. "You check out Global Financial and I'll see if I can get a rise out of Mr. Tunstall."

It was a few minutes past eleven when Gabe walked into his office. As he passed Monica's desk, he said, "Get me the governor's office in California."

She looked at her watch. "It's only eight o'clock out there."

"That's all right. He gets up early. At least he says he does."

As soon as he sat down behind his desk, Monica buzzed him and said, "The governor's not there. He's in New York. They said we could reach him at the Sherry-Netherland."

"Good . . . go ahead. No, wait a minute. I've got a better idea. He has an aide named Ethel McIntire. I'll talk to her."

"Does she get up early too?"

"She will this morning. Just make it sound very official."

A few minutes later, when Mrs. McIntire came on the phone, Gabe said, "This is Senator Treptow. I met you in Denver a year or so ago when my brother was giving a speech at the Western Governors' Conference. . . . That's right. . . . Thank you. . . . Well . . . things are going slower than we'd like, but we're making some headway, I think. . . . That's right. Look, Mrs. McIntire, I need a favor. I know your park patrol helicopters fly a regular schedule this time of year up and down that long stretch of beach below Santa Cruz. . . . That's right. . . . Here's what you can do for me. For the next few days, each time they pass Leo Hartwig's house . . . that's the one . . . ask the chopper pilots to hover there for a few minutes, just over the house, before they go on. Is that any problem for you? . . . Good—that should be helpful."

Late that afternoon, Darby Roush, a senior official in the Federal Bureau of Investigation, arrived, precisely on time, at Gabe's office.

"I appreciate your coming," Gabe said. "I know you people have busy schedules. I wouldn't have asked you, but I felt this might be the best way to proceed. Nothing official. Just a one-to-one talk."

Roush, managing to look ill at ease and aggressive at the same time, said, "We try to cooperate with the Senate members whenever we can."

"Good. I'm glad to hear that." Gabe picked up his intercom phone, said, "Excuse me just a second," and when Monica Cullen came on, said to her, "Place that call to California in about ten minutes. Oscar Tunstall. Person-to-person. That's right. The number Kosta gave us."

Gabe turned back to Roush then. "Now," he said, "here's the

situation. My office is conducting an investigation on those two H-14 crashes that happened last January. You may have seen something in the papers about it."

"No . . . I don't think I did."

"We released a list of people we planned to interview, people we hope will give us some pertinent information. You didn't see that list?"

"The bureau wasn't involved in those investigations. That's FAA territory."

"Yes, I know that, I just thought—never mind. Anyway, one of the individuals we're anxious to talk with is Leo Hartwig. His company manufactures the H-14. After the planes crashed he said he believed that both of them had been sabotaged."

Roush was impassive. No reply at all. Gabe went on. "Since those statements were made, Mr. Hartwig has been replaced as head of Hartwig Systems. He and his wife are believed to be at their home in Watsonville, California. But when one of my people went there recently, she was told that the Hartwigs are not there and the house is for sale. The two men she talked to claimed to be employees of a security organization in Santa Cruz. But one of these men, it turns out, was Oscar Tunstall. I believe you know Mr. Tunstall."

"No, I don't think I do," Roush said.

"Are you sure?"

"I may have met someone by that name. But if I did I don't remember him. I've been with the bureau for twenty-three years . . . "

"I know that," Gabe said. "You were one of Hoover's chief lieutenants, I understand."

Roush nodded. "Mr. Hoover hired me and trained me. We worked together for a long time."

"That's why I'm surprised you don't remember Tunstall. He was a close friend of Hoover's. I'm told they worked together on quite a few projects, including the Martin Luther King surveillance."

Roush answered quickly. "There was no project like that. There was never any *surveillance,* as you call it, of King. On a few occasions we were asked to send men to help out with security. But that was all. And there was nobody named Tunstall working for the bureau. Not then and not now. Not ever, since I've been there."

"I didn't say he was one of your agents. His association with Mr. Hoover, as I understand it, was unofficial. The fact is, he's been in Washington for thirty years. He's been attached to half a dozen different agencies and departments. And always, it seems, in some kind of *unofficial* capacity. The government personnel center lists him as an advisor to the Justice Department. But nobody there seems to know who he is."

Roush squeezed out a tight smile. "Good. I'm glad I'm not the *only* one."

"It's a slim chance," Gabe said then, "but maybe Mr. Tunstall uses more than one name. Maybe you'd recognize his face if you saw it." He took two photographs out of his desk drawer, walked across to Roush's chair, and handed them to him. "That's him, right there, with Sam Giancano. And in this one, taken in Peking, he's standing just behind Richard Nixon."

Roush pointed at a face on the China picture. "This is Tunstall?"

"That's right."

Roush shook his head. "I know half a dozen men who look a little like that." He studied the picture more closely. "But I don't know *this* one."

"You're sure?"

"Positive."

Gabe's intercom buzzed them. He went back to his desk and picked up the receiver. "There's a man holding at that California number," Monica said. "He says there's nobody there named Tunstall."

"Tell him it's a person-to-person call for Oscar Tunstall. Tell him it's extremely urgent. From Washington. Tell him Darby Roush is calling."

Gabe sat back with the receiver at his ear, looking across the desk. Roush was trying to look detached and unperturbed. But he wasn't doing very well.

Monica's voice clicked on again. "Mr. Tunstall's on the line."

Holding one hand over the mouthpiece, Gabe said to Roush, "I've got Tunstall at the other end. Do you want to talk to him or should I?"

"I told you once . . . " Roush began strongly, then dried up. Into the mouthpiece, Gabe said, "Oscar . . . ?" and the voice at the other end said, "What's the problem, Darby?"

"Darby Roush is sitting here in my office," Gabe answered. "I'm Senator Treptow."

The line went dead suddenly. When Gabe hung up, he turned to Roush and said, "Mr. Tunstall doesn't want to talk to me. I'm not surprised." He buzzed Monica then and said, "Do you want to come in and bring your book?"

To Roush he said, "I'm going to dictate a telegram to Tunstall. I think you'll be interested in what I have to say."

"Senator Treptow, I came here in good faith because you asked me to. But if you're playing some kind of a game . . . "

"There's a game going on, but *I'm* not playing it. I'm just trying to figure out what it *is.*"

Monica came in then and sat down with her pad and pencil ready.

"You have the Hartwig address," Gabe said to her. "I want to send this telegram there. It goes to Oscar Tunstall. To be phoned in to the number we just called. I also want the message hand-delivered, top priority, from the telegraph company's office in Santa Cruz. And I want to mail a copy from here, express mail, so the postman will deliver it tomorrow. Send a Xerox copy to Mr. Darby Roush at the Federal Bureau of Investigation and another copy to Arthur Garrigus. Got it?"

"All set."

"Here's the message.

Mr. Tunstall: This will inform you that we know you are holding Mr. and Mrs. Leo Hartwig captive in their own house, depriving them of their freedom and their civil rights. I have arranged twenty-four-hour surveillance of the Hartwig house. Including an air watch by beach-patrol helicopters.

If you try to move the Hartwigs to another location you

*will be arrested and formally charged with kidnapping. I
will contact you later to arrange a meeting with Leo Hartwig. Darby Roush knows that I am sending you this wire.
Signed, Gabe Treptow, United States Senate.*

As soon as Monica left the room, Roush said, "You're running
a bluff. You can't authorize a surveillance. And you can't have
anybody arrested. For kidnapping or anything else."

"You're right," Gabe said. "I'm sure Tunstall knows that, too.
If he doesn't he *will* as soon as you get back to your office and
call him. But that won't keep Garrigus from printing the telegram."

Roush stood up. "What the hell are you trying to do?"

"I'm lighting fires all over the place. Trying to smoke out the
rats."

"You light too many fires, you might get your ass burned."

"That's not a threat, is it?" Gabe stood up and walked to the
door. "I hope not, because so far all you've done is tell a few lies.
But if you start making threats you could paint yourself into a
corner. You know what I mean?"

Gabe opened the door and stepped back. Roush, his jaw
thrust forward and his mouth clamped in an iron line, walked
stiffly out of the room.

 "Wait a minute, God damn it." Lasker's hand was
gripping the telephone receiver like a weapon.
His neck was very pink suddenly, and the color
was spreading up into his cheeks. "Who the hell do
you think you're talking to?"

"I'm talking to *you*," Tunstall said, "and I hope you're paying attention. Because if you people don't get into action back there that whole fucking building you're sitting in is going to come down on your head."

"What does that mean?"

"It means things are coming unstuck. We're springing leaks all over the place."

"Treptow's guessing. That's all. He's on a fishing expedition. Running a bluff and trying to get us to jump at it."

"Bullshit. When I see my name in the paper, to me that's more than a bluff. I don't like to see my name in print. When I hear helicopters hovering over this place every hour on the hour, and when a United States senator calls me direct on an unlisted number that nobody knows except you and Dalrymple, I start to get nervous as hell. This guy's got a bead on me. I'm telling you that. He knows exactly where I am and what I'm up to and those goddamned choppers are all over us like buzzards."

"We can stop that," Lasker said. "I don't know how he pulled that one off but we can stop it. I guarantee you."

"Too late," Tunstall said. "The damage is done. I'm getting telegrams phoned in to an unlisted number. How do you peg that one? And you want to know what the message is? Senator Treptow says he's going to nail my ass for kidnapping. What do you say to that?"

"He's crazy. He can't nail you for anything."

"Good. I'm glad you're feeling so confident. I'm *not*. Tyson and I are bailing out of this fishbowl. And we're doing it tonight."

"Don't do it. It's a bad move. That's what he wants you to do. Look, we know about the telegram. Roush came to us as soon as he left Treptow. Dalrymple and I went over the whole thing with Newquist. We agreed you have to sit tight and let us handle Treptow at this end. Don't make a move."

"I told you. I'm going."

"I hate to pull rank on you," Lasker said, "but that's an order. Straight from Newquist."

"You tell Newquist for me he can kiss my ass. I've been in these fire drills before. If the shit hits the fan on this thing, it's gonna be every man for himself. It always is. So I'm getting a head start. If you give me a go-ahead I'll take Hartwig and his wife with me. At least that will give you a little more breathing room. If you try to fuck me up I'll leave them here with the number of the nearest police station taped to the telephone. What'll it be?"

"What about Tyson?" Lasker said. "What does he . . . "

"He's no idiot. He's going with me. He's standing right here and he's as pissed off as I am. You want to talk to him?"

"No, that's all right." Then, "Look, I'll have to get back to you. I'll call you back in half an hour."

"No good. I'm not answering the phone. I'll call *you* back in fifteen minutes and you'd better have an answer. 'Cause that's the last time I'm calling."

Tunstall called again in exactly fifteen minutes. "I talked with Newquist and Dalrymple," Lasker said. "They think you're making a mistake, but we'll support you. If you agree to take the Hartwigs with you."

"That's better. Now you're using your head."

"How can we contact you?"

"You can't. I'll be keeping an eye on the situation. If you manage to pull the plug on Treptow we'll see where we go from there. And let me give you some advice about that bird. He's a germ. And you'd better find a way to vaccinate yourselves or he'll have you on your back. You can't just build a wall and hide behind it. With that guy you have to go on the attack. Hit him with every club you can get hold of. The girl too. I have a hunch she'll turn around once you unload on her folks.

"One more thing," Tunstall said then. "If you get your tails in a crack, don't get the idea that you can wrap everything up in a package and hang it around my neck. If I go under, the President and the Secretary better be ready to go with me."

When Lasker told Newquist and Dalrymple the details of his telephone conversation with Tunstall, Newquist said, "I don't like it. I thought Tunstall was a rock." He picked up his telephone. "But he's right about one thing. We have to push harder on Treptow." Into the phone he said, "Lola. Call Lennie and find out if Angela Marks is in town. I have to talk to her."

When he hung up the phone, he said to Dalrymple, "Get hold of Senator Bright and tell him what we have in mind. If he gives you any static let me know. Then see how fast you can set up an appointment with Treptow. Play it loose. But try to sit down with him as fast as possible." He turned to Lasker. "And let's move on the Kosta thing. The quicker we pull that off the better."

The offices of Global Financial Horizons were in a corner suite on the penthouse floor. The heavily carved teak doors were locked. But they clicked open with a soft buzz a few seconds after Kosta pressed the signal button beside the entrance.

The foyer was thickly carpeted and forty feet long. One glass wall with sliding doors opening out on a wide terrace with grass like a thick carpet, dwarf trees and shrubs in urns and ceramic planters, bright clumps of flowers, and a sculptured fountain bubbling blue and white in the afternoon sun.

At the back of the room, softly lighted, at a desk against the wall, sat a beautifully chiseled black woman, her gray hair pulled back in a loose knot, diamond earrings glittering, and a jade necklace double-looped around her throat. When Kosta identified herself, the woman said, "Yes, of course. From Senator Treptow's office. Mrs. Tamuri is expecting you."

Oni Tamuri, behind her mahogany desk, nestled in a soft leather chair, like a perfectly mounted stone from some remote corner of Peru. Soft but slender under a pale-blue silk tunic with a high neck; her hair, blue-black as a crow's wing, was cropped short as a boy's. Her only jewelry was a wide diamond band, channel set, a narrow sapphire guard on either side of it.

On the linen-covered wall behind her desk, a Pissarro landscape swam in a pool of soft light, a Brancusi bronze on a pedestal just below it. On one side wall there was a fine van Dongen, a woman with a macaw, and opposite that, a cluster of five Cézanne watercolors.

"What can we do for you?" she said. Kosta explained briefly about the H-14 investigation.

Mrs. Tamuri nodded. "Miss Sugarman in Senator Treptow's office told me something about that."

"Good. Then you know what we're up to," Kosta said. "One of the loose ends we're trying to clear up involves a passenger named Ralph Benedict." She paused and tried to gauge what reaction, if any, she was getting from Mrs. Tamuri's flawless face. All she could see was total composure. Bright, attentive eyes. Innocence and contentment.

"Mr. Benedict insured his life for two hundred thousand dollars before the SAI plane took off from Indianapolis. I'm sure you've seen those insurance machines they have in airport terminals."

"Of course."

"In the section of the contract where you must indicate a beneficiary, Mr. Benedict wrote the name of this company, Global Financial."

"You can't be serious."

"I can show you a photocopy of the contract if you'd like to see it."

"No, of course not. I don't *doubt* you," Mrs. Tamuri said. "It's just that I . . . are you saying that GFH can claim that money?"

"They already have. The claim was paid last February. The check was deposited ten days later."

"But this man, Mr. Benedict—who is he?"

"I was hoping you could help me with that one," Kosta said. "I assume he had some connection with your company."

"It's possible, I suppose. I thought I knew all of our people, but we do have a large staff in Zurich, more than two hundred employees, and nearly a hundred in Tokyo. So it's possible. . . . "

"How many people work here in Washington?"

"Oh, we're just a token operation. We have perhaps half a dozen clerical and stenographic people. But aside from them, there are just the three of us. Mr. Hopewell, Mrs. Garvin, and

myself. Mr. Hopewell is our United States director. But he
spends at least half his time, maybe more, in Tokyo and Zurich.
Mrs. Garvin is the handsome lady you met outside."

"When I came down the corridor there seemed to be a great
many offices."

"Oh, yes. Sometimes we have ten or twelve corporate officers
in Washington at one time. On those occasions we need all our
available space."

"Do you mind telling me something about the structure of
your company?"

"Not at all. We are an international investment organization,
incorporated in Liberia, licensed to function in twenty-one
countries on five continents. We have been in operation for
nineteen years, and I'm delighted to tell you we're thriving."

"Is it Mr. Hopewell who oversees the day-to-day operation of
this office in Washington?"

"Mr. Hopewell is a key officer in the corporation. But as I said,
he is seldom here. So much of the responsibility rests with me."

"You would supervise the banking routine, then? You would
know about the financial details of your local accounts?"

Mrs. Tamuri's smile lost none of its warmth, but her voice
cooled slightly. "This *is* a *financial* organization, Miss Kosta.
And I'm sure you realize—"

"Of course I do. I assure you I'm not investigating your business operation. Neither is Senator Treptow. But we are puz-
zled. Because Mr. Benedict's insurance check was stamped for
deposit in this office and deposited in the GFH account just
downstairs in the Maryland Federal Bank."

"I'm sure you're mistaken."

Kosta took a piece of paper out of her bag and handed it to
Mrs. Tamuri. "This is a photocopy of both sides of the check. It
came from the files of the insurance company that issued it."

Mrs. Tamuri studied the piece of paper carefully. Then she
picked up the phone and said, "Can we reach Mr. Rhyzdani
now? Good. As quickly as possible."

"All I can say," she said then, resettling in her elegant chair,
"is that there must have been an oversight. Our accounts often
deposit or withdraw large amounts in a single day. Sometimes
millions of dollars in a few hours. I can only guess that one of

our clerical people handled this check as routine and deposited it routinely with a number of other checks. I simply missed it when I reviewed the accounts."

"But that tells us nothing about Ralph Benedict."

The phone rang then, and Mrs. Tamuri picked it up. Before she spoke into the mouthpiece, she said to Kosta, "No, it doesn't. But perhaps Mr. Rhyzdani can help with that."

She spoke into the phone for several minutes, her voice almost inaudible, using some soft, guttural language that Kosta could barely hear and could not identify. Then she sat curled in her chair, like a freshly bathed kitten, and listened. Longer than the time she had spent talking. She had been on the telephone for almost thirty minutes when she hung up at last.

"Ahh . . . well . . . " she said. "Some of the mystery is solved. Mr. Rhyzdani *was* aware of the check. He knew that our company had been named Mr. Benedict's beneficiary. He suspects that the check was originally mailed from the insurance company to our Zurich office, and then was deposited by one of our Zurich people when he or she was here in Washington. That is not our standard routine, but it does happen on occasion.

"Regarding Mr. Benedict, no information, I'm afraid. Mr. Rhyzdani confirms that no such person has ever been employed by GFH. A thorough search of personnel files was made. We feel that the man was perhaps a former employee who for some reason decided to use another name. Why he selected us as his beneficiary, no one will ever know. Perhaps he had formed a genuine affection for the firm. Or . . . perhaps it was an ironic gesture toward an organization he had come to hate. Perhaps he had a twisted sense of humor. Maybe he was angry at his wife. Maybe he was drunk. I guess we'll never know, will we? I'm sorry I can't be more helpful."

When the telephone call came from Mark Dalrymple, Gabe told Monica to say he'd call back. When he hung up, he said to Jud, "What's the poop on Dalrymple?"

"State Department."

"That much I know. What else?"

"Up and coming. Maximum achiever. Ambitious as hell. Takes a lot of crap from the Secretary but keeps turning the other cheek. Very bright. Very tough. His friends call him Killer and he likes it. Used to be the resident genius on the Middle East. But he shot his mouth off once too often about Israel, Begin leaned on the President, and Dalrymple got repositioned. But now he's in a stronger slot than ever. Sticks his nose in anyplace he wants. Troubleshoots for the Secretary and handles liaison with the White House. He keeps everybody on their toes, but they like him over there. The book on him is that he'll never get the top job at State but that he'll never go hungry in Washington."

"What does that mean exactly?"

"He's got notes on everybody. Knows where the bodies are buried and *who* buried them. What's he want from you?"

"I was counting on you telling *me* that."

"I'll give you an educated guess. If your hunch is right, if somebody's trying to hide something about the H-14, then maybe he wants to lean on you a little."

"Good. I'll let him lean on his phone for a while."

Dalrymple's office called four times before midafternoon. Finally Gabe took the call.

"Sorry I couldn't get back to you," he said. "Crazy day over here."

"No problem," Dalrymple said.

"What can I do for you?"

"Nothing at all. Just tag this as a social call. Sooner or later I get to know most of the men on the Hill. And since you and I haven't met yet, I thought maybe we should schedule a lunch. On me."

"Sounds great. I'd like that."

"What's your calendar look like?" Dalrymple said.

"Well . . . that could be a problem. We've got a heavy work load over here right now. I've been putting in some brutal hours."

"I know what you mean. We have weeks over here when my kids forget what I look like. But we still take time to eat lunch." Gabe didn't answer, so Dalrymple went on. "Tell you what I'll do. I'll come over that way and save you some driving time. We'll grab a steak at The Monocle."

"That's nice of you," Gabe said. "But here's the situation. As we've been talking I checked my calendar. I don't have a free lunch for five weeks. Can you believe that?"

There was a thick pause. Finally Dalrymple said, "Maybe we should settle for a drink. Or we could have dinner one night if you'd like that."

"I think that's probably better. Let's meet for a drink some afternoon."

"You name it. Anytime you say."

"Let's do this," Gabe said. "Let me sit down with my appointments lady and work something out. Maybe I can finesse one of these lunch dates. I'll get back to you."

"Try to work it out. I really do want to sit down with you."

"Is it something pressing?" Gabe said. "Because if it is . . ."

"No. Nothing heavy. Just what I said. A little get-acquainted meeting."

As soon as he hung up, Gabe called Monica in. "From now on, when Dalrymple calls, I'm not here."

"No matter what?"

"No matter what."

"Are we going to be nice about it, cool, or nasty?"

"Very nice," Gabe said. "Sweet as sugar. Tell him I feel very remiss and extremely apologetic. Tell him anything you want. Just make sure I don't talk to him."

 At two thirty in the morning, Tunstall awakened Leo and Louise Hartwig. While she was in the bathroom putting a robe on over her pajamas, her husband, still not fully awake, was shouting at Tunstall.

"What do you mean we're leaving? It's the middle of the night for Christ's sake."

"That's right," Tunstall said. "You have about twenty minutes to get yourselves together. We're pulling out at three."

"No we're not. We're not going anywhere."

"Suit yourself. If you're not dressed when it's time to leave, we'll take you in your pajamas. If you try to make a fuss about it we'll chloroform you and carry you. One way or another, we'll be on the road at three o'clock."

It was a heavy summer night, misty and hot even along the ocean, an off-desert wind pushing the cool air back from the shore. At precisely three o'clock, Tunstall and Wib Tyson walked the Hartwigs out of the house, locked it behind them, got into the car, pulled out into the road, and headed north toward Santa Cruz, Hartwig in the front seat with Tyson, Mrs. Hartwig in back with Tunstall.

Forty minutes later, they turned into the parking lot at the Santa Cruz airport. Tyson drove to the north end of the lot and parked there. Sixty yards away, an unmarked eight-passenger jet sat waiting. "That's it," Tunstall said to Tyson. Then, "You take Mrs. Hartwig on board. We'll be along in a minute."

"I don't want to do that," she said. "I'll wait for Leo."

"We'll just be a minute," Tunstall said. "I have some things to discuss with your husband. You can listen if you want to, but I think he'd like it better if you didn't."

She turned to her husband. "What does that mean? What does he mean by that?"

"God knows," Hartwig said. Then, "Go ahead. Get on the plane. I'll be right there."

He sat in the car watching her as she crossed the landing area with Tyson, climbed the boarding steps, and disappeared inside the plane. As soon as she was out of sight, Tunstall took an envelope out of his inside jacket pocket and said, "There are a couple things here I'd like you to sign."

"Not a chance," Hartwig said. "I'm not signing anything."

Tunstall slipped two neatly folded pages out of the envelope. "Nothing objectionable about it. Read it for yourself." He unfolded one of the pages and handed it to Hartwig.

> To Whom It May Concern:
>   I understand there has been some speculation as to my whereabouts, some questions about my safety. In answer to these concerns I would like to say that my wife, Louise, and I are perfectly well and happy. But since my retirement from Hartwig Systems we have chosen to live a secluded life. After many years of social and business activity we welcome the chance to be alone, to have some much-needed privacy. We are enjoying ourselves immensely and we would deeply appreciate not being disturbed or even speculated about. Thank you.

"Jesus," Hartwig said, "this is a joke. What makes you think I would sign this? And what's the point anyway? Who would you send it to?"

Tunstall held up the other page. "Two copies," he said. "One to a senator who has been anxious to find out where you are and what you're up to. And the other copy to a lawyer friend of mine to file for future reference."

"You don't think the authorities—"

"I'm not concerned about the authorities," Tunstall said. "I just like to plan ahead. It keeps things neat."

"Well, I'm not going to sign it."

"Suit yourself." Tunstall took the piece of paper from him, folded it neatly with the second page, and slipped them back inside the envelope. "But I don't think you're going to like the alternative."

He rolled down the car window, put his hand outside, and waved. Out on the runway, a man in red coveralls ran up the portable stairs, closed the door of the jet, and began to secure it from the outside.

"Wait a minute," Hartwig said, "what's he doing?"

"I told you you wouldn't like it. But you've just changed our plans. Now your wife and Tyson will be making the trip by themselves. You and I are going back to the house."

"You son of a bitch . . . you can't do that."

"Yes I can. I'm *doing* it."

The attendant came back down the stairs and began rolling them away from the side of the plane.

"Stop him," Hartwig said quietly. "Don't let the plane take off."

Hartwig reached outside the window and signaled again. Wi'' his other hand he took the envelope out of his pocket and gave it to Hartwig.

In a television interview with Angela Marks, Senator Bright began the public counterattack against Gabe Treptow. In answer to a question about bipartisan cooperation in matters affecting defense and national security, he said:

"To address your question directly, when a situation arises where the national security is at issue, the membership of the Senate is quick to recognize that fact. In such instances, the welfare of the nation has clear priority over party differences.

"We're talking about character now, aren't we? Personal integrity. I am proud to tell you that in my sixteen years in the Senate, my colleagues have been, almost without exception, men of remarkable character."

Miss Marks picked up on his phrase "almost without exception" and asked him to expand on that. The senator frowned with concern, dropped his voice a full tone, and went on.

"In a republic such as ours where almost every man or woman is free to seek public office, it is inevitable that on certain isolated occasions an unfit person will be elected. In the Senate this happens rarely. But I confess it *does* happen.

"I am embarrassed to tell you that we have at the present time such a man in the Senate. A man who simply should not be there."

When Miss Marks asked him pointedly if he was referring to Senator Treptow of Illinois, Bright at first refused to acknowledge that. But finally he capitulated.

"When we listen to Treptow's irresponsible statements, monitor his shameless use of the media, and witness his careless amorality, we can be thankful for one thing. He shows us, by contrast, the decency and character of the other ninety-nine men in the United States Senate.

"I do not, however, intend to dignify Treptow's activities by discussing them in detail. I sympathize sincerely with the good people of Illinois who sent him here. I can only assume they were as thoroughly deceived as the leaders of the Democratic Party were. I do caution all of our citizens, however, as well as members of the media, to think twice when you read Senator Treptow's unsubstantiated theories about deception and dishonesty in the federal government. I would not call him a traitor, as some people have, but I do believe he is a seriously disturbed man."

In the Chicago area, a local news program followed the Angela Marks interview. It was reported there that a Moslem businessman named Jamal Hamad, formerly a resident of

Bedaki, had been found dead in his hotel apartment on Fullerton Street, along with his wife and two children. All four had been strangled.

No connection was made between these deaths and the earlier killing of Harun Haikal. Or with the limousine explosion in Washington, D.C. Only in a small part of the Moslem community on Chicago's North Side was the connection made. And of course the Kaskar knew.

 Gabe received Hartwig's letter the day after it was sent, express mail, from Santa Cruz. When he checked with the California park patrol, they reported that the Hartwig house seemed deserted.

Gabe's staff talked with flight control at the Santa Cruz airport. They learned that a private jet, four passengers aboard, had taken off at four o'clock that previous morning. The pilot's name was Rod Greber. His flight plan showed Albuquerque as his destination. Further checking with Albuquerque airport officials revealed that Greber's plane had not landed there.

Gabe called London then and spoke to Roland Casper in his office at Peddicord Industries; he asked him if he knew where Leo Hartwig could be reached.

"I'm quite sure he's at his home in California."

"I'm afraid not. He and his wife left there yesterday and no one seems to know where they went."

"Holiday, I expect," Casper said. "Leo's keen on deep-sea fishing, you know. I wouldn't be surprised if he's in a motor launch somewhere right now. Pulling in a marlin. Mazatlán's a good bet, I should think."

"Do you mind telling me when you saw him last?"

"I'd be happy to, Senator, but I'm not sure I can remember precisely. I know it was sometime last winter."

"Have you spoken with him on the telephone?"

"Of course. I must have. But again I would have to look up those dates."

"I see," Gabe said. Then, "According to a clipping I have here from *The Wall Street Journal,* you succeeded Mr. Hartwig as president of Hartwig Systems on February 12 this year."

"That was the official date, yes. But I was simply an interim officer. Since then we've moved Peter Sidney into that post."

"Are you saying you haven't *seen* Leo Hartwig or spoken to him since February twelfth?"

"Not precisely. I did say I had not seen him. I believe that we have talked on the telephone but I cannot give you the exact dates. In deference to your office I'm trying to be helpful, Senator Treptow, but I'm not quite clear what information you want from me. We admitted our culpability in both those H-14 crashes."

"I have a clipping in front of me from the *Los Angeles Times,* the day after the FAA released their final conclusions. They quote Leo Hartwig. I'll read you what he said."

"That's not necessary, I'm familiar with that interview," Casper said. "It made things very awkward for us."

"Is that why Hartwig was retired so quickly?"

"His retirement was voluntary."

"That's not the impression I got," Gabe said.

"Mr. Hartwig seemed to be feeling a great deal of tension. That is the principal reason we agreed to accept his resignation. We thought perhaps his health was in jeopardy."

"Then you have no idea why he implied that the H-14's were sabotaged?"

"None whatsoever. The facts are these. We were at fault. The aircraft was at fault. The hydraulic system failed. It's as simple and tragic as that."

When Gabe arrived for his appointment at the Federal Aviation Administration, the director, Ernest Mossler, was well prepared. Along with his chief investigator, Wesley Duggan, he escorted Gabe to an elaborate conference room. There, with the help of two assistants, Duggan put on a detailed, hour-long presentation of slides, graphs, statistics, and probability charts, intricate case histories of the two crashes, all the facts and evidence that had led the investigators to their final conclusions.

When the presentation ended, after the assistants had been dismissed, Gabe said, "I understand there were no witnesses to the Air Force Three crash in West Virginia. Is that correct?"

"We interviewed more than a thousand people around Elkins," Duggan said. "Eleven hundred and fourteen to be exact. We really combed that area. But no one saw the plane come down. Or if they did, they didn't feel like telling us about it."

"Those mountain people can be very secretive," Mossler said.

"If there weren't any witnesses," Gabe said, "how can you be sure the plane didn't explode before it crashed?"

"A midair explosion tortures the fuselage metal differently than a contact explosion. An expert can tell the difference on even a small piece of aluminum."

"Also," Mossler said, "if there had been a midair explosion, debris would have scattered over several miles."

"That's pretty wild country," Gabe said. "Isn't it possible that debris could have fallen in the woods or the mountains and nobody's discovered it?"

"It's possible, but—"

"Let me ask you this," Gabe cut in. "What if a witness came forward now who *had* seen the plane in flight? What if he said it exploded in midair and *then* crashed?"

Mossler spoke slowly and carefully. "In some circumstances we might reopen the investigation. In this case, if no new evidence supported the witness's story, I think we would stand behind our original conclusions."

"We've done this many times," Duggan said. "We have experience. When we combine that experience with our knowledge of flight and the laws of probability, when we feed all the data through our computers, we are convinced we can come up with a foolproof picture of exactly what happened. We trust ourselves and our process more than we do the emotional reporting of most eyewitnesses."

"In both the H-14 crashes," Mossler said, "we are absolutely certain that the plane was at fault. The hydraulic system failed. It's as simple and tragic as that."

"It was scary," Gabe said. "Like two robots. Programmed to say the same words. I mean, it was word for word. Letter-perfect. As though somebody had written it down and handed out copies to be memorized. Except those two clowns must have taken it literally. They recited it like the multiplication tables—'The hydraulic system failed. It's as simple and tragic as that.'"

"Who do you see next?" Kosta said.

"General Stecko."

"Any problem getting to him?"

"No problems anywhere. All of a sudden I'm as welcome as the prodigal."

"Why not?" she said. "They've got nothing to lose. They've all got their stories straight."

"It's all right. We're chipping away," Gabe said. "I think we're moving ahead."

"Not me. I feel as hung up as I did at the beginning. If somebody blew up the SAI flight to kill Benedict, why did they do it? Who are they and who the hell is *he?* With Air Force Three we're in worse shape. Same scenario. Who would want to get rid of anybody who was on that plane? So far the answer is *nobody.* All the passengers and all the crew check out pure as a lily.

"So we say, 'All right, somebody who was *supposed* to be on that plane didn't make it. The plane was booby-trapped before the passengers got on, so when the real target didn't show the plane blew up anyway.' That makes as much sense as anything, doesn't it?"

"It does to me."

"But who the hell was it they were after?"

"Any news from your friend at the Pentagon?"

"Bad news. They transferred her two days ago. Just at the wrong time. She had an idea she could find out from the catering service how many meals they loaded on that flight. If there were more meals than passengers . . . "

"We still wouldn't know who the missing passenger was. There has to be a flight manifest filed somewhere. That would show the passenger list."

"Terrific, all we have to do is locate it. And then try to get our hands on it."

"Maybe I can do a number on Stecko. I will if I can."

"We may have an in at Andrews Air Base. Nellie's friend Jackie Rovach has a boyfriend out there in traffic control. I'll follow up on that."

"Are we all clued out on Benedict?" Gabe said.

"I don't know. I hope not."

"Is there any point in going back to Global Financial?"

Kosta made a face. "Not unless I want to play sandwich with Mrs. Tamuri and that sensational-looking black lady at the reception desk. When I left the other day, Mrs. Tamuri walked me out to the reception room. And once those two made eye contact they started flashing signals like a couple of radar transmitters. I felt like the daily special at the top of the menu."

Gabe grinned. "You're in a chancy profession. Sometimes you have to make a few sacrifices."

"Thanks a lot," she said. Then, "One thing I'd bet on. If Mrs. Tamuri knows who Benedict is, she's not about to confide in me. My hunch is she *doesn't* know. I think the answer's in Zurich."

"With Rhyzdani?"

"With somebody. But a lot of good it does us. We're not there."

"We can be. There are planes leaving all the time."

"I thought of that. But Rhyzdani's on his guard now. He's not about to roll out the red carpet for me."

"Maybe not. But if the front door slams we'll try the back. An old friend of Chet's is on the Banking Committee. International finance. He can muscle us in to see Rhyzdani. I'd bet on it. It's a long shot, but so is everything else. There has to be a reason why Benedict made GFH his beneficiary."

Amenable and expansive in his Pentagon office, Major General Craig Stecko was also well prepared and articulate in his meeting with Gabe.

"Of course we reviewed all the possibilities of pilot error," he said. "Our experience has taught us that personnel is subject to error more often than equipment is. In this case, however, there were three first-rate people in that cockpit. Pilot, copilot, and flight engineer. Between them, these men had logged thousands of hours in jet equipment. So . . . although we reviewed all aspects in the area of pilot failure, we felt from the start that the chances were one in several thousand that all *three* of these capable fliers could have failed to respond to whatever emergency came up that day."

"Copilots and flight engineers are always present on large jets, aren't they?"

"Yes, they are."

"But still they crash."

Stecko nodded. "But if you study those cases you'll find that in almost every instance there was a critical *time* factor involved. *Reaction* time. Takeoff or landing, for example. Or a midair collision. A problem develops in seconds and *only* the pilot can deal with it. There's no time for anyone else to take over. In that split second, any coordination failure on the pilot's part, any lapse in judgment, means almost certain destruction for the aircraft."

"But in this case you're saying the time factor was *not* critical."

"How could it be? Air Force Three was at thirty thousand feet, almost her cruising altitude. So whatever flight problem came up, there should have been more than enough time and altitude for the crew to function, to make adjustments."

"But they didn't."

"That's my point. That's why our independent conclusions agreed with those of the FAA and NTSB people. Only one thing could have happened. A sudden, massive equipment failure. The aircraft went into a power dive and could not be stabilized."

"You're talking about the hydraulic system?"

The general nodded. "A critical failure there. A hydraulic leak seems to have developed in the right wing area. That meant the forward slats could not be controlled from the cockpit. Those slats moved suddenly into the airstream, the plane veered, rolled to the right, and went into a seventy-five-degree power dive. It could have fallen at a speed of eight hundred miles per hour."

"What you've just described to me," Gabe said, "almost word for word, is the official explanation for why that TWA 727 almost crashed over Michigan in April 1979."

"I'm aware of that. We think the circumstances must have been very similar."

"What about the possibility of a midair explosion? Was *that* considered?"

"Every possibility was reviewed. But we found absolutely no on-the-ground evidence of such an explosion."

If Gabe had expected to hear from Stecko's lips the same litany he'd heard from Ernest Mossler and Roland Casper, he was disappointed. If the general had been briefed or rehearsed, he was clever enough to rephrase, to put the key conclusion in his own words. Or at least in a different order. "We're convinced there was a failure of the hydraulic system. No amount of skill or experience could have averted it. It's tragic but true."

Just before leaving Stecko's office, Gabe said, "I know the full list of crew and passengers was published in the papers, but I wonder if it would be possible for me to see a copy of the flight manifest?"

"No problem."

"If there were any last-minute cancellations or additions among the passengers it might be valuable to know those names."

"Of course."

"We have some information indicating there was a discrepancy between the number of meals ordered from the caterers and the actual number of passengers and crew on board."

The general said he didn't know anything about that. "But I'm sure that kind of mistake happens all the time."

"I suppose so."

"Anyway, I'll have a copy of that flight manifest in your office first thing tomorrow morning."

Next morning the manifest did not show up. But an Air Force officer did. Captain Merle Fairchild. "General Stecko sends his apologies. There could be a slight delay in delivering the papers you requested. There's some construction going on out at Andrews and a lot of our records are being transferred. But no more than a few days' delay, General Stecko says. Two weeks at the most."

 The night before she was scheduled to fly to Zurich, Kosta called her mother in Harrisonburg. "It's no big deal," she said. "Just a fast trip. I should be back in four or five days. A week at the longest. I just wanted you to know I'll be away in case you tried to call and couldn't reach me."

"It sounds like a nice trip. Switzerland's pretty."

"I don't expect to see much of it. I'll be too busy."

"Well, anyway, you watch out for yourself. From what I see in the papers, those European airports are no place to be. Hijackers and crazy people everyplace you look. You couldn't pay me to climb into an airplane. But I'd just about as soon do that as sit around in an airport someplace with the bullets flying."

"Nobody ever gets shot in Switzerland, Mom. People just go there to visit their money."

"Well, your dad will be all excited. You know how he is. Every time you go to some new place he marks it down on that big map he keeps down at the café. Gives him something new to brag about. To hear him tell it, Barbara Walters can't hold a candle to you. Too bad you didn't call ten minutes later. I expect him home anytime."

"It's only a little past seven. What's he doing, locking up early?"

"No. But he's got a new girl working for him and she's a crackerjack. Only been there a week or so and he's got her closing up, dropping the money off at the bank, and everything."

"Where'd she come from?"

"Georgia, I think he said. Maybe North Carolina. Only been up here a few weeks. But she's taken a load off your dad's back, what with Garnet being four months pregnant and only able to work mornings. And Lizzie's arthritis has got her bunged up so she can't work the counter more than an hour at a time."

"Well, let me see if I can catch him before he leaves for home."

"No need to do that. Just sit tight and I'll have him call you back soon as he comes in."

"I can't, Mom. I'm ready to go out. I'm due someplace at seven thirty and I'm late as it is."

When she called the restaurant, a girl's voice answered. "He's just about to go out the door. I'll get him back here."

"Just caught me," her father said when he came on the phone. "I was heading for the house."

"Bankers' hours," Kosta said.

She told him about her trip then, repeating everything she'd told her mother. When he ran out of questions finally, she said, "I'll write a card from there. And I'll call you as soon as I get back." Just before she hung up, she said, "What about this new girl you've got working for you? Mom says she's a whiz."

"No doubt about it. Gwen Pickett's her name and she's really saved my bacon. Picked up the slack for Garnet and Lizzie. Took over like she's been here all her life."

"Where's she from? Mom said she's from out of town."

"That's right. North Carolina. A town called Monroe. It's just down Highway 74 from Charlotte. And this'll give you a laugh. Remember that red-haired girl you were looking at when I drove you to the airport, the one driving the light-blue Dodge camper? Well, that's her. She came in here looking for work the day after you left. I would never have recognized her if I hadn't seen her car parked out in front. Then I remembered about the red hair. It's no wonder you thought you'd seen her before. She told me she'd been here four or five days, driving all over, looking for a job."

"Well . . . I don't know," Kosta said. "Just make sure she's not a fly-by-night. She could clean out the cash register some night and be long-gone back to North Carolina."

"Not this girl. She comes from a good family. Says her great-grandfather was a Greek."

 On Friday afternoon, when Gabe and Kosta checked in at the Ambassador's lounge in the TWA terminal at Dulles, the young woman at the desk said, "There's a message for you, Senator Treptow. Call Mr. Rimmer in your office."

As soon as Jud came on the phone, he said, "I've got lousy news, Gabe. They called from Fort Beck about an hour ago. It's your dad."

Half an hour later, Gabe was on an American Airlines flight to Chicago. Forty-five minutes later, Kosta was on her way to Zurich.

She had started to cry when Gabe came out of the phone booth and told her his father was dead. She wanted to put her arms around him. But all she could do was stand there with her hands at her sides, her face tilted down, and cry like a child.

Sitting in her plane seat, her cheeks still tear spotted, her eyes blurred and pink, she gave in at last to the turmoil she'd been fighting off for days. It had started God knows when, she didn't want to speculate, and it had spun out of control the moment Gabe walked away from the telephone at Dulles Airport, his eyes flat and wounded, and told her about his father.

Looking down at the ocean, trying to concentrate on external things, but trembling inside in a way that was totally new to her, she told herself that hers was a normal reaction, the quick empathy that any sensitive person would feel in the presence of someone else's sadness. It was true. She had been affected by Gabe's words and the way he looked at that moment. And it *had* happened before. She had felt strong reactions to someone else's grief. Many times.

But this was different. New and foreign. And stubbornly persistent. It refused to be redefined or explained away. The simple truth was, whatever may have triggered it, however specifically linked it was to Gabe's shock about his father, the fact was that her reaction had been sensual. Clearly that. Sexual. What she tried now to label as an impulse to console and commiserate had been, in truth, something remarkably different from that.

Standing there crying in the air terminal, her hands in her raincoat pockets, Kosta had felt a pulsing hunger, a need to hold on to someone, to Gabe, to touch him, to fuse herself to him, to begin at last the naked animal life she had avoided for so long. Whatever self-deceptions and elaborate detours she had used to sublimate her sexuality, they all, quite suddenly, lost their effectiveness.

Still she struggled. In the cool cocoon of the transatlantic flight, she settled deep in her chair, sipped orange juice, listened to recorded music, and waited for the well-trained systems of her intelligence to resume command.

Her mind had never failed her. She could always find an *idea* to fasten on, a life-saving rationale. Or if all else failed, a joke. Laugh it off. Find the humor. No emotion or syllogism, no sacred precept, was impervious to a smile or a giggle. Perilous situations had been tested in the past, notes kept, and case histories carefully filed. Kosta's survival kit was sophisticated and foolproof.

But not now. Now the center would not hold. Wherever her brain tried to lead, some soft, undisciplined part of her pulled it back. Through that entire flight from Washington to Zurich, she half-floated, asleep and awake, through a sea of crème caramel.

With no sexual memories to refer to, her subconscious lazily stuck together a schoolgirl collage of ballet dancers, trapeze artists, and track athletes in skimpy shorts, Tchaikovsky's themes superimposed. And all the while, Gabe Treptow, fully clothed and serious, strolled back and forth in the middle distance, dislodging those stuck-together pictures and images.

In Zurich, in her fifth-floor hotel room looking out across the lake, her mind busy with the questions she had brought with her and the answers she was finding, she discovered that her newfound sensuality would not be silenced. Her body was insisting now on a life of its own.

She took hot baths in the deep tub, soaped and rinsed and cologned herself. And stood naked outside on her balcony late at night, surrounded by mountain peaks and a low purple sky, the lake, black and gleaming, down below.

She preened herself, a new pleasure for her, stood in front of the long mirror and appraised, as well as she could, her small, well-shaped body, tried to envision it as a fully activated sexual weapon, a link, a cushion, a receptacle.

And in her soft Swiss bed, under the eiderdown, she touched herself, explored her body with her fingertips, not for the first time, but differently. Now she imagined that the warm hands belonged to someone else. Now she closed her eyes and murmured a name as her nipples tingled, her stomach quivered, and the lovely agony began between her legs.

Gradually, the very real fears she had lived with since that terrifying childhood moment in the Big Flat forest seemed to wash away. She still remembered, of course. But she was able now to paint a clear picture of that bloody scene in her mind and still function. She was able to say to herself, "That was an ugly day in my life. But it wasn't my *whole* life. I won't let it be."

In Chicago, Gabe connected with the Illinois-Wisconsin commuter line that flies to Fort Beck. When he landed at the airport, his Uncle Wayne and Aunt Nancy were there to meet him.

"We thought maybe you'd like to drive over to our place," Nancy said. "You could stay there with us till after the funeral and everything."

"Or we could bunk in with you for a few days," his uncle said, "if you'd like that better."

"I appreciate that," Gabe said. "But you don't have to worry about me. I won't come apart."

"It's just a rotten shame," Nancy said. "Everything happening at once. Chet and his little family going the way they did. And now, just a few months later . . . "

"I feel awful you won't at least let us buy you some supper," his uncle said when they let him out at his house. "Or I could run to the store for a few things and Nancy could fix you something right here."

"It's all right. I ate on the plane coming in to Chicago. You go on home and I'll see you tomorrow. I want to drive over to the nursing home and see what needs to be done."

"Your car's all gassed up for you. I ran the engine five minutes or so and it's in good shape."

"Thanks for everything," Gabe said. "I'll call you in the morning after I've made the arrangements."

Forty minutes later, when he saw Dr. Throckmorton, Gabe said, "I don't understand why he's still lying here like a dead animal. My uncle said he gave instructions to send him to the Brownridge Funeral Home six hours ago."

"We're just following the coroner's instructions. He told us to keep your father here till he'd had a chance to talk with you."

"What's the coroner have to do with it?"

"He thought you might want to have an autopsy."

Gabe found the coroner, Dr. Segal, at home. He was pink cheeked and solemn, just up from his dinner table.

"It's not unusual in cases like this," he said.

"Cases like what?"

"I'm not sure what you've been told about your father's death," the doctor said carefully, "but we have reason to suspect that Mr. Treptow may have . . . that the cause of death may have been an overdose of barbiturates."

" 'Reason to suspect'—what does that mean?"

"According to Dr. Throckmorton, your father had been experiencing no pain. And he slept well. So there was no reason to prescribe even a mild sedative."

"Then what makes you think . . . ?"

"A bottle of powerful barbiturates was missing from the night nurse's prescription cart. And when they cleaned out your father's room . . . when they . . . the empty barbiturate bottle was found in the wastebasket by the bed. Carefully wrapped in a Kleenex."

"Are you saying he committed suicide?"

"He died peacefully in his sleep. That's all we're sure of. It could have been simple heart failure. On the other hand . . . "

"On the other hand he could have swallowed a handful of pills and killed himself," Gabe said.

"If you authorize an autopsy we'll have the answer."

"I don't need an answer. You say he died peacefully. That's good enough for me. *Why* he died is his business."

Through all the funeral details, the open-coffin viewing, the eulogy with the relatives weeping, through the damp-eyed condolences of hundreds of people he scarcely knew, and through the stark ashes-to-ashes ritual of the burial itself, Gabe did not break down. No one looking at his face could fail to see the sorrow there. But no one was able to go home, review the day over supper, and tell his family, "Howard's boy just broke down and bawled like a baby."

The twenty or so closest relatives, the uncles and aunts and cousins, mostly Furmans and Knights, who came back to Gabe's house from the cemetery for coffee and pie and ice cream, all spoke among themselves, that day and later on, of how well Gabe had held up. Admiring him, respecting him for his strength and self-control, they didn't admit, even to themselves, that it disappointed them. But it did. Their own grief was not enough. They needed to witness his, to see his shoulders shake, to watch his hands come up and cover his face.

But Gabe refused to perform properly. He stood stiff and pale through all the long hours before and after the burial, nodding his head when someone told an anecdote about his father, smiling when it was an amusing anecdote, consoling his aunts and nieces and cousins. But he continued to keep his grief to himself.

When the women had carefully cleaned up the kitchen and put away the dishes and silver, when all the family members had trailed away to their cars and rolled down the long driveway toward the river road, even then Gabe did not let down.

After the last car left, he went inside, mixed himself a Scotch and soda, turned on the television set, and watched the last four innings of a White Sox–Cleveland Indians game from Comiskey Park. He went upstairs then, turned back his bed, and took a shower. With all the lights off he stood in front of the window, drying himself with a thick blue towel, and looked down across the summer fields toward the river, shining silver in the heavy blue night.

After the movement and turbulence of the past several days, the unending drone of hushed voices, the funeral music and earnest singing, the insistent reverence, the tension of watching people mourn, after all that, this silent, dark moment almost exploded in his ears. The shimmering stillness folded around him like a silk net. The familiar downslope scene he had gazed at thousands of times before tilted now and undulated strangely, the colors shifting and bleeding together, the distances expanding and compressing in soft waves.

Then, filtering through the open grassy stretches with bordering elm and sycamore, the river always silently there at the bottom, the remembered images of the graveyard floated into focus, enlarged themselves and moved closer. For just a shredded instant he saw the cluster of graves. Howard and Alice Treptow, the parents. Their son, Chet, and his wife, Evelyn. And their son. Crazy, whirlwind Sam. Buried there, what was left of him, with his Johnny Bench catcher's mitt.

Gabe sat down then in the chair by the window, the towel slipping to the floor by his feet. Sitting naked in the dark, his eyes fixed on some blurred nothingness on the wall in front of him, he felt his chin quiver. And the corners of his mouth pulled down. Then a sound like a death cry from some ancient cave came grinding and tearing its way up from the most locked-away inside part of him.

It was eight fifteen at night, late for Harrisonburg. In the last booth of Kosta's restaurant, in the back, a man and a woman were drinking coffee. No other customers. Up front, near the cash register, Gwen Pickett had come out from behind the counter and was sitting on one of the customer stools, sipping a glass of soda water. Mr. Kosta, looking concerned, was just opposite her, behind the counter.

"I don't know what got into me," Gwen said, pushing her red hair back from her forehead. "All of a sudden I just felt all hot and funny. Kind of woozy. You know what I mean?"

"Well, you just sit there till you feel better," Mr. Kosta said. "Is there anything I can get you? How about a cup of coffee? Or some tea maybe?"

"No, I don't think so. That fizzy water tasted good to me. I'm a lot better already. I just feel silly. That's not like me. I'm usually healthy as a horse. Never get sick from one year to the next."

"You sure you feel like driving? Because if you don't I'll take you home as soon as I close up here."

"No, that's all right. I'll be fine. I'll be good as new in a minute or so. And *I'll* close up."

"Not tonight you won't. You've been spoiling me as it is. I've been sneaking out of here early every evening for over a week. But tonight I want you to go on home. Get some rest and take care of yourself."

"All right. If you say so." She stood up, walked around the counter, and put her glass in the dirty-dish container underneath. "But just let me finish up what I started before I got dizzy. It'll just take me five minutes to restock that cigar and candy case. Then I'll take your advice. I'll go straight home and get a load off my feet."

While Mr. Kosta scraped the grill and tidied up behind the counter, Gwen made two trips to the storeroom behind the kitchen. She brought out three fresh boxes of cigars and half a dozen boxes of candy bars and put them in the glass-topped case by the cash register. She opened two of the cigar boxes. The third one she put in the storage cabinet underneath the display case.

When she left the café, she got into her camper parked at the curb in front. She tooted her horn twice and Mr. Kosta waved at her through the window. Then she backed up, turned right and drove south to the corner of the square. Instead of turning left, however, toward the trailer camp where she parked her camper every night, she drove straight ahead for two blocks, then right for three blocks, then back north toward the square again.

She switched off her headlights and parked across the courthouse square from Kosta's café. From where she sat she could see the inside of the café, no customers there now, Mr. Kosta moving around doing his last-minute clean-up chores. But she knew that if he looked out he would not be able to see her, all the way across the poorly lighted square, partially concealed by a corner of the courthouse itself and by the shrubs that grew on the lawn along the sidewalk.

She took off her wristwatch and strapped it on the big steering wheel in front of her, where she could clearly see the luminous hands and numbers. Exactly eighteen minutes later, Mr. Kosta switched off all the lights except the lighted clock on the back wall, came out through the front door, and locked it behind him.

As he turned away from the door, Gwen picked up a small box, the size of a cigarette package, from the seat beside her. The box resembled a pocket calculator; there were ten numbered buttons on its face.

She waited until Mr. Kosta was a hundred feet away from his café, walking up the sidewalk toward the corner lot where he always left his car. Then she switched on the dash lights and carefully pressed a combination of seven numbers on the box in her hand. As her finger pushed the final button, the front of Kosta's café flamed yellow and scarlet, the glass shattered and blew out across the sidewalk, and a black cloud of smoke poured out through the ugly burning hole at the front of the building.

She took her watch off the steering wheel and strapped it to her wrist again. When she saw Mr. Kosta running back down the sidewalk toward his burning restaurant, she started the engine of her car and backed out slowly, her headlights turned off; she drove to the first corner and turned right, away from the square.

At the edge of town, she switched on her headlights and drove southwest on Highway 42. At the intersection of Highway 250 she turned east and drove thirty miles to a spot a mile outside Staunton. There she turned off onto a gravel road, then to a rough wagon road that twisted into a thickly wooded area.

Moving quickly then, she took off her clothes and shoes and peeled off the red wig she had worn since the day she arrived in Harrisonburg. Her natural hair was brown and curly, cut very short. Getting out of the camper, she redressed herself in a blue shirt, work shoes, and a well-worn suit of Levi's. On her head she put a crumpled man's hat.

Out of the back of the camper she lifted a five-gallon can of gasoline. Uncapping it, she drenched the inside of the car, front and back. Then she splashed a pool of gasoline on the grass and threw the can, with at least a gallon still inside it, underneath the chassis. Wiping her hands carefully on the waitress uniform she had taken off, she dropped it on the gas-soaked grass. Moving twenty feet away then, she took a cardboard packet of matches out of her pocket, lighted all of them at once, and tossed them in a high arc back toward the camper.

She started to run while the little torch of matches was still in the air. When the flames roared up behind her, she fell flat on the ground and lay there till the fire had licked up into the fuel tank and the camper exploded. Then she got up and stood, half-behind a tree, felt the heat on her face, and watched the flames crackle and moan up into the darkness.

She turned back toward the highway then, walked into the town of Staunton, and caught the 10:15 bus to Richmond. There she bought a ticket to Jacksonville, Florida, ate two cheeseburgers, drank a cup of coffee while she waited in the terminal, and boarded, at one fifteen in the morning, Greyhound's Sunland Express, only five stops between New York and Miami.

Two days after his father's funeral, Gabe had a telegram from Kosta:

STRUCK GOLD IN ZURICH. HEADING HOME. SEE YOU IN D.C. KOSTA.

Three days later, arriving at Dulles on a morning flight from Chicago, Gabe tried to call her from the airport. A recorded voice told him the number he was calling had been disconnected. On a hunch he dialed the number of his own phone in the apartment. Also disconnected. Before he left the booth, he called the telephone company. A supervisor assured him his telephone would be back in service in no more than thirty minutes. But when he walked into his apartment and picked up the receiver, there was no dial tone.

Arriving at his office just before noon, Gabe told Monica he was expecting a call from Kosta. "Has she called in the last day or so?"

"Not a word."

"Well, we should hear from her today. If I'm in the Senate Chamber have one of the pages bring me a message."

As he turned away from Monica's desk, she said, "Jud's waiting for you. He wants to see you before you go into your office."

Jud briefed him quickly on what had happened while he was gone. "The public transportation bill came up, but they sent it back to committee. The Puerto Rican Aid Program is having tough sledding. If they vote tomorrow as scheduled it won't have a chance."

"What about the defense budget?"

"The Pentagon is pushing hard and making progress. There's talk of an increase as big as 40 percent."

"Have you talked to Kosta?"

Jud shook his head. "Not since she left for Zurich. Is she back?"

"Supposed to be. But her phone's disconnected. Mine, too, as a matter of fact. Put Sugarman on that. She likes to yell at people. Ask her to call the executive office of the phone company and tell them that if both those phones, mine and Kosta's, aren't working by three this afternoon, I will recommend a full-scale probe of the telephone company's proposed rate increases." He stood up. "That should get their blood circulating."

"Just a second," Jud said, "before you go into your office. There's somebody waiting in there. You know Jim Lasker?"

"No."

"But you know Mark Dalrymple."

Gabe nodded. "I don't know him but we talked on the phone a time or two."

"Lasker's his gunfighter."

"So what's he want from me?"

"I don't know. He talked his way into your office before I got in this morning. We can ease him out if we have to, but I wanted to check with you first. He implied that you were expecting him."

"Wrong," Gabe said. "But I'll talk to him anyway. Give me ten minutes. Then come and call me out."

"A meeting with the grain brokers' association . . . "

"Something like that."

When Gabe walked in, Jim Lasker stood up, all smiles and affability, and introduced himself. "I work with Mark Dalrymple at State."

"That's what I hear," Gabe said, sitting down behind his desk.

"I hope you don't mind my waiting for you in here, but—"

"As a matter of fact I *do* mind. I mind a lot. I keep an appointment schedule. If your name isn't on it, you're screwing up my whole day."

"I'm sorry you feel that way. If I'd known—"

"Don't give me that. You know how things work around here. If you decide to barge into my office and wait for two hours you must have a good reason. What is it?"

Lasker positioned himself in his chair and carefully laced his fingers together. Then, "As you know, Mr. Dalrymple has been trying for some time to set up a meeting with you."

"No, I didn't know that."

"I believe you've talked on the phone."

"That's right," Gabe said. "Strictly social. He talked about us getting together for a drink sometime. I said fine, and that was that."

"But there has been some problem getting you on the phone since then."

"This is a busy time for me. We're coming up to a recess and I'm snowed under."

"We appreciate that. Mr. Dalrymple has a tight schedule himself."

"Good. Then we understand each other."

Lasker managed a cardboard grin. "I'm sure it's occurred to you that Mr. Dalrymple had some impulse other than a social one."

"Meaning what?"

"I'm not authorized to speak for him, but I would guess that he had something to discuss with you."

"Why didn't he say that?"

Another starched smile. "This is Washington, Senator. The direct approach is not a popular tactic here."

"It is with me. It saves a lot of time."

"In our area, most of us are career diplomats."

"You don't have to be diplomatic with me. Just tell me what's on your mind."

"I would prefer to set up a meeting between you and Mr. Dalrymple."

"Fine," Gabe said. "I told him I'm agreeable to that." He looked at his calendar. "How about Wednesday, October twenty-second?"

"For some reason you're being difficult."

"No I'm not. I'm being impossible. And I'll tell you why. I don't like to be manipulated. I'm not a Boy Scout and you're not a scoutmaster. So let's either talk straight or let's not talk at all. What do you want from me?"

"It isn't a question of *wanting* something. Matter of fact, we're aware of the investigation you've started and we thought perhaps we could be of some help."

"Good. I need all the help I can get. What did you have in mind?"

"I think the most productive notion would be for us to take our cue from you," Lasker said.

"You mean if we could go over what I've found out so far, then maybe you could help me get the answers I *don't* have yet. Is that right?"

"Something like that, I suppose. That would be up to you. It's *your* investigation."

"Are you saying you'd give me public support, or would it be kind of an unofficial thing?"

"Our office doesn't do anything unofficially. If you decide that we can be helpful we would be forthcoming about it. We would take whatever public position the situation might require."

"I couldn't ask for more than that," Gabe said. Then, "There is something that bothers me, though."

"What's that?"

"One of those crashes involved a commercial carrier. The other one was an Air Force plane assigned to the executive branch. In other words, we're dealing with a completely domestic, *internal* matter. Don't you feel there might be some media speculation if the State Department suddenly involved itself? Wouldn't there be a suspicion that there was some *international* aspect to those H-14 crashes? I'll tell you the truth. The mere fact that you and Mr. Dalrymple are so interested makes *me* suspect that there's an international connection. If there is, then I'm sure you already know some things I don't know. So maybe you're more interested in *hiding* information than you are in helping me find it."

"Then why would I be here?"

"Very simple. You want to know how much *I know.*"

There was a tap on the door then and Jud came in. "Sorry to break in, Senator, but you're late for your meeting."

"No problem. Mr. Lasker and I are just winding down."

He stood up and walked around the side of his desk. "Please tell Mr. Dalrymple I appreciate his offer. I wish it had come sooner because I'm sure you could have helped me a lot. But now, I'm happy to say, our investigation is about over. We have all the pieces we were looking for. It's just a matter of sitting down and pasting them together. I expect to make a public disclosure of our findings within a week."

As he and Gabe walked down the Dirksen Building corridor a few minutes later, Jud said, "Was that on the level, that little speech you made to Lasker?"

"On the level, Jud."

When Jud turned to look at him, Gabe winked and said, "If anybody asks you, you can quote me."

Twenty minutes later, Jud called Jim Lasker. As soon as Lasker hung up, he called Newquist from Dalrymple's office. Newquist listened carefully till Lasker stopped talking. Finally he said, "He doesn't leave us much choice, does he?"

Gabe stayed in his office till almost nine o'clock that night. Every ten minutes or so he tried Kosta's home number. It was in service now. It rang each time he called. But there was no answer. His own number at home was also back in service. An odd tone to the ringing, but ringing without question when he called home to test it.

Finally he left the office, got into his car, and drove to Anna Maria's for a plate of rigatoni and a bottle of beer. On his way home he stopped at Kosta's apartment. No lights. No answer when he rang the bell.

He tried the apartments on either side of hers. At the first one there was nobody home. At the other one there were lights on behind the blind slats, but no one answered until the third ring. Finally, a soft, pale girl in a short cotton robe came to the door.

No, she didn't know Kosta. Yes, she had seen her two or three times. "I just moved in here first of the month." Although she hadn't seen Kosta in the past few days, she thought she had heard someone moving around in her apartment.

Heading back toward his car, Gabe looked in through the windows of Kosta's garage. Her yellow Volkswagen was there.

On Wisconsin Avenue, running noisily and brightly through the center of Georgetown, Gabe went into four or five restaurants and coffeehouses that Kosta frequented. No one had seen her for more than a week.

The druggist on the corner of Wisconsin and Volta Place hadn't seen her either. In fact she had ordered a prescription ten days before and hadn't picked it up. Nor had the henna-haired lady at the all-night dry cleaner seen her. No one, it seemed, had seen her or talked with her since she left for Zurich.

Back in his apartment, Gabe shuffled through the litter of cards and memos in his center desk drawer. Finally he found what he was looking for, one of Kosta's business cards. On the back she had written two names. Naomi Guterman and Nellie Arvidsen.

Gabe found both numbers in the D.C. telephone directory. Naomi Guterman's recorded voice told him she had gone to New York for ten days. She could be reached there, nine to five, at the offices of *The Village Voice.* Nellie Arvidsen's voice, also recorded, said she had gone out but would be home at ten thirty that night.

At exactly ten thirty Gabe called Arvidsen's number again and got the same message as before. He called every fifteen minutes till midnight. At last Nellie Arvidsen's live voice answered. Of course she remembered him from the Hinshaw program. But no, she had not seen Kosta for over a week. "I did talk with her, though. A couple days ago. She called me from the airport. There was some problem with her family. She was on her way to Virginia."

Gabe had no trouble at all with the information operator in Harrisonburg. There was only one Kosta listed. A. C. Kosta on Bridgewater Street. When Gabe dialed the number, an older woman's voice answered, a sleepy voice with a soft accent. When he asked for Kosta, remembering to call her Rosemary, the woman said, "It's very late. Do you know how late it is?"

"I'm sorry. I wouldn't call if it weren't important. Is this Mrs. Kosta?"

"Yes. Who is this?"

"Mr. Treptow. I have to talk to your daughter."

"She's sound asleep."

"Please," Gabe said. "She won't mind if you wake her up. It's really important."

There was a hollow silence at the other end of the line as he waited for Kosta to come to the phone. When he heard her voice finally, he said, "What's the matter? You sound strange."

"I'm still asleep."

"I'm sorry to call so late. But I was worried about you."

"I'm all right."

"You don't sound all right. Your voice sounds different."

"I *feel* different."

"What's the matter?"

"I don't want to talk about it."

"Okay," he said. "Go back to bed. I'll see you when you get back to Washington."

There was a long pause. Then she said, "I'm not coming back right now."

"What does *that* mean?"

"Just what it sounds like. I have to stay here for a while."

"How long?"

"I don't know."

"Wait a minute. What's going on? The last thing I heard from you was that gung-ho wire from Zurich. Now all of a sudden—"

"Forget about Zurich. I was mistaken. I was off base about everything."

"I don't know what you're talking about."

"I'm *scared*," she said. "That's what I'm talking about. I'm backing off. That's what I'm telling you. I already know more than I want to know. This thing is bigger and dirtier than we thought it was. It's too much for me. And it's too much for you, too. If you're smart you'll walk away from it."

"Walk *away* from it? Are you nuts? You got me into this. You sold me on it. Are you saying that it's a bigger mess than we expected so we should tuck our tails between our legs and go back to reading *Newsweek*? I'm telling you . . . I don't recognize you. Did somebody get to you? Did somebody buy you off?"

Her voice stabbed at him through the telephone, a strained, hoarse whisper. "I'll *tell* you what happened to me. Somebody planted a bomb in my dad's restaurant. Four days ago. He'd just locked up to go home. If he'd stayed two minutes longer he'd have been splashed all over the walls. *Now* do you know what I'm talking about? I've been hassled and humiliated for ten years because I said what I thought. I'm used to it. I'll take my chances. But when they start sharpshooting at my folks, I turn into the biggest coward in town. *Nothing*'s that important. Not to me. I'm through with the whole mess. *Finito!* And if you have any brains you'll drop it too."

"I'm not dropping *anything.*"

"Suit yourself. But don't expect me to stand around and watch you bleed."

The line went dead then. When he dialed the number again, it was busy. He kept trying for almost an hour. Busy. Finally, when he had the operator check the line, she told him what he'd known all along. The receiver was off the hook.

89 In Zurich, Kosta had reveled in her newfound self, in the moment, in the future. When she sent the cable to Gabe, "Struck gold in Zurich," she was, on one level, referring to the information she had found there. But also, happily and secretly, she referred to the magnificent change she could sense inside herself.

Later, however, flying back to Washington, she began to lose momentum. When she'd flown east toward Zurich, toward a new place, a country she'd never seen, she had taken on security and strengthened identity with every hour in the air. As she headed home again, however, the coin lazily turned over. The thought of familiar places and people stirred up old doubts. The fantasy she had gorged on in Zurich no longer tasted sweet in her mouth as the plane dropped low over Chesapeake Bay and curved south toward Washington.

As soon as she was back in her Georgetown apartment, as soon as she'd called her parents and heard the news about the restaurant explosion, she left at once for the airport. Stunned as she was, anxious as she felt about her parents' safety, as she boarded the Harrisonburg flight some perverse angel inside her celebrated the fact that she would not have to test herself as quickly as she had feared. She could flee. There would be more time to crystallize the new Kosta, to shore her up, to build her back to the reckless level she had reached in Zurich.

In Harrisonburg, however, she did a full turnaround. That place, those surroundings, those rippling associations, took their toll. By the time Gabe called, she had persuaded herself that she was a permanent product of her background, of her internal conflicts and her own hateful memories. When she told him she was afraid to go on with the investigation, afraid for her family, afraid for herself, she didn't mention her greatest fear. She didn't allow herself to consider that at all.

 The morning after he talked to Kosta on the phone, Gabe booked a seat on the noon flight from D.C. to Harrisonburg. Just as he was leaving his office to go to the airport, Monica handed him a letter.

"Will you look at this poor specimen. It looks as if it's been through the wars. No wonder the post office is showing a profit. They've gone back to pony express."

Heading down the corridor toward the elevator, Gabe glanced at the return address on the dirty envelope. Dr. August Throckmorton. Gabe put the letter in his jacket pocket and forgot about it till he was on the plane. When he opened the envelope there was another letter inside. Sealed and addressed to him. His father's handwriting. A note from Dr. Throckmorton was paper-clipped to it.

    Dear Senator Treptow:
      This letter from your father was mailed the day before he died. For some reason it was returned here. So you'll be

sure to get it, I will send it along to you c/o the U.S. Senate.
We all miss your remarkable father. I hope that reading
his letter will not bring you any additional sadness.

Best wishes,
August B. Throckmorton

Gabe sat looking at the enclosed envelope for a long few minutes. The handwriting, clear and firm, was achingly familiar to him. Through the years he'd had hundreds of letters from his father.

The grammar, the spelling, the syntax, were all self-taught. Simple, declarative, sometimes beautifully awkward. But the drive to communicate was unmistakable. The feel for language was strong and personal. In his letters, his father achieved the most difficult thing. With just pen and paper, he managed to present, always, an accurate portrait of himself. His letters said, "This is where I stand. This is how things are today. If things change tomorrow, I'll let you know."

Knowing what he did about his father's death, Gabe was apprehensive about this last letter, afraid it might tell him more, after the fact, than he needed or wanted to know, might reopen cabinets he had permanently closed. His father was solid and vivid in his memory. He did not want some new revelation to blur that image.

He considered not reading the letter at all. But he resisted the idea of tearing it up. Or burning it. So at last he slit the envelope, took the letter out, and read it.

Dear Gabe:

Hot as hell in Illinois. No place hotter than this cornfield country when the summer decides to hit hard. Still, the heat's not as bad as those damned things they've invented to keep a person cool.

Air conditioners should be outlawed. And I hate an electric fan like a snake. Especially the kind that turns back and forth. Oscillating, they call that. I'm sure that's no news to you but it was to me. Just looked it up yesterday. And in case you're interested, osculate means to kiss. I guess that's no news to you either.

I envy you all that reading and soaking yourself in books you've been able to do. I always thought you had a little head start on Chet in that department. Not taking anything away from your brother. I don't mean that. But all the things that really got him steamed up seemed to require people around. Nothing wrong with that, I guess, but it's not for me.

I always thought a man who could sit in a room by himself and do something with his hands or his brain that would put clothes on his back and bread on the table was a lucky son of a bitch.

When I was a kid up in Sterling there was a little sawed-off stump of a guy, I guess he was a dwarf, who was our town shoemaker. Had a cubbyhole shop about six feet by eight feet, right on the courthouse square.

Everybody felt sorry for him. Otto, his name was. People used to take him shoes to fix that didn't really need fixing just because they figured he had a lousy life. Living alone. Cooking for himself. Dragging himself up and down on that stool he sat on while he worked. I guess Otto was the most pitied man in town.

But not by me. I always thought he had the world by the ass. He knew he'd been short-changed but he'd worked out a way to deal with it. And best of all he'd learned how to function and survive by himself.

I don't know how all that connects with you except I think you're a solitary ape, too. At least you're capable of it. And like I say you've got all those books, all that fine language and those beautiful ideas, crammed into your system. And it's never going to dry up and blow away. So you're a lucky duck. That's what I mean. Remember when you used to say that when you were four years old? "We're lucky ducks, Dad."

What I really want to tell you is that no matter what happens to you there in Washington it's not going to change you much or cripple you. You had yourself pulled together before you went there. And when you leave you'll still be pulled together.

I've been following you pretty closely since you sent me that subscription to the Washington Post. *I'm not sure what you're going after with that H-14 investigation but it must be something worthwhile because you're getting a lot of people sore at you. Even Chet's old friend, Senator Isbell, has been taking some potshots in your direction. He made a speech in Springfield last week that hit a new low even for him.*

I suppose that's the way it is in politics, everybody scrambling around to protect his own ass. But I'm glad it's you instead of me. I wouldn't want any part of it. On the other hand, I'm just as bullheaded as you are. If I thought they were trying to scare me off, that would make me twice as anxious to finish the job I'd started. If I know you, that's what's buzzing around in your head.

Speaking of that, I've got a little information for you. It may not mean anything but I'll pass it along for whatever it's worth. I was going through some old papers yesterday and I found a letter from Evelyn, the last one she ever wrote me. Right at the end of it she was saying they'd be coming to Chicago on the sixteenth of January and they planned to drive down to Fort Beck that same day.

The thing that caught my eye was this. I've got her letter right here so I'll copy it for you exact. She wrote, "These government jets are really fancy. Instead of two hundred and sixty passengers, they're re-vamped to carry only a hundred or so. And on our flight only about fourteen were booked. So we were looking forward to a real luxury trip. But Chet just called this morning and said the plane's going to be full. Every seat taken. And wait till I tell you who the other passengers are. You'll get a laugh, I bet. Or maybe you'll cuss a little."

What do you suppose all that means? When the plane went down there were only fourteen passengers. So does that make sense? Not to me.

That's about it, I guess. I'll sign off before I start writing a lot of sentimental crap. I don't want to do that.

Let me just put it this way and you'll understand everything. I've had a problem here the last couple months. The doctors didn't tell you about it because I told them not to. It's the old circulation thing again. You remember they stripped the arteries in my legs in March. They thought that would take care of it but it didn't. My feet are swelling up again and getting discolored just like before.

Now there's a new development. They've all put their heads together, these doctors, and decided the only way they can keep me alive is to amputate my leg. Just the one leg they said, but Agnes Doty, the night nurse, who's a buddy of mine, says they almost always end up whacking off both legs before they're finished.

Well, I've thought it over, Gabe, and I don't want that. I'm not going to let it happen. I'm very sure in my mind that I don't want to spend the rest of my life as an oversized paperweight.

Beyond telling you that much, I won't dwell on it. You've always understood me pretty well and I'm counting on you to understand me now.

I'm proud of you, Gabe. I was always proud of both you boys. I could have had a crummy life after your mother died. But you and Chet made it good.

Take care of yourself and don't let them box you in.

Lots of love,

Dad.

When his plane landed in Harrisonburg, Gabe went straight from the airport to Kosta's home. It was a modest, neatly kept house in a family neighborhood. But the window shades were all pulled down. And when he rang the doorbell there was no answer. He walked around the house to the back and knocked on the kitchen door. No answer there either.

As he stood in the driveway looking up at the second story, a window in the house next door slid up and a woman's voice said, "They're not there, mister. They went off someplace this morning early."

"Do you have any idea where they are?" Gabe said, walking closer to the open window. "It's important."

"They didn't say nothing about it to me and I never asked. They just went off in their Chrysler with the daughter driving. They asked me to take in their mail and their paper every day and I said I would."

"Did they say when they might be back?"

"Not a word. I know they felt awful about those goings-on down at the café. I figure their daughter just thought it was a good notion to get them away for a while."

"Is there anybody else who might know where they've gone?"

"If they didn't tell me," the woman said, "you can bet they didn't tell anybody."

Back at the Harrisonburg airport, Gabe turned in his return air ticket and rented a car. Then he drove slowly north through the Shenandoah Valley. At Strasburg he angled east across Virginia toward Washington.

When he got home, the lock on his front door was broken. Inside the apartment, the contents of all the drawers and closets had been dumped in the center of the living room and soaked with dirty machine oil.

In the kitchen the refrigerator door was open, all the food scattered and spilled on the floor. The dishes and silver were piled in the double sink and the oven door had been wrenched off and left on top of the stove. When Gabe picked up the telephone to call the police, the line was dead.

The following morning, in the Washington, D.C. segment of *A.M. Report,* Lester Ainslie did five minutes on Gabe.

Last spring, Senator Gabe Treptow was sworn in as the junior man from the state of Illinois. He was, by his own admission, a political novice. But he had the endorsement of the Democratic Party in Illinois, particularly Senator Rafer Isbell, a widely respected and influential member of the Congress.

Even the people who didn't support him conceded that Treptow was a bright, personable man and a forceful speaker. And he proved in his underdog victory last spring that he is a vote getter.

He did have some eccentric ideas. No question about that. And an inclination to speak his mind. And that raised some hackles in the Congress. But the Senate had seen mavericks before. They come and go. One-term wonders, they're called.

In Treptow's case, however, it seems unlikely that he will complete even *one* term. It seems possible that he will be recalled before he has served even one *year.* In an unusual announcement, his colleague, Senator Isbell, said this morning that petitions have been circulating in Illinois for three weeks and that soon they will have the required number of signatures to institute recall procedures against

Treptow. So we have a Washington first. Democratic Senators supporting the recall of a fellow Democrat.

What's behind it? There is no question that Treptow has been critical of Senate traditions and operations. He has gone so far as to question the integrity, even the honesty, of some of his fellow senators. He has refused to compromise, to play the Capitol Hill game, to play ball. On the other hand, no one will say that he hasn't done his legislative homework. No one questions his intelligence or his courage.

So why this movement to recall him? It all seems to boil down to one thing—Treptow's investigation of the H-14 crashes last January. Repudiating the FAA conclusions, Treptow has insisted that the evidence was incomplete, that significant facts were withheld. And last night on a late news broadcast here in Washington, he pulled out all the stops.

Treptow accused the federal government, up to and including the White House, of conspiring to conceal evidence about the H-14 crashes. He maintains that both planes were sabotaged, that all the passengers and crews, two hundred and forty-five people, were murdered, and that government officials are accessories after the fact to those murders.

Senator Treptow promises complete details and full disclosure later this week. Until then, no final judgment can be made regarding the validity of his accusations. But many Washington observers feel today that Treptow, however well intentioned he may be, has given his critics substantial ammunition for their charges against him of incompetence and irresponsibility.

Later that morning, Jud Rimmer came into Gabe's office. "I just had a call from the White House. Joe Newquist's office."

"What's on his mind?"

"He didn't say. His secretary asked if you could come over there this afternoon."

"What did you tell her?"

"I said I'd have to get back to them," Jud said.

"You think they're ready to answer my questions?"

"Maybe they want you to answer some of theirs."

"Either way it's progress," Gabe said. "Tell them I'll be there at three o'clock. You want to come along?"

"I think I'd better hold the fort here."

"I guess you're right."

At the door Jud turned and said, "Is all the stuff true? That interview you gave on the local news last night?"

"You know me, Jud. Poor but honest."

"I just meant . . . I don't know . . . you're good at running a bluff. Chet could do it too. He'd pretend to *know* something and the next thing you knew somebody would *tell* him because they thought he already knew."

"I'm not bluffing, Jud." He laid it out very precisely. "I know exactly what happened now. Every detail. I've got it all nailed together."

Newquist sat, loose and cool and benign, behind his glass-topped antique desk, his jacket off and draped across the high back of his chair, his dark-blue tie loosened, his hands toying with a silver letter-opener.

"I saw a lot of your brother when he was in Washington. Did he ever mention that?"

"Yes, he did," Gabe said.

"We played quite a bit of tennis."

"That's what he told me. He said you have a killer serve."

Newquist grinned. "I wish I did. I'm not a very big guy. I

decided I needed an equalizer. So I used to work on that serve for days. I can sneak it through once in a while, but it doesn't win any matches for me. You play?"

"Not since I came to Washington. But I played every day when I was teaching."

"Could you beat Chet?"

"Some days I beat him. Some days he beat me."

"You must be pretty hot then. I don't think I ever won a match from Chet."

"He was good," Gabe said, "but if you kept chopping to his backhand you could beat him."

"We'll have to play a few sets sometime."

"Anytime."

Newquist got up and adjusted his window shades so the afternoon sun didn't glare through on his desk top. After he sat down again, he said, "Lester Ainslie did quite a number on you this morning. Did you see it?"

"No. But I've been hearing about it."

"Is there anything we can do for you?"

"How do you mean?"

"It sounds as if you're in some trouble. I mean, if they're serious about this recall business . . . "

"They're serious," Gabe said. "The word from Illinois is that they're getting a lot of petitions together."

"Well . . . that's just the first step. It's a long way from there to the finish line. The whole thing has to come back here to the Congress. Once that happens there are some things we can do."

"I appreciate your interest. But to tell you the truth I'm willing to let it play itself out. If my constituents want to tie a can to my tail and if the other senators want to get rid of me, I'm sure they'll find some way to do it."

"Not necessarily. These things can be choreographed so they peter out in committee. Just like a piece of legislation."

"Like I say, it's damned nice of you. I know you were a friend of Chet's."

"Wait a minute. Nobody's throwing you a rose. We have a Democratic administration here. You're a Democratic senator from a key state. The President doesn't want to see a Republican in that seat. Either before November or after November.

We know you haven't made many friends in the Senate, but that can be turned around. Everybody gives a little ground and all of a sudden the problem goes away. You know what I mean? You could take a page from Chet's book. He was just as hard headed as you seem to be. He wouldn't give an inch. But he had a way of making people *think* he was agreeing with everything they said. And before he finished, *they* were agreeing with *him*. It's all a matter of style. If you try to butt heads you're bound to lose out to anybody who has a harder skull than you do."

"You said something about 'giving a little,' " Gabe said. "What do you think I'd have to give?"

"I'm not sure. I'm just talking about procedures and attitudes. You know more about the specifics than I do. You'd have to decide about those."

"Yes, I guess so."

Newquist waited for him to go on, but Gabe didn't say anything. He simply looked pleasant and nodded his head slowly.

Newquist resettled himself in his chair and lit a cigarette. Then, "As I say, I don't know all the details of your situation. But I did see that television show this morning. According to Ainslie you've unsettled a lot of people with that H-14 thing you're trying to stir up."

"It's already stirred up. I'm trying to settle it."

"Whatever. I'm just repeating what I've heard."

"From Ainslie?"

Newquist nodded. "*And* from the Senate people. The consensus seems to be that if you'd back off from that investigation everything else could be worked out."

"Do you agree with that?"

"It's hard for me to say. All my information is secondhand. I think it's a decision you have to make."

"But if I decide to proceed, you think the recall procedure will move ahead too."

"It's not a question of what *I* think," Newquist said. "But that seems to be what I'm picking up."

"Then if I asked your advice you would advise me to walk away from the H-14 investigation."

"I would advise you to use your own best judgment. *My* best judgment is that you should probably apply your energy to other areas." Sensing that he was beginning to turn the situation around, Newquist took one additional step. "From what I understand, those accidents were thoroughly investigated and there is no reason to question the conclusions that were presented by the FAA and the NTSB."

"That's the problem," Gabe said. "Those investigations were manipulated and I can prove it. Evidence was suppressed and I can prove *that*. Those two planes were sabotaged and some key people in government knew about it. I admit I don't have all the names and numbers yet. But when I go to the *Post* or *The New York Times* with what I *do* have, I'm sure they'll be happy to help me find the rest. I may be recalled, but the H-14 story will be out long before that can happen."

The intercom buzzed softly then. Newquist picked up the receiver, listened, and said, "I'll come out." To Gabe he said, "I have to take an overseas call. I'll just be a few minutes." He put on his jacket as he went out the door.

When he came back into the office a few minutes later, Newquist perched on the front edge of his desk, one foot up, the other one barely touching the floor. "I haven't been completely candid with you," he said, "and I apologize for that. But that's one of the disadvantages of this job. Very often, I'm outer directed. Now, however, I will tell you the straight situation. As much as I'm able to.

"Your instincts are correct. All the details of those H-14 crashes were not made public. Not because we are trying to suppress the truth. Not because the facts are too agonizing to reveal. Nothing dramatic like that. Actually, the truth is quite simple. There was no sabotage. Each crash truly was an accident. But . . . there are some interacting elements, after the fact, which must be dealt with.

"It has never been a question of *whether* we would come forth with all the details. It has always been a matter of *when*. When that moment comes, when the proper agencies agree that there is no risk involved in releasing the material we have, I promise that I will tell *you* personally, in *this* office, everything you want to know. I'll answer any questions. When that happens you'll understand why we've had to move slowly."

"When will that be, exactly?" Gabe said.

"Soon, I think. A month perhaps. Maybe as long as six months. But I guarantee you that all of us in the executive branch are anxious to see this situation resolved as quickly as possible. Until that time, however, until it's wise, and *safe* for us to make full disclosure, I have to ask you to ease off on your own investigation."

"I can't do that."

"What do you mean?"

"I mean that this kind of manipulation is what got me into this thing in the first place. I suspected that somebody was screwing around with the truth. For you to sit there and *admit* that I was right doesn't make me want to kiss the President's ring and go suck my thumb in the corner. It makes me want to move ahead to the finish. Before you started talking I *suspected* there was a conspiracy to conceal the facts. Now I *know* it. So if you expect me to roll over and play dead, you're going to be disappointed. Either you go public with the straight story or *I'm* going to."

Newquist went back to his chair, sat down, and touched a button on his desk. Gabe heard a soft buzz in the outer office. The door opened then, and a middle-aged woman came in. Gray hair and glasses. Wearing a blue silk dress with a turquoise necklace. Behind her, a slender young man in his thirties, neat brown hair and shell-rim glasses. They stopped just inside the door and closed it behind them.

"This is Mrs. Brock," Newquist said. "And Mr. Gaines. Two of my associates. I want them to witness what I'm about to say to you." He touched a switch at the cover of his desk. "I am also advising you that what I'm saying will be recorded."

After a pause, Newquist went on. "I have been authorized to inform you that your investigation of the H-14 accidents that took place last January is to be terminated at once. Critical international issues are involved here. The President and his advisors feel that secrecy is vital, that we face a situation where national security could be jeopardized. As a responsible member of the United States Senate you will certainly understand the need for your cooperation."

Gabe nodded. "I'm starting to understand."

"Then we can count on your cooperation?"

"Let me put it this way. I know there are times when secrecy's the only answer. There are other times when secrecy is *not* necessary. It's just *convenient.* I'm convinced that most of the time the best security we have is the truth. When Iran decided to hold fifty Americans hostage, that certainly looked like a national security crisis. It was also a public event. I didn't hear anybody say that situation could have been resolved more easily if nobody in the United States knew about it."

"This is a totally different problem."

"Sure it is," Gabe said. "The details are always different. But I'm saying that the strongest weapon we had in the Iran situation was public indignation."

"I'm telling you—this is not the same."

"Maybe you're right. Maybe if the country finds out that two hundred and forty-five people were needlessly killed on those two planes, they won't be curious about the reasons. If they find out the government was responsible maybe they won't ask how. If they see that an elaborate cover-up was arranged to keep the truth from getting out, maybe they won't ask why. What do you think, Mrs. Brock?"

The woman, startled at being singled out, glanced toward Newquist. But she didn't say anything.

"How about you, Mr. Gaines?" Gabe said.

No reaction at all from him. Just a fixed stare at some point on the wall.

"Maybe everybody will just say ho-hum and go back to their television sets," Gabe said. "But I don't think so. I think a lot of people will feel the same way I do. I think they'll be sore as hell." He stood up and buttoned his jacket. "You want my cooperation? All right. I'll cooperate to this extent. I'll pretend this meeting never happened. *If* you stay out of my way. But if you try to obstruct my investigation I will have all three of you subpoenaed as witnesses."

He walked to the door then and opened it. Turning back, he said, "I will also subpoena that tape you just made. And if you decide to erase it just remember something. For all you know I could have made my own recording of this meeting. *All* of it." He patted the breast pocket of his jacket. "Think it over."

He left the door open behind him as he walked out through Newquist's outer office and down the corridor of the Executive Office Building.

Late that night, almost three in the morning, Gabe's telephone woke him up.

"Is this Senator Treptow?"

"That's right. Who's this?"

"Sergeant Minafer. Georgetown police. We're holding a young woman here who says she works for you. According to her driver's license her name is Kosta. R. M. Kosta."

"What do you mean, you're *holding* her?"

"Does she work for you?"

"Yes, she does. What's the problem?"

"We can't go into that on the telephone."

"Well, can I talk to her, then?" Gabe said.

"I'm afraid she's not able to come to the phone."

"What the hell does that mean?"

"There was an accident. On the Whitehurst Freeway . . . "

Gabe hung up the phone and quickly got dressed. Locking his apartment door, he ran down the outside staircase and hurried along the dark driveway to his garage.

Raising the overhead doors, he took his keys out of his pocket and moved to the side of his car.

He'd started to unlock the door on the driver's side when he sensed a movement behind him in the dark. Before he could turn, something blunt and heavy struck him at the base of the skull just behind his ear.

Part Five

93 As soon as Kosta saw the story about Gabe in the Winston-Salem paper she called Nellie Arvidsen in Washington.

"I thought I'd be hearing from you," Nellie said. "I'd have called but I didn't know where you were."

"What happened to him?" Kosta said. "The paper down here just said he'd been hurt and he's in the hospital."

"There wasn't much in the D.C. papers either. But there's a lot of chatter going on. The word is the police found him in the gutter at five in the morning, outside that raunchy leather bar on Farragut Square. Dead drunk, the story goes, and badly beat up. You know Jack Sternhagen at the *Star*. He was at Edgewood Hospital when they brought him in. He told me somebody had really worked him over."

"Oh my God . . . "

"Don't fall apart. Jack says he'll be all right. He just has some serious healing up to do."

"There was nothing in the papers about who did it?"

"Not a word. Like I said, after the first break, the papers have stayed off it. You know the routine. They decide the less said about it the better. So instead of facts, everybody settles for gossip."

"What are they saying?"

"What do you think they're saying? I told you where they found him. He's not married. He's living alone. You know this town. They're having a field day."

When Kosta told her parents she had to go to Washington, she said, "But I want you to stay here in Reidsville with Aunt Stella."

Her father nodded his head and looked at her mother, and she nodded too. But an hour later, when Kosta put her suitcase in the car, her parents' luggage was already in the trunk.

"Wait a minute," she said. "We made a deal. You said you'd stay here."

"No we didn't," her father said. *"You* said it."

"You don't have to leave just because *I'm* leaving."

"We're *not,"* her mother said. "We talked about it since two days ago. We've been here long enough. We don't want to wear out our welcome."

"It's true," her Aunt Stella said. "They told me day before yesterday they wanted to get back to Harrisonburg."

When they were inside the car, heading for the Winston-Salem airport, Kosta's father said, "Remember when you were in college and we worried all the time that you might get hurt in some protest or demonstration, you told us you couldn't always do things that were safe? You remember saying that?"

"Yes. But this is different."

"Not so different. It just seems different because it's you worrying about us for a change."

"We haven't done anything to be ashamed of," her mother said. "So why should we run and hide someplace?"

"I told you," Kosta said. "Nobody planted that bomb because of something *you* did. It was something *I* did. Something I'm *doing."*

"Maybe that's right," her father said. "But you've been shaking people up since you were sixteen. And I've only had my business bombed once."

"Once is enough. What kind of logic is *that?"*

"It's *my* logic. I say to myself, I've been in business thirty years and never any trouble. Now I have some trouble maybe. But that's no reason to go out of business. You think we should run away to Mykonos just because some fool put a bomb in my shop?"

"I don't know what you should do. I just hate the idea that you could be hurt."

"When you were three years old we felt the same way," her mother said. "*Me* especially. I was worse than Angelo. Afraid to leave you out in the yard, afraid to let you go up and down stairs by yourself. All mothers are the same. Till finally they realize they have to stand back, look the other way, and let things happen. People get hurt sometimes."

"No way to avoid it," her father said.

Kosta laughed then. "Oh my God . . . you two are impossible! I'm trying to take care of you and you're smothering me with gypsy fatalism. I want nice ordinary parents and I end up with a couple of lunchroom philosophers."

"The philosophy isn't much good maybe," her father said, "but you've got to admit I run a first-rate lunchroom."

"Sure you do. Only last time I looked, the whole front of it was wrecked."

"So I'll fix it. It can be fixed. The only thing that can't be fixed is if I'm scared of my own shadow. There's no way I can think of to fix that."

An hour later, as her plane circled to land at National Airport, just south of the central city, Kosta managed to focus sharply on the situation at hand, what she told herself was the *real* situation. Zurich had been an aberration. It had nothing to do with her as she really was. Nothing to do with her and Gabe as two serious people trying to solve a difficult problem.

In the taxi she took from the airport to Edgewood Hospital, she spelled all this out for herself. And she believed it. Every word of it. At least she believed very sincerely that she believed it.

94 "Don't sugar me, Dr. Sharkey," Kosta said. "I need to know the truth. I know I'm not his wife or anything. I'm not related to him. But I'm the closest thing to a relative he's got here in Washington. I want to help him and I *can* help him. But you've got to level with me."

Dr. Sharkey, in his mid-forties, lean, brown, and deliberate, tilted back in his chair, hands clasped behind his head, and grinned. "I haven't told you anything yet. You haven't given me a chance."

"I'm sorry. I'm nervous. I can't shut up when I'm nervous. The nurse took me into his room and I thought he was dead. He looks like hell."

"Looks pretty good to me. You should have seen him a couple days ago."

"Why does he look like that? Is he doped up or what?"

"We call it *sedated.*"

"Why are you doing that?" Kosta said.

"Because he needs rest. He came in here with a concussion, a broken nose, three cracked ribs, and a nasty fracture of the wrist. We were afraid of internal injuries, but there's no evidence of that yet. Still, until his bones start to knit, we don't want him moving around any more than necessary. Light meals, mild sedation, and lots of sleep."

"How much longer will he be here?"

"If there are no problems he should be able to go home in four or five days. He's a young guy. He should recover pretty fast."

"How about me staying here with him till he goes home?"

"I don't think there's any need for that. He's not in any danger and he's getting plenty of attention."

"I just hate to see him in there all by himself." Then, "Look, I didn't exactly tell you the truth. I'm not just a friend. I'm his fiancée. We live together. He's used to having me around."

"Like I said, in a few days . . ."

"Come on, Dr. Sharkey—if I was his wife you'd let me stay with him. Give me a break. It means a lot to me." When the doctor didn't answer, she said, "Besides, I'm afraid those crazies who beat him up might decide to take another crack at him."

"In the hospital?"

"Why not? It's happened before."

"You're volunteering as a bodyguard—is that it?"

"Don't laugh. I can yell like hell. I'm a mean Greek when I get started."

Dr. Sharkey picked up his phone, buzzed the outside office, and said, "Ask Mrs. Wheeler to have a guest bed put in Senator Treptow's room. That's right. His fiancée will be staying in there with him."

The first time Gabe woke up and saw Kosta sitting by his bed, he smiled groggily and said, "How'm I doing?"

"Terrible. You look like a chef's salad."

There was a wide strip of tape across his nose, bruises under his eyes and on his cheekbones, and a blue lump on his jaw. On his left arm there was a light cast. From mid-forearm to his knuckles.

"You should see the other guy," he said.

"That's not the way I heard it."

Later that day, when she came back from her apartment with a small bag of toilet articles and her pajamas, he was sitting up in bed, clear-eyed and wide awake. "You moving in?"

"Somebody has to look after you. You're not much good at looking after yourself."

"What's this routine about your being my fiancée? You've got the nurses all excited."

"I just told the doctor that so he'd let me stay here. Don't worry. I don't have a yen for your bod." She walked over to the side of his bed. "You look better than you did this morning. The first time I came in here you looked like a cadaver."

"I feel better now. A couple more days and I'll be back in the ring."

"Sure you will." She tapped his cast with one finger. "With a broken wrist, a beat-up nose, and bells in your head. You should stay out of fights."

"That wasn't a fight. It was an ambush."

"Did you get a look at who did it?"

Gabe shook his head. "I started to unlock the car door and bang, the lights went out. Beyond that, all I know is what I read in the papers."

He told her about the telephone call he'd received that night.

"They said *I* was at the police station in Georgetown?" she said.

"That's right. They told me you'd been in an accident."

"But you knew I wasn't in Washington."

"No I didn't. I knew you left town and went to Harrisonburg. And I knew you left Harrisonburg and went *someplace.* But I didn't know *where.*"

"Then you hadn't been drinking like they said?"

He shook his head. "I was in bed asleep when they called. After they knocked me out, I guess they poured some booze down my throat and sprinkled some more on my clothes. Then they dropped me in the gutter outside a bar. They had it all worked out."

"Who do you think did it?"

"Who ransacked your apartment and your car? Who wrecked my place? Who planted a bomb in your father's restaurant? The *who* doesn't matter. *Why* is all that counts. And you and I both know the answer to that one. That's the reason you ran off to hide someplace, isn't it?"

"I took my folks to my aunt's house."

"That's not what I mean. I'm surprised to see you come back here at all. I thought you'd walked away for good."

"I have. I just came back because I found out you were in the hospital."

"Here today, gone tomorrow. I won't be out of action long."

She sat looking at him. Silent and concentrated. Then, "You're not going to stick your neck out again, are you?"

"Not if I can help it. But I expect to finish what I started."

"They won't let you."

"Yes they will. They've played all their cards. The more they panic, the more I realize how important it is for me to hang on. If you won't tell me what you found out in Zurich then I'll have to ride with what I have. A few facts and a lot of guesswork. It's not perfect, but it's better than backing down and pissing little holes in the snow."

"That means you're going ahead. Either with me or without me."

"That's right."

Kosta got up then and walked out into the corridor, down its entire length to the sun room on the south side of the building. She stayed there, in a deep chair, looking out the window, for more than an hour. When she got up finally and walked back to Gabe's room, when she sat down beside his bed again, she said, "What if I'm wacky enough to go along with you, then what?"

"I think I know the scenario now. I can plug up the holes and wing it if I have to. But anything you can tell me about Ralph Benedict will help a lot. And if we've still got a shot at that flight manifest for Air Force Three, that would stitch it up, I think. But regardless, whatever new hard evidence we come up with, I want to hole up in my apartment for four or five days as soon as they spring me from here. Just you and me. We'll start at the beginning, with the SAI crash in Indianapolis, and go on from there. We'll nail it all together till it's solid and right. Then I'll walk into the Senate chamber and read it into the record."

"They won't let you do that."

"Yes they will. They can't stop me. It's a government matter, government agencies are involved, and until they drum me out, I'm still a United States senator."

The next day Kosta left the hospital early and came back late. And the day after that. The afternoon of the second day, on a hunch, she went to the offices of Global Financial. At the reception desk there was a slender blond woman in her early thirties. Kosta identified herself and asked if she could see Mrs. Tamuri.

"I'm sorry," the receptionist said. "Mrs. Tamuri is in London. She's due back in ten days. Perhaps I can help you."

"No, I don't think so. It's sort of a personal matter."

"Are you a friend of Mrs. Tamuri?"

"Yes," Kosta said. "But mostly I'm a friend of Mrs. Garvin."

"Who?"

"You must know her—uh . . . *Mary* Garvin."

"You mean Esther Garvin?"

"That's right. I always confuse her with her sister."

"Esther doesn't have a sister," the blond woman said.

Plowing straight ahead, Kosta said, "Perhaps I could talk to her. Is she here?"

"No, she's not. She's not here any longer. She was—she resigned."

"I can't believe it. She and Mrs. Tamuri were so close. I mean, I know how closely they worked together."

The blond woman answered quickly. "Actually, Mrs. Garvin was a receptionist. She didn't—"

"I know that. She had the job you have now."

"Not exactly. I was hired as Mrs. Tamuri's executive assistant. I'm only filling in here at the desk while the new receptionist takes a coffee break."

"I see." Then, "Would you have any idea where I could reach Mrs. Garvin?"

"I thought you said you were friends."

"We are. But I've been away for a while and I understand she's moved."

"I wouldn't know about that."

Downstairs in the lobby a few minutes later, Kosta called information. They told her Esther Garvin's number was unlisted. But in the public library an hour later, in a 1977 telephone directory, she found her address, an apartment building on Corcoran Street.

When she went there and rang the bell, Esther Garvin came to the door, wearing a bright-orange hostess gown with a blue flower in her hair. "Of course I remember you. I'm just having a Drambuie. Perhaps you'd like to join me."

96

In November 1975, Mrs. Oni Tamuri was invited to a dinner party at the home of two women friends. There she was introduced to Esther Garvin. Later they left the party together, kissed for the first time in a taxi, and went to Oni's apartment on Massachusetts Avenue. They drank brandy and shared a marijuana cigarette. Then they undressed each other and made love on the low couch in front of the fireplace.

Three weeks later Esther was persuaded to leave her job at the National Gallery and come to work for Global Financial. "You're too beautiful," Mrs. Tamuri said. "I want to look at you all day long. I can't stand to have you halfway across town being stared at by strangers."

The pattern was set from the start; the delicate Japanese woman, soft-spoken and fragile as porcelain, was the dominant, passionate, insistent partner. And the heroically sculptured Esther, black and beautiful, tall as a Masai, submitted and smiled, held out her arms, spread her legs, and fell more helplessly in love each day with the tiny golden hands that bathed her and massaged her, that stroked and seduced and punished her.

For almost five years they lived together, tenderly, in a climate of genuine warmth and kindness, sharing their lives with no one, guarding their privacy, each maintaining her own address, each of them careful to lead some superficial social life totally apart from the other.

In the offices of GFH they took perverse pride in their ability to function as dispassionate business associates. No looks, no touching, no clues whatsoever to the curious. No surrender to their feelings from the time they kissed good-bye after breakfast, each arriving separately at the office, till the moment that evening when the apartment door closed behind whichever one of them arrived home last and they could laugh again, kiss and have cocktails and turn off the phone.

They were truly contented, peaceful and loving and truthful, concerned, each of them, for the other's needs, no impulse to compete or humiliate or injure. They didn't shout or scream or weep. No rebukes or recriminations. Not until the end. Not until the last two hours they spent together, on a humid and sultry Saturday morning, as Oni Tamuri prepared to leave for her trip to London.

"I don't *recognize* you," Esther said. "I don't know what you're saying."

"Yes you do. I made it as plain as I can."

"I'm not just a piece of office furniture you can send back to the warehouse."

"*I'm* not doing it," Oni said. "I explained that to you. It wasn't my decision."

"I don't believe that. Don't insult me with a story like that."

"It's true. Rhyzdani tells me what to do. You know that."

"No. I *don't* know that," Esther said. "Did he tell you to hire me five years ago?"

"No, but—"

"That's right. He didn't. And he's not telling you to let me go now. It's *your* idea."

"Why would I want to do that?"

"I don't know," Esther said. "That's what I'm trying to find out."

"You can get another job in a minute and a better one. All you have to do is pick up the phone."

"I know that. I'm not worrying about a paycheck. That's not what we're talking about, is it?"

"I don't know what you mean."

"All right. Let me put it this way. Let me see if I've got it straight. You're going off to London for three or four weeks. I'm going to leave Global Financial because Mr. Rhyzdani says so. But I'll get another job and everything will be smooth. I mean, when you come back I'll be waiting here for you and nothing will be changed between us. Is that right? Is that what you're saying?"

Oni carefully folded a silk shirt and placed it in her bag lying open on the bed. Then she began folding another shirt. Esther sat staring at her. Finally she said, "Jesus, Oni . . . " She got up suddenly and walked across the room to the window.

"Don't start that," Oni said. "Don't start crying. What good does *that* do?" She followed Esther across the room. But as soon as she touched her, the black woman turned and walked into the bathroom, closing the door behind her. When she came out a few minutes later, Mrs. Tamuri had finished packing and was sitting at the mirror putting on eye shadow.

"Did I *do* something?" Esther said. "What did I do?"

"It's nothing like that. You didn't *do* anything."

"My contract just ran out, huh? Time for a change. Some new blood. A new face. Somebody a little younger maybe. Not so black. A little white chickie with pink nipples."

"For God's sake, Esther. I told you. It's not like that. Give me some credit. Don't wreck everything. We've been friends for a long time."

"No we haven't. Not *friends*. That's not what it was. That's not what it *is*. Not for me. I can't just press a button and make everything go away."

"Neither can I. You're twisting things around," Oni said. "You're making me feel awful."

"Jesus, I'm sorry, baby. I don't want *that* to happen. I mean, one of us feeling lousy is enough. I certainly don't want you to get on that airplane with anything *bothering* you. I'd feel guilty as hell if that happened."

Oni turned away from the mirror. She sat with her hands in her lap looking at Esther. Finally she said, "I'm sorry, Essy, I really am. But I . . . I can't help it."

Sitting in her apartment with Kosta, the shades closed to keep out the summer sun, Esther Garvin said, "Don't get me wrong. I'm not proud of my own record. I've been married three times and I've had a lot of what my daughter calls 'relationships.' I'm not saying that I haven't acted like a jackass more often than I like to remember. I've done some bad things to people. Careless things. But I found out a long time ago you can break up with somebody without cutting them in strips. There's always a better way to do it. Some decent way to behave. I figure it's better if the other person ends up hating *me* than if they end up hating *themselves.* That's the toughest rap of all. That's the thing that's hardest to get over."

She got up and walked to the bar for the Drambuie bottle. She poured a little in Kosta's glass and refilled her own. "I was crazy about Oni," she said. "I still am. But I never fooled myself about her. I never cheated on her and I don't think she cheated on me, but I knew in my heart it was just a question of time. I saw the way she looked at people. She couldn't help herself. I saw the way she looked at you the day you came in. She knew you were straight and she didn't like it. At heart she's a chaser. She'll be looking at young girls when she's eighty years old. And some of them will be looking at her.

"What I'm saying is that people break up. I know that. Oni's entitled to do whatever she wants to, to sleep with whoever. I didn't *own* her. She didn't own me. But she didn't have to do what she did. Not the *way* she did it. She didn't have to humiliate me. Have the locks changed at the office and her apartment. Have my stuff sent to me in cardboard boxes by some goddamned messenger service. She could have talked to me like a human being and *told* me how she felt. If she's got the hots for that little blond number she hired to take my place, that's her business. But she could have been decent about it. She could have had some respect for me. Some respect for all the time we spent together. We could have parted like grown-up women with some good memories of the life we had. But instead she turned it into something crummy. She made me feel rotten about myself and about her. I'm not going to spend the rest of my life trying to get even with her, but I don't have any urge to protect her either. If you still want to find out about Ralph Benedict, I'll be tickled to death to tell you."

 Later that afternoon Kosta had coffee with Nellie Arvidsen and Jackie Rovach, the girl whose boyfriend, Lee Dobler, worked in traffic control at Andrews Air Base. Later still, she and Jackie drove out to Andrews and spent an hour with Dobler while he ate his supper. And at eight o'clock she met Naomi Guterman for dinner at the Publick House in Georgetown.

It was after eleven when she came back to the hospital. She stopped at the night desk down the corridor from Gabe's room and asked the nurse how he was.

"He couldn't sleep. Said he slept too much this afternoon." The nurse looked at her watch. "So I gave him a sleeping pill a few minutes ago."

He was lying on his back in the dim light when Kosta went into the room. Regular breathing. His left arm, heavy in the cast, lay across his chest.

Kosta was exhilarated. Wide awake. Eager to tell him what she believed, what she suspected, what she knew. She was tempted to wake him, but instead she undressed quietly, draped her clothes across the screen that divided her side of the room from his, and slipped into her pajamas.

Lying in bed then, the crisp sheet pulled up to her waist, she listened to the hum of the air conditioner, heard the heavy whir of the elevator down the corridor, the squeak of rubber soles on the high wax of the hall floors, and soft laughter occasionally from the nurses' station.

Starting with her feet, she began to isolate and relax each section of her body, moving slowly up her legs, past her hips and stomach, past her chest and shoulders and neck and on into her brain, a self-induced hypnotic paralysis that could simulate sleep and turn itself at last into genuine sleep.

She had used the technique many times before, had mastered it, she felt. Sleeping on the ground, in vans and boats, on hard floors, in bad beds and bus seats, all through her school years, she had, more times than she could remember or count, slowly nudged herself through discomfort and fatigue and found a way, *some* way, to fall asleep.

There in the hospital room, she called up all those old skills, isolated her consciousness, and turned off the crackling power of her nerve endings. But she stayed vividly awake, all senses tingling, acute, and alive.

Finally she got out of bed and moved to the window. Across Pennsylvania Avenue, across nearly three quarters of a mile of buildings, monuments, and public gardens, she could see a soft halo of light from the end of the mall to the Potomac, the city beneath it quiet and dark, all the power and turbulence temporarily unplugged and stored away.

She turned away from the window then and stood beside Gabe's bed. He still lay on his back, breathing steadily, the night light behind him edging his profile in blue. She felt, or imagined she could feel, the warmth of his body. Under the white sheet, she could trace, in the dimness, its angular contours. Wide chest. Flat stomach. The fabric falling away softly to delineate his legs. Without touching him she moved one hand slowly through the air from his shoulders to his feet, her fingertips just inches from his body, gently sculpting in the cool half-light of the room his long outlines.

Like a nurse checking the temperature of a sick child, she

held her hand out then and felt his forehead. It was cool. And his cheek felt flat and cool when she touched it.

Suddenly she bent forward and brushed his cheek with her lips. He didn't move. She leaned over again and brought her mouth down on his. Kept it there. When she straightened up she could feel the warmth flooding through her veins and down into her body. She stood motionless, for long throbbing seconds, a vein pulsing in her temple, her stomach muscles tight and her legs trembling, her lungs hot and raw with breath she was afraid to let out.

The sound of a nurse's rubber soles outside startled and released her. Like a swift shadow, she was across the room, behind the screen, and into her bed. She lay there trembling, her cheeks flushed, her heart thumping, and her lips still tingling. And miraculously, in a matter of seconds, she was asleep.

Across the room, still inert on his back, Gabe opened his eyes. He stared up at the ceiling for a long moment. Then he closed his eyes again.

For five days after Gabe came home from the hospital, a bright orange Volkswagen panel truck, rigged inside to sleep three, was parked in his driveway, just at the foot of the outside staircase leading up to his apartment. In neat red letters on either side of the truck it said LOBBY FOR HUMAN SURVIVAL.

Day or night, there were always two young, wide-awake people in the front seat of the truck, smoking and talking, their eyes on the driveway and the street beyond. And two others slept in the back, waiting their turns to stand guard. Each person was on four hours and off four. They also took turns going to the store for food and newspapers which they delivered upstairs to Gabe and Kosta.

In Gabe's living room, two eight-foot folding tables had been set up facing each other. Each was partly covered with stacks of newspapers and magazines, folders of clippings, typewritten sheets, and penciled notes on yellow legal pads. There was a portable tape recorder, a typewriter, a desk-size calculator, and, just to one side, a school blackboard, easel style. And on one wall a huge map of the world had been tacked up.

In the bedroom, Gabe's bed was unmade. In the living room, the convertible couch where Kosta slept was open and unmade, a tangle of sheets and pillows at one end and newspapers and file folders spread across the mattress at the bottom, all within reach of Kosta's chair, which sat centered on the long side of one of the tables.

Once a day Kosta cleaned the kitchen and the bathrooms. She insisted. "I don't mind working like an animal, but I don't want to live like one. Not all the time, anyway."

Also once a day—at least once—usually at night, when they were both red eyed and worn out, one of them would say, "Is it worth it?" and the other one would say, "No. Of course not." But each morning, as they sat with their coffee, Kosta said, "Are we gonna make it, Senator?" and Gabe said, "I wouldn't be surprised."

On the fifth day, late at night, when Kosta, reversing the normal routine, said, "Well, *are* we gonna make it?" Gabe grinned and said, "We *have* made it. Starting from zip, with one chance in ten thousand, we have bloody well, I *promise* you, *made* it."

"So when do you do your number on the Senate floor?" she said.

"Not till tomorrow. You want to drink to that?"

"I'm superstitious. I'll wait till tomorrow. *Late* tomorrow."

An hour later, when she was lying awake in the dark living room, the door to Gabe's bedroom opened and he stood there in a rectangle of light in his robe. "You asleep?"

"Not yet."

He walked over and sat down on the edge of the bed.

"We forgot something important," he said.

"Too late. I'm already on rewind."

"There's one question we didn't answer yet."

" 'What's that?' the lady said, putting the pillow over her head."

"What about *us?*" he said.

"What does that mean?"

"You know what it means. It means what are we gonna do about you and me?"

"Let's take you first," she said. "When you walk off the Senate floor tomorrow I think they'll ship you straight back to the cornfields. As for me—"

"Bullshit, Kosta. The jokes won't work anymore."

"Hey . . . I'm not—"

"Yes you are. And it won't work."

She pulled herself together then. Very deliberately. She sat up, leaned back against the head of the couch, pulled the sheet up over her, and made one last stubborn attempt to stay the way she'd always been. "Wait a minute," she said. "I'm not sure what you're up to, but if you're trying to change the ground rules all of a sudden, it won't work. I mean, we had a tough job to do. And we did it. At least I *hope* we did it. I told you before, if you want to have a drink and shoot out some streetlights tomorrow night, that's fine with me. That's terrific with me. But as far as anything else—I mean, if I did something to give you the wrong idea . . . God, I'm really terrible at this. What I'm struggling to say is, I don't jump in bed with somebody just because they happen—"

"I didn't say anything about that," Gabe said. "Who said anything about going to bed?"

"Well, not in so many words."

"Not in *any* words. I didn't say anything at all about that. We've been shut up in this apartment for almost a week. We've known each other for months. Have I made any kind of a move on you at all?"

"I didn't say—"

"You know I haven't," he said, "and I'm not making one now. I just asked what we're going to do about you and me. Just that. Nothing else."

She made one last try. "If you're asking me if I have some

feelings for you . . . if I . . . well, I *don't.* I'm sorry to just blurt it out like that, but I . . . "

"Go on. You *what?*"

"I don't know. I mean, I can't handle these games."

He got up and started for the door.

"Oh, for God's sake," she said. "Don't get mad and go pout in your room."

"I'm not mad." He went into the bedroom and closed the door behind him. As he took off his robe and got into bed, he heard her voice, faintly through the door. "Oh, for God's sake."

Turning off his bed lamp, he lay back with his head on the pillow. Suddenly she wailed from the living room, "You're crazy. Do you know that? You're really a pain."

He lay there and didn't answer. A moment later he heard her mattress squeak. Then a light knock on the door. "Are you asleep already?"

"Not quite."

"I don't want to come in. I just think it's boring for two people to go to sleep mad."

"I'm not mad," he said.

"Neither am I."

"That's good."

"Good night," she said then. Very faint through the door.

"Good night."

After a long silence the knob turned and his door eased open. She came through the doorway and stood just inside, wearing a robe over her pajamas. "What I should have said is this. I like you a lot. I admire you and I respect you. And I'd hate it if I thought I'd never see you again. But it's different from . . . I mean, I don't just jump into somebody's bed."

"There you go again," Gabe said. "That's at least *twice* you've jumped into my bed, and I haven't asked you *once.*"

"Well . . . come on," she said. "I'm not stupid. I didn't just pop out of the egg five minutes ago."

He turned his bed lamp on then and sat there looking at her. For a long time. Finally, he said, "Come here." When she hesitated he said, "Come on. I'm not going to jump on your bones."

She walked across the room and stood beside his bed, her

hands in the pockets of her robe. "Let's stop kidding each other," he said. "I didn't just hatch out of the egg either. Do you remember last week at the hospital when you came in late?"

"You were asleep. Sleeping pill and everything."

"That's right. I was *almost* asleep. But I woke up when you came into the room. I heard you getting undressed and getting into bed. I could tell you were having trouble going to sleep, and that kept *me* awake. So when you got up and walked over to the window—"

"Oh, my God."

"When you came over to my bed, my eyes were squinted open just enough so I could see you in the night light. I could see your face and I saw what you did with your hands. When you bent over and kissed me I pretended I was asleep. But I wasn't. I was awake. Just as awake as you are now."

She sank slowly down to the floor beside his bed and sat there like a crumpled cloth doll, her face turned down and away from him.

"What is it?" he said. "What's the matter?"

"Nothing."

"Are you crying?"

"No."

"The hell you're not. What are you crying about?"

"I don't know," she said.

"What do you mean, you don't know?"

"Just what I said, damn it. I don't know."

"Look at me," he said.

"I can't."

"Are you crying because I told you I was awake the other night?"

"It's not just that," she said.

"Then what *is* it?"

"You don't understand. You don't understand *anything.*"

"You're right. I sure as hell don't understand *you.* I don't know what you're talking about."

She came up on her knees suddenly beside the bed. "I'm talking about *me.* About the way I *feel.* I'm embarrassed. I never kissed anybody like . . . I mean, I never wanted to . . . I just . . . "

"I know what you mean."

"No you don't. Because it's *weird. I'm* weird. I don't know anything about men. I'm scared of them. I always have been. I'm scared to *death* of men. I mean it. I've never . . . I've never *done* anything. I never *wanted* to. I was afraid to."

She slumped down by the bed again and stayed there for a long time, looking at the floor. Finally Gabe said, "Let's go in the kitchen and have some coffee."

"I don't want any coffee."

"Yes you do."

They sat across from each other at the kitchen table and he told her about Sam. The whole story. Then he told her about Helen, how they'd met, what their life together had been like, and how they'd broken up and divorced.

Finally, then, in the deepest hours of the late night, Kosta told him, haltingly at first, and at last in what seemed an endless flow of tortured words, the ugly details of what she had seen that late afternoon in the mountain forest, how it had affected her, stunted her, twisted her away from herself, away from touching, away from feeling.

When they stood up to leave the kitchen, it was almost morning. Faint light bled in around the window shades. As they walked into the living room, Gabe stopped, turned her to him, and kissed her. Then he held her away a little and looked down at her. "Are you scared of me?"

"I don't think so."

"You're not sure?"

"Yes, I'm sure. I'm not scared."

"I don't want to rush you."

"You're not rushing anybody." She pulled his head down and kissed him.

"I don't want to sleep out here by myself," she said then.

In his room, when he switched off the bed lamp, she said, "Leave it on. I don't want to miss anything. I want to see how you look."

Standing by the bed, he took off his robe. She stood staring at him for a long silent moment. Then, without taking her eyes from his, she slipped out of her robe and took off her pajamas. "You're beautiful," she said. "I'm funny looking."

"You're crazy." He put his arms around her and held her close to him.

"I hope I'm not too little," she said.

"You're not too little."

He eased her down on the bed and she lay close against him with her arms around him. "I'm stupid," she said. "I don't know anything about anything."

"How do you *feel?* That's what matters."

"I feel terrific. I mean, *you* feel terrific."

"That's all there is to it."

"You mean if it feels good to me it will feel good to you? Just like that?"

"Just like that."

"Even if I don't *know* anything?"

"Nobody *knows* anything."

 At two thirty that afternoon on the Senate floor, debate resumed on the Petersen-Mullaney farm subsidy bill. Less than half of the senators had come back from lunch, but the press gallery was packed when Senator Kitchin from Montana, taking his turn at the chair, recognized Senator Treptow from Illinois.

Gabe organized the papers on his podium, glanced up at Kosta in the press section, and began to speak.

"Thank you, Mr. President. I would like to say, first of all, that I've consulted with both Senator Petersen and Senator Mullaney. I think their subsidy bill provides for a well-worked-out program and I've assured them that I will support it. Before we come to a final vote I will be more specific in my comments."

Again he glanced up at Kosta. "First, however, I would like to focus on another matter, one that on the surface seems to have no relevance to the bill before us. I can only say that what I will present to you is relevant to *everything* we do here, to everything we *are*, to everything the Senate stands for."

Senator Basenfelder was on his feet suddenly. "Mr. President . . . would the senator from Illinois yield?"

"With all respect to my colleague from Nevada," Gabe said quickly, "I will *not* yield. My remarks shouldn't take more than fifteen minutes. I beg the chair's indulgence."

Basenfelder walked slowly across to Rafer Isbell's desk. Senator Bright joined them there. With their backs turned to the front of the chamber, they talked quietly as Gabe went on speaking.

"I'm aware of my standing here. If we had a sour apple award or a poison ivy citation I'm sure I would win it. I've made a serious error for a member of the Congress. I've tried to use my own standards as a measuring rod for this legislative body. I've suggested that the United States government should be at least as honest as *I* am. Since I've never pretended to be a paragon of virtue, I can't believe those standards are too high."

A soft cloud of approval and some subdued laughter floated down from the press gallery.

"Today, however, I don't plan to give a lecture on integrity. I will simply present a series of facts about some events that have taken place in the past few months. I ask that all this material be entered into the *Congressional Record.*"

A soft buzz of conversation started, then subsided, as Senator Kitchin tapped his gavel on the block. Both Senator Small and Senator Fletemyer joined the group around Isbell's desk.

"As all of you know, I've been conducting an investigation into the crashes of two H-14 aircraft last January. In one of those accidents my brother and his family were killed. The total number of dead in both crashes was two hundred and forty-five."

With his right hand, Gabe held up a thick, accordion-pleated file envelope. "The pertinent information has been assembled and reviewed. The H-14 investigation, as of today, is concluded."

This time Senator Isbell spoke up. "Would the senator yield?"

"Mr. President," Gabe said. "I explained my position. I will not yield at this time."

Kitchin tapped the gavel again. "The senator will proceed."

"Our investigation is now finished," Gabe repeated. He paused, then went on. "The conclusions are these. Neither of those H-14 crashes was an accident. Both the SAI flight and Air Force Three exploded in midair. In each case explosive devices had been planted on the planes before takeoff. The two hundred forty-five passengers and crew were *not* accident victims. Those people were murdered. I accuse the United States government of complicity in those murders. Before the fact and after the fact.

"With the knowledge and cooperation of the executive branch, various government agencies and departments conspired to conceal evidence, to bribe witnesses, to distort the truth. There is evidence of kidnapping, burglary, harassment, and in my own case, as you can see, of physical assault. All this with one purpose. To cover up an enormous lie with a blanket of smaller ones. To conceal a dangerous and cynical act, a massive international deception."

Senator Isbell moved up the aisle to the exit door, pushed it open, and exited into the cloakroom, followed by seven of his colleagues. As Gabe continued speaking, the other senators in the chamber quietly left, one by one. At last it seemed that only Senator Kitchin was present, presiding from behind the huge elevated desk. Two parliamentary reporters, at a long table in front of Kitchin, also remained. And the recording stenographers at their desks on the floor. Both the party secretaries stayed too, Republican and Democrat, at their desks in opposite corners at the front of the chamber. But apart from these individuals, the crowd in the press gallery, and a sprinkle of tourists and students in the visitors' sections, only Gabe remained in the chamber.

"I have mixed feelings," he went on, "about presenting this material. I take no pride in revealing a national disgrace. I know there could be international reverberations. Serious economic consequences. Those prospects sober me and frighten me. But something else frightens me more. Government by subterfuge and falsehood, by deliberate perversion of meaning and intention and purpose.

"There is no one living who has never told a lie. There is no government that doesn't lie to other governments. There is no government that doesn't lie to its own people. But, God help us, there has to be an end to it somewhere. *Someplace, sometime*, at *some* point along the line, *somebody* has to say, 'Wait a minute. I've had enough. You can't keep doing this to me. I won't stand for it.'"

Gabe took a sip of water from the glass in front of him. "I promised I wouldn't moralize," he said. He looked around the chamber. "But most of the people I made that promise to are gone. I thought they were *all* gone till I just spotted the senator from California. If one of the pages will wake him up and escort him to the door we can make it a hundred-percent desertion rate. Then I can say whatever I like."

A sustained rumble of laughter from the press gallery this time. And some uncertain chuckles from the visitors' seats. Until Kitchin rapped for silence. Then Gabe began to speak again. More briskly now.

"Here's what took place. All documented. All verified. On January sixth this year, at two forty-three in the afternoon, a Simison Air International jet, flight number three forty-six, destination Los Angeles, crashed on takeoff from International Airport just outside Indianapolis.

"Just after that crash three eyewitnesses reported that they'd seen the plane explode in the air. By the time the FAA issued its final report, one of those three witnesses, Arloa Anderson, was confined to a mental institution. Her sister told my investigator that Miss Anderson's condition had not changed since childhood. Nonetheless she was suddenly confined and kept in isolation. No visitors permitted.

"The other two eyewitnesses were Avery Buck and Ellen Perigo. Not long after the SAI crash Mr. Buck sold his farm to a company that's owned by the United States Department of Agriculture. They paid him, according to local real estate agents, at least *four times* what the property was worth.

"In Ellen Perigo's case, she, too, had a remarkable stroke of luck. Less than two weeks after witnessing the H-14 crash, she received in a lump sum all the overdue payments from her husband's black-lung compensation. Plus a generous lifetime pension for herself. In addition, a long-standing claim against a strip-mining company which had allegedly destroyed her home in Tennessee was suddenly settled. She was told that a government agency had intervened on her behalf. All in all, Mrs. Perigo was suddenly richer by several hundred thousand dollars.

"In the FAA's concluding report, both Mr. Buck and Mrs. Perigo testified they had made a mistake. The midair explosion they had reported actually didn't take place till the plane hit the ground. That was their final conclusion.

"Early in their investigations, both the FAA and the NTSB had indicated publicly that they believed the SAI crash was due to pilot error. After the Air Force Three crash, however, on January 16, the two agencies announced that a failure of the H-14's hydraulic system had caused both crashes. At that time, Leo Hartwig, president of the company that builds the H-14, said to newspaper reporters in California, *quote*, 'There was no failure of our hydraulic systems. I defy the FAA to *prove* what they're saying. Those two H-14's crashed for only one reason—because somebody *wanted* them to crash.'

"Shortly after that interview, Hartwig was replaced as the head of his own company. Since then no one has talked with him. It was assumed that he was living quietly with his wife in their home outside Watsonville, California. My investigators concluded that the Hartwigs were in fact there. But they seemed to be living under a kind of house arrest, guarded day and night by two men who claimed to be private security officers hired by Mr. Hartwig.

"Our investigation showed that these two men were *not* employed, as they said, by an agency in Santa Cruz. One of them, in fact, was identified by my people as Oscar Tunstall, a former friend and unofficial associate of J. Edgar Hoover. Mr. Tunstall is at present an employee of the Justice Department. But no officials at Justice will admit that they know him or that he works there.

"I personally called the Hartwig house in California and had a short conversation with Mr. Tunstall. Shortly after that call, the Hartwigs were seen leaving their house with two men. We have no idea where they are now, but it seems likely that Mr. Tunstall has added the charge of kidnapping to whatever others will eventually be brought against him.

"Tunstall had other duties, it seems, related to the SAI flight. Before going to California to oversee the Hartwigs he was in Indianapolis. While he was there, shortly after the crash, he made contact with a young man named Dick McCann, the editor and publisher of an underground newspaper called *The Belated Truth*.

"Dick McCann, just after the SAI crash, had interviewed Avery Buck and Ellen Perigo. And he was the only newspaper person who managed to talk to Arloa Anderson. He had already published a short item about their original testimony and he'd promised a complete story on what he called 'The Exploding Airliner.' But . . . he suddenly decided to give up his newspaper. The reason? He was offered a truly remarkable job. With an astonishing salary. Working for the Department of Health, Education, and Welfare. Indianapolis office. The man who recruited him, who identified himself as a senior official with HEW in Washington, was Oscar Tunstall.

"No matter how sure we were that the SAI plane had been blown up, we still didn't know *why*. Not till the people who were orchestrating the cover-up *told* us. They knew what *we* didn't know, that the plane had been destroyed to kill just one man. So to cut off all questions before they were asked, a decision was made. They would pretend that *that* man, the target, had never actually been on the plane. After originally listing two hundred fourteen passengers and twelve crew, the FAA and the airline later revised the list down to two hundred *thirteen* passengers.

"That might have worked for them if one of the specialists who came in to sort out and identify the bodies hadn't told a reporter from the *Indianapolis Star* that there were two hundred fourteen passengers after all. This reporter snooped around the SAI offices and bribed someone to let him see the original passenger list. When his story came out, the FAA said they'd made a mistake. There *was* one more passenger. His name was Ralph Benedict.

"Nobody claimed Benedict's body. He was cremated in Indianapolis almost as soon as he was identified. After a week or so the newspapers forgot about him. But when my people started digging they discovered that Benedict had bought two

hundred thousand dollars' worth of life insurance twenty minutes before his plane took off from Indianapolis. The beneficiary
of that policy was not a relative or a close friend, however. It
was a company called Global Financial Horizons.

"We found out that GFH had received the insurance check
and had deposited it in a Washington bank. But nobody in their
office here seemed to know anything at all about Ralph Benedict. Next step, one of our people went to Zurich, to the home
office of Global Financial. No luck there either. No one knew
Benedict. No one knew why he had made the company his
beneficiary. But on that trip we found out some interesting
things about Global Financial.

"The company does function, as its charter indicates, as an
international investment service. If you have a lot of cash on
hand, they will bank it for you, invest it, or simply lock it away
in a vault inside some Swiss mountain. That is their business. At
least it's a *part* of their business.

"But the main function of Global Financial, it turns out, is as
a holding company for three billion Swiss francs, for two billion
British pounds in banks in London and Liverpool, and for nine
billion dollars in the Chase Manhattan and Morgan Guaranty
banks in New York. An astounding amount of money. But most
astounding is the fact that it all belongs to one man. Prince Abu
Khamufa.

"Till last November, the Abu was the sole ruler of Bedaki, one
of the richest of the United Arab Emirates. Since then he's lived
in Switzerland in exile. Until he moved, with his entire family,
to Costa Rica. We've all seen pictures of his villa on television,
surrounded by soldiers with automatic weapons.

"We still had no real link between Khamufa and Benedict.
There was no trace of such a man. No one knew who he was or
where he came from. Then, a few days ago, we found out. Not
through skill or wisdom. We suddenly got lucky. Or maybe
Global Financial got dumb. Three weeks ago they discharged a
woman who had worked for them here in Washington for nearly
five years. An intelligent woman and a loyal employee. And not
only did they discharge her, they managed to humiliate her."

Gabe took a business envelope out of the folder in front of
him and held it up. "This lady turned out to be the jigsaw-

puzzle piece we were looking for. This is her sworn affidavit giving undeniable proof that the airline passenger who called himself Ralph Benedict was in fact Ibn Khamufa, the Abu's younger brother. He was described by Bedaki's present leader, Ishaq Rashid, as an enemy of the Bedaki people, a man whose guilt is on the same level as that of the Abu.

"We all know that Rashid denies the existence of any assassination squads. But other Arab sources disagree. They say the squads are real, well trained, and determined. And at the top of their target list are two names—Abu Khamufa and his brother, Ibn.

"Once we had this information about Khamufa, our investigation of the Air Force Three crash went very quickly. The FAA says there were no eyewitnesses. Therefore no reason to suspect a midair explosion. We are convinced that there was such an explosion, but we can't prove it. So we counter the FAA by saying, 'If there are no eyewitnesses, how can you be *sure* there was no explosion?'

"A midair explosion, the FAA says, would have scattered debris in a wide area. They say no such debris was found. That is not true. In the past few weeks we have collected signed statements from three West Virginia farmers, one near the town of Beverly, one near Junior, and one near Mabie. All these farms are just a few miles from Elkins, where Air Force Three went down. And on each one, small pieces of burned and twisted aluminum have been found, the kind of wreckage an exploding airplane would scatter. None of these farmers, or any of the other West Virginia residents our people talked to had ever been questioned by government inspectors. No previous search for debris had been made.

"Air Force Three's passenger list gave us no clues. But when we found out about Ibn Khamufa, when we concluded that *he* had been the target in the SAI explosion, some things we'd learned earlier began to make sense. My brother's wife had written to my father saying that Air Force Three would be crowded. The pilot's wife had been told the same thing. And the airport caterer's records showed that more than a hundred in-flight meals had been ordered. But there were only fourteen passengers on that plane when it went down, all of them scheduled to disembark in Chicago. And from Chicago the empty plane would have flown on to Seattle according to the flight plan registered at O'Hare Airport. It didn't make sense. Not until we got this copy of the flight manifest for Air Force Three. Departing Washington, D.C., January 16, an interim stop in Chicago, continuing to Seattle."

Again Gabe held up some papers. "Almost one hundred passenger names are on this manifest for Air Force Three. The explosives that were planted on that plane were intended to kill more than eighty passengers who didn't show up for the takeoff.

"On this list are the names of Abu Khamufa, two of his brothers, five of his sisters, four uncles, seventeen wives, and more than fifty children. These were the passengers who were to go on to Seattle. In Seattle, they were scheduled to board a ship and go by sea to Costa Rica. But the Abu changed his mind. When the Air Force Three took off from Andrews he and his family were not on board."

Gabe paused, glanced at his watch, then went on. "If this were a play in a theater, or a motion picture, I would give you the names of the people who planted explosives on those two planes. I can't do that, because I don't know. I would also show you dental records of the man who called himself Ralph Benedict, *proving* that he was in fact Ibn Khamufa. Since his body was cremated, that's impossible too. Apart from what I've told you, apart from the information I have in this file, there is no *physical* evidence at all—just two black, burned-over fields, one in Indiana and one in West Virginia.

"If we were in court it would be argued that everything I've presented here comes under the heading of circumstantial evidence. From a strictly *legal* point of view, that may be true. But I contend that when all other evidence has been destroyed or concealed, then circumstantial evidence becomes *best* evidence.

"This investigation started because there were all kinds of unanswered questions in my mind. There are still questions. Lots of them. Why would the Abu pretend to be living in Costa Rica when he was actually in the United States? Why couldn't he just say, 'I like the United States. That's where I'm going to stay'?

"There's an easy answer to that one. Our government wouldn't let him stay here. They *couldn't*. Because the President had assured the world, the United Nations, and the people of Bedaki that Abu Khamufa would never be allowed asylum here.

"But now we find out that he *was* granted asylum in this country. Why? I say it's *money*. That *has* to be the answer. What would happen, for example, if the Abu's three billion Swiss francs, two billion pounds, and nine billion American dollars suddenly broke loose and began to float in the world money market?

"What if he deposited all that money in Johannesburg? What if he decided to buy gold? What if he converted it overnight to German marks or Japanese yen? Tough questions. Difficult to answer.

"Next question. No easier than the last one. After his brother's death on the SAI plane, did Khamufa decide that the United States wasn't such a safe place after all? Was that why ten days later he was scheduled to fly to Seattle and go from there to Costa Rica? If so, why didn't he take that flight? And where is he now?

"If Bedaki agents were responsible for those two crashes, if they knew that Khamufa and his family were here in the United States, then Ishaq Rashid certainly knew it too. So why didn't he make it public? Why didn't he carry out the threats he made when he took office, that he would cancel oil shipments and cut off all relations with any nation that harbored the Abu?

"And finally, the question that's most important to all of us who had relatives on either one of the H-14's: Who *are* the people who actually put the explosive devices on those planes? Does our government know their names? Where are these people now and how will they be dealt with?

"I can't answer these questions. Not yet. But I know that someone can. Somewhere the answers are available. So I call on the executive branch, the Congress, and the agencies involved to come forward. I call on the media to be aggressive and alert. And, most important, I call on the people of this country to send a message to their elected representatives. If *you* are concerned, *they* will be concerned. They *must* be. And just at the bottom of whatever card or letter or telegram you send, write the following message:

"*Inform* me . . . *Represent* me . . . *Respect* me."

That evening, in his commentary on the seven o'clock news, Marvin Hepworth began by saying:

> '*Inform* me, *represent* me, *respect* me.' With that slogan, heard for the first time today in the chamber of the United States Senate, it's possible we may have seen the beginning of a new relationship in this land between the voters and the people they send to Washington to represent them.
>
> We are not a nation of scholars and idealists, but we usually know a good slogan when we hear one. Many people here believe that this one, coined today by Senator Treptow of Illinois, could hang around to haunt the political community for a long, long time.

 Twenty minutes after Gabe finished speaking in the Senate chamber, Dalrymple and Lasker were meeting with the Secretary in his office. From there they placed calls to Roland Casper in London, to the American embassy in Caracas, to the Mexican embassy in Washington, and to Ishaq Rashid in Bedaki.

An hour later these three men went to Newquist's office in the Executive Office Building. They were joined there by Darby Roush, Wesley Duggan, and General Stecko. Newquist placed a second call to Rashid, and both he and the Secretary spoke with him. Then the Secretary called Abu Khamufa to set up an appointment for later that night.

The meeting in the Oval Office started at six o'clock with all the men who had been in Newquist's office, plus Mossler of the FAA, Slayback of NTSB, two senior officials from the Justice Department, and the President. They stopped the meeting long enough to listen to Marvin Hepworth, then went at it again.

By midnight, Lasker and the two men from Justice were on a jet for Mexico City to meet Roland Casper, who was flying in from London; the Secretary, in Air Force Two, was on his way to Bedaki; Newquist was in an all-night strategy session with the presidential press secretary and his staff; Dalrymple was coordinating events from the communications room at State; and two White House aides, a national security advisor, and General Stecko were just arriving by helicopter at the estate in central Virginia where the Abu was waiting to talk with them.

Forty-eight hours later, television audiences had seen Abu Khamufa and his family boarding planes that would take them to Costa Rica, they had seen Leo Hartwig announcing that he and his wife had never been illegally detained, that they had gone voluntarily to Mazatlán from their home in California, that Mr. Hartwig would soon be resuming his position as president of Hartwig Systems, and that neither he nor his wife had ever met a man named Oscar Tunstall.

Viewers then saw a satellite interview from Caracas. An American embassy official there testified that both Tunstall and Wib Tyson had been in Venezuela since January third on special assignment for the Department of Energy. Their passports proved that they had never left Venezuela since their arrival there.

Finally, the President, on all three networks, had explained to the world that leadership is painful, that the demands of national security often necessitate difficult decisions. He concluded with assurances that world stability had been maintained, that restraint had won the day, that economic chaos had been averted, and that all guilty persons had been apprehended and would pay for their crimes. As a final note he closed his eyes and offered up a prayer for the innocent people who had perished in the two airplane crashes and for their families who had suffered such tragic losses.

The following Sunday, in the opening portion of *Forefront*, Bert Culbertson, said, "Tonight I'll be talking with a gentleman you met first on this program several months ago—Gabe Treptow. At that time he was a candidate. Running for a seat in the United States Senate. Today he's a senator who may be in trouble. Or he may be a hero. Depending on who you talked to last. But whatever he does from now on, he'll be remembered, I think, as the man who uncovered what has come to be known as the Khamufa conspiracy, the biggest scandal to unfold in Washington since Watergate."

During the interview segment, Culbertson began by saying, "I keep hearing that you're a political misfit. And two minutes later somebody tells me you may be the only honest man in Washington. What do *you* say?"

"I say they're both wrong."

"Have the events of the past week surprised you?"

"I'm not surprised at what's happened. But I didn't expect it to happen so fast."

"Without your investigation, without the speech you made on the floor of the Senate, do you think this whole story would have come out?"

"It might have," Gabe said. "But you can't be sure. The more time goes by, the tougher it is to dig out the truth."

"Were you surprised that the Federal Bureau of Investigation knew about the bombs on those planes, that they already had the five men in custody?"

"Six months ago I would have been surprised. Now . . . "

"Now *nothing* surprises you," Culbertson said.

"I wouldn't say that. Let's just say that the time I've spent in Washington has changed some of my reactions."

"The words *cover-up* and *conspiracy* have just about been worn out in the papers and on television these past few days. How do you feel about it? Do you think the spokesmen for the White House and the State Department and the FAA are being candid now? Are we getting the whole truth finally?"

Gabe shook his head: "No. Of course not. But the big stuff, the *important* facts, couldn't be covered up any longer. They had their tails in a crack. The same people who'd been pressuring them to lie, the banks and the Pentagon and the oil companies, all started pressuring them to tell the truth. Once the boat started to leak, everybody wanted to bail out in a hurry, take their losses, and start over."

"You were the architect of this whole thing. You did a lot of guesswork, but most of it turned out to be right. Tell us exactly what happened."

"Well, there's still some guesswork involved, but not much. At the beginning I think the President was shooting straight when he said we wouldn't give Khamufa asylum. But then Abu started throwing darts from Switzerland, threatening the banks with what he could do. So the money people got nervous and began running scared to the White House. They painted such a disastrous picture for the President that he knuckled under and agreed to let Khamufa come in on the sly.

"They took every precaution they could once the decision was made. All the Khamufa family came on military planes and landed on government bases. And they took them to that big estate in Virginia in Army trucks. In the middle of the night. The place itself had been a CIA safe house for years, so nobody was surprised to see guards around it."

"So everyone was fooled."

"Everybody but the Bedakis. They never bought the Costa Rica story for a minute. But when Rashid called us on it, the State Department lied to him. And they kept on lying till some Bedaki dissidents zeroed in on the Abu's brother and blasted the plane he was on. The State Department says they didn't know what had happened to the plane till Rashid told them. Maybe they did and maybe they didn't. Anyway, they had to scramble to keep him from going public with the whole thing right then, cutting off the oil, the whole works, just the way he'd promised he would."

"What stopped him?"

"He was having some troubles of his own. He was nervous about the Pakistanis and a little bit leery of his Cuban advisors. And mostly he was scared that Iraq was going to make a move against him. He decided he'd better keep us on his side. Just in case. So he told the President he'd look the other way if we promised him Khamufa would be out of the United States within a week. The President promised, the cover-up of the SAI crash got underway, and the State Department started putting pressure on Khamufa. That's when they arranged the Air Force Three flight and the ship from Seattle to Costa Rica."

"Why did Khamufa accept it?"

"He didn't. But he went through the motions. Then, just before his whole tribe was about to load up for the trip to Andrews Air Base to get on Air Force Three, he called the White House and said he was going to float his nine billion dollars right out of Morgan Guaranty and Chase Manhattan. The President said, 'Sorry, you can't do that. I've frozen those funds till you arrive in Costa Rica.'

"But Khamufa had another card. He said if they forced him to go to Costa Rica he would talk to the press as soon as he got there and tell them his brother had been assassinated by Bedaki nationals. And over two hundred Americans had been murdered with him."

"That's when the cover-up really got going," Culbertson said.

"That's right. The State Department had to keep Rashid in the dark about Khamufa and they had to keep the American people from finding out that all those passengers had been killed by Bedakis. Oil or no oil, money or no money, they knew the country would be in an uproar. Then Air Force Three went down and that had to be dealt with too."

"And Rashid found out that Khamufa hadn't left the country after all."

"Not exactly. The State Department told him there'd been a last-minute change in plans, that Khamufa and his family had gone on a direct flight to Costa Rica. They did fly a bunch of his relatives down there and they were seen in San José, so that made the story look good."

"Did Rashid believe it?"

"He pretended to. Mostly by then he was trying to save face. The Iraqis were still looking down his throat and his Bedaki enemies had made him look bad by blowing up Air Force Three. Rashid had promised the President he could control those people once we said we'd ship Khamufa to Costa Rica."

"But what about now?" Culbertson said. "Now he knows we lied again. Doesn't he have to act?"

"No. We gave him an out. This time the whole world knows that Khamufa and his family left from Andrews. A hundred cameras saw him get on the plane and take off. We admitted publicly that Khamufa had been here 'temporarily . . . for humanitarian reasons,' and Rashid accepted that. Publicly then he got the President off the hook with the people in this country who wanted to hit back at Bedaki by saying the five Bedaki terrorists did not, in any way, represent his government. He said they were right-wing Islamic purists working for an Iraqi takeover of Bedaki."

"Do you believe that?"

"Who knows what's going on over there? Maybe Rashid's telling the truth. Maybe he's not. The important thing is that those men will be brought to trial. The other important thing is that the people got a firsthand look at how the government operates. The name of the game is Overkill. Never try a simple solution. Don't risk telling the truth. The more things can be complicated and screwed up, the better. Welcome to the squirrel cage."

"Just one more question. After all that resistance, why did Khamufa finally leave so peacefully for Costa Rica? He got on that plane with a big smile. What do you think brought *that* on?"

Gabe smiled. "That's an easy one. I'm sure somebody *promised* him something."

"Like what?"

Gabe shook his head. "Who knows? But I guarantee you we'll find the answer someplace down the road."

"What about down the road for you? You're a national figure

all of a sudden. But they say there's a good chance you'll be recalled from office by your constituents. Do you think that will happen?"

"No, I don't. My term in office expires in 1984 and I expect to complete that term."

"That means you'll fight to stay in office?"

Gabe nodded. "Sure I will. Nobody likes to be fired. Especially when two hundred million people are watching. But I know I'm in for a battle. I know what I'm up against. It's hard to talk principles to somebody who only cares about keeping his gas tank full. Remember that lady in New Mexico a few years ago? She said she didn't mind risking radiation from a nuclear plant if it meant she could keep her second toaster. Maybe that's just the way people are. Maybe I can't change anything. But I think it's worth a try. Maybe I can't change things in the Senate either. But I'm gonna fight like hell to stay there till the end of my term. I can make a lot of noise in four years."

"*If* you stay in office."

"That's right. *If* I stay in office."

"And if you *don't?*"

Gabe grinned. "If I don't, I have my teaching job waiting for me whenever I want it. And besides that I'm getting married next week."

"Well . . . congratulations. Maybe we should make the announcement right here. Finish up this interview with a social item."

Gabe leaned back in his chair and laughed. "I don't think we'd better do that. Matter of fact, I've talked too much already. You see, there's one little problem. I haven't really . . . I mean, I haven't actually *asked* her yet."

"God, are you off the wall," Kosta said. "I never heard such a routine." She lowered her voice a full tone. " 'I mean, I'm sort of thinking, maybe, if the rain don't hurt the rhubarb, of getting sort of *married* next week'—*God!*"

"You're overdoing it," Gabe said. "I thought I was pretty smooth."

"Mortimer Snerd. 'I've got this uh—little—uh—*problem*, Mr. Bergen. I—uh—well, you know . . . I ain't really *asked* her yet.' *God in heaven!* I mean, I wasn't even in the same *room* with you! I'm sitting there in the clients' booth at CBS with a couple of pinstripe yo-yos from God knows where and you come out with *that!* What a proposal! Prime time. Full network."

"You can top it. I'll get you on *Meet the Press* next week and you can turn me down."

It was early evening. Almost sunset. They were driving west on Dolly Madison Boulevard. They'd left the television studio half an hour before.

"The truth is," she said then, "the *real* truth is, I thought it was a gorgeous proposal."

"Too late. I just took it back."

"Fat chance." She moved closer to him on the front seat. "Where are you taking me? Why are we driving all the way out here?"

"There's this restaurant I know. Just past Pimmit Hills. I thought you might like to eat a big dinner and drink a lot. Celebrate."

"What are we celebrating?"

"All kinds of things. You're smart and I'm beautiful."

"I hate to tell you, but you've still got that bump on your nose, and your nice purple bruises are turning yellow. You're not too beautiful."

"Suit yourself. *You* be beautiful and *I'll* be smart."

"You know what an egress is?" she said then.

"A white bird with long skinny legs."

"Perfect. You see that egress down the road? Let's egress there."

"Why?"

"I want to talk serious. I want you to look at me while I tell you something."

When he pulled off the boulevard into a grassy area with a drinking fountain, a picnic table, and an outdoor grill, when he switched off the engine, she turned to face him in the seat.

"I hope you don't think you have to marry me."

"That's *exactly* what I think," he said. "Why shouldn't I think that?"

"Because you *don't* have to. I mean, just because you wrecked my virginity and turned my life around and like that . . ."

"That doesn't mean anything. I've done those things to lots of people."

"Seriously, folks . . ."

"Seriously, folks, I think the shoe is on the other foot. *You* don't have to marry *me.* Now that you're not scared of men anymore, maybe you should shop around a little, try the water, as they say—study the landscape."

"I've been thinking about that."

"What did you decide?"

"I think I'd better stay put. Some famous preacher once said, 'When you make a bad choice, stick with it. That's how you prove you've got character.' "

"Makes sense to me."

She slid close to him, put her arms around his neck, and said, "How'd you like to kiss a Greek?"

She stayed where she was then, her head on his shoulder, the sun burning blood red suddenly as it edged behind the trees to the west.

"You think I'll like it when we're living in Fort Beck?"

"You'd better. I don't want to hear you crying all the time in the kitchen."

"Will I fit in?"

"If you don't, we'll get rid of all the other people."

"I can't wait to see your house."

"You'll like it," he said. "It's a good house."

She moved away from him on the front seat, then put on a very serious expression and said, "Before we go too far there's something I've been meaning to tell you. I come from a very fertile family. Greeks all over the place. My grandmother on Mom's side had thirteen kids. My dad's mother had eleven. All boys. I mean, I think it's important for people to know exactly what they're letting themselves in for. Before they let themselves in for it. You know what I'm trying to say?"

"Sure I do."

"So what do you think?"

"I don't know," he said. "What do you think?"

"I say the Treptow clan is gonna rise again."

Gabe turned the key and started the car engine. Then he turned and looked at her. "I wouldn't be surprised," he said.